RIDE A
FAST
HORSE

RIDE A FAST HORSE

❖ A CAPTAIN TOM SKINNER WESTERN ❖

KEVIN WARREN

PINNACLE BOOKS
Kensington Publishing Corp.
www.kensingtonbooks.com

PINNACLE BOOKS are published by

Kensington Publishing Corp.
119 West 40th Street
New York, NY 10018

First Printing: June 2023
ISBN-13: 978-0-7860-5026-0
ISBN-13: 978-0-7860-5027-7 (eBook)

10 9 8 7 6 5 4 3 2 1

Printed in the United States of America

For Amy

CHAPTER 1

Arizona Territory, 1889

In the bottom of a small depression, two fires burned twenty feet apart. Sweat-stained horses tied to creosote bushes and saguaros stood with their heads hung low around a cluster of filthy, exhausted men. The ground beneath them was hard and cold and covered with small sharp stones that worked on making the human body miserable and unshod hooves sore. The only firewood available had been scrounged from dead saguaros, which burned quickly and had to be procured at progressively more distant locations. For those who made wood runs, there was an anger-inducing suspicion that their share of meat had gotten smaller upon their return. The men had all made chairs out of their saddles and saddle blankets, but such seats took up room, and resentment flowed at those closest to the warmth. Woodsmoke, cooking meat, horse sweat, and the odor of unwashed men drifted on crisp desert air.

Jessup Henry sat with his back against the blackened base of a saguaro. Crooked yellow teeth ripped at a small piece of tough, poorly cooked meat. His long, thin face and beard were covered in layers of dust, and his hands were blackened with filth, except on the tips of his fingers, where the meat had washed them clean. The few mouthfuls of flesh in his stomach had helped calm the burn of hunger pains, but the satisfaction of a full stomach and the promise of renewed strength remained to be had. Jessup studied the camp and the men and schemed.

Jessup took heed of the rising tone of irritation in the terse conversations. He noted the quick, angry body language of the men, and he read and understood the tightness of their facial expressions. Sixteen men were sharing two small javelina, and the meat for some had spent little time on the cook fire. His blue eyes descended on Grady Hobbs, sitting to his right. Grady was a powerfully built man with a huge head, a short neck, thick forearms, and broad shoulders. At two hundred and ten pounds he was the biggest man in the group, and he never hesitated to use his size to intimidate. He sat motionless, but his eyes, like Jessup's, remained restless. Jessup stayed patient, engrossed in his study of the men, and a confidence rooted in experience assured him that sooner or later an opportunity would rise.

Ricky Waters, one of Jessup's followers, broke through the small talk and announced to the gathering of men in a loud voice, "You would think one of us coulda hung on ta something we could cook with."

The meat was being cooked in various ways at both fires. At one fire, a large flat rock had been placed on its side near the edge of the flames. A few strips of meat draped from the top edge sizzled.

"Don't know why you're cryin' about a cook pot, Ricky, cause dinner's over," a man named Pepper responded from the far side of the fire.

"You better be lying." Ricky stood and walked over to the carcasses of the javelina.

The small animals lay on their backs, and their skins

had been folded outwards flat on the ground to serve as a butchering table. With a hard blow from his sheath knife, Ricky broke the backbone up near the neck. He stepped on the hide with both feet, reached down, and gave the skeleton a hard tug and tossed it aside. Now he could extract the last bits of meat from around the head and up behind the ears at the top of the neck.

A small, skinny, gray-haired man named Colin groaned in frustration. He stood stiffly, stretched his curved spine for a moment, then, with a hunched body, walked over and repeated the process on the other carcass. Colin was the oldest man among them, and he was worn out riding with this bunch. He survived on the dregs: weak horses, used women, and the worst food and drink.

I'm leavin' first chance I get. Maybe I'll kill that wise ass when I do, Colin thought. He looked at Pepper, who was watching him intently with a broad, tight-lipped smile spread across his face.

The two of them got inquiring looks from others as they worked the carcasses.

"Anybody want to cook this gut?" asked Ricky. He gestured towards the gut pile that had slid into the gravel.

"I'll be damned if I'll eat guts," said Colin, sensing the question was directed at him. "You can kiss my ass."

Cusco, half Comanche and half white, and also low on the pecking order, came over to the butchering area. His knife dug into the gut pile, and he lifted a long piece of white intestine off the ground. He adjusted the slippery organ over his knife edge for grip and then, with a forefinger and thumb squeezing the gut flat, he ran his hand down its length, and emptied all of the contents. He flicked his hand vigorously to rid it of the partially digested food and then bit off a mouthful.

"Be better hot," he said with a grimace, and moved back to the fire.

Jessup eased himself around so his pistol was easier to grab. He reached down and pulled the leather thong off the hammer, and his hand rested just above the deeply stained ivory grip. He looked towards Grady. The big man's eyes were now focused on him.

In Jessup's hand was a small pocketknife that he brought out for every meal. He used it to cut food that he could swallow in pill-size chunks because of a lack of upper teeth. Jessup tossed the pocketknife into his other hand and shifted his position, his eyes narrowed, the corners of his mouth curled downwards.

Silence momentarily reigned, the fires crackled, and far to the east the three-quarter moon had risen high enough that moonlight now swept down into the depression and over their camp.

Jessup snapped the pocketknife shut and slipped it into a vest pocket. Behind a thick dark beard, his jaw clenched. His gaze swept over the men a final time. He stood, stepped around the fire to where Colin and Ricky worked the carcasses, and stared down at them.

Ricky froze and avoided looking up at Jessup. Colin, crippled with fear, fell backwards from a squat into a sitting position, mouth wide open. Jessup ignored them and looked out at the others sitting by the fires. He gestured at the skin and bones of the carcasses and announced to the men. "These two little pigs ain't enough."

Three more steps put him next to a small chestnut colored-horse tied to a saguaro. He pulled out his sheath knife and buried it to the hilt in the front of the horse's neck. The chestnut squealed, its hooves slid on the loose gravel as it sat back against its lead rope and tried to pull away. Jessup jerked the knife downwards and opened a three-inch tear in the carotid artery. Without pause, Jessup pulled his pistol, crouched, and drew back the hammer with a loud click. He leveled it at Cusco, who scrambled to his feet and tried to pull his own gun, but he was too slow. Jessup had the drop on him and the moonlight at his back.

Cusco froze. His hand gripped the pistol still in his waistband.

"Whatcha gonna do half-breed?" asked Jessup.

Tense seconds passed, and every man in the camp had a hand on a gun. Blood ran down the chestnut's neck and leg, it coughed, staggered sideways, and pulled back on its lead rope.

Pepper stifled a nervous smile. "Hell, oh dear. We're goin'..."

"The horse was lame, Cusco. We need the food." Grady cut Pepper off in a loud voice. He'd seen Pepper encourage killings too often, and he didn't like his chances in a shootout in these tight quarters.

The chestnut's blood rolled down its neck and legs. A gurgling sound emanated from its throat. It lurched forward putting slack back in the lead rope, lowered its head, wobbled, and spread its legs into a wide stance. The fires crackled and popped. Cusco's hand remained on his gun.

When the horse collapsed, a hoof struck Jessup's calf. He stepped forward just enough to get away from the horse, knowing it would soon begin to thrash.

Wardell, another half-breed and friend of Cusco's provided the break. He stood slowly with his hands held wide, looked towards Jessup, and said in an even tone, "Why do you got to go about everything the wrong way?" Wardell remained silent for only a moment, then his voice doubled in volume. He addressed Cusco and made the request: "Let's eat."

On the heels of Wardell's words, Jessup offered a truce.

With a quick wrist movement, he tilted his pistol straight up and let the hammer down with another ominous click, yet he remained poised and ready and continued to stare down Cusco. "You want to eat or die?" The last two words slid from Jessup's mouth one at a time, this was not a negotiation.

Cusco cussed under his breath and backed down. He pulled his hand away from his gun, slunk back into his seat, and looked away towards the moonlit hillside on the other side of camp.

Wardell leaned down over the sorrel with a knife in hand. In pursuit of the tenderloin, he cut a long slice along the side of the backbone before the last sign of life had left the sorrel's body.

He planned that whole goddamn scene, thought Grady. *He planned that as the easiest and quickest way to get a damn meal without an argument.*

The huge amount of food eliminated the tension born of hunger from the group, but many eyes glanced at Cusco, who continued to brood in the moon shadow of a huge saguaro.

The fires crackled with piles of added wood, the smell of cooking meat was once again thick on the air, and more subdued conversations flowed as bellies filled. Cusco ate last. When he stood and moved to his dead horse, he wisely let Jessup see his gun jammed deep into his waistband. He jerked out his sheath knife and cut a large portion off the front shoulder, then squatted by the fire and cooked a meal. He would need his strength, for he would be afoot until the next raid, maybe longer: Horses were hard to come by.

By the time the moon was straight overhead no one could eat any more. Full-bellied men made themselves more comfortable. Several began to snore. Jessup rolled off his saddle pad and walked away from the group to urinate. He returned walking on the balls of his feet and carried his pistol in the shadow of his body, close to his side. When he achieved a predetermined spot among the sleeping men, he swung his pistol up, took a second to aim well, and shot Cusco in the back of the head while he slept. Startled men erupted off beds and scrambled away from the center of the camp, seeking cover, clawing for their guns. Horses pulled back, several broke free and skittered away, trampling men in their path.

Jessup's voice rose above the commotion. "I got tired of watching my back."

CHAPTER 2

Dawn, the time of day when unbroken horses are most alert, found Tom Skinner headed for the round corral. This morning work promised to be more interesting than usual. There were eight new geldings bunched together in the main corral. They were all between four and six years old and were good-sized, well-put-together animals. Four had been ridden a few times, and the rest had been broke to lead on the way to Fort Verde.

The horses tensed and watched his approach. Their winter coats, raised for maximum warmth, looked clean and healthy. The dim light made their eyes hard to judge, but there were other ways to gauge temperaments. The compact buckskin on the near side of the bunch let its breath out quickly and spent more time and effort taking in scent than the others. Skinner valued a wary temperament; experience had taught him that horses mentally composed to question each and every stimulation usually offered surefootedness, quick reactions, athleticism, and trainability. Right away the buckskin became his top pick. Skinner peered under the highest rail and studied the horses. His forearms rested on a lower rail in the same spot they had many times before, a large worn metal coffee cup warmed his fingers while he waited for Chaco.

A door creaked open and lantern light spread onto the porch. Skinner saw his friend step out, stretch, and put on his floppy, narrow-brimmed hat. Skinner noticed that the short, leather riding whip Chaco wore throughout every day was already dangling from his wrist.

Chaco was a small man with a slim build, short-cropped black hair, and an inextinguishable smile.

"Morning Chaco," Skinner called out.

"Buenos dias," replied Chaco in a tone affected by the previous night's lengthy poker game.

"How you feelin'?" asked Skinner, smiling.

"Un poco mal. How about you?"

"Hell, I didn't drink that much. I've been looking forward to getting into this bunch," answered Skinner, gesturing towards the horses. "Muggs up yet?"

"He's awake, but he ain't too happy about it. Why don't you let someone else top off these horses?"

"Why would I let someone else have all the fun?"

The horses jerked their heads up, spooked at the sound of a bucket striking the side of a plank wall.

"Damn it all!" Muggs rubbed his head with one hand as he appeared out of a small room that adjoined Chaco's. His shirt hung open and exposed his full belly covered in dark curls of black hair. He looked up to see Chaco and Skinner greeting him with huge grins.

"Damn it!" he repeated, and strode around the side of the barn.

"Rider came in last night." Chaco's statement cut through Skinner's chuckling.

"Is that right?" Skinner swung a hundred and eighty degrees to look across the parade ground at Col. Brickman's office lit up by lanterns. "The big man's up early. What

time did that rider come in?" Skinner's eyes swept over the
rest of the fort. The administration building was completely
dark. A lantern burned at one of the officers' quarters, and
from Chaco's house. Weak light shone through the windows of the long bunkhouse where all the unmarried
soldiers slept. Other than Brickman being in his office so
early, nothing seemed out of the ordinary.

"A little after midnight," said Chaco.

"I guess we'll know about it soon enough. In the meantime, let's get that buckskin into the round pen. Time to go
to work."

The buckskin skittered into the pen and took two fast
laps around the enclosure looking for an exit.

Skinner eased into the pen carrying a six-foot length of
woven cotton rope. Corralled and now confronted by Skinner, the horse's ears flattened, and his nose came up. He
was ready to defend himself, but Skinner never gave him
a chance. Skinner positioned himself near the rails and
moved up behind the buckskin's hip, which allowed the
animal to move away from him. He pursued the animal
along the rails and twirled the rope. Skinner changed the
horse's impulse from fight to flight with ease.

After four laps Skinner commented, "This is a pretty
nice horse, Chaco."

"He's off the Harlow place. I guess they rode him a time
or two, but they think he's an outlaw."

"Hell, this horse ain't no outlaw. He's just a thinker."

"You sure you don't want to let someone else be first
up?"

"Nope."

Skinner continued to move the horse around and around.
The buckskin responded with a brisk high-stepping trot
along the rails. Then, in frustration, it kicked out at Skinner
with a hind leg. Skinner responded by flinging a loose end

of his rope at the horse's rear end, and pressuring the animal to move faster. After two more laps, the buckskin moved boldly and much closer to Skinner and kicked out again.

"Got some attitude, do ya?" Skinner spoke to both the horse and Chaco.

On the ends of his words the buckskin stopped hard, reared, and struck out at Skinner with his front feet. Skinner moved sideways, closer to the fence, and slapped the rails with the rope, then threw a loose end at the buckskin's head. Frightened, the horse again sought distance and fled along the edge of the pen.

"Time to show him who's boss." After one lap Skinner made sure to escalate his conduct before the horse had a similar notion. Abruptly he crossed the round pen and confronted the animal head on, swinging the rope in small, fast circles by his side. The horse brought his hind legs forward, braked hard and reversed direction. Skinner and Chaco studied the pivot, and both noted that the inside hind foot had carried the horse's weight all the way through the turn.

"Handles himself pretty good don't you think?" said Chaco.

"Yep."

Skinner kept firm control by rolling the horse back several more times, but he also took some pressure off by allowing the buckskin to slow its pace.

"He's about over it."

"Yep." Chaco shook his head and grinned.

"Hell, he was easy."

Controlled by the human, the horse lowered its head and ceded the battle for dominance. Skinner immediately quit pressuring the buckskin. He stopped and turned sideways to the horse to reward the behavior. The animal faced

Skinner and snorted. Skinner took more pressure off, turned his back, and took several steps directly away. The horse followed him with short tentative steps. Skinner encouraged him and stepped backwards. The horse moved towards him. Skinner stepped back again. The horse twitched its ears, and nodded its head a few more times, and then walked right up to its new master.

"Easy now. No one's gonna hit ya," said Skinner. His voice was low and quiet. He allowed the horse to take in the scent of his hand.

After a few light touches to the horse's nose Skinner spread his arms and advanced on the horse head on, "Back. Back." The buckskin took two steps back, and immediately Skinner quit pressuring him.

Perched on the upper rail of the corral, Chaco watched with a wide smile.

"That a boy. Easy now." Skinner turned his shoulder and moved away from the horse. The buckskin eased up closer to him.

It was clear to Skinner that this horse had been beaten. He could see it in the horse's eye and sense by the quickly evolving attitude that the buckskin was a good-minded horse but had damage to repair from previous bad handling. He began stroking the animal on both sides and desensitized it to his touch. He reached over the horse's neck with one hand and handed the short rope underneath with the other and pulled back, applying pressure to the buckskin's lower neck.

"Back. Back." As soon as the horse complied, Skinner instantly rewarded the animal by stopping the pressure. Skinner stepped back and moved to the rail. He picked up a halter and returned to the animal and was able to slip it on without trouble. This time when he applied pressure to the chest, he also pulled on the halter lead, and the horse made the connection.

"He's tough on the outside, soft on the inside," said Skinner stroking the horse's neck. "I think I'll go ahead and ride him right now."

"You got it." Chaco jumped down from his perch and picked up Skinner's saddle and a blanket and pushed them under the bottom rail. He grabbed the mecate and bosal and hung them on one of the higher rails while Skinner continued desensitizing the horse. Both men ignored the newest recruit, Charlie, who trotted towards them from Brickman's office.

"Captain Skinner, Col. Brickman wants to see you in his office right away," he said.

"Thank you, Private."

"You're welcome, sir." Charlie saluted crisply and waited for Skinner to salute back. Charlie wanted, even wished, that he could make a comment about horsemanship that wouldn't sound inept. Perhaps something that would make these men's opinion of him rise, but as usual nothing came to him except the deep feeling of inadequacy, so he spun around and moved off.

Skinner and Chaco both watched Charlie walk away. Charlie had only been at the fort two weeks, and so far, he had managed to annoy just about everyone. His all-consuming military correctness was only appreciated by Col. Brickman, who had been using Charlie as his personal servant.

Skinner looked at Chaco and jerked a thumb in Charlie's direction, then shook his head.

Chaco smiled back, "Gonna be a rough week for that little *cabrón*."

Skinner hated to break away from the buckskin while he had his attention, but he reached up and slipped the halter. The buckskin—released physically but more to its liking, psychologically—mustered some of its former attitude and bolted for the far side of the corral.

With Charlie quickly forgotten, Chaco tilted his head towards Brickman's office. "How's anyone supposed to get any work done around here?"

"Gotta go, damn it."

"Hope it ain't bad news." Chaco added.

"Me too. Got a lot on my plate right now, I don't need any distractions."

Chaco chuckled. "You got Veronica on your plate is what you got. Make sure you pay attention over there and quit thinkin' about her for one minute."

"Shut up, Chaco."

Skinner chuckled to himself and walked towards the colonel's office, leaving Chaco with the buckskin. Chaco was right, he thought. Over the last four months he had become besotted over Veronica, ever since they met on the streets of Prescott, and he had withdrawn by degrees from those around him. A smile spread across his face as he thought back once again about the first time he laid eyes on Veronica.

"Dad, can I drive for a while?"

"Not now," replied Leon.

Veronica took no offense at her father's quick dismissal of her request. On this heavily traveled road the ruts were deep, varied in width, and it took considerable skill to keep a four-horse hitch moving in rhythm. And she was fully aware that her father not only loved the challenge of handling the reins, he was also coaxing the team into their best performance for their imminent arrival in Prescott.

Veronica took a strong grip on the rolled canvas cover above her head. She stood precariously and looked backwards over the top to check on Viking.

Trotting outside of the wagon ruts and ahead of the dust on a strong ten-foot lead, the family's bay stallion kept pace. His chest, neck, and shoulders were blackened with sweat, but high on his sides and rump, dapples glistened beneath a layer of trail dust. The stallion took no notice of Veronica. His gaze remained focused on the land ahead. Veronica rolled her eyes in response to the stallion's single-minded obsession, but she continued to stare, enthralled by the animal's silken carriage and how the ends of his curly black mane and tail bobbed each time a hoof struck the earth.

From the corner of her eye, Veronica saw her father take off his leather glove and reach back to grab Muriel's hand in an affectionate squeeze, acknowledging her fortitude now that the journey was almost over. He held her hand until the team broke rhythm in a short patch of deep sand. He quickly put his glove back on, reached forward, and then slid his hands backwards along the reins to a precise spot. In one choreographed motion, he flicked the left rein up and brought it down on the hip of the left wheel horse and lightly tugged on the right rein to chasten the lead mare.

"Maggie," Leon called out in a firm voice. The mare's right ear flicked backwards at him. "Ease up," he said in a softer tone. When all four were once again on the same lead, he pushed his arms forward and shook the reins. "Hupp, hupp, git."

As a team, the horses applied more speed, and the heavy wagon burst out of the patch of sand, back onto firm ground, and rolled on at a furious pace.

"Sit down, Veronica," said Muriel, pulling at the folds of Veronica's dress with one hand and gripping the bottom of her seat with the other.

The family had left their remote ranch on the Mogollon Rim three days ago. They'd traveled west along most of the rim's length the first day. On the second day, they'd dropped into the sunbaked Verde Valley and then crossed to its western edge. This morning they'd climbed up onto the higher forested slopes that surrounded the Prescott Valley and then out onto the windswept plateau. It was a long trip between their ranch and Prescott, but other than the challenges of dealing with intense summer heat, the journey had been without incident.

Three years prior to this trip, on a hunting foray with friends, Leon had fallen for the Mogollon Rim, dead center in the Arizona Territory. The limestone outcrops, guarded by untouched stands of ponderosa pine, the hunting opportunities, and the idea of raising both his children and fine horses in this incredible landscape had become a goal for him.

It wasn't until after Geronimo's surrender to Gen. Miles that Muriel had agreed to move there. For years, her fear of Indian attacks and her stern business sense had trumped Leon's desire to give up his lucrative but unrewarding job as director of Prescott's only bank. Eventually, and to Leon's utter astonishment, her hard-won blessing arrived, but it had come with conditions, one of which included a trip to Prescott every two months to combat the isolation of living in such a remote location. The timing of this visit had been dictated by Prescott's now-famous Fourth of July rodeo and the opportunity to sell stud fees.

The sun was low on the horizon as the family rumbled into the busy streets of Prescott, where a loud and eager *young crowd, composed mostly of cowboys and miners, was descending on the town square. In the opposite direction, an older generation had begun to work its way home after a day of conducting business. Leon slowed the sweat-soaked team to a walk and threaded his wagon through the commotion.*

Veronica smiled at her mother's expression: Her lips had drawn tight, and her brow had narrowed. It was a predictable response to the looks they got from those who admired their perfectly matched four-horse hitch and Viking, who now cantered in place at the end of his lead and wrung out his mane with every other stride.

"Everyone's looking at us, Mom," she said.

"It's 'cause of Viking," said her brother Monte, gesturing at their stallion.

"You shook me near to death, Leon," said Muriel on the final turn off Gurley Street.

"You have to admit they're fine horses. We made record time, and look at the energy they still . . ." Leon's voice trailed off.

Immediately recognizing that her father had become concerned, Veronica's green eyes swept forward.

Forty yards beyond them an elderly man with a scraggly white beard straightened from under a horse he was fitting a shoe for. He watched as the wagon and horses approached, shook his head, gestured at the overcrowded stockyards behind him, and waved Leon on to the last empty spot.

When Veronica saw the offered corral had been built with old gates hastily tied together, she knew right away it was going to cause problems.

"This isn't good," said Leon. "That's not going to hold Viking."

The wrinkles across the tops of Muriel's cheeks grew

*deeper. "This means you won't be sleeping at the hotel,"
Muriel scoffed. "Why don't you geld that horse? He's
ruined more opportunities for us to enjoy ourselves. I'm
tired of it."*

*"Honey, he's the best stallion in the territory. Whoa
now, whoa," said Leon as he lifted the heavy reins.*

*The team braked, the wagon lurched to a stop, and for
the first time in more than two hours the trace chains
slackened and swung idly over the trampled soil. The four
mares' legs, still running full with blood, remained restless beneath them, and their mouths, thick with saliva,
toyed with the bits while their hearts slowed from a working pace. Viking moved to the end of his lead, away from
the wagon, stiffened his frame, raised his head, and took
in the surroundings. He stomped a front foot, kicked at the
soil with a hind, and announced his arrival with a loud
snort.*

*"Look at this team, Muriel. They have more to give."
Leon jerked the wagon brake back and deftly tied a clove
hitch with the reins around the top of the long wooden
brake handle.*

*Monte vaulted off the wagon and spoke over his shoul-
der in midair. "Yeah Mom, we ain't cuttin' Viking."*

*"The word is not cutting, it's gelding." Educating the
kids up on the Mogollon had fallen to Muriel, and, always
concerned she was inadequate to the task, she'd become—
to the dismay of her family—relentlessly educational.*

*Veronica wanted to direct a familiar complaint at her
mother, but she stifled the impulse and waited while
her mother climbed down from the wagon ahead of her.
She noted with a touch of concern that her mother's
haste was impeded only by the need to be mindful of
her dress sweeping against the rough boards on the
wagon sides.*

"Oh no," she murmured under her breath to Laura, "watch out."

"Veronica, hand down that bundle." Muriel found her small money purse, which she had tucked away in a pocket of her pleated gray traveling dress. "Here," she said, and handed the bundle back. Avoiding eye contact with Leon, Muriel looked at Laura. "You can go with me all day tomorrow."

Laura had already been told she would not be accompanying her mother, but she remained convinced it was stupid reasoning that she should be left behind just because they were in a hurry. She could run circles around her mother. Cautioned by her sister, however, she didn't argue and kept her young eyes, brimming with tears, hidden beneath her sun-faded red bonnet.

Not bothering to use the lazy board as a step, Veronica gathered her indigo dress that her mother had insisted she wear that day with one hand, placed the other on the edge of the wagon's sideboard, and sprang down. She patiently endured a look of disapproval over her exit from the wagon and indulged her mother's need to fluff the ends of her long, dark-brown hair so it draped over each shoulder in equal amounts.

"Why you can't take better care of yourself I don't understand," said Muriel, admiring Veronica's cheekbones and strong jaw.

Veronica continued to be patient while Muriel wiped dust from her cheeks, but when her mother licked her fingers, she recoiled.

"Mom."

"Go wash your face then," said Muriel curtly as her hands rose to fluff her own hair, which had just recently begun to gray at the temples.

Veronica moved to the back of the wagon, pried off the

lid to the water barrel, gave her face a quick rinse, and dried it with a sweep of the sleeve of her dress.

"Let's go," said Veronica in a voice now tinged with impatience. She put an arm through her mother's, tugged her forward, and together they walked off, shaking wrinkles and dust from their dresses.

Veronica knew her mother's annoyance that the shops were closing was part of the reason she had been so short with her father, but there was another larger issue as well. She had also reserved two rooms at the Granite Creek Hotel, far enough away from Whiskey Row that they could sleep, but close enough to town that they could walk anywhere. It had been a long, muddy spring on the Mogollon Rim, and she had planned to be treated like a lady on this trip. Now, with her husband's need to tend to a stallion, probably throughout the night, her mood had darkened.

"Keeping a stallion is just not worth it. If your father believes I came all the way down here to sleep by myself while he tends to that horse, he's got another thing coming," ranted Muriel, fully aware that her husband could still hear her.

"That corral is pretty flimsy. What if Viking gets out?"

"I don't care if he gets out. I'm sick and tired of having a stallion run my life. Good God, I spend enough time alone when he's off camping with you kids. I deserve better, Veronica. You better take note of his failings and make sure you don't make the same mistake I did."

"Mom."

"Veronica, you better find someone soon. Twenty-three is practically an old maid anymore."

"Mom. Stop."

"We need to move back to town. Living up there you don't meet anyone."

"Mom. Please stop."

"Don't you try and shut me up. I'm really upset, and with good reason."

Just ahead of them was the town square and Whiskey Row. To the left was the business section of Prescott and the best shopping. Veronica let her mother grumble, fully aware that the sight of men and women beckoning pedestrians to enter their stores before closing was doing more to change Muriel's mood than anything Veronica could do or say.

On the right side of the square, bars and restaurants lined the road for two blocks. Horses crowded the hitch rails, and the narrow boardwalks were full of people jostling for room as they passed one another. Laughter and music poured onto the street from every open door.

A young man emerged from the crowd and strode directly at them. He moved his six-foot frame with a confident stride. Tan, callused hands swung at his sides, and the sleeves of his worn-thin cavalry shirt were protected by stamped-leather cuff guards. He wore a brand-new gray felt hat clamped down over collar-length black hair and three days' growth of beard. He looked directly at them, and his wide-set hazel eyes captured and held both their attentions. They stared until the young man tipped his hat and acknowledged them as he passed.

"Evenin'," he said.

Veronica pulled her mother to a stop and made a quarter turn to ostensibly take in the view of the shopping area, but her head twisted farther, so she could take a look at the young man's back. He had turned as well, and a furious hot blush sprang into her cheeks when their eyes met. Her mother's fingers sank into the flesh of her bicep, and she felt the stern look of disapproval bore into the back of her neck. She'd been caught looking by both of them. Veronica pulled out of her mother's grip, pushed her *chin forward, stepped up onto a wooden boardwalk, and moved on without a word.*

Skinner pulled his new hat down tight, stretched out his stride, and charged up the lane of the stockyards. He sprang effortlessly up the rails between the first two corral set posts and looked back, just in time to see the girl and her mother disappearing into a fabric shop. When she turned sideways to enter the store, he exhaled audibly, "I gotta meet her."

Skinner swung a leg over the rail and watched the storefront. He could feel the blood in his veins moving quickly, and his mind was suddenly and inexplicably befuddled with too many thoughts at once, and he was sweating more than the heat of the day called for. "Make a plan, you stupid idiot," he whispered, "Cause she sure as hell looked at you."

The loud squeal of a horse behind him broke his thoughts, and he swiveled his head to look. Across the lane a young girl, two young boys, and a man were anxiously watching what was almost assuredly a stallion get acquainted with horses in the next corral.

The big bay's sweat and dust-caked hide could not conceal the fine muscling that lay beneath; he was a beautifully conditioned animal. Skinner saw a quiver run through the animal's flanks as it stretched its neck over a rickety gate to nicker at a petite gray mare emerging from the cluster of horses in the next pen. The dark bay's flanks heaved, and the penis dropped as the gray mare stretched out her neck to greet him.

The stallion and the mare tensed. Their necks now arched across the rickety divider between them. In short heavy breaths they took in each other's scent. The stallion nickered again, then squealed and struck a forefoot against a board. The gray mare laid her ears back, bit the stallion's neck, and pivoted away before she suffered any retribution. She swished her tail, stomped a foot, then she curled her neck back and took a final glance at the stallion. After a quick appraisal the mare shook out her mane and trotted away to the safety of the herd.

Viking lifted his front hooves a foot off the ground, pivoted, and began circling the enclosure. His head lowered until his nostrils were inches from the ground. Spurts of dust rose from the dry earth after each heavy breath. With ears pinned flat to his head, the stallion charged across the confines of the corral. At the last second the stallion decided not to jump the fence. His hind end lowered, his rear hooves slid along the ground, and his front feet tapped the earth as he came to a hard stop. His ears came forward, and his head rose above the dust to lock his eyes on Skinner across the lane, up on the rails. The stallion blew. The sharp exhalation whistled on the air.

Skinner's mouth fell open, and his eyes held the stallion's glare. "Damn, You and me both. . . ." he murmured. His head swiveled briefly to look at the storefront, then he turned back to watch the stallion. He was about to jump off the fence and go for a closer look, but he hesitated. His eye had been drawn to the wagon next to the stallion's pen. It had been hastily unpacked, and on top of a pile of duffel lay a girl's red traveling bonnet. Skinner looked back toward town again. This was the other half of the family.

"That sure is a nice stud, mister."

"Well thank you," said Leon as he looked up at the stranger sitting on a rail. "I have a real reasonable stud fee if you're interested."

"Not sure that pen is gonna hold him."

"No, it won't for long. He's acting like a young buck." Leon shook his head. "This flimsy corral is causing more problems than you can imagine. What's your name?"

"Tom Skinner." Skinner jumped down from the rails and walked over to shake hands.

"Leon Sharp, this is my daughter Laura, and my twin boys Monte and Courtney." Leon beckoned sternly for the boys to come to him.

Monte and Courtney came over and shook hands. Monte was dressed in a faded blue shirt, cut-off pants, and leather work boots with no socks. Courtney wore cowboy boots and long denim pants, and his face was clean compared to Monte's, which was black with dirt. When Skinner introduced himself to Laura, he was convinced he was right about this being the other half of the family. Her long, dark-brown hair was the same color, and it hung below her shoulders and curled upwards at the ends, just as that girl's had. Her bright-green eyes were identical. If I can stall around the family for a while, I might be able to see her again, Skinner thought.

"If you're willing to pack up again, I know a better place to keep a stud, on the other end of town. Closer to all the action too; might even help your sales a bit." Skinner pointed in the general direction. "It's small, but it'll hold him. You'll need to highline your mares."

"That's mighty kind of you, Tom. How much you want for the spot if we take you up on it?"

"Don't know, it ain't my place. Let's go find out." Skinner looked Leon in the eye, trying to assure himself this was the girl's father. Leon was tall and slender and wore a stiff brimmed hat with a crushed in crown on the front end. He had at least two weeks growth of graying beard hiding his face, but like the girls, he too had green eyes. "If you like it, I'll come back and help you pack up."

"Well thank you," said Leon, slightly taken back by this stranger's friendliness. "Let me tie my stud to the wagon.

We're headed for a wreck. Kids, stay here. I'm going to go look at another spot. I'll be right back."

"Hurry Dad, we're hungry."

"I will. Leave everything as it is, we might move. Tom Skinner, you say. You stationed at Fort Verde?"

"Yes, I am." Skinner reached up and removed his hat. He swept his hair back and pulled the hat back down so the brim was a bit lower over his eyes. *"Been there quite a while now,"* he added.

They worked their way across town and arrived at a small inn that had a sturdy five-rail corral built onto the side of the building. Inside a lanky lined-back dun dozed.

"Looks like we're too late, Tom. Someone's already using that spot."

Skinner let out a short, sharp whistle. The dun moved to the gate with his ears pricked forward and searched him out. *"He's my horse; I can put him anywhere. Let's talk to the owner, explain what's going on. His name's Cliff. If you pay me for leavin' and pay him for stayin', he'll be fine with it."*

"He's a nice-looking horse, Tom. Looks like he could cover some country," said Leon.

"He can. About as good as they get."

"You don't see lined-back duns with that tall build too often. Where'd you get him?"

"He was a gift."

"Who'd gift a horse like that?"

"Glen Tulin gave him to me."

"Tulin. I knew him. I didn't think that horse-trading son of a gun would give anyone anything."

"Me and a friend worked for him for quite a while."

"What'd you call him?"

"His name is Too Tall."

"You ever raced him?"

"Nope. He's too good a traveler for me to risk it. Besides, I'd just clean up. Then everyone would be pesterin' me to buy him or be tryin' to swipe him."

Leon chuckled. *"I've got some money that says my stud can beat him."*

Skinner hesitated. *"How much money?"*

Leon laughed. *"I've got to say it was a piece of luck running into you, Tom. Now you have to find a place for your horse, I feel obliged. Could I buy you dinner tonight? We have reservations at the Palace Restaurant. All I have to do is let them know we are going to be one more for the evening. We can talk about racing over a good meal."*

"Ah, sure. I can pay my way though." Skinner stammered.

"No. You're going to be our guest. You pulled me out of a bind. We'll meet you at eight."

Skinner chuckled to himself over the memories of the discomfort of that dinner with Veronica and her family. He shook his head vigorously and prepared himself to pay attention, to follow Chaco's advice as he walked up the steps to Colonel Brickman's office and entered.

"At ease, Captain," said Brickman.

Brickman was short and heavyset. He wore a manicured mustache and goatee to help conceal a double chin. He had restless eyes and never held eye contact with anyone for more than a second.

"I have a couple of letters here. The first one is out of Sante Fe, New Mexico, telling all forts, outposts, and local law enforcement to be on the lookout for a group of outlaws. This bunch has been on the run for some time in

New Mexico. They have reason to believe they may now be headed west in a hell of a hurry."

Brickman moved to his desk chair and finally looked Skinner in the eye, expecting questions, but Skinner remained silent. Brickman cleared his throat and continued. "The second one is from General Miles, who's down at Fort Lowell right now. He wants this bunch arrested or killed if they come anywhere near us. He's calling for regular patrols north and south between forts from the Mexican border to Colorado. He's mad as hell about this bunch and getting pressure from Washington to deal with them in an urgent manner. You and I both know Washington is worried sick about relations with Mexico. If these outlaws go across the border and start something bad, who knows what might happen. It's a long letter," Brickman tapped his fingers on the envelope sitting on his desk. "You read it so you can get a sense of his urgency."

Skinner kept his eyes lowered. He was thinking hard, and he didn't move to pick up the letter.

Brickman continued, "They're leftover gunhands from the Lincoln County War."

"Billy the Kid has been dead for more than eight years now. He was behind most of that trouble," said Skinner.

"I know it, but just because he's dead doesn't mean every gunhand that hung around him is gone too. That whole fight produced a bunch of men with nowhere to go, no open doors. It appears some of them partnered up to steal horses and cattle both sides of the border. Then they went too far and killed a bunch of ranchers. Now everyone is on their trail."

Brickman paced back and forth as he spoke. "The whole situation is spelled out in that letter. The main point, the huge concern, is that they could start something bigger." Brickman stopped pacing and looked at Skinner, and then sat down at his desk chair. "Relations with Mexico are tense enough, that's why we are getting involved. General Miles is determined to not let this gang of miscreants become the spark of something that could be hard to stop. He's going to head north himself and try and put an end to this fast."

From a habit rooted in orneriness, and a fort-wide effort to cause Brickman every discomfort possible, Skinner reached out for the letter, but only far enough that the colonel had to raise his bulk out of his chair to hand it over. This morning, however, Skinner took no pleasure in the game. His intellect and his emotions had suddenly collided within him in an unfamiliar way, and he understood that any urgency the letter contained would never match his own need to go. To go now.

"Sir, does the other letter say how many outlaws there are?"

"Between twelve and twenty. Why there isn't a better number on that is anyone's guess," answered Brickman.

"Sir, if they have loose stock with them and maybe some pack animals, and if no one is getting a good look at 'em, it could be hard to tell how many of 'em there are unless . . ." Skinner paced as he spoke.

Concerned by how Skinner paced and clutched the still-unread letter in his hand, Brickman interrupted him with a raised voice. "Captain, that Gila country is a long way from here, and if these outlaws are getting pressured, they're probably going to stay south so they can dodge into Mexico if they need to. All we have to do is send out patrols as ordered." Brickman gestured at the letter in Skinner's hand. "The chances of them coming this far north are remote, to say the least."

"Yes sir," Skinner replied.

"This is what I want, Captain. Take six men. You pick 'em. Go south. Cut for sign all the way to where the Verde meets the Salt River, then keep going south until you bump into patrols coming north. I don't know what General Miles will send out of the valley. Take Chaco and them two scouts with you as well. If you get held up for any reason, send one back to let me know why. Otherwise I'll expect you back in two weeks. If you cut sign don't lose them. Stay on them, leave us a big trail, send word back here, and we'll come as fast as we can. If you confront them, you're going to have a fight on your hands. There's no doubt about that. You leave today. Any questions?" Brickman rocked back in his chair, placed his elbows on the armrests, and folded his hands on his gut.

"Yes sir. Sir, when and where were they last seen?"

"Last seen December fifth. Six days ago, headed due west into the desert just south of Sante Fe.

"Yes sir." Skinner kept pacing. "Sir?"

"What is it, Captain?"

I need to be ready for anything, thought Skinner. "You said there were twelve to twenty outlaws. Why are you sending me with such a small troop?"

"All right, Captain. Take two more men, if it makes you feel better." Brickman gestured as though his statement was a gift. "But that's it, I'm not going to send out half the command to chase around looking for outlaws that might not be within four hundred miles of here."

"I got a bad feeling about 'em already, sir." Skinner stopped pacing and looked at Brickman. He watched the colonel's furrowed brow relax and the hint of a mean-spirited smile held in check take its place. Skinner's fists tightened at his sides.

"If you were to find them, I don't think these are the

kind of men that are going to engage the United States Cavalry." The words slithered from Brickman's throat.

"What did they do in New Mexico, Colonel?"

"They're raiding as they go. On a killing spree. Homesteaders, women, children, it doesn't matter. They're killers, taking what they need and living on the run."

Skinner turned his back, not wanting Brickman to see his reaction, but the obvious, the unsaid, had been hung on the wall for both of them. Any big group of men and horses headed due west from the headwaters of the Gila would have to turn north or south for water once they reached the deserts of eastern Arizona, and if they turned north, they would be headed towards the Mogollon Rim country, where Veronica lived.

"Captain, any questions?" Brickman taunted.

"No sir," Skinner replied through tight lips and clenched teeth.

As Skinner reached for the door, Brickman called to him once more.

"Captain!"

"Sir!"

"I'll be sending Sweeney north towards Flagstaff under the same orders. He'll be leaving tomorrow morning."

"Yes sir," said Skinner. He hesitated with his hand on the doorknob. Then he turned, faced the colonel, and in a soft voice made his request. "Colonel, maybe it would be smart for me to head east into the Mogollon country, if those killers are headed due west, they'll hit desert about . . ."

"Listen to me, Captain, I got orders from General Miles. He wants patrols going north and south—don't second guess me or him. Got it?" Brickman stood, rounded his desk, and confronted Skinner. "Let me remind you that General Miles is used to having private dinners with presidents. He's met with everyone from Lincoln to Chester Arthur." Brickman saw Skinner's demeanor remained unchanged, and he pressed his point. "Fredericksburg. Appomattox. Chancellorsville. A Medal of Honor recipient. I don't want to hear any ideas you might have that are contrary to his orders. Do I make myself clear?" Brickman waited but got no response. "Captain, do I make myself clear?"

Brickman's raised voice jarred Skinner. "I was just thinking out loud, sir. They'll need water before they get this far west. Might be smart to scout areas where they're more likely to end up."

"Captain Skinner, I know exactly where this is going. Your girl lives over that way, but we have no idea where this gang is. Whether they broke up or not. Nothing. We don't know within five hundred miles where they are. They might be headed back east for all we know."

"You told me the letter said 'believed to be heading west in a hell of a hurry,' sir." Skinner took an aggressive half step forward.

"Captain," Brickman shouted and took his own step forward. The two men stood toe to toe. "One change to my orders: I'm assigning the new recruit, Charlie, to your patrol. If you deviate from your orders, he will let me know when you return. You will head south. Is that clear?"

"Yes sir. I hear you but it doesn't make any sense." Skinner made no effort to hide his tight lips and clenched jaw.

"I don't give a damn what you think makes sense. I have been given orders from General Miles, and they will be followed."

"Yes sir," Skinner replied over his shoulder as he reached for the door.

"Attention."

Skinner turned back, faced the Colonel, and stood at attention.

"You always think you know better than anyone else what should be done."

"It's a curse for sure."

"You insolent hothead. You deviate from your orders, and I'll end your career, you hear me?"

"I hear you."

"You hear me, sir." Brickman waited.

"Sir. I hear you, sir." Skinner saluted.

"Dismissed, Captain."

CHAPTER 3

Skinner's pace and determined stride across the compound alerted everyone who saw him that there were developments. "Chaco, round up Skeeter, Vance, and Boomer. Meet me in the barn." Skinner yelled across the packed earth at Sunny and Greg standing outside their barracks. "Get over here on the double. Bring Victor, Brooks, and Wade with ya."

Fort Verde, just north of dead center in the Arizona Territory, was awakening to bad news. Men, still coming to terms with the severity of whiskey-induced headaches, scrambled towards the barn where Skinner began to assemble gear.

Boomer came through the door first and tucked a worn thin cavalry shirt into faded gray pants. Boomer had a compact build, red hair, and thick forearms. His neck was so short it looked like his head grew right out of his shoulders. No one at the fort could beat him at any of the games that required strength, but despite his physical power, Boomer was usually the peacemaker when angry disputes rose among the men.

"Captain," Boomer came to attention and saluted.

Skeeter rushed through the door next. "They're coming, Captain." Skeeter was the opposite of Boomer both physically and mentally. Skeeter had a tall thin build, talked incessantly, and was invariably a prime suspect when tensions arose among the enlisted men.

"What's up, Captain?" asked Chaco, who rushed in next, followed by Vance and Sunny.

Skinner briefed them on his conversation with the colonel.

"Well hell, Captain," said Chaco. "Going out on patrol looking for some bandits is no big deal. How come you look like you're gonna puke?"

"I got a bad hunch," began Skinner. "If these killers travel due west of the Gila country, you and I both know that they are going to have to turn north or south when they hit the lower desert. If they come north—well, I'm worried for those ranches on the Mogollon Rim."

Chaco smiled and rocked back and forth on well-worn boot heels. His dark eyes twinkled with pleasure as he slapped his riding whip against his calf. "Well hell, Captain, I knew you was sweet on her, but this looks like a serious case of love jitters."

Skinner let out a sigh, and a smile came across his face. He stood and moved closer to the five of them. "Look fellas, I know it's long on paranoia and short on possibility but"—Skinner leveled his gaze at them—"we're swinging that way first thing."

Sunny pushed his filthy cavalry cap back on his head and took a step forward, "Brickman ain't going to go easy on us if'n we do."

"Somehow, I don't think he's gonna know," said Chaco while hammering Sunny with his eyes.

For the next two and half hours the fort bustled with activity. Skinner had a checklist in his pocket that he constantly referred to as he put his men to work. The entire horse herd had been wrangled off the surrounding desert, and now a cloud of dust rose above the corrals and drifted among the buildings and across the parade ground. Muggs was bent over nailing the last shoe on a horse tied to a strong hitch rail. Outside, in front of the tack room, a growing pile of gear was being assembled. Food was put into sacks meal by meal. Doctoring kits, shoeing kits, and pots and pans were added to the piles. Skeeter and Vance moved through the piles and lifted the duffle sacks and various boxes to test the weight so they could produce balanced loads. The heavier items disappeared into the bottoms of six sets of panniers, and again, Skeeter and Vance lifted all the panniers to test their weight. Individual bedrolls and lighter personal gear were placed on top of each set of panniers for top loads. Six mules were brought up and tied to a sturdy set of posts near the panniers. They eyeballed the loads, stomped nervously, laid their ears back at everyone near them, and tugged on lead ropes as the cinches of pack saddles were drawn tight. On a bench near the packing area, Boomer had assembled piles of sixty bullets for each soldier to pick up and put in their ammunition belts.

Skinner's men glanced at Brickman's office window as they packed and they caught him looking out at their preparations more than once, but he never ventured outside. Women and kids mingled among the men. Soon every man's pockets were crammed with candy, chunks of bread, and other treats. Skinner's two scouts, Victor and Brooks, each held a Springfield balanced in the crook of their arms as they scooped up their bullets and filled their ammunition belts. Brooks was thin and taller than his companion and wore his hair in two short braids. He had a long nose that accentuated the narrowness of his eyes.

Victor had a more compact build, and despite a broad scar running across his face, he looked more amicable than Brooks.

Almost ready, thought Skinner. He looked over his shoulder towards Brickman's office and saw the colonel duck away from the window. He sighed and walked to his horse with a loaded set of saddlebags hung over his arm.

Too Tall tucked his chin and angled his head in Skinner's direction. His frame rose with the double expectation of work and a possible treat, and his nostrils vibrated with a low whicker.

"Hey, buddy, time to go to work." Skinner slipped Too Tall a lump of sugar and then swung his saddlebags over the cantle of his saddle. He threaded the saddle strings through the cutouts on his saddlebags and tied an overhand knot, but when he jerked the knot tight, the saddle string broke.

"Damn it." Skinner pulled out his pocketknife and cut slits in the broken ends of each string. He threaded one through the other and made the repair. "I hate these hurry-up-and-get-out trips. My knife is dull. What am I forgetting? How am I going to handle his little spy, Charlie?" Skinner whispered out loud as his mind ran negative scenarios in a familiar ritual. He reminded himself that he always did this just prior to a departure and experience made him shake the failed thinking away. He needed to check out with Brickman before they left, and he didn't want Brickman to get any sense his angst had grown worse.

He placed a hand over Too Tall's nose, pulled the horse's head closer, and whispered to him. "Hey, you ol' sidewinder. You look happier about this than I am." Despite an already-festering anger at Brickman and his unease over Veronica's safety, Skinner took some solace knowing that with all the preparations behind him, once out on the trail astride Too Tall he would be able to think without distractions. He gave Too Tall's dun-colored chest two pats, then put his attention back on his men. It was time to go.

"Chaco, mount 'em up nice and neat. Right out front!" Skinner bellowed out the order in a voice loud enough to be heard across most of the fort.

Cinches got one last tug, a last piece of gear got tied on, and in three minutes everyone was mounted. Often the mules were tied together in a string, and only one man could lead them all, but Chaco didn't want to fight it today. The mules were rank from a lack of recent use, and there were just too many indications for a blowup, so he gave six men one mule each to lead. Leather saddles creaked, and more dust rose as the soldiers jockeyed their horses into the straight line demanded by Chaco. Six soldiers lined up side by side, each with a loaded pack mule behind them. When the rest of the troop was lined up in front of them in a tight formation, Chaco, riding as though five hundred people had their eyes on him, made a pass across the front of the line on his stocky chestnut, Turns Good. When he passed the last man, he spun Turns Good hard, loped back to the other end, pulled up sharp, and gave Skinner a salute.

"Ready, Captain."

Skinner stood by Too Tall, who was still tied to the hitch rail. "Be right back." He turned and walked into Brickman's office. Brickman was looking out the window at the patrol with his hands clasped behind his back. He didn't turn to look at Skinner.

"Patrol ready to depart, sir."

"Got everything you need, Captain?" Brickman asked. "Yes sir."

"Looks like you're headed out on a major campaign." Brickman paused, "Six mules for a two-week patrol?" He twisted away from the window to face Skinner and added, "Is there any gear left for Sweeny?"

"Men and equipment always in short supply, Colonel but he should find what he needs." Skinner handed Brickman a list of the men. Including Charlie, the patrol would be comprised of twelve men.

Brickman read the list out loud. "Sergeant Chaco Velez. Corporal Boomer Dinning. Privates. Skeeter O'Brian, Vance Brewer, Sunny Korfanta, Greg Legerski, Willy Klingbell, Wade Evans, Charlie Oberling. Scouts Victor Chenoa. Brooks Odin. Captain Tom Skinner." Brickman brought his eyes up from the list and stared at Skinner.

"We're prepared to engage a numerically superior force unsupported, sir," said Skinner. When Brickman didn't answer, Skinner spoke out. "Permission to depart, sir."

"You aren't unsupported, Captain Skinner. We don't have any idea where this bunch is. You just follow the orders I gave you and keep your men safe. Main thing is that if you find them, don't lose them. Stay on their trail. Send for help. I wrote it out so you can carry this with you," said Brickman. "Here." He held out an envelope for Skinner. "I'm quite sure you don't have any questions."

"No sir."

"Get on down the trail, Captain," said Brickman.

From beneath a thick forelock Too Tall eyeballed Skinner as he approached. His tongue began to toy with the bit at a furious pace. Too Tall's head lowered, he shook out his mane, then he jerked his head high and arched his neck. When Skinner untied the lead rope, Too Tall lifted his front left foot and pawed at the soil.

Skinner coiled his lead rope and tied it to his saddle. He reached over Too Tall's neck and pulled the offside rein up to the front of his saddle. As Too Tall made an eager half circle around him, Skinner gathered himself and leapt aboard. Too Tall tugged on the bit and pranced sideways down the row of men as Skinner settled into his well-worn saddle.

Skinner looked back and saw Chaco stop at the front porch of his living quarters, pull his floppy hat off, hold it at arm's length, and bend down from the saddle to kiss his wife, Maria.

"Hasta pronto mi amor," said Chaco in a voice loud enough for all to hear.

"Hace mucho cuidado hombre," said Maria, standing on her toes to kiss her man.

Skinner smiled at the display of gallantry and watched Chaco line the column out.

Chaco rolled Turns Good away and caught up to the rear of the column. *"Mula,* hup, hup." Chaco swung the riding whip that hung from his wrist and brought it firmly down on the rear end of a gray mule. The animal's tail tucked between its legs, and it lurched forward to the relief of Skeeter, who'd refused to let go of the lead rope and had been nearly pulled from the saddle. Once again, Chaco put Turns Good into a run, charged to the front, and pulled up alongside Skinner, who was yards ahead of everyone.

Too Tall, on a tight rein, cantered sideways. Skinner looked over at his friend rolling easily with the smooth motion of Turns Good. Skinner pressed his spur into Too Tall's ribs and moved the big horse sideways, back towards Turns Good.

"You still worried?" Chaco said in a low voice.

When Skinner's stirrup bumped Chaco's, Skinner replied, "Don't worry. I got a plan."

"Does it include you gettin' there as fast as you can?"

Skinner grinned. "That's pretty much it altogether."

"Pony Express?"

"Yup. Pony Express."

"That's what I thought. You do what you need to. I'll take care of everything else."

"Thanks, Chaco."

"Yeah, we'll be fine," replied Chaco, "as long as I don't let things fall completely apart." He turned and yelled back at the men trailing behind. "Close it up. Column of twos. Boomer, take point."

Boomer, astride his prancing black-faced blue roan, raised a thick forearm, pulled his hat down tighter over his close-cropped red hair and moved to the point position behind Skinner and Chaco.

"You won't," said Skinner. He looped his reins around the saddle horn and then slipped the ends under his thigh to keep a tight hold on Too Tall and free both hands. He reached up and swept his hair back under his hat and adjusted his collar higher on his neck. Chaco's full support for him in his dealings with Brickman pulled his thoughts back to their childhood together and Glen Tulin, the man who adopted them both so many years ago. "I guess we're gonna put a few Tulin lessons to work," he said. He looked over at Chaco and winked.

"Which one?"

"How to get somewhere quick."

"Hell, we go everywhere quick."

"I got this boilin' feeling makin' me wanna break into a run, to tell ya the truth."

"That's your protective instincts talking to ya," said Chaco. "You're in love, *amigo.*" Chaco laughed, but Skinner didn't. "This will be your third time up there, and you know what they say."

"Yeah, I know. Last time didn't go so good though. She's probably done with me anyhow."

"I doubt it."

"What would you know? You weren't there."

"What the hell did you do?"

"I ain't tellin' you anythin' about that."

"What the hell did you do?"

"Shut up."

"People get over stuff. Women are more forgiving than men. Sometimes, anyway." Chaco changed the subject. "Don't forget what else he taught us."

"Who? Tulin?"

"Yeah," said Chaco looking over his shoulder, making sure the men closing in on them were still out of earshot.

"What's that?" asked Skinner.

"Remember that shootin' lesson? Remember when he told us there would be no doubt in our mind if it was time to shoot?" Chaco looked over at Skinner. "Don't forget that one."

"You got a bad feelin' about this, too?"

"Yeah."

Skinner looked straight ahead, "This is the one time I wish I didn't trust your intuition."

When he felt his rider's tension increase, Too Tall danced sideways and jerked the bit forward to put slack in the reins. "Going to be hard to make the Edge Camp before dark." Skinner looked over at Chaco, lifted his hand and pointed forward. "Trot."

Chaco raised his arm straight up, turned around in his saddle, and yelled out the order. "Column of twos. Trot."

Skinner's voice rose. "His orders are if we find them, stay on them and send for help. I guess we can handle that."

"Yeah, sure. Maybe." Chaco looked at Skinner, shook his head, and rolled his eyes.

CHAPTER 4

Jessup and Grady took the lead as they moved on from another desolate desert campsite. They had traveled a long way since Jessup killed Cusco, and their horses were now in critical shape. Lack of water, poor forage, and hard use had rendered most of their horses unusable. Ribs protruded on all of the horses, and several had open withers sores that oozed yellow pus and coated their hides in a sticky mess not easily cleaned without hot water. Despite frequent inspections and quick fixes, only two horses were still shod with four shoes. The outlaws wound their way through the cactus-filled desert, every man walked and led their horses as they worked their way up a long-inclined valley.

At midmorning the outlaws arrived on the crest of a low pass between two outcrops of black volcanic rock. Towards the west the desert stretched out to a blurry dust-filled flat and featureless horizon. To the south, tall gray mountains rose from the desert floor, devoid of vegetation, and cut by deep side canyons that held the promise of water.

Despite their predicament, Jessup couldn't keep quiet for long.

"Well boys, what do you think this country is going to provide for us?" Jessup's speech was altered by a dry mouth and swollen tongue.

Grady grunted, "Not much."

"It better provide some water and grass pretty quick, or we're all gonna be done in," said Pepper.

Jessup looked at Pepper and sneered. "Think so, do ya?"

Grady saw Jessup's eyes narrow, the corners of his mouth curl downwards. He recognized the look. Grady intended to be the last man alive in the group. *I better back him for my own good,* he thought.

To the north loomed the rugged, boulder-strewn, Mazatzal range, and beyond it rose the Mogollon Rim. Its forested slopes invited the thirsty traveler. A few spots showed the whitish color of cottonwood trees. The leaves had fallen for the winter, but the white trunks of these water-loving trees contrasted vividly with the deeper green of ponderosa pine and could be seen from a great distance.

"I don't think we got much choice fellas. I ain't goin' out there." Jessup threw his arm out to the west. "Looks like weather building, but we can't count on it. South looks like a gamble. I seen a lot of them side canyons be dry as a bone. If we go northwest, we're gonna find water and grass."

"I thought we was going south to the border towns." Pepper wasn't intimidated by Jessup. "We need fresh horses."

He must be losing it for lack of water, thought Grady.

Jessup delivered another hard look Pepper's direction. "We are headed down there, but we don't wanna die of thirst on the way. You don't know a damn thing about this country. We head south and don't run into water real quick, we're done for."

"We head up that way and don't find it, same thing,"

said Pepper. "The Salt River has to be somewhere close, an' it's going to rain."

"I like my chances going northwest. What you say Jessup?" Grady tried to manipulate the conversation.

Jessup shook his head towards the northwest and looked around at the others for support but didn't need it. Three of them made their opinions known by jerking their horses heads up and trudging northwest towards the Mazatzals, not bothering to give Pepper another opportunity to whine. Single file, they traveled on.

After the descent off the pass, they came upon a dry wash with a stand of grass on both banks where the outlaws put the horses out to graze. Even though they were confident no one was on their trail, out of pure habit, Grady and Jessup moved to a high spot.

Jessup lay back on one elbow next to Grady, both chewing on pieces of grass and looking back at the country they had just crossed. Jessup's pistol sat easily across his lap as he tried to get some conversation going.

"If the weather had been hot, we'd all be dead by now."

Grady grunted.

"You know, Grady, it's an amazing thing this group. How in the hell did we ever get together? How come we ain't split up yet?"

Grady still didn't reply.

Jessup continued to talk. "We sure left our mark back in New Mexico don't ya think?" Jessup adjusted his position so the collar of his coat came up higher around his neck. The sun was out, but it wasn't strong, and a slight breeze kept a chill in the air. "I wonder what the hell people are saying about us back there. We sure left our mark."

"You said that already." Grady sounded irritated.

Jessup looked at Grady, slightly surprised. "Yes, I did.

But the fact of the matter is that if I wasn't talking, we wouldn't be having any conversation at all."

Grady let a faint smile lift the corners of his mouth. He fell to one side on the ground, making his position more comfortable. He had grown accustomed to Jessup's incessant talk. Sometimes it made him angry, but at other times, like now, it was entertainment.

Jessup raised a finger to his nose. Using it to hold one nostril closed, he turned his head slightly and tried to blow snot out the other. Nothing budged. It was too dry. Annoyed, Jessup picked with his index finger and kept talking. "I wonder if anyone's still chasing us? What do ya suppose they're calling us? I mean, they must have a name for us by now. Every gang gets a name, especially after all those people we killed. I want notoriety."

Grady scoffed. "You don't even know what that word means."

"Hell I don't. It means being famous, kinda."

"Why do you use words you don't know the meaning of? You trying to impress me or something? It ain't working if that's what you're doing."

Jessup had been silent too long traveling single file, and the words flowed out of him. "Ya know, since Geronimo give up, well somehow . . ." Jessup brought his legs up underneath him with a quick nervous motion, muttering unintelligibly for a few seconds. "Somehow, I just don't think this country is ever going to see the likes of us again. It's kind of like we're the last of the worst."

Grady sat up. "The last of the worst, huh? Well, that would be a poor name for a gang, wouldn't it?"

"You're damn right it would." Animated by Grady's response, Jessup pulled a fresh piece of grass out of the ground. He broke the thick end off sharply so it would last longer in his mouth. He rolled to one side, facing Grady directly. "Hell, they don't even know our names. How are we going to get any notoriety if they don't even know our names?"

Grady spoke up again. "Who's they?"

"The ones chasing us. If I'm going to be an outlaw, I wanna be a famous one. That's all."

"You ain't an outlaw."

"No? Then just what the hell am I?"

Grady raised his eyebrows and looked straight at Jessup. "You're a killer. Fodder for a lynch mob."

CHAPTER 5

The flat plain where Fort Verde was located slid out of sight behind the patrol as they worked their way south. Two decades ago, the immediate area around Fort Verde had been covered in juniper and piñon trees, but nearly every tree within three miles of the fort had been cut down for firewood. Prickly pear cactus had grown rampantly in its place, and the patrol snaked along on trails that wound through huge patches of the hardy cactus.

From mountains on both the eastern and western flanks of the Verde Valley, large ravines cut gouges in the earth that ran towards the center of the wide valley. During rain storms the bottoms of these ravines filled with water and fed the usually tame Verde River, turning it into a torrent that ran south to merge with the Salt River, and then on to the Rio Grande, along the border with Mexico. Remote sections of the Verde River loomed ahead, and here the river cut through some of the roughest terrain in the Arizona Territory, an area where the Apache had been able to elude pursuit on many occasions. After two hours of travel, the land became drier and rockier, and the hardiest of desert species now dominated. The patrol threaded its way among stands of agave, yucca, creosote, and ocotillo.

The patrol had gotten out of the fort late, and it would be close to dark before they arrived at the Edge Camp. Despite a faster pace than usual, the horses would handle this distance without problems, and if they rested for most of the night, they would have plenty of energy for the long hard ride into the high country the next day.

In the morning, Skinner would lead the patrol another five miles south, then he intended to break orders and head east up Hardscrabble Ridge and onto the timbered flats between the Mazatzals and the Mogollon Rim. They would come to the Parson ranch first, and the next day they would ride farther north and east to Veronica's ranch. It was a long way, two full days of travel off the assigned route, plus the return trip. Skinner was under no illusions about what would happen if Brickman found out. He'd been warned not to do it both verbally and in writing. This was a major offense. He also had the new recruit, Charlie, sent as a spy, to deal with.

Skinner had considered various ways to keep Charlie quiet and had come up short. He posed the question to Chaco. "Chaco, how are you gonna shut up that new private?"

"Got two weeks. Should be able to find ten or twenty ways to keep his mouth shut."

"He's gonna know we're going east tomorrow. I'm thinkin' we tell him we gotta skirt some narrow sections of the river bottom. Get as far as we can before he gets wise to us."

"Four days of hard riding oughta get us around them sections."

Skinner chuckled and changed the subject. "Think Sweeny is going to be mad when he sees how bad we Burt Turnered him?"

To Burt Turner someone was an expression used at the

fort that referred to the practice of the first group out taking the best equipment, horses, and guns, and it was done out of pure good-natured cussedness. Burt had been the best at the game, but that was a while back now, for he got killed in a runaway-wagon accident six years ago. But his name had stuck in a strange sort of epitaph. He and his companion McIntyre had been the heart and soul of Fort Verde, and now it was Skinner and Chaco who tried to fill the void.

"You weren't really in a mood to argue with if you recall, Capt'n."

"That's true enough," Skinner said and then added, "I just got a bad feeling about these outlaws, Chaco. Can't shake it."

"I know."

"The other thing that could be a big problem is if they split up and scatter."

"I don't think they'll scatter. Men who murder women and children are like cur dogs—they only feel safe in a crowd."

"Cowards!" Skinner spit the word out as the comment registered. Chaco could always be counted on to summarize given situations with a few choice words. His mind worked tirelessly, gauging which human instincts were at fault in every situation. Skinner gave Too Tall his head, barked out an order, and the pace increased.

By sundown the patrol had traveled twenty-one miles south and approached the final stretch of a wide, flat plain. The Verde River ran to the east of them, its course outlined by a long string of cottonwood trees. The soil beneath them had turned white, and to avoid breathing the chalky dust stirred by seventy-two hooves, Skinner had allowed the formation of the column to travel on an angle.

The pace was brisk—brisker than usual—and both man

and beast alike checked and rechecked their mental and physical composure as they trailed along behind two men— one riding a stocky chestnut, the other a tall lined-back dun—that were covering ground with a hint of urgency. A metal item wiggled loose in one of the packs and started to clink against the coffee pot. The mule slowed enough to take the slack out of its lead rope and pressed one ear back to examine the danger level this noise might present. A firm tug on the lead rope assured him that it was okay.

Near the tail end of the patrol, Charlie kicked his horse up alongside Vance, "My horse is tired."

Vance looked over at Charlie, "He ain't that tired, he's building attitude 'cause you're riding like a sack of potatoes. You're gonna' get an ass chewin' tonight."

"What?" Charlie frowned and looked forward, at Skinner and Chaco in the lead.

"Captain don't tolerate lazy riding."

Charlie had ridden out of necessity a lot in his life, but he had never considered riding something that a person should do well. He looked around and saw how the other men were making an effort to stay balanced, easing their horses forward. He tried to smooth out his riding, but his legs and the small of his back began to tire quickly. He sensed that he was the only one feeling incompetent and out of place. *I'll be all right,* he thought, but his anxiety rose, and he was unable to suppress it. He reached into a pocket and felt for the small blue stone. His thumb caressed the stone three times upward and three times downward.

The sun had been hidden by the mountains to the west for more than two hours when the patrol suddenly slowed way down. Charlie was the last man in line. He peered ahead in the fading light. They had arrived at the Edge Camp. Charlie was in pain. His calves had been rubbed raw against the new stirrup straps of his McClellan saddle. His lower back muscles were in knots.

Everyone dismounted and as they went to work setting up camp, Charlie could tell that the others had all been to this place many times before. The mules were unloaded in the center of the campsite and the panniers were put neatly in a row near the cooking area. A well-used fire pit was at the base of two large rocks with flat tops that had been pulled together at one end forming a *V*. In the gap, the sides of the rocks were blackened by soot, and there was a thick mat of coals from previous fires. Between the creek and the camp was a huge trunk of a fallen cottonwood tree, and its length was used to hold all the saddles. A worn trail made by frequent trips to the river for water led around the end of the tree trunk. Behind camp, where they tied the horses when they weren't out on hobbles, cottonwood trees held scars from the rubbing of highline ropes, and the ground around their bases held thick layers of dry manure.

Charlie kept a nervous eye on Skinner and Chaco and made sure he was being attentive.

Skinner's voice was loud and gruff. "Charlie, Skeeter, Vance, Boomer, let's get these horses out. Tomorrow's gonna' be a long day; I want 'em on grass now."

Chaco began issuing orders of his own. "Greg, you and Jimmy take sentry. Sunny, make a wood run. Vance, Boomer, picket the wrangle horses."

Charlie hustled behind Skinner and helped him pull a pile of hobbles out of a pannier and carry them to the long string of horses and mules already tied to highlines made from the pack lash ropes. He knelt by a black-faced roan and started putting on the first set. He'd hardly begun before Skinner critiqued him.

"Stay off your knees when you do that. Sometimes when you put that second strap on, they'll take a step and get surprised by the hobble and then have to lunge to recover. Hobble them from the side, not right in front of 'em. I don't need you to get hurt doing something dumb out here. That would just slow us down."

Charlie quickly got to his feet and moved to one side of the horse, "Yes sir, Captain."

"One thing I need out of ya: Your ridin' is wearing your horse out. When we trot, I want to see you standin' up and balanced. Don't make that horse tire 'cause you're being lazy, ya understand?"

"Yes sir."

"All right then, put more energy into your riding. Another thing: Quit looking at the trail; let your horse have that job. I wanna see ya watchin' the country." Skinner waved an arm towards the horizon. "Dust clouds, movement, maybe someone will skyline themselves for just a second. We need to keep our eyes peeled for anythin'. These are bad people we're lookin' for. I need yours and everyone's help watchin' the land."

"Yes sir. Sir, permission to ask a question?"

"Don't ask for permission, just ask."

"Yes sir. Sir, what's your plan to catch these men?"

Skinner briefly dodged the obvious direction of the question. "We're going to ride a lot of country fast. See if we cross their trail. If we do, we're gonna try an engage 'em and bring 'em in." Skinner paused and stared Charlie down. "Might not be much left to bring in. These are real killers, is what I been told. They ain't gonna' be the type to give up without a fight. You got concerns about that?"

"Captain, sir, I've never been in a fight before." Charlie kept his head ducked so Skinner couldn't see his expression. "I mean one involving guns, anyway."

"Don't think about that too much. I tell ya what to do,

if needed, and how to do it. All you're gonna have to do is shoot straight. You can shoot, can't ya?"

"Yes sir. I can shoot. I'm just not too sure how well if someone's shooting back. You know how everyone talks about the difference between shooting targets and shooting when someone's shooting back . . ."

"Yeah, I know. Main thing is to remember to actually aim. It's amazin' how people just start firing off bullets and don't even look down the barrel of their gun. You remember to aim, all right?"

"Yes sir."

"In the meantime, all I need you to do is ride well and keep a keen eye out. Me an' Chaco will tell you everything else as we go."

"Sir?"

"Yeah, last question, though."

"Have all these men been with you before?"

Skinner knew the private was uncomfortable with the lack of strict military correctness among them, and again he deflected the direction of the question. "You pay attention to what they tell ya. Unless they're trying to get ya riled."

"Sir, I don't understand what you mean."

"You will." Skinner turned his back and started hobbling another horse.

Charlie stood and pulled the halter on the roan horse he'd just hobbled.

"Private, wait until they're all hobbled before ya let one go. The others get restless if they see one leaving, makes it hard to get the hobbles on 'em." Skinner lectured him in a gruff tone and moved on to the next horse.

Angry at himself for making another greenhorn mistake, Charlie quickly caught the gray.

When all the horses had been hobbled, they pulled halters and gently hazed them up a narrow side canyon above camp. Too Tall, as usual, in the absence of any mares, went to the front and led the herd.

Charlie kept his eyes on everyone, determined not to make another mistake. He found himself unexpectedly impressed with how quickly everything was done. Within twenty-five minutes of their arrival, the horses were out, the area secured, and the camp set. Chaco's wife, Maria, had stuffed the panniers with salt pork, biscuits, and dried fruit, which required minimum prep work to prepare a meal.

Charlie lingered near the cook fire and ate his meal slowly, continuing his observation of the men. Seated near him, Boomer and Vance had busied themselves sewing torn clothing and repairing a bridle. Skeeter hovered nearby trying to get anyone to listen to his long list of jokes until Vance had had enough and told him to shut up. Everyone else had moved to a warming fire a few yards away, where a deck of cards had appeared.

Charlie put down his plate and rubbed his sore calves. "How far is it to where the Verde joins the Salt?" he asked Skeeter.

"If you're saddle sore already, you're gonna be half dead by the time we get there," answered Skeeter. "You're a soft one, ain't ya?" Skeeter looked over Charlie's short build and blond hair.

"I'm fine."

"You're gonna hafta be. When you ride with the captain and Chaco, you better count on staying tough. You start whining, you'll get hammered quick. The captain don't tolerate any whining. Chaco neither."

"I won't whine."

"You're here to spy on us, ain't ya?"

"I wish you would just shut up." Charlie's face turned red.

"How about you wish in one hand, crap in the other.

See which gets full first." Skeeter took a step towards Charlie. Clenched fists hung at his sides.

"Leave him alone, Skeeter," said Boomer.

"Hell, it ain't no secret why he's along. I'm just trying to let him . . ."

"Shut up Skeeter, or I'm going to bust your chops." Boomer stretched his broad shoulders back to emphasize his annoyance.

"What's it matter to you?"

"I ain't in no mood for you and your pot stirring."

Charlie circled the stones of the cook fire, sat near Boomer, and wisely changed the subject.

"The captain and Chaco act like they been around each other a long time. Sure seem to have nice horses too."

"Those are two of the best horses you're ever going to see," said Boomer. He looked straight at Charlie, and his eyes glinted in the firelight as he studied the new private.

"They known each other since they was kids. Captain saved Chaco's life last summer, too," added Skeeter.

"Shut up Skeeter," said Boomer.

"I'll say whatever I want."

"Why you bringing that up anyhow?"

Charlie pushed to hear the story. "What happened?"

"You tell him, Boomer. I've told that story enough times already," said Skeeter.

Exasperated with Skeeter, Boomer stopped sewing and dropped his hands into his lap. "If I get up, I'm going to thump ya."

"I'm shuttin' up. I'm shuttin' up." Skeeter's voice softened. "Tell him the story, Boomer."

Boomer sighed, "It ain't about knowing each other good that makes 'em close. It's about what they've been through." Boomer looked out from beneath his hat brim and saw both Chaco and Skinner were out of earshot over

at the warming fire, helping a card game get started. "Long
time ago they ran away as a couple of orphans. Left in the
middle of the night after an accident that killed a boy
named Sydney. Horse trader named Glen Tulin adopted
'em. Taught 'em a lot about horses. You have a problem
with a horse, ain't no one better than the captain to sort
it out."

"How'd they kill a kid?" Charlie interrupted.

"Thought you wanted to hear about how the captain
saved Chaco's life?"

"I want to hear it all."

"That early part is a different story, an' a sore subject
with 'em. You wanna hear it, ask them, 'cause you won't
catch me telling it. Might tell it wrong. Wouldn't be right
to get it wrong." Boomer jerked his coat around and dipped
his needle into the edge of another tear in the sleeve.

"Tell me what you're willing," said Charlie.

Boomer hunkered down in his seat. He covered his
thighs with folds from the lower portions of his jacket and
continued to sew. "Last year, Chaco got the sweet eye on
Maria when she moved to the fort. She was working tables
at the Come and Get It. Been raining for days, but there
was still a fair amount of people passing through on their
way to other parts. Mud was everywhere. Like usual,
Chaco and the captain were up first . . ."

*Heavy cloud cover blocked most of the sun's light as it
rose, and a dull gray light spread over the valley.
Woodsmoke billowing from multiple chimney pipes clung
to the rooftops in the cold, windless drizzle that continued
to fall. The forlorn crowing of a single rooster rose above
the sound of shovels sliding over wood as two soldiers
working off demerits pushed the heavy mud off sidewalks.*

Others, in equally bad standing, chopped wood under the dripping roof of a dilapidated woodshed near the barracks. There was little talk; the soldiers finished quickly and retreated to the dry warmth of their bunks, and soon the only sound at Fort Verde was rain hitting the rooftops.

Chaco, all alone, was out at the corral with a lariat in hand. He stomped into the corral and tossed a loop on Turns Good.

"Let's go, amigo. I'm gonna give you the best grooming you ever had."

Chaco led his horse back into a dimly lit tack room with one thought on his mind: Maria. She was the prettiest thing he'd ever seen.

He spent considerable time brushing out Turns Good's long mane and tail and grooming his thick winter coat. When his coat was slicked out as much as it could be, Chaco began oiling his saddle. Twice he put down the oil rags and went to the doorway to look at the weather.

Turns Good bent his neck to eyeball his master.

"It's okay, boy," Chaco said. "All you gotta do is show off a bit."

Chaco lingered in the doorway waiting and hoping for the rain to taper off. He intended to then take the horse out for a training session near the restaurant. With a well-timed tickle from a sharp spur, Turns Good would spin both ways, and if Chaco put him into a run and then asked for a big stop, Turns Good would stop so hard his butt scraped the ground. Any woman would be impressed. He kneeled and began to clean the last of the mud off Turns Good's coronets just as Skinner walked into the tack room.

"Morning," said Skinner.

"Morning," said Chaco, looking at the thick mud clinging to Skinner's boots.

Skinner ran a hand over Turns Good and admired his brushed-out coat. "Gonna be hard to spin your horse in mud, ain't it?" he asked. "He'll probably pull a muscle and start limpin'. If I was you . . ."

"Why don't you mind your own business?"

"You're wasting your time gussying him up like that. He ain't gonna be anything but mud-splattered by the time you get over there."

"I'm real frustrated, so shut the hell up."

Skinner laughed, "Here's another idea: How about we just go over there for breakfast and talk to her? How's that for a plan?"

"Might be a little obvious two days in a row, don't you think?"

"Oh, I get it. You was gonna use a more subtle approach. Go out there all gussied up and start spinnin' your horse by her window in the mud and rain." Skinner shook his head, "You sure got a lot to learn. Go have breakfast, Chaco. Quit planning it out. Just go over there and eat."

Wanting more grooming, Turns Good stepped back towards Chaco and pushed him with his rear end. Chaco bumped into Skinner.

Chaco's shoulders sank. "You got any money I can borrow?"

"Not on me. Tell you what—I'll meet you over there. You go first. Tell her you're waiting for me. That'll give you time to drink coffee and visit." Skinner winked at Chaco.

Chaco frowned. "Don't leave me in there too long. By myself, I mean."

"I won't. Now listen to me, Chaco. Don't rush anything. Just go easy. Make sure you ask her about herself. Don't just talk about you. Talk about her."

"Like what?"

"Tell her she's pretty," said Skinner with raised eyebrows and pursed lips.

"Shut the hell up." Chaco's frown turned into a scowl as he stripped his saddle off Turns Good. "Slip me some money when she ain't lookin'. I wanna pay. I'll pay you back come next week."

"All right. See ya in a bit." Skinner moved towards the door.

"She ain't pretty; she's beautiful," said Chaco over his shoulder.

"She shore is," said Skinner, grinning. "That's why I made that suggestion." Skinner grinned and raised his eyebrows at Chaco, but he didn't have much opportunity to indulge his mirth due to a brush flying his direction. He managed to avoid the brush and duck out the door unscathed as more projectiles slammed against the flimsy wood walls behind him.

Chaco stepped under the awning of the Come and Get It, pulled his hat down low over his dark eyes. With a shaky hand he rubbed the small amount of stubble on the point of his chin. He could hear lots of voices coming from inside. Unable to see through the steamed-up windows, he shrugged, took a couple of deep breaths, and walked in. Drawn in by the smell of side pork, sourdough, and coffee, and seeking warmth and shelter from the rain, people filled the tiny restaurant.

Chaco squeezed through the tight spaces among the tables and sat down at the only empty table. Moments later Maria appeared from the kitchen with her arms full of plates. She acknowledged him with a faint smile but moved to a table on the far side of the room.

"She's working so hard, I ain't ever gonna get a chance to talk to her. Damn," Chaco muttered to himself. He turned his metal coffee cup over and waited. He looked around. There were several people he knew, but most of the faces belonged to strangers. Four men sat at a table to his right. The biggest man had a wide, thick beard that hung well *below his neck. He looked at Chaco and stared. Chaco ignored him.*

"Morning," said the man with the beard.

"Morning." Chaco nodded at the man then looked away.

"Names Harvey. Harvey Pleasant."

"Chaco."

"We're outta Santa Fe. Heading' to Yuma."

"That's a long way, mister." Chaco looked at Maria's backside as she disappeared through the swinging doors into the kitchen. He didn't look at the stranger.

The man seated to Harvey's right spoke up. "Trail's getting longer too, slow as this place is."

"I ain't got all day for some food," Harvey yelled towards the kitchen, then he grinned at Chaco.

Maria swept out of the kitchen with more orders.

"Hey, little woman. Get over here," Harvey called out.

Maria handed out the plates of food and then moved to Harvey's table. "Yes?" she said.

"We been waiting long enough. Where's our food?"

"It will be ready soon," Maria replied.

Harvey reached out and slapped her butt as she turned back to the kitchen. "Maybe that'll help you hurry up about it," he said.

Maria gasped and turned back; red faced. "Don't ever do that," she said, and slapped his face.

Harvey grabbed her wrist, spun her around, and pulled her hips onto his lap. He wiggled her closer, so her hips were up tight against his belt, and pushed his bearded chin over her shoulder. He spoke with his lips just an inch from her ear. "What did ya say little woman? I didn't hear ya real good."

The busy cafe got quiet, and all heads turned towards the center of the room . . .

"Let her go." Chaco's chair sliding back grated on the floor as he stood.

"Whatcha gonna do about it, little man, if I don't do like you say?"

"I'm gonna kick your ass is what I'm gonna do about it. Now let her go."

"It's okay Chaco. I'm okay." Maria squirmed trying to wrestle herself away from Harvey's grip. "Let go of me."

"I don't think you're going to kick my ass little man. Ain't that funny. A little man and a little woman," said Harvey.

"Let her go." Chaco spoke loudly.

"What about them? They'll back me." Harvey gestured at his companions and held on tight to Maria as she squirmed harder to get away. "You gonna take on all four of us?"

"Let go of me." Maria yelled.

Chaco eyed the man's companions, sucked in a huge, strained breath, and over Maria's protests kept talking. "No. When I'm done with you, I'm gonna just be getting warmed up. Ol' toothless there, I'm gonna break his leg. Then I'm gonna hurt that scary-looking idiot real bad. Might break both his legs." Trembling Chaco took in the last of Harvey's companions. "If you was an Indian, I guess they'd call you One Eye That Sags." Chaco focused back on Harvey. "If I'm able to catch him before he turns tail, I'm gonna use his nasty-lookin' face to scrape the mud off this floor."

"And if I let her go, then whatcha you gonna do about it?"

"You need me to repeat all that, you foul mannered ignorant fool?"

Harvey threw Maria off his lap and lunged out of his chair.

Chaco swung hard. His fist slammed against Harvey's

nose, slowing the big man down long enough for Chaco to step to the side and hurl his chair in front of Harvey, breaking his momentum. Harvey stumbled over the chair, smashing it to pieces. Before his companions could get into the fight, Chaco picked up another chair and whacked Harvey in the back of the head, knocking him out. Chaco swung around to meet his companions who took him in a rush, knocked him to the floor, and began pummeling him. The customers were all stampeding for cover, except Maria.

"Pare! Pare! Stop it!" she screamed. She too picked up a chair, swung it over her head, and brought it down on the nearest man trying to get at Chaco. He turned, grabbed her around the waist, and pushed her backwards until they crashed into a table.

Chaco, kicking and squirming, managed to get back on his feet. He moved left and right, and swung wildly, matching them blow for blow. He hurled a table in between them and him, then tried to pick up another chair and use it as a weapon, but they were too close and hitting him relentlessly. One of them undid the leather thong to his sheath knife and pulled the blade out. The knife panicked Chaco; he took a vicious swing at the knife with the riding crop hanging from his wrist, but the man held on to the weapon. Chaco pushed backwards, sending more chairs and tables skittering across the floor as he tried to get away, but he took a vicious hit to the stomach from the second man, which knocked the wind out of him. Adrenaline kept him on his feet, and he lunged for the door, trying to buy time to get his lungs working again.

Shouting, furniture legs sliding on the floor, and the sound of dishes breaking filled the restaurant. Unable to catch his breath, Chaco fell out the door, rolled across the boardwalk, and landed in the mud. One of his attackers fell on top of him and squeezed the last air from his lungs.

Unable to breathe, he curled up, rolled sideways, and gagged.

The skinny man saw Chaco was done and put his knife away. Moving up beside Chaco, he planted one boot solidly in the mud and then delivered a vicious kick to Chaco's head with his other foot.

Chaco collapsed unconscious facedown in the wet mud.

Boomer put his needle away and took a swig of water from a canteen. "Chaco would have died if the captain hadn't been on his way over. That mud was deep. Water filled every hoof print. Be a hell of a thing to drown in a few inches of mud."

"Chaco took on three men all at once?"

Skeeter sat straight up and glared at Charlie. "Took on four. Are you deaf or something? You calling us liars?"

Charlie recoiled. "No, I'm not calling you liars."

"You think we're all crooked, you come to spy on us, and you don't know what the hell you're doing out here. We gotta take care of ya. I oughta take you down by the river and bust some sense into you."

"Ease up, you jumpy knucklehead. You're getting on my nerves more than him." Boomer pulled a red-faced Skeeter back into his seat. "You're right, he don't know nothing yet, but he will. Relax will ya?" Boomer swiveled his head and looked at Charlie. "Might help if you don't feel a need to put a negative comment on every subject that don't sit just right with ya. You could relax that head of yours a bit. We got a long ride ahead of us."

With Charlie and Skeeter silenced, Boomer went on with the story.

"Captain got there just in time. Told me he come around the corner, first thing he saw was Chaco getting kicked

upside the head. Told me he just went on the fight, never
thought about nothing. The two outside, still hovering
around Chaco, probably woulda crapped themselves if
they'd a known what was coming. Captain took the first
one out with one punch. I never saw his face, but I sure
saw Captain's hands later on. I bet that piece of dirt is still
hurting. He took the second man out quick too and never
got cut."

"Whatcha you mean cut?" Charlie leaned in.

"Second one drew that skinning knife again. He took
one big swipe at the Captain with that blade, and that was
all he ever got done. Knowing he had to get to Chaco
before he drowned, Captain just waded in behind that first
swipe and took him out. He kicked both their asses fast."

Skeeter leaned in closer to Boomer as well. In a hushed
voice he encouraged him to continue with the story "Tell
him what happened next, Boomer. Tell him."

Skinner slid down on his knees by Chaco, rolled him
over, swiped the mud from his face, and saw that Chaco
wasn't breathing. Skinner pinched his nose, covered
Chaco's mouth with his own and blew a breath down his
windpipe. Chaco coughed and took a ragged breath.

People emerged from the restaurant and stood to the
left and right of the door on the sidewalk, under the
awning and out of the rain. Brushing through them, Maria
rushed over to Skinner and dropped on her knees by
Chaco's head. She leaned forward and sheltered Chaco's
face from the rain with her torso.

"Ay Dios mio!" she stammered.

Chaco only took two breaths on his own, so Skinner
breathed in another lungful of air. Chaco coughed and

gagged but continued to breathe on his own, and his eyes flickered open.

"He's coming back. He's going to be okay. Oh my God look at his cheek," said Maria as she cleared the mud from the wound with a fold of her dress. She looked up at Skinner, but her eye was pulled by the sight of Harvey walking out the door of the restaurant holding a pistol in his right hand. "Tom," Maria gasped, and stared straight at Harvey.

Harvey's nose dripped blood. It rolled over his lips, down his beard, and onto the front of his shirt. Skinner stood and took three steps towards him, shielding Chaco and Maria. Fifteen feet separated him from Harvey.

"Was this you're doing? Did you start all this?" Skinner asked in a loud voice.

"Who the hell are you?" Harvey asked as he wiped blood off his face with his free hand.

"Captain Skinner. I been looking for this man all morning," Skinner pointed at Chaco.

"Well, ya found him. I ain't sure ya found him quick enough 'cause . . ."

Skinner interrupted him, his voice full of authority. "Because what?"

The skinny man who'd pulled the knife groaned audibly and rolled to his side. "Do these men work for you?" Skinner gestured at Harvey's companion and took a nonchalant step to the right so if Harvey shot at him, Chaco and Maria would be out of the line of fire.

Harvey's legs wobbled. His hand twitched.

Skinner calculated as he talked and took another step forward and to the right. The pistol was a single action Colt, which required the man to cock the hammer before pulling the trigger. The man was unsteady, his movements slow, the pistol was not cocked. Skinner took another step forward and kept talking. "Pull in your horns, mister. Don't need a shooting over this little scrap." Getting no response, Skinner yelled. "Drop that gun." He took one more step forward. Only ten feet separated them now; his body shook with nerves.

"Shut your mouth and get out of my way," said Harvey.

When Harvey raised his free hand to wipe blood off his mouth, Skinner lunged for his knees. A shot roared above his head; the bullet plucked at the back of his coat. Skinner drove forward and pushed Harvey's legs out from under him. When he fell, Skinner kicked wildly at Harvey's head and gun hand, not giving him a chance to aim and shoot again. When Harvey wrenched his gun hand around, Skinner caught his wrist and held it with both hands. Harvey coiled his free arm and slammed his elbow into Skinner's ribs, but Skinner held onto his wrist, absorbed the punishment, and kept his focus on the weapon. He had to get the gun out of the fight. Skinner contained his rage while Harvey delivered blow after blow with his elbow against his ribs. Skinner slammed Harvey's hand repeatedly against the boardwalk, trying to get him to let go of the pistol. Then he saw a jagged piece of wood that protruded off the edge of the boardwalk. He slid Harvey's hand across it and drove the sliver into the back of his hand. Then Skinner pounded his hand down again and drove the sliver deeper. The gun fell out of Harvey's hand. Skinner kicked at it and saw it slither off the boardwalk and into the mud. With the weapon now out of the fight, Skinner was free to fight. He wrenched free of the big man, pivoted, and attacked.

Moments later Skinner felt other men grab his arms, "Pull him back," said a voice. More hands grabbed him and pulled him backwards. "He's done Captain. Stop," said another voice.

Skinner stood and looked down at the big man lying on his back. Harvey was barely breathing. Unfocused eyes blinked against the blood pooling in both his eye sockets. Two men knelt by Harvey, one looked up at Skinner. "He's not going anywhere. He's done." A third man pushed Skinner back.

Skinner turned and walked a short distance away with his arm held tight against his ribs.

Soldiers that had arrived from the fort had already secured Harvey's companions. Men, women, and children emerged from hiding places. Two young boys peeked around the corner of the restaurant and gaped at Skinner with open mouths.

Maria was still kneeling in the mud by Chaco. "Tom . . . Tom are you okay?"

"Yeah. Come on let's get out of the rain."

With Maria and Skinner's help, Chaco stood. He placed his hands on his knees and moved his head from side to side. "Someone whacked me good."

Skinner and Maria each put an arm around Chaco, and they moved to the porch and sat on a bench out of the rain. Maria rushed inside the restaurant. Steam rose off Skinner's head and neck. Chaco began to shiver. They both stared out towards the horizon.

Skinner felt Chaco's elbow press into his side.

"Hey?" said Chaco.

"What?"

"Next time let me spin my damn horse."

Skinner took a deep breath, the corners of his lips stretched into an exhausted smile. He chuckled and examined his bloodied hands.

Maria emerged with coats and a clean, wet towel. She draped a coat over Chaco's shoulders and another over his knees. Crooning in whispered Spanish, she began to

clean the blood and mud off his face and hands. Chaco
stared into her eyes as she worked.

The rain began to lighten, and towards the west, rays of
light broke through the clouds for the first time in two days.
"I don't know, Chaco," said Skinner as he watched the pair
of them. "I'm thinkin' my idea done worked like a charm."

Chilled, Boomer pulled the repaired coat on. "That
Maria, she doesn't leave Chaco's side." Boomer buttoned
his coat and looked at Charlie. "The captain and Chaco are
a team; you'll see how they are. We happen to get in a
scrap, you'll see."

Visibly impressed, Charlie looked towards the warming
fire and saw that Chaco was now directing the card game.
He saw Chaco toss a couple of coins. Skinner was nowhere
to be seen. *No one salutes around here, they're gambling,*
their uniforms are a mess, they cuss and fight among them-
selves, but those two have everyone's respect, Charlie
thought. He felt Skeeter stand and move behind him.
When Skeeter spoke, the words floated around his head
like the smoke from the fire.

"When you ride with the two of them, you better stay
tough. You go get some shut-eye. We'll be moving again
before you know it." Skeeter hesitated, then continued in
his serious matter-of-fact tone, his voice lowered to just
above a whisper, "It ain't a small thing what he done for
his friend."

Charlie rose, pulled his hat brim low over his eyes. He
shoved his hands deep into his pockets, walked past the
card game, and went to his bedroll.

CHAPTER 6

Skinner never slept well at the Edge Camp, and tonight it was doubly hard. After tossing around in his bedroll for hours, he gave up. He needed to move. Out of habit, he decided to test the sentry, to make sure he was awake. Since the Apache had given up, sentry duty had gone from being a terrifying experience to monotonous and boring, the most miserable job a soldier could be given. But the Arizona Territory wasn't safe yet; trouble could come in a variety of forms, one of which was horse thieves. There was also the possibility that the horses would come out of the side canyon and drift back towards the fort; they had to be watched. After quietly pulling on his boots, Skinner rolled onto his hands and knees and crawled across the camp, passing by the stack of saddles and working his way towards a small high point where the sentry would be.

A voice spoke softly out of the night "You lose something, Captain?" It was Skeeter.

"Just checking on ya, Skeeter. Wouldn't be the first time you fell asleep on watch." Skinner got to his feet. "I'm going for a walk."

"Yes sir, Captain," said Skeeter.

"Don't shoot me when I come back in."

Skeeter replied in a whisper as Skinner moved off, "I ain't feeble minded, sir."

Skinner walked fast and summited a low ridge to the north of the camp. He found a place to sit where he could lean against a boulder. He looked over the starlit valley that spread out to the north and tried to clear his mind of negative thoughts, but an emotion that was new to him wouldn't allow it. Skinner knew his worry for Veronica was based on his knowledge of the land. The dry deserts to the east and south dictated how people traveled; areas had to be skirted for the sake of water. If he could just get to Veronica, warn her, and then head south in a hurry, he might get away with it. If he got caught it would be bad. It might get Chaco in trouble as well; everyone knew they'd grown up together. That idiot Brickman just didn't think. If he knew the lay of the land and what it took to move horses through it, he would know he's sending me the wrong way. Least of all he could have asked him for an opinion. Brickman's problem, Skinner thought, was that he was so nervous that someone would challenge his authority that he isolated himself in his own stupidity. He kicked at a rock with his boot heel. Maybe he was making a bad call. Maybe, though, if he got there and warned her and her whole family, it would make up for his behavior the last time they were together. Skinner knew Leon would heed a warning and take serious precautions to protect his family, Leon would probably think the same way he had about what direction a big group of men traveling due east out of the Gila country would need to go.

The howling of a wolf pack on the mountain behind him broke Skinner's thoughts.

"Wolves." he spoke out loud.

He stood abruptly and started to walk back to camp.

Sometimes he wished he weren't superstitious, but he hadn't seen so much as a wolf track in two years and hearing them now he took as a bad omen. The wolves had put another rush of adrenaline into his already overloaded system. Again he spoke aloud into the starlit night. "Get ahold of yourself soldier. Get a hold of yourself now."

A minute out of camp Skeeter challenged him again.

"Is that you, Captain?"

"Yeah, it's me."

"Go ahead and get some shut-eye. I'll take watch," Skinner said.

"You sure?"

"Yeah, it's okay."

Skinner felt Skeeter eyeballing him.

"Hey, Captain, did you hear all of them wolves howling?"

"Yeah, I heard them."

"Sounded like a bunch of them killing beasts out there."

"Probably so, Skeeter." Skinner looked away, to the east.

Skeeter pulled his hat off and balled it up. "I'm sorry Captain. I. . . ."

"Go get some shut-eye, Skeeter."

As Skeeter moved off, Skinner watched him descend the slope to camp. He grunted an approbation of the soldier's comment and hammered his fist against a rock. More anxiety swept over him, and the temptation to roust everyone and go immediately became huge, but he knew from experience that another four hours of rest and feed for the horses would see them to the Mogollon Rim country sooner than if they left right away. A slight breeze found a hole in the clothing around his neck, and he pulled his collar a little higher. He sensed a change on the air. *Weather coming,* he thought. "Damn."

Soon after Skinner had settled in on the rocky outcrop, the solitude of sentry duty, the brilliant starlight circling above, the hoots of a distant great horned owl, stress, and the strong likelihood of being wet and cold in the near future began to take a toll on Skinner's mental discipline. For the thousandth time, his mind trapped him into reliving the events of that crisp sunny day two months ago, after he'd accepted an invitation to join Leon, the boys, and Veronica on a fall hunt up on the Mogollon. The day had gone well, but just after dark he'd behaved badly, and their perfect day had gone all wrong. Skinner tilted his head back and exhaled sharply, then grunted in frustration. . . .

The hunting camp was a four-hour ride north of their home on the Mogollon Rim. In a sheltered spot, Leon and the kids had built a small frame out of pine logs and then cut and sewed a canvas skin that could be stretched over the frame in a matter of minutes to create a warm and comfortable cook tent. During the course of three fall hunting seasons, a table, chairs, and stove had been added. Water was available in all but the coldest months of the year from a spring that trickled out of the ground outside the tent. Just behind the spring a high point looked out over a vast piece of land to the north that was cut with steep-sided canyons, all of which had small streams running through them. Expanses of land between the canyon's limestone and granite rims consisted of dense stands of scrub oak, alligator juniper, ponderosa pine and meadows usually thick with grass. This remote area still held large numbers of deer and the last remaining elk that had eluded an ever-increasing number of meat hunters.

The cook-tent stove and rusty stovepipe had tiny leaks,

and small amounts of woodsmoke carried the aroma of frijoles and beefsteak to every corner of the tent. It was Veronica's nervous energy around Skinner, however, that filled the tent to the bursting point. Veronica worked without pause and made a quick fuss about any inefficiencies in cooking dinner, caring for the horses, or preparing for the hunt in the morning. It was clear to her brothers and Leon that on this trip, she intended to rule over every job, including leadership. Leon and the twins cautiously indulged her nervous energy with patience and humor, for they knew she wanted to impress their guest. Veronica was dressed in a tan shirt and gray wool vest. Below her waist, a faded brown riding skirt swirled above her calves and high-topped boots each time she made another hurried turn. With a heavily stained apron tied around her waist, Veronica moved from task to task, and a barely audible hum emanated from her throat that she hoped would help her to appear aloof from the conversation going on between Leon and Skinner behind her.

"Which way do ya think we should go tomorrow?" Skinner asked Leon.

"I been thinking on that. As little game as we're seeing, I think we probably better split up. Why don't you and Veronica stay up high on the canyon ridge, and I'll take the boys and we'll work down inside. Maybe we'll flush something towards each other."

Veronica reached for the pan and grabbed the hot handle without using a glove. "Ow," she squealed.

Leon leapt to his feet and went to investigate the burn.

Veronica was frequently amazed by her father's wild thinking, but this was pushing it. Mom would kill him. She knew instinctively, however, that he must approve of Skinner, or he wouldn't have suggested it. There was something else to it as well, some other reason why he would let her go like this. She questioned herself, her upbringing, her understanding of her father's eccentricities, looking for answers, but her thoughts were addled by the prospect of being alone with Skinner, and by the pain in her hand.

"It's not too bad," said Leon. He held his daughter's burnt hand and with his other hand he grabbed her bicep and squeezed. He looked directly into her eyes. "You'll be all right."

Veronica understood, and tears welled in her eyes. He's letting me go because he trusts me. Trusts me to make good decisions. She suppressed an urge to hug him because of Skinner's presence, but she had never felt better complimented in her life. "Yeah, I'm fine, Dad," she replied in a whisper. "I'll be just fine."

Veronica turned back to the cooking area. She swiped a forefinger along the congealed grease on the bottom of the stove and spread it on her burn. She blew on the injured spot and felt the cooling effect. Prompted by touches of guilt and concern, her thoughts turned to her mother. This would definitely not be happening if she'd been here. Mom must have a wild streak in her somewhere to have married Dad, she thought.

"I think I'll go check on the horses," said Skinner, stumbling out of the tent, needing space and air.

"Hurry up, dinner is ready." answered Veronica. "Courtney. Monte. Get your plates. How hungry are you?"

"Not as hungry as you are," said Courtney in a voice only Veronica could hear. He put a thick slice of bread on the side of his plate and held the dish out, chuckling.

Veronica scooped a huge amount of beans and meat up with the spoon and, giving her brother a hard look, she slapped the food on top of the bread and his thumb, which was curled over the edge of the plate.

"Good one," said Courtney, still chuckling. He raised

his thumb to his mouth and sucked the beans off as he stared at his sister.

Veronica squinted, the corners of her mouth stretched tight, and she whacked Courtney on the side of his head with the spoon. She pulled her arm back for another blow and waited.

Courtney flopped down in the dirt next to the stove to eat. He was done with his taunts but was unable to suppress a mischievous grin.

Sunrise was half an hour away as the five of them prepared their horses for the day. Cold saddles were lifted into place, and bridles were put on over the halters. Chaps, canteens, rain gear, and saddlebags full of food were all tied securely to saddles. Loaded rifles, ready for a quick dismount and fast shot, were shoved into scabbards, and pistol belts were fastened around waists, holding thick layers of clothing tightly against their bodies. Skinner was ready first, but he fumbled with his gear and stalled, not wanting to make them look slow or make him appear too eager to go. He didn't step aboard Too Tall until Monte and Courtney had mounted their horses.

"I would say let's meet for lunch, but I don't think they would go for that," Leon said to Veronica, gesturing at his two sons.

"Not a chance, Dad," said Monte.

Leon smiled and gave his cinch a final check. Today his boys would show him everything they knew about themselves as horsemen, hunters, and brothers. He was happy for his daughter as well, and despite having tossed and turned most of the night second-guessing his decision to allow her and Skinner to go alone together, his confidence that he'd made a smart choice returned. Encumbered by heavy clothing, Leon mounted Viking awkwardly and struggled to get his leg over the back of the saddle. The stallion seized the opportunity, his neck arched, and he moved aggressively towards Veronica's mare. He snorted, and his flanks began to heave before Leon could get seated and pull him up. "Cut it out." Leon gave Viking a hard slap, pulled the reins, and turned the stallion away from camp.

Courtney rolled his eyes. "Let's get out of here."

"You want me to go first?" asked Skinner when Leon and the boys were out of earshot.

"Yeah, sure," Veronica replied.

Too Tall put his nose down and moved off, angling away from Leon and the twins. They traveled for an hour in silence, with Skinner in the lead. To the east a crest of light began forming along the length of the horizon, and a half hour later shooting light found them on the eastern slope of a small hill. A dense ribbon of scrub oak ran all the way down the hill to a gully at its base. The nameless canyon where Leon and the boys had gone was to the south and far below them. In the low light, the outline of the snow-capped San Francisco Peaks far to the north looked two dimensional and bold. It was an ideal place to set up and watch for deer.

Veronica's heart started to pound against her rib cage. It wasn't merely Skinner's suggestion that they get off and watch the meadows that started her heart racing; it was the large, twisted root that protruded up and out from the base of a huge old alligator juniper. The root, having grown up and over a rock, had created a perfect place for two people to sit, but they would be hip to hip. Veronica wondered if Skinner had noticed the spot as well, and she began to stall.

Skinner saw the seat; he felt his adrenaline rise but didn't say anything. To appear relaxed, he attempted a choreographed move that included pulling his rifle out of the scabbard, swinging his leg across the back of his saddle and stepping down in one smooth motion. But his cold-weather hunting boot hung up in the stirrup, and he had to hop on his other foot to get his balance before he could jerk it free. Too Tall questioned the dismount with a turn of his head and a step to the side.

He's nervous too, thought Veronica when she saw Skinner hop like a beginner rider. She mobilized every ounce of courage she could, tied her horse, moved over to the tree, and took a nonchalant look around. "Shall we sit here?"

"Looks like a good spot to me," said Skinner. He turned his back and led Too Tall to a tree, taking his time tying the big horse so he could get control of a huge, nervous grin that gripped his face.

Veronica sat down on one end of the root, leaving room for him. She raised her chin and did not look at Skinner as he approached, keeping her eyes focused down the slope. Her body was reacting in an unfamiliar way, and she found it hard to breathe, yet she most certainly wasn't going to allow herself to draw in a deep breath and expose the way she felt. When Skinner sat, their hips touched ever so slightly, and Veronica in her most mature, ladylike fashion slid to the very edge of the seat, up against the trunk of the tree, only to discover there was a small, sharp point sticking into her hip on the far side. The only way to relieve the pain was to move closer to Skinner, so she endured the discomfort, but she was unable to subdue the need for a deep breath any longer.

"The air is so fresh out here, don't you think?" Veronica took in a deep breath.

"Yeah, I guess so." Skinner took a quick look at Veronica from the corner of his eye. "This is a perfect spot."

Skinner quickly added to his brief statement. "To watch for deer."

Skinner could feel nervous energy radiate off Veronica; it hit him full in the face like a warm wind. He didn't know what it meant, because as far as Skinner was concerned, the correct feeling one should have right now was fear, not nerves—at least that's how he felt about it. He needed to say something fast. "I didn't see any fresh sign on the way in here, did you?" he asked in a quiet hunting voice.

"No."

"Let's give it about half an hour here, and if nothing shows, maybe we should move on."

"Okay."

They both remained quiet, relieved by the need for silence as they watched for deer. But after a few minutes, Veronica started to fidget.

"Are you comfortable? Here, you want me to move over?"

"Just a little."

Their hips touched for the second time, and Skinner was sure Veronica's head had tilted his direction just a fraction of an inch. One of her hands slid onto the top of her thigh and remained still, but the way she held it looked unnatural; it looked uncomfortable. It looked like an invitation, and Skinner's heart began to pound hard.

Skinner slid his own hand down along his thigh and rested it just inches from hers. She didn't move her hand away, so Skinner slid his over hers.

"Tom?"

"What?"

"You like me, don't you?"

"Yes, I do." Skinner sensed rejection, but then the tips of her fingers suddenly curled into his palm.

Veronica increased the pressure of her leg against his. "Do you want to kiss me?" she asked. Her voice was higher than normal and a little bit hoarse.

"Yes, I do." He waited.

Barely breathing, Veronica waited.

Scared, Skinner didn't move.

"I'd like to kiss you, too," she said. Her eyes closed and her head turned. She smelled his breath first—it was strong, but not unpleasant. She felt his hand let go of hers and slide around the back of her waist then his lips pressed against hers.

His kiss was gentle at first, then it became a bit awkward, but he didn't stop for a full minute. When it was over Veronica stood and took a step forward to hide the smile on her face—for some reason, she didn't want him to see it. Desperate for a distraction, she reverted into the previous night's bossy demeanor and blurted out an order. "Let's travel."

Too Tall had taken the break as an opportunity to nap. He lifted his head when Veronica suddenly stood, and with heavy eyelids studied her.

"Have you ever let anyone ride your horse?" she asked.

"Nope."

"Will you let me try him?"

"You sure?"

Veronica pushed her idea with a hugely enthusiastic tone of voice. "Let's switch horses."

"All right," said Skinner after a slight pause. "If we're going to do it, let's switch saddles too."

"Sounds good to me," said Veronica as she studied the big horse.

Too Tall yawned, then arched his neck and stretched out his spine. His nap was over. He straightened a hind

*leg and held it out behind him, giving the leg a good
stretch as well.*

"Has anyone ever ridden him besides you?" Veronica
asked again as she watched Too Tall stretch and flex his
muscles.

"Chaco has a few times," said Skinner with a smile.
"He'll test ya, but I don't think he'll buck."

"Oh great." Veronica's voice was a little shaky, but she
bravely moved to her horse and pulled her saddle.

Skinner pulled his own saddle and tried to shake his
thoughts of what she thought about the kiss.

"You better not buck," said Veronica as she approached
Too Tall with her saddle in her arms.

Skinner smiled broadly and asked, "What's your horse's
name again?"

"Her name is Maggie, and she's going to buck for sure!"

The horses both shook out their manes and bobbed
their heads to wake themselves and absorb this new turn
of events. Too Tall bent his neck and took in the scent of a
nervous, distracted female human. The big horse stepped
away from Veronica until he reached the end of his lead
rope. His left ear twisted back and lowered over his skull
as he studied Veronica.

Maggie moved to the end of her lead rope as well. Her
short, finely tapered ears flicked back and forth when the
unfamiliar saddle tree pressed onto her back. She did not
bend her neck as Too Tall had, but her eye was turned back
in its socket and the white portion showed in front of the
cornea. Maggie held both of her ears backwards and
slowly lowered them closer and closer towards the top of
her skull.

Skinner sized her up easily. She wanted to remain dom-
inant and had adopted a rotten attitude. Poised to pivot

away if she tried to kick him with a hind foot, Skinner pressed his thumb into her ribs and kept it there until she responded with a step away from the pressure. When she did, he relented, to reward the behavior. Maggie twisted her head around and looked Skinner over.

"Whoa, little horse." Skinner spoke softly in a soothing tone. He pushed her head back to straighten her neck and show his dominance. "Whoa."

He circled the mare to shorten his cinch on the offside, his hand touching the mare at all times. When Maggie bent her neck a second time, Skinner pushed it back once more and then paused to see what she would do. When she held her head forward, he stroked her neck twice. He tightened his cinch, then reached for the lead rope and asked her to take a step back with a light tug. The instant she moved he released the pressure. Dominating her mind with clear commands and small rewards, Skinner won the test of wills in the time it took to saddle her. More importantly, however, in Skinner's mind, it had been done without Veronica noticing. "You ain't gettin' in the way of anything right now little horse," he whispered. Skinner also kept an eye on Too Tall, ready to intervene if the horse acted up. With a touch of concern, he observed Veronica doing just the opposite of his technique in her handling of Too Tall.

Veronica stroked Too Tall's neck a couple of times. "Hello handsome. You're going to be just fine, aren't you? You won't buck."

Veronica had to swing her saddle hard to get it over Too Tall's high wither, and the big horse tensed and snorted when the offside stirrup banged into his ribs. She tightened the cinch and continued to speak to the horse in an improper manner, as far as Skinner was concerned.

"Okay, Too Tall, don't buck me off." Veronica looked over at Skinner and winked. "You ready?"

Too Tall lifted his tail and swept it down between his legs twice in rapid succession. His neck rose higher on his shoulders, and his ears flicked alternately back and forth.

Well aware of Skinner's eye on her, Veronica gave Too Tall a couple more affectionate pats, then looped the reins around his neck. She had to grab her knee to get her foot high enough for the stirrup and slightly off balance, she reached awkwardly for her saddle horn to haul herself aboard. She plonked into her saddle with a small jolt, and Too Tall's spine hardened.

The big horse stood still with his ears now trained backwards at Veronica, waiting for a cue. His tail flicked up and down again. Veronica gathered the reins and prepared to move out, but the horse was ahead of her and backed up at her first touch on the rein. "Wow," she said in reaction to his responsiveness. She put her hand forward, but again Too Tall misunderstood the aid; he interpreted her voice as wanting to stop, yet she had released pressure. He took two steps sideways. Veronica pulled the reins firmly to stop him, but she hadn't yet gathered her reins properly, and her offside rein was shorter. Too Tall pivoted hard and fast to the right. Veronica's reaction was to squeeze with her lower legs and give her right rein a sharp tug. Too Tall started scrambling sideways, building speed toward a rough patch of rocks.

"Whoa. Stand." Skinner commanded. Too Tall jerked to a stop. "Touchy, ain't he?"

Flushed with a touch of fear, Veronica knew she had to relax. She took off all pressure and sat still.

"That's it, just relax. Let him do all the thinkin'. He'll be all right now," said Skinner as he made a final adjustment to his own saddle.

"I'm okay. He's just so sensitive. I just wasn't ready for that."

"Yep. He's got a real good handle on him."

Veronica's head was tilted so it appeared she was looking down at Too Tall's neck, but her eyes had swiveled, and she peeked at Skinner from under her hat brim as he gathered his reins and prepared to mount. She reached up, swept her fingers across her lips and thought about the kiss. She watched him swing his leg effortlessly across the saddle and settle in with ease. "He's so sensitive and big," she said, stroking Too Tall. "You can just feel his power."

Skinner turned Maggie and when his gaze fell on her, she felt her body tighten in that new and unfamiliar way again. Sweat formed under her hat brim. She drew in a lung full of air and swung her eyes out to the views beyond them. "The way you're watching me is making me nervous," she said. "Let's go," Veronica summoned all her riding skill. She gathered the reins lightly and with renewed confidence pushed Too Tall out into the meadow and away from him.

Skinner urged Maggie in behind them with another irrepressible grin spread across his face. He watched Veronica's long hair catch the early morning sunlight and swing across her back and shoulders. She swayed easily with the motion of Too Tall, and he fantasized at what her hips and legs would look like in the absence of her riding skirt.

For the next hour Veronica put Too Tall through his paces. Rarely did she have to guide him. Instead, once pointed in a direction, he would take over and pick the path, and then he would take it at whatever speed she asked. Veronica was astonished at how Too Tall would lengthen not shorten his strides to accommodate a rough piece of terrain. He was effortlessly tearing through this rough country.

"Hey, you know we're going to scare away any deer long before we see them at this pace," Skinner, who had started lagging behind, called out.

Maggie was a fine horse, but the rocky terrain made it difficult to trot for any length of time, which was what she needed to do to keep up with Too Tall. It wasn't really deer hunting on Skinner's mind, but it sounded good as an excuse to get closer to Veronica.

Veronica slowed, then stopped and patted the big horse. "He's really wonderful, Tom. He travels so well," she said. "He just goes."

"Serious about his work is how I describe him."

"That's a little dull."

Skinner laughed. He could not stop his mind from complimenting this woman. She'd easily conquered her fear of his horse and seemed at ease in a wild piece of country. "You did a good job gettin' him to relax. He likes you now."

Veronica twisted in her saddle and watched Skinner ride Maggie up to her. She would have been so disappointed if he had tried to show off or become impatient with her horse. Maggie just wasn't the same caliber of horse as Too Tall, but Skinner had remained patient and worked her at the top of her ability and no more. Maggie had responded and left her sour attitude far behind. She seemed to be the one who was showing off now. Her ears and eyes were forward and concentrated, her finely tapered legs flashed among the rocks, and Skinner remained perfectly balanced so as not to interfere with her effort. Veronica was reminded of her father telling her Skinner was one of the best horsemen he had ever seen, and she now saw it for herself. We're all showing off, she thought.

"How about we get up to that ridge and put a sneak on the opposite side. Maybe we'll see something." Skinner pointed to a spot a couple of miles away.

"All right. I guess we should do a little hunting."

As they approached the summit of the ridge they quit talking, and twenty yards out they got off and tied the horses. It was time to creep up to the crest of the ridge and peek over the side for game. Skinner couldn't contain his desire for another kiss, and he had a strong hunch that Veronica expected him to do something—and more importantly, that she wasn't going to say no. They tied the horses to a bush, their bodies got close together. Skinner pulled her to him, and they kissed again, and some of the awkwardness of their first kiss began to recede.

"You're kind of pushy," Veronica said when she pulled away.

"You want to go over there? We could get comfortable and . . ." Skinner changed the subject. "Belly up there and watch the other side for a while. Sun is warm now."

They settled onto a small patch of ground that had no rocks. They both rested their chins on their arms so just their eyes could be seen by anything below them. In the distance they could see the San Francisco Peaks, now fully lit up by sunlight. Directly in front and below, the land fell away steeply for a short distance and then flattened out. Stands of scrub oak and pinon trees grew in abundance in the rockier sections, and a long meadow thick with grass, weaved its way to the north.

"This looks like as good a spot as any," said Skinner. He rolled to his side and stared at Veronica. He reached an arm over her and tried to pull her closer, but she resisted. "You okay?" Skinner asked in a low voice.

"Just thinking is all."

"About what?"

"Stuff."

"How about thinkin' about one more kiss. One more?"

Skinner kissed her and rolled up against her, pressing

his body against hers. He buried his head in her neck and kissed the soft skin below her ear. His hands reached under her coat and pulled at the blouse tucked firmly into her hunting skirt. He felt her stiffen. She pushed an arm defensively between them, and pushed his hand away, then sat up. She reached into a pocket, pulled out a hair tie and pulled her hair back.

Skinner reached up and took the tie from her hand. "Leave it loose. I like the way the sun shines on it."

Veronica crossed her legs and folded her arms across her chest. "Are you surprised? What I let you do?" she asked.

"You didn't do anything bad," said Skinner.

"Oh, I'm bad. Is that it?"

Skinner reached out and held her by the shoulders. "No. That's not what I mean."

"What do you mean?"

"Why did you stop me?"

"I don't know."

"Can I kiss you again?"

For a minute nature trumped Veronica's upbringing, and she indulged the new feeling that swept through her and at times made it hard to breathe. When his hands moved over her body, she audibly sucked in lungsful of air with no fear of what he would think of her. But then suddenly, Skinner's lust became too much, and she pushed him away again. "That's enough. Stop." Veronica retucked her blouse and rolled onto her belly. She looked out at the view without talking or looking at Skinner.

"You okay?"

"Yeah."

"Whatcha thinkin'?"

"I'm thinking I don't know much about you." Veronica rolled onto her back and looked at him.

"Like what?"

"Where were you born?"

"Where were you born?" Skinner turned the question around.

"Virginia" answered Veronica.

"Why you want to ask questions like that right now?" Skinner could feel her waiting for his reply. "Your stubborn, aren't ya?"

"My father says no one knows a thing about your past, but he thinks you are a good man."

"Did he say that?"

"Twice." Veronica put an arm over her eyes. "He also said you ran away from home when you were just a kid. He said something bad happened."

"I was born in Prescott."

"And?"

"If I tell ya, you might not like me anymore."

"Yes, I will."

"Oh you like me then?" Skinner eyes opened wide, and he directed a huge smile at Veronica.

Veronica's jaw dropped before she punched him in the shoulder. "That's called manipulation. I might not like you if you do that again."

Skinner laughed and reached out for her, but she pushed him back.

"Tell me a little about your life," she said.

"Like what?"

Tell me about your parents."

"My pa died before I was one, so I didn't know him at all. My mom died when I was twelve. She got sick, no one knew what was the matter. She just died. Doctor said it was probably her heart gave out." Skinner paused and took a deep breath. "I lived with a guy named Ron before I left."

"Left for where?"

"You're not going to like this story." Skinner looked at Veronica, frowned, and waited for her response.

"Why not?"

"Because of what I did."

"What?" Veronica whispered. "Tell me."

"I figure you'll hear about it sometime. I killed a kid. Name was Sydney. Ran a loaded wagon over his leg, and I couldn't stop the bleeding. When you're a kid you never see things coming until it's too late, but that ain't no excuse. It was my fault. We was wrestling. Me and him and Chaco after drinking some whiskey. I pushed him out of the wagon, and he fell kind of awkward. That big wagon smashed his leg. There wasn't much we could do."

"I'm sorry Tom. That is a really painful memory, I can tell."

"Yup." Skinner stared up at the sky.

"Is that why you ran away?"

"That sure hurried the event along."

"Is that when Glen Tulin adopted you and Chaco?"

"You know more about me than I know about you now. That ain't fair. I figure you owe me," Skinner said as he reached for her. Suddenly his eye caught movement way down the hill. "Deer," he whispered. He rolled away and scrambled for his rifle.

Veronica suddenly felt that shooting the deer would mar the day or bring bad luck. "Leave it be."

"No."

"Tom, I don't want you to shoot it. Not today."

"Well, I'm gonna. You dad wants meat." Keeping his profile low Skinner rolled away and minutes later appeared forty yards down the slope.

Veronica watched him with her head poking over the lip of the hill. She felt a momentary sadness for the animal, as she knew he was going to shoot. After the *peaceful atmosphere of the day, the report of the rifle was incredibly loud. She looked to the horses, whose heads were up. She stood and went to them, wondering if Tom was as hardheaded as she suspected.*

Skinner watched her riding towards him. Her saddle was back on Maggie, and she was leading Too Tall by the reins. She had retied her hair behind her head.

"She's in good shape, she ought to be good eating," he said quietly as she pulled up.

Veronica was always deflated by the death of one of these beautiful animals, and she didn't answer. Skinner had the doe on her back and was nearly finished dressing her out. He was very proficient. Only his fingers had any blood on them by the time he had pulled the gut pile loose from the carcass. She watched him cut through the hide and the tendons around the knee joints and one by one break off all four lower legs. Then he made a small cut behind a tendon above the knee as a place to tie the doe onto the saddle and sacrifice little hide. She was pleased to see he handled the animal respectfully, and there even seemed to be ceremony involved in his work. She was sure of it when he placed all four legs on top of the gut pile with each one pointing one direction of the compass. He cut the head off the doe, and then placed the head facing east on top of the legs.

"Why do you do that Tom?"

"I do it to be respectful. Keep my hunting luck up. I guess it's just a way to say thanks for the food. I ain't real religious if that's what you mean. Is it . . ." Skinner's voice trailed off when he looked up and met Veronica's eye and saw the fixed smile she had directed at him while he rambled.

"I'm glad to see you actually give a damn."

"You're getting feisty."

"*I can cuss just as good as anyone.*" *Veronica smiled.* "*The Parson boys shoot everything they see . . . It's awful the disrespect they have.*"

"*I know the type. How about we load her on Maggie, and you and I can ride double on Too Tall?*"

"*Okay.*" *Veronica remained quiet but was unable to shake the feeling that killing the doe on this day was bad luck.*

They spent the afternoon working their way back to the hunting camp on a long slow route, riding double on Too Tall and trailing Maggie, who packed the deer. Veronica couldn't stop her mind from compiling information about her day. Her preconceived notions of him had been mostly wrong, and she regarded what she had just learned as a big step in her adulthood. She felt she could be herself and he would like her. It was too perfect. She steeled herself, not wanting to be let down. He was going leave the next day, and that thought hurt. Skinner rocked gently behind her with the motion of Too Tall, who eased along faint game trails on a loose rein. Veronica leaned back so her shoulder blades pressed against his chest, his arms were around her waist, his hands rested on the saddle horn. Veronica felt confident that his affection was sincere, and she liked him. She was excited about the future.

A full moon rising in the east flooded the land in soft, blue light. To the west a crescent of sunlight hung stubbornly above the horizon. They threaded their way through a maze of huge ponderosa pines and moon shadows, and neither spoke for some time. When they topped out on a small hill above the hunting camp at full dark, Too Tall stopped on his own accord. In the distance they saw weak lantern light shining through the walls of the cook tent below them. Leon and the boys were already back.

Skinner gathered the reins and held Too Tall where he was. "What's your story Veronica?"

"If you want to hear it you have to come back." Veronica swept a hand over his and squeezed.

"I'm coming back. I'm coming back soon."

"You better." She gently elbowed him.

"You can count on it."

"Sometimes after a long day the glow of that lantern is the most welcome sight on earth," Veronica said with a sigh.

"I was just thinking the same thing."

"Let's not go back yet."

Skinner swung his leg and dropped off Too Tall. He reached up for Veronica, and she slid off the horse into his arms. Skinner pulled her to him and kissed her. He pressed her tighter against his body and tugged her shirt out of her belt.

Veronica pushed him back, opened his coat, and undid the buttons on his shirt front, then she pushed her arms inside and let his skin warm her cold hands.

Chilled air rushed in through the gaps in their clothing and goose bumps rose over Veronica's arms and chest. The kissing became more intense. Whenever the cold air penetrated they shrugged, rearranged their clothes, and pressed closer together to block it out.

Veronica felt his callused hand slide down her back until it was stopped by her belt, but his fingers reached under and slid over the skin on the top of her hip. His lips pressed against the side of her neck with more strength, his mouth opened wider with each kiss on her lips. He had become too fierce, and she suddenly didn't feel comfortable.

The soft smooth feel of Veronica's skin warmed Skinner's hand and filled his mind. He wanted to feel more. He felt strong and indefatigable. His hand dug at the top of her skirt.

Veronica was now uncomfortable; he was going too far, but she didn't stop him right away, fearing he would feel rejected. His hand pushed inside her skirt and slid across the back of her bare hip.

"Tom," she said. "Tom. Don't."

Skinner heard her, but he didn't stop. He covered her mouth with his to cut short her tiny protest. He felt her hands push on his chest, and she told him to stop a second time, but he pulled her to him with more strength, and his hand squeezed her hip.

"Stop," Veronica squealed, and struggled away.

"I stopped."

"No, you didn't."

Skinner stepped back and looked away. "I stopped."

"I had to yell to get you to stop. I'm going back right now."

"I'm sorry. I'm sorry."

"No you're not."

Skinner looked at her and, in the moonlight, caught the glint of a tear as it slid down her cheek. She turned away from him and walked towards camp, leaving him to bring the horses.

CHAPTER 7

Skinner looked into the sky at the Big Dipper and with great effort pushed the memory of his misbehavior away. The four stars that comprised the handle had swung and were now parallel with the northern horizon. It was time to go. He whistled at Boomer doing sentry duty on the other side of camp.

"Stay put another ten minutes. I'll wake 'em up," Skinner said.

"Yes sir, Capt'n."

When he stood, the cold air found a hole in his clothes and trickled down his neck, and a hard shiver ran along his shoulders as he descended off the high point. Along the way he grabbed clumps of dry grass that he would use to restart the fire. At the fire pit he piled wood on top of the coals, then shoved the grass in underneath. He dropped to his knees and blew the coals back to life. The noise awakened Chaco, who was sleeping nearby.

"Hey," Chaco murmured from deep under his blanket.

"Morning."

"Did ya sleep?"

"Little bit," said Skinner.

"Gonna get plenty a saddle time today, huh?" said Chaco.

"We'll have time to talk."

Skinner grabbed the big coffeepot and went to the river. He never liked having it filled the night before because there were always bugs floating in it by morning. When he returned Chaco had the fire roaring. Skinner put the coffeepot down so it straddled the two big rocks, with the handle out of the flames. He stood and greeted Victor and Brooks as they walked into the firelight.

"Morning," Skinner said. Then he resumed his breakfast preparations. "Where's the bacon, Chaco?"

"Third pannier over," Chaco replied.

"Okay, let's get 'em up."

Chaco yelled out at the camp of sleeping men. "Drop your cocks and grab your socks, boys. We're burning daylight!"

Five of the men had elected to set up one of the tents while the others all slept out. Chaco grabbed the cross pole of the tent and shook it violently. He pulled back the flap and stuck his head to yell at them. "Hey, up and at 'em. Get your butts out of . . . Damn, you guys stink." Chaco jerked his head away from the tent opening, then moved among the others who had elected to sleep out, kicking their feet.

"I don't see any daylight!"

"Ow! I'm up, I'm up," Skeeter complained.

Skinner cut a slab of bacon into small pieces and dropped the pile into the pan. He lifted the lid to the coffeepot and saw the water rolling. He pulled it back from the fire and poured in grounds from a bulging wax-lined cotton bag. He slid the brew back over the flames, putting just the front edge of the pot over the fire to keep the water barely rolling. After a few moments, he pulled the stirred-up liquid back from the fire and poured some into his tin cup. Holding his cup well above the coffee pot, he poured a long slow trickle back into the pot to settle the grounds.

"Coffee's ready," Skinner announced so the entire camp could hear. He stood with his back to the fire and drank from his own mug as he filled mug after mug with the hot, black liquid. Skinner made a point to greet each man by name and acknowledged each flippant complaint about the early departure with an equally flippant remark, a smile, and nods of his head. Every few moments Skinner stirred the bacon and added wood to the fire. The men responded to his care and took a few unhurried minutes to linger by the fire's warmth and wake themselves.

"Greg refill this pot will ya?" Skinner said. "Skeeter, Victor, Brooks—get going. Bring the horses in." As they made ready to leave camp, Skinner turned his attention to Charlie. "Help me tie the wrangle horses. They get excited when the others come in. Those pickets won't hold 'em. Chaco, finish off breakfast, will ya?"

Minutes later Skinner could hear the horses lumbering towards camp, still restrained by hobbles. The first two horses, a buckskin and Turns Good, balked at the perimeter of the firelight; both pivoted and tried to move in another direction. Skeeter and Brooks ran to the left, their voices loud and cross as they got ahead of the fleeing horses.

"You knothead, don't you even think about it!" Brooks flung a handful of gravel ahead of the buckskin's path to stop it.

"Whoa, you peckerwoods!" shouted Skeeter.

When the buckskin stopped Victor came in from the right. "Easy does it. Easy does it." He walked up to the buckskin and slipped on a halter. He removed the hobbles and tied them around the horse's neck before leading him back to camp in a slow, deliberate manner. "Come on. Come on," he called out to the others farther behind, lulling them into following the buckskin.

The dull jingle of hobble chains and the sharper sound of shod hooves striking rocks told those still drinking coffee that the main bunch was close; it was time to grab halters and catch their mounts. Again, at the edge of the firelight's reach, the first horses stopped, and the others piled up behind them. With raised heads held at odd angles to the firelight so they wouldn't be blinded, they watched and evaluated the approaching soldiers, all of them looking for another excuse to turn and leave.

"Easy now. Whoa." Calm voices spoke out from all sides. Soldiers slipped on halters and led the animals to the highlines, where they would be saddled.

Skinner remained by the fire drinking coffee and watching the actions of his men. He couldn't help but wonder what the next couple of weeks would bring, how his men would fare, and what Veronica would think of him riding all the way to her ranch to deliver a warning that might not even be needed.

Vance, always the last one out of bed, avoided Skinner and coffee and stumbled directly from his bedroll over to the highlines. Skeeter had already caught his horse, Mousy, and was leading it towards the firelight.

"What happened?" he asked.

"Came in lame," answered Skeeter. He led the horse closer to the fire.

Skinner filled his cup for the third time then moved in behind Vance, who had knelt to inspect the leg and peered over his shoulder. Long abrasions ran from the ankle to the hock, and the lower third of the leg was swollen. Vance looked carefully among the abrasions for deep cuts but could find none.

"We got lucky," said Skinner. "He'll walk that swelling off in a mile."

"Mind if I stand him in the creek for a while, Captain?"

"Go ahead. Grab something to eat first." Skinner said. He filled a mug of coffee, handed it to Vance, and made no mention of him remaining in his bedroll until the last second.

Skinner gulping his coffee didn't go unnoticed by Chaco, who had taken over preparing breakfast. Chuckling, he picked up the big pan of bacon and scooped the meat onto the side of a canvas pannier near him, careful to not spill the grease. He set the pan to the side, opened a bag of cold biscuits, and placed them beside the meat. With breakfast served, he caught Skinner's eye, picked up the pan full of grease and held it over the fire. *"Buena suerte,"* he said, tipping the pan and pouring the hot bacon grease on the fire, creating a sheet of flame.

"You're just funny as hell," Skinner said, seeing Chaco's broad smile.

Charlie whispered to Vance. "What's that all about?"

"Lots of coffee helps the captain work up a big you-know-what before we leave. Chaco's trying to help him along."

Chaco giggled to himself and used his leather gloves to wipe the last of the grease out of the pan before he shoved it into a pannier. He pulled his gloves over his hands, massaged the grease into the leather, and moved closer to Skinner. "This storm coming could foul us up good."

"You smell it comin' too?"

"Yeah."

Skinner cursed under his breath and flicked the last swallow of cold coffee from his cup. He poured himself one more and grabbed a handful of bacon and a biscuit. With his back to the fire, he gulped down breakfast and watched his men finish saddling the mules and horses. A final swig of coffee washed down his last bite, and then he began to bark orders.

"Greg, leave them mules hobbled until we get 'em loaded. Boomer, throw a double diamond on every load. Skeeter, reroll that tent nice and tight. Who in the hell did it like that in the first place! Was that your work private?"

"Yes sir. I'll do it again, sir."

"No. Let Skeeter do it. You take those last two pack saddles over to Greg."

"Yes sir." Charlie hustled over to get the pack saddles, followed by Vance, who had returned from the river leading his horse.

Vance whispered to Charlie. "You better start doing things right or he's gonna let Victor and Brooks give you some lessons."

"What?"

"Yeah, last time we had a new recruit, the captain had them two give him an education," said Vance in a low, serious tone. "They got ways of making you pay real close attention."

Skeeter slipped up behind them. "Yeah. They can make a person learn real, real fast."

"We wouldn't kid ya Charlie," said Vance.

"You wouldn't?"

"No, you're our favorite turd." Vance and Skeeter laughed until they saw Boomer walk up. They quickly grabbed their riding saddles and moved off into the dark, leaving Charlie to bring the pack saddles and pads.

"Hurry up private," said Skinner. He moved past Charlie and walked off into the woods above camp.

"Yes sir, Captain."

Moments later Skinner returned to camp, grabbed his saddle, and approached Too Tall, who was tied to the high-line.

"Morning." Skinner greeted his horse.

Too Tall turned one ear back and forward, then lowered his head and held a front foot forward for a moment before pawing the ground.

"Ready aren't ya?" Charmed by the attention of his horse Skinner gave him a good rub down with his hands before saddling. "I'm twisted tight. Probably won't be paying much attention; you're gonna have to do your best the next couple of days," Skinner whispered. "Get me up to the ranch, then I'll relax."

Too Tall lowered his head, pulled his ears back against the top of his skull, and shook out his mane. With more vigor than usual he pawed the earth. First the left foot, then the right, hurling chunks of manure onto Skinner's boots.

Skinner gathered the reins, "You always understand." he said. He led Too Tall over to his bedroll and personal gear and let him stand close by while he rolled everything into a bundle, which he tossed to Boomer, who was already packing the mules.

Skinner stepped aboard and rode Too Tall below the camp, to a wide section of the river where the water was ankle deep. Yards away, the current was swift and indicated a deep portion of the channel. Reflected starlight sparkled on the dark surface as it gurgled by. While his saddle warmed and Too Tall took a long drink, Skinner studied the river, trying to pick a place to cross that wasn't more than belly deep to a horse. Ten minutes later, his men and the horses and mules began to quietly gather around him.

Some of the horses lowered their heads and playfully pushed the water with their muzzles, others drank deeply. Soldiers made final adjustments to gear tied around their

waists and to their saddles. When every horse had raised
its head from the water's surface, Skinner's voice rose
above the subdued talk of the men.

"I'll take point. Single file."

The Verde River was subjected to frequent floods and
the footing in the bottom of the channel changed with
every one. Deep holes formed frequently that could soak
a horse and rider, and in the dark it was impossible to get
a feel for where they might be. Skinner rode Too Tall five
yards in front of the men. If he walked into a hole, then
the patrol would wait for him to find a different route; this
way only one man would get wet on this chilly morning.
Skinner could have let one of his men take this job, but
part of his leadership style was to periodically show the
men that he was not above nasty jobs. His taking point for
this early morning crossing did not go unnoticed by any
of them.

Too Tall jerked his head forward and tugged the bit,
wanting to cross no matter what the obstacles. "Easy does
it," Skinner said as he shortened his reins, holding Too
Tall to a slow walk along the shoreline. The horse tossed
his head to protest the bit pressure. Skinner's hand slid
onto his neck and stroked the dark fur. "Easy boy. That
water is mighty cold," he said. He kept his weight as far
back in the saddle as he could and eased Too Tall slowly
towards the center of the river. As they approached the
middle of the channel, he felt Too Tall's front shoulder
begin to drop into a hole, and his other front foot was
caving in the ground it was standing on. Sensing his
horse's left hind was farthest forward Skinner pulled on
the reins and pressed with the offside spur to ask for a left
pivot. Too Tall's haunches dropped, transferring his center
of gravity and the weight of his rider to his hind end, and

he swung back up onto solid footing. Immediately Skinner put slack in the reins. "Good boy, good boy."

"You're a lucky cuss," said Chaco behind him.

"Yep," said Skinner. He stroked Too Tall's neck again. "Come on, boy, keep me dry." He jiggled the reins, then gave them a quick short tug coupled with several light squeezes from his lower legs without applying spur. He reached forward and gave Too Tall a couple of quick pats on the neck and then put him on a loose rein.

Too Tall's head dropped. His nose hovered just above the surface of the river; the edges of his nostrils fluttered as he took in the scent of the river. The big horse traveled a dozen yards downstream before attempting another crossing. As he headed for the opposite bank, he kept his weight back and placed each forefoot onto solid ground before moving a back foot. His snorting increased in volume and frequency as the water became belly deep. Near the middle of the channel, Too Tall again turned directly downstream for ten yards before he attempted to angle for the far side of the river. The patrol snaked along behind, following Too Tall's exact route. As they neared the far side and the water depth decreased, Too Tall quit snorting, emerged from the river, and resumed his ground-covering walk.

"Attaboy, Too Tall." Skinner twisted in the saddle and looked back. "Your turn next, Chaco."

"That's bull."

Chuckling for the first time since the previous day, Skinner put more slack in the reins and allowed his horse to choose a path through a dense stand of leafless cottonwood trees lining the river. Too Tall merely snorted at the owls, ringtail cats, and racoons scurrying for their hideouts, but he shied hard when three deer rose from warm beds and moved rapidly away from the patrol. Occasionally, shod hooves clattering across the bottom of rocky washes broke the quiet of the predawn hour, but soft, chalky soil predominated over the land, and muffled hoofbeats were the norm as the horses and mules carried the patrol, all their camping equipment, food, and weapons downriver. The faintest stars, and the gray outlines of the Milky Way galaxy disappeared first, and soon only the brightest stars remained visible as soft gray light loomed ever brighter to the east.

Midmorning, Skinner called a halt on a rich stand of grass. "Let 'em graze dragging halter ropes. Skeeter, Vance—you two wrangle. Sunny, up above." Skinner pointed to a lookout on the rocks behind them. "Rest of you, take a break. We're gonna rest thirty minutes." Skinner walked over by Vance to inspect Mousy's leg. "How's he doing?"

"He's fine, Captain," said Vance as he ran a hand down Mousy's leg to show Skinner that the swelling had gone.

"All right, turn him loose."

Direct sunlight was still blocked by a tall, rugged mountain to the east, and the air remained cold, but most of the men lay down on the damp grass for a miserable attempt at a nap. The horses, trailing lead ropes, scuffled among themselves over choice spots of grass, but there was plenty and soon they all relaxed and pulled at the grass in earnest. Skinner paced back and forth along the river's edge. His gaze was frequently pulled to the fork in the trail just beyond where his men rested. When he saw Chaco rise from his nap, Skinner caught his eye and motioned with a jerk of his head for Chaco to follow him to a private area.

"I'm feelin' paranoid and irresponsible. These outlaws are probably down in Mexico. What the hell do you think?"

asked Skinner with his hands rammed into his pockets and shoulders hunched.

"I think you are right about these killers going north or south once they hit the desert." Chaco paused.

"Brickman is such a fool," said Skinner.

"Let's go warn 'em, then we'll just make a beeline south. Brickman might never know, if we can find a way to shut that private up."

"Chances are slim he won't find out. He'll bury me if he does. Bury my career in the cavalry is what he told me," said Skinner.

"What if you don't go and these killers end up riding into their area and . . ." Chaco gestured with one arm towards the east as his voice trailed off. He grabbed Skinner's shirt and pulled him up close. "If that happens, you're gonna have another real bad feeling to deal with. Trust me, it'll last a lifetime."

"Another bad feeling. Another to add to the pile."

"Your damn right that's what I mean." Chaco jerked off his hat, held the brim in a tight fist, and shook it in Skinner's direction. "Trust your instincts, Tom Skinner."

Skinner watched the horses begin drifting towards the river for a drink. They were full and ready to travel. He looked back at his friend. "If it goes really bad, you might get in trouble too."

"I don't care." Chaco scratched his head and then clamped his hat back on.

"Yeah, you do."

"We ain't got a choice, Tom. Sometimes that's just how it is. It's time to make a run for the Mogollon."

"You got a choice."

"That's the dumbest thing you said yet."

To the southeast of where they stood, the first ridges of the rugged Mazatzal Mountains rose above them. To the northeast, a series of equally rocky and rugged nameless canyons cut through the land haphazardly. In between these formations a long, steep ridge ran directly away from them. This ridge would take them up to the rim country and the Parson ranch.

"We'll be in the malapai soon," said Chaco eyeing the trail named Hardscrabble that led up the ridge. Malapai, a sharp-edged. mostly fist-sized volcanic rock, covered vast areas of the Mogollon Rim country and created treacherous footing for travelers. The trail out of the river bottom was particularly bad, but was by far the shortest route to the Parson Ranch.

"Yep. I hate it."

"Me too."

"Probably gonna get wet tonight too," said Skinner, looking west at the storm clouds building on the horizon.

"Yup, I aint looking forward to that. Oh well, we need the rain."

"Hey, Chaco. Thanks."

"What for?" Chaco slapped his riding whip gently against his leg.

"For backing me up."

"The way you operate, I ain't got any choice."

Skinner laughed. "That's probably true."

"Damn right it is," said Chaco. "We're gonna get away with this if we can find a way to shut Charlie up before we get back. Why the hell did you agree to bring him?"

"Brickman gave me no choice."

Chaco took a deep breath. "That snake head spends his whole life putting others down trying to make himself feel good."

"I call that being a jackass."

"Needs to get thumped, far as I'm concerned."

Skinner laughed again. "We'll think of a way to shut Charlie up. We could be out here a long time."

"I'll put Skeeter on it," said Chaco, smiling.

"That's good. He'll find somethin' to hold over him." Skinner hesitated. "Let me talk to Skeeter about it. I don't want that on you if things go bad."

"Nothing's going to go bad." Chaco stared up the long ridge.

"We'll see, I guess." Skinner hesitated. "Okay, I'm listening to ya. Let's go east. We'll stay at the Parson ranch tonight. Then go up to Veronica's tomorrow. They can pass the word around from there. Then we'll head south and try and make it look like we never went up there." Skinner looked Chaco in the eye. "Let's ride. Let's get it done."

Skinner and Chaco walked back among the men, and Chaco yelled out the order to catch horses and climb aboard. In less than five minutes the patrol was mounted and lined out behind Skinner. Skinner laid his right rein against Too Tall's neck and turned left at the fork in the trail. This trail took them directly away from the river bottom, narrowed to a single track, and began to climb. Forced to go single file, the men behind jostled for position, and every man suddenly grew quiet as well. All of them, with the exception of Charlie, fully aware of the choice their captain had just made.

When the small talk behind him stopped, Skinner felt his adrenaline rise and mix with the anxiety that wouldn't leave his body. He felt sick to his stomach, his spine tensed, his fingers squeezed the reins hard, his legs felt rigid. Too Tall arched his back under the saddle and began to prance, his frame bent to one side despite the narrow trail. A nervous smile creased Skinner's face as he thought about his recent conversation with Chaco. *Chaco,*

you're a wise one. Got a set of balls too, he thought. Too
Tall continued to respond to Skinner's tense frame. He
lunged up a rough spot in the trail and tried to break into a
trot. Skinner checked him with the reins and realized that
now that he had made the turn—now that he was on the
way to Veronica's ranch, coupled with Chaco's backing—
his mindset was changing. "Easy boy," Skinner whispered.
He checked his horse again and relaxed his body. It was
time to quit second-guessing himself. It was time to focus
on something he and Too Tall were really good at. It was
time to concentrate on covering a lot of miles fast. Skinner
drew a deep breath, reached forward, and patted Too Tall's
neck.

The patrol traveled east and steadily uphill until they
arrived at Stinking Springs. Here Skinner called for a
short rest. The spring water trickling out of a pile of rocks
gave off a sulfurous odor and left red streaks on the rocks
before gathering in a small pool. On the far side of the
pool, more red-streaked rocks spread the water over a wide
area, and ten yards beyond that the water disappeared
under a rock ledge, back underground. Despite the odor,
the water was drinkable, and it was the last they would get
until the Parson ranch. Before the horses were led in and
allowed to drink, the men filled their canteens and washed
the dust off their faces, necks, and arms.

Skinner had avoided Charlie while the men washed, but
the young private sought him out and caught his eye.

"Captain Skinner, may I have a word with you?"

"Sure." Skinner faced Charlie.

"In private. Sir."

"No. You go ahead and say what's on your mind."

Charlie felt the eyes and ears of the patrol turn to him.
"I don't think we are on course." Charlie waved his hand
out at the land below them. From their high point they

could see the Verde River far below them. Its tree-lined
course meandered south towards the sprawling deserts that
spread out towards the Salt River, Tucson, and Mexico.

"We have to ride east to get around them rough sections," answered Skinner. "We'll be heading south again
soon enough."

"Sir, we are a long way from the river."

"It's a long way around them rough spots."

"Sir, I don't think we're on course."

"Well I guess you got a decision to make then, don't ya?"

"Sir?"

"You can go on back and tell Brickman you wanted to
ride through them rough sections, or you can shut your
mouth and follow orders." When Charlie didn't answer
right away, Skinner dished out an order. "Let's get these
horses in here for a drink then mount up."

As soldiers walked by Charlie, none looked at him
except Boomer, who grabbed a handful of Charlie's shirt
sleeve and propelled him towards his horse.

Skinner watched Boomer check Charlie's cinch and
talk to him while they all prepared to ride on.

At four in the afternoon one mule was unpacked
briefly and each man was handed out chunks of jerked
meat, a piece of bread, and a handful of rock candy to eat
as they traveled on. The slope of the ridge became much
steeper about halfway up, and the malapai lay thick on the
land. The horses protested with increasingly foul atti-
tudes, letting the riders know with certainty they saw no
good reason to travel over this section. Two miles before
they topped out, fist-sized malapai rock lay in foot-thick
piles, and Skinner ordered the men to get off and walk the
horses through the treacherous footing. At the top of the
ridge, they scrambled over one final pile of rocks and

gratefully entered a forest of ponderosa pines and a firm, soil-covered surface.

"Dismount. Boomer, Sunny, check the mules. Everyone else check your clinches." Skinner jerked the clinching tool out of his saddlebags and walked down the line of men. Malapai tended to roll upwards against the horses' hooves and straighten the crimp on horseshoe nails. Skinner handed the tool out several times so his men could re-crimp nails and avoid losing a shoe. Beyond some evident fatigue after the long climb and a handful of minor rock-inflicted cuts and abrasions to their coronets and heels, the horses and mules had done well.

Skinner stopped alongside Skeeter. "Skeeter. I need ya to do somethin' for me," he said in a low voice.

"Name it, Captain."

"Shhh." Skinner put an arm around Skeeter and pulled him to the far side of his horse. "Charlie's smart enough to know we ain't followin' orders. I need you to find somethin' we can hold over him. Some way to keep his mouth shut when we get back to the fort."

"You mean get him to do something stupid? Get him in trouble some way so we can blackmail him?"

"Yeah."

"Got anything in mind?"

"No. But I'm figurin' you'll come up with a good idea before I can."

"I'll try and think of something, Captain. Don't have any good ideas right off. It's gonna have to be something pretty bad."

"Keep it in mind. Don't pass up an opportunity is all I'm asking." Skinner slapped Skeeter on the back and put his attention back on the horses and mules.

Minutes later everyone was mounted and moving eastward. On the smoother footing Skinner lifted the pace to a trot. Each time the forest thinned, he caught glimpses of the limestone and sandstone outcrops ahead; the Mogollon Rim was finally in sight. This limestone formation separated huge portions of the ponderosa pine forests that spread north from the sandy deserts to the south and ran for more than two hundred miles across the center of the Arizona Territory.

Skinner loved the utter beauty of this country and noted how it was helping to calm his angst, and he felt a huge amount of mental relief to have done so well on the trip up Hardscrabble Ridge. The horses were tired, but they'd made good time and would arrive just before dark. The men would enjoy camping at the Parson ranch, which was now just a few miles down the trail. The Parsons always had lots of food, and they enjoyed company. Even better, the Parson ranch was a big outfit, and they would be able to shelter from the storm that was bearing down with certainty now. It was cold enough to snow and it would be a rough night to be outside. Veronica's ranch was another eight hours beyond, and they could be there by tomorrow afternoon. If Skeeter could find a way to compromise Charlie and shut him up, Skinner was beginning to think that he might just fool Brickman and he started to relax while on this final stretch.

Just minutes from the Parson ranch Victor trotted up beside Skinner with haste. He sat bolt upright and stared straight ahead. "What is it?" Skinner asked, his eyes forward.

"Don't know," answered Victor.

Brooks came up beside Victor.

Skinner called out, "Chaco."

"Right behind ya."

They rode in silence for another minute, all of them trying to gauge what Victor had picked up on. Skinner directed them off the trail, and they all moved up a side hill to gain a better view. A lazy pall of smoke could be seen rising from where the Parson ranch would be located. Smoke drifted southeast just above tree level. "Vance, Greg, go right. Skeeter, Chaco . . ." Skinner gestured to the left with a motion of his head. They continued forward, spread out in a skirmish line.

"Big bunch of riders passed over this way, Captain," said Chaco in a low voice. He and Skeeter had come across a stretch of ground full of horse tracks forty yards to Skinner's left.

Skinner's adrenaline soared. He called Chaco back to his side. "We got smoke coming from the ranch, and a big bunch of riders. You think we just ran into this gang?"

"Hope not."

Victor jumped off his horse to study the tracks. The prints looked fresh, but there had been little weather to disturb them all day. Victor pressed his thumb into the dirt by a clear hoofprint. He swung back onto his horse and looked at Skinner. "Last night," he said.

Skinner halted the patrol, pointed one hand in the air, made a small circling motion, then pointed towards the ranch.

Charlie looked over at Vance and asked, "What's that mean? What's going on?"

"Means, Victor is gonna recon the ranch and come back. It also means shut up. Do what I do."

Victor swung off his horse again, handed his reins to Boomer, and moved towards the Parson ranch on foot.

"Brooks, follow those tracks until you get a feel for how many," said Skinner. He drew his rifle and hissed at everyone else to do the same. "Move right." He gestured with his rifle to the right and moved the patrol into thicker timber that afforded better cover.

Skinner needed to give Victor time to do a reconnaissance

and get back to him before he approached with the entire patrol.

"I can't think of any reasons for what we're seeing except bad ones," Skinner whispered at Chaco.

"Me either."

Skinner waved at the men to move forward beside him. He shortened his reins and let Too Tall creep forward as he studied the scene ahead and watched for Victor.

The clink and rattle of equipment, the squeak of saddle leather, and hooves settling on the pine-needle strewn forest floor were the only sounds. The sun low in the sky was moments from disappearing behind a solid bank of storm clouds that rolled up behind them. A cool breeze flared up, flapping the collars of shirts and jackets and chilling necks. The horses moved with ears pricked forward, nostrils flared as they took in scent. Skinner saw high in a ponderosa pine two black vultures looking down from comfortable roosts. Being shy birds, they normally flew away quickly when humans approached, but Skinner knew they often waited until the last minute to flee if their bellies were full.

"This is bad," Skinner grunted. Too Tall started to act up under him.

Brooks appeared and motioned with his rifle. All clear. Two more vultures soared up and over the smoke that drifted through the trees held low by the breeze. Skinner let Too Tall canter forward. The patrol broke out of the forest and rode up on a massacre.

Flames still worked the end of the main house beam, which had broken in half and fallen into the center of the ranch house. The roof and most of the walls were burned up, along with everything that had been inside. Ash and debris lay two feet thick on what had been the floor of the house.

Skinner pulled Too Tall to a stop at the center of the ranch buildings. He dismounted and walked forward, drawing the reins through his hands over and over. He'd seen atrocities chasing the Apache before, but nothing like this.

Mrs. Parson lay by the shed, naked and sprawled. The vultures had eaten her eyes and worked her face and groin. The hired hand, Matt, lay nearby, and vultures had done their work on him as well. Mr. Parson had been a big man, and it was only the size of the corpse that enabled Skinner to identify the body lying by the house; one half of his body was burned through, the other half was blackened by heat. The family's three boys were nowhere to be seen.

A strong gust of wind swept over them as the storm rolled closer. Skinner's men moved in around him.

Chaco was the first to speak. "You four take the horses down to that pasture. Strip the tack and hobble 'em. Let's get 'em fed and watered."

Skinner grabbed the closest soldier by his shirt. "Charlie, take my horse and walk him back and forth right here. Keep him loose."

"Oh no. No." Chaco spit the words out.

"Hold on. Before any of you go, listen up," said Skinner. "Looks like we run right into this bunch. There's nothing we can do for these people but bury them. Then we're gonna get after whoever did this and put a stop on 'em. Stay focused on that." Skinner took a deep breath. "This family had three boys; keep your eyes out for them. Skeeter, Vance, get these people ready for burial. Hunt up some shovels and a pick. Chaco will show ya where to dig. Everyone keep your eye out for their three boys," he repeated. "Their names are Timothy, Justin, and Douglas."

The wind swirled and the horses got their first whiff of blood; several shied and pulled back. Boomer, who held four horses by the reins, fell and was pulled down on his side, but he didn't let go. "Whoa now! Whoa."

Skinner, followed by Chaco, walked to a small shed and kicked open the door. Scattered on the floor were Mrs. Parson's clothes. "Where in the hell is Victor?" Skinner stepped back out and looked Chaco in the eye. "I gotta go."

"I know."

"If they fall apart on you . . ."

"If they do, I'll handle it."

"Chaco, I don't know what to say. I . . ."

Chaco cut him off. "Just go, Tom. And remember: You get shot, you can't do any good."

"Yeah." Skinner's chin fell to his chest, his fingers pinched the bridge of his nose hard. He shook his head then turned and stared at Chaco. Neither spoke for a moment.

Chaco's cheeks swelled as his lungs emptied. "This is bad."

"Bad as it gets."

They moved back to where the rest of the patrol stood. Skinner waited for Victor, who jogged up towards them from the forest. "Whatcha got?"

"More than a dozen, probably less than twenty, riders headed north. Ten hours gone. Hard to tell much else. They're going single file."

"Okay, here it is: I'm going up to the Sharp ranch now. Brooks, you're leaving now as well. Go back to the fort and tell Brickman to hurry the hell up here. We'll leave a big trail no matter where we go. If he wants to know how we found them, tell him I followed a hunch. Chaco get moving at daylight, and you'll be there midafternoon. I'll meet ya a mile or less out from Veronica's ranch. What we don't want to do is let them know we're on their trail until we're ready. We also have to be careful in case they double back on us. Any questions?"

The storm bank rolled over them, and the light dropped immediately. The first big raindrops pelted their hats and shoulders.

"What are you going to do by yourself, Captain?" asked Charlie.

Skinner looked straight at Charlie but didn't answer.

Chaco spoke up. "Captain, we don't need to stay here until morning. We did real good getting here. How about we leave two hours before daylight? That'll give the horses a good rest, and we can get there easy by midday."

"Sounds good," Skinner nodded a silent thank-you at Chaco.

The wind gusted hard, and a plume of swirling gray ash rose above the house, only to be swept away by wind from another direction. Some of the horses spooked again. Rain began to fall harder, and the horses, as one, all swung their butts to meet the rain. Skinner moved to his horse and took the reins from Charlie. He could feel the men watching him. "Steady now, Charlie."

"What are you going to do?" Charlie stared at Skinner, his mouth was pulled tight, his eyes wide.

"Chaco's in charge; you do exactly what he tells you. Got it?" Skinner ignored the private's mumbled additional questions and reached for his slicker on the back of his saddle.

Chaco shoved Charlie back and away, then stepped up close to Skinner, grabbed his shirt sleeve and spoke. "You better get a lid on your hotheadedness this time, Tom. Don't you go pile into some situation you can't handle. Use your head, you hear me?"

Skinner nodded, but it wasn't enough for Chaco.

"Don't you get yourself killed, Tom. You can't help

anyone if you're dead. Are you listening?" Chaco jerked Skinner's arm, pulling him around until they were face-to-face. "You hearing me?"

"Yeah, I'm listening." Skinner said as he turned back to his horse.

Agitated by the storm and the tension among the men, Too Tall held his head high, body tense. Keeping a firm grip on the reins, Skinner untied his slicker and swung it on seconds before the storm let loose and rain poured down. "Damn weather isn't going to help."

"No it ain't. You be smart Tom. Don't get yourself killed. Take what you can get," said Chaco, raising his voice to be heard over the rainfall. "Don't get yourself killed." Chaco yelled. "You hear me?"

Grabbing a handful of mane along with the reins, Skinner swung into the saddle. Too Tall bolted, taking four big strides before Skinner could get a firm seat and haul him down. Looking back through driving rain, Skinner saw Chaco standing apart from the other men holding his arm up, his riding whip dangled from beneath his clenched fist. A bolt of lightning and ear-punishing thunder crashed onto the hillside behind the house. Too Tall reared straight up in the flash of light. Skinner gripped the saddle with his knees, pulled off his hat and held it high above his head, acknowledging Chaco. His agonized gaze remained fixed on his friend until Too Tall's front end came back to earth, then he loosened the reins and jammed his spurs into Too Tall's hide.

CHAPTER 8

Jutting out from a section of the Mogollon Rim, huge slabs of limestone etched with multicolored lichens provided a platform for Leon's exotic house and outbuildings. The location offered unparalleled views in three directions. At night, looking far to the west, faint lights could be seen twinkling from the mining operations of Jerome, high on the side of Mingus Mountain. A crisp, gray line outlined the crest of the Dragoon mountain range, a hundred and twenty miles to the south. Huge expanses of the Sonoran Desert and spectacular views of the rugged Mazatzals could be seen between the Dragoons and the house. To the east an undulating deep-green canopy of ponderosa pines stretched to the horizon.

The heavy log construction of the buildings had weathered quickly and now gave the house a seasoned look beyond its four years, of age. On either side of the house, two ancient cedar trees' massive roots spiraled down into cracks in the limestone and their branches spread over the house. These ancient treasures, as Leon referred to them, were surrounded by fences, protecting them from the family's four milk goats. Interspersed among the buildings, in stark contrast to the flat slabs of limestone, lay several large boulders. Two of the outbuildings had been built to incorporate the boulders as part of their structures. The back end of the house butted up against a wall of limestone as well and enveloped a crack running down the rock face. From the bottom of the crack a trickle of water flowed, which was directed into a catch basin. This seep provided the family with an indoor supply of water. It was an improbable place to build and had been done with such care and creativity, it possessed a magical quality that amazed every guest.

Outside, in Muriel's fenced-off vegetable garden, now flattened and drab in winter, a variety of tin pots, stone figures, and oddly shaped pieces of driftwood hauled from the lower valleys sat idle, waiting to lend character to the garden when spring arrived.

Between the garden and the house, Veronica sat on a padded bench. Her legs were tucked under her, and two faded red wool blankets covered her body and shoulders. One hand poked from beneath the blankets and clutched a mug full of coffee beneath her chin. She stared into the distance, watching the light grow over the land below her.

Leon returned from letting the goats out and approached the bench. "Hey, where's my coffee?"

"In the pot," said Veronica, snuggling down deeper under the heavy blankets.

"Don't go away, you rat."

Moments later Leon emerged from the house with his own mug and slipped under the blankets next to his daughter. Veronica leaned against her father's shoulder, and they sipped strong coffee in silence, both fully content to let nature and the rising light entertain them. As full daylight approached, Muriel could be heard waking Laura and the boys.

"I guess we better get to work," said Leon.

"Five more minutes?" suggested Veronica.

"You know your mom. Come on, let's go."

They rose, folded the blankets and left them neatly stacked on the bench, then went to the barn to greet their five horses who, restrained by hobbles, were shuffling in from the night pasture ready for the daily ration of grain that brought them in at the same time each day. Leon and Veronica pulled off the hobbles, led each horse to their individual stall inside the barn, and dished out tiny rations of the hard-to-acquire grains.

"Seems like such a measly amount for them to come all this way for," said Leon, dishing out portions.

"I'm going to skip breakfast this morning, Dad," said Veronica, changing the subject.

"What's the matter, honey?"

"I've got a lot on my mind. Just need some alone time is all."

"You want to talk to me about it?"

"No. Tell mom I'm fine."

"Okay, honey. See you in a while."

Veronica slipped away and went around the side of the house to an area that blocked wind and collected the sun's warmth. She slid into a familiar spot, with her back against the base of a ponderosa pine. Clutching her knees in her arms, she rocked gently back and forth and for the thousandth time her mind relived the end of that cold, sunny day with Tom. She filled her lungs and pushed the air out slowly as she looked west, towards Fort Verde. No matter how many times she relived that moment in the moonlight above the hunting camp, she could find no resolution. It was all her fault. She'd egged him on, then blamed him for going too far, then dismissed him, and she had achieved nothing by doing it. All she'd accomplished was to demonstrate her own immaturity, and that was tormenting her.

Veronica remembered every feeling, emotion, and word spoken between them in those moments. She clutched her arms over her midsection, leaned forward, and cried out.

Only the raven that suddenly glided up from below the edge of the rim heard her. It squawked, caught her attention, then hung on an updraft and eyeballed her sitting under the tree. The scraggly bird was close enough that Veronica could see the shine of its black eye, and the hair on her neck prickled. It squawked twice more then broadened its wings and lifted up and over her.

Unsettled by the raven, Veronica questioned her intuition and convinced herself the bird's appearance was confirmation that she'd been immature with Tom, that she had turned him away for good. The raven's sudden appearance had rattled her thoughts, scared her as well, and yet she'd never felt afraid of Tom. Just as quickly, Veronica rejected the tortuous twists her thoughts were taking, stood abruptly, and returned to the house.

"Dad," she called. "I have to get out of here today."

"What's the matter with you?"

"I don't know, I need to walk. I think I'll go out to the big slope."

"That's an all-day walk. Talk to me, baby."

"Quit calling her baby, Leon," said Muriel from the back room.

"I'm all right, Dad. I see a storm coming and I want to get out before it rains."

"Can I go too?" asked Courtney.

"Me too," said Monte.

"You can, but you may not," said Muriel, correcting Courtney's English.

"Might be a good idea to get out before the weather rolls in. Why don't you all go. Just keep an eye on the weather and be back before it hits," said Leon.

Still in her pajamas, Laura called from the back of the house, "Not me."

"Get some gear together and go. I'll walk to the top of the bluff with you," said Leon.

Near the top of the bluff above the house where the trail narrowed, Leon subtly put Courtney and Monte in front and then stepped in behind Veronica.

"What's going on now, honey? Come on, talk to me."

"Same old thing, Dad."

"You want to move back to town?"

Veronica abruptly spun around in the trail to face her father, tears springing to her eyes.

"You thinking about Tom?"

"We had a problem."

"I know. I remember. Don't know what it was about, but I remember." Leon pulled her to him and hugged her. "Let's go to Prescott. Let's go there and see if we can find you a place to live, and a job," he said pushing her back and giving her a wink. "I bet Tom can make the ride to Prescott in ten hours."

"If I didn't ruin it."

"I seriously doubt that. I bet he can't get you off his mind for a second."

Veronica embraced her dad. "You're not disappointed if I want to go?" she whispered in his ear.

"Why would I be?"

"Thanks, Dad," she said, crying even harder.

Leon looked ahead at Monte and Courtney, who stood patiently listening and watching them. "Come on everyone—this is how life is. You kids grow up and then it's time to move on. You can't stay with us forever. This is how life works. It's okay this is supposed to happen," said Leon. "It's not like we're never going to see you again. Go on over to the big slope. Enjoy yourselves. I'll go tell your

Mom about this little conversation, and we'll expect you back this afternoon."

Veronica hugged her father harder. "Thanks, Dad. I love you."

"I love you all. A lot," Leon said. He waited and watched them until they started up the trail leading to the top of a small bluff that loomed over the house. He waved and called out. "Love you all."

Leon returned to the house, stepped inside the living room, and slammed the door behind him. He didn't go to his wife right away and instead stalled and waited with a smirk on his face, predicting she would call out for him within seconds.

"Leon come talk to me." Muriel's stern voice carried from the warmest room, just off the kitchen.

"Be right there."

Leon poured himself another cup of coffee then filled the doorway of the room where his wife was sitting in a huge homemade sewing chair, knitting a sweater.

"You look like you're going to be sick, Leon. What's going on?"

Leon chuckled. "Had a pretty serious conversation with Veronica." He eased into a chair across from his wife, sipped his coffee, and waited for her to dig.

"What did you two decide without me?"

"She wants to move to Prescott and live on her own."

"Was that your idea or hers?"

"I don't know how it came up," said Leon. "She's worried about disappointing us."

"Well, what did you tell her?" Muriel quit knitting and let her hands drop into her lap. "Give Leon. Give."

"I told her we'd look into it."

Muriel ignored the tactical inclusion. "Did you tell her that Courtney would have to go with her?"

"Courtney! Hell, he wouldn't go. Where is Laura anyway?"

"He'd go, Leon. That's the part you aren't going to like. Laura will be back soon. I asked her to slaughter the turkey."

Leon wanted to protest killing their last turkey, but he let it go. "What about Monte? I don't think he would stay if Courtney went. Why would Courtney have to go anyway?"

"To give her strength when she finds out that it's not so easy to be on your own in a big town. Monte won't go, and you know it."

"Lots of people make it on their own. The place is growing like crazy."

"Lots of men, Leon. Not women. When was the last time you saw a young woman arrive in Prescott, find a place to live and a job? For heaven's sake, I'm not sending my daughter over there all set up to fail and get her spirit broken. You men don't realize how difficult it is for women to live in the Territory." Muriel picked up her knitting needles and attacked the sweater with speed. "I have been doing everything—"

"You're right," Leon cut her off. He knew how she felt, knew how all women felt about living in the west. It was a man's world. He got up and kissed his wife. "I know it's been hard on you. I know it's not easy for you here, or in Prescott." Leon drained his mug in one big gulp. "Do you want to move out too? Back to Prescott?" he asked.

"Not yet," she replied. "Let them get some independence first. We can follow them when we get too old to run this place. Which, by the way I'm feeling lately, isn't too far off."

"That's why I married you."

"What's that supposed to mean?"

"I love the way you think. How about we have a really big dinner tonight?"

Muriel produced a tight-lipped smile, looked at Leon, and raised an eyebrow. "Why do you think I had Laura butcher the turkey?"

"I'm tempted to sweep you off to the back of the house."

Muriel stood and gave her husband a hug. "That sounds nice, but we haven't got time. Laura will be back any minute," she whispered. She grabbed his ear in her teeth and gave it a slight tug before kissing him on the lips. "Add more wood, will you please? I'm chilled."

"You sure you don't want to go back there?" Leon pointed towards their bedroom, "It would be warmer."

"Shh. Stop. Laura might come in," she said. Breaking out of Leon's tight hold, Muriel grabbed the coffee cup from his hand and went to the kitchen. "You want more coffee?"

"Yeah." Leon looked over his shoulder at his wife. "This is what you call a milestone day."

"I don't like milestone days. Never have."

Leon lingered a moment and looked out the window towards Prescott and Fort Verde. "I love you," he said, then he blinked away tears before they could fall on his cheeks and give him away. He moved towards the stove to add wood.

"I know. I love you more."

Leon filled the wood-stove, and as the flames rose, warmed himself. His eyes fell on a familiar gouge in the wooden floor caused when they had moved the stove in. He remembered being so disappointed by the mar. Since that day the house had been scarred a thousand times by the children, but the blemishes no longer bothered him. He'd achieved a dream of bringing his kids to this improbable place. It had been a successful parenting effort, but this morning's events had shown it was coming to an end. The home was too remote for ambitious kids full of curiosity about the larger world. It was especially too far away from a young man named Tom Skinner who Veronica could not get out of her mind.

The soft thud of horse hooves and riders approaching interrupted his thinking.

Who in the hell would be coming now, thought Leon? He was moving towards the front door when a pistol shot exploded outside.

"Leon!" Muriel screamed, and she rushed out of the kitchen.

Both of them charged to the front door. Leon arrived a second before his wife and burst outside. He saw Laura lying sprawled on the ground between the barn and the house. Men and horses were swirling into the tight space between the house and outbuildings. More riders were streaming up over the lip of the rim.

A roar emerged from Leon's throat as he rushed to his daughter. One step out the door a bullet tore through his collarbone and knocked him backwards into Muriel and down onto the floor. "Grab the gun. Grab the gun," he called to his wife, but with the air knocked out of him, his voice was lost.

Muriel screamed and pushed past him, also trying to rush to Laura.

"There she is, hold your fire," a gang member shouted. "Don't shoot."

Leon got himself off the floor and lunged across the room. Unable to keep his feet, he crashed into the side cupboard before he could open the drawer that held his pistol. From where he fell, he could see men climbing out of their saddles and swarming towards the front door.

Pepper and Jessup were the first to enter. Jessup had

an arm around Muriel's waist and carried her bodily back
inside. Pepper's gun came up and he shot Leon again where
he lay, filling the room with the smoke and the smell of
gunpowder.

Muriel broke away from Jessup and dropped beside
Leon, who lay motionless on the floor, eyes closed. "They
shot Laura. They shot Laura," she screamed at Leon. She
saw blood spreading underneath him and grabbed his head
and pulled it towards her shielding him from the men in
the house. "I love you," she cried into his ear.

Filthy hands grabbed her and jerked her off the floor.

Pepper held her throat with one hand and pushed her
against the wall, holding her solid, so her feet barely
touched the floor. "Where do ya keep the whiskey? Where
do ya keep the damn whiskey?" he demanded.

She shouted, "You damned—"

A slap in the face cut off her words but brought out
the fight in her. She kicked at the man's groin and clawed
his face.

His hand squeezed her neck violently, and he pressed
his body against hers to subdue her struggles. He pushed his
bearded, pockmarked face an inch from hers. "Whiskey?"
he growled.

Muriel clawed at his face again with one hand, digging
her fingernails into his cheek. Her other hand grabbed his
ear, which she tried to rip from his scalp.

Pepper recoiled and hit her hard in the stomach.
"Tramp," he yelled. Blood trickled from his ear and cheek.
He hit her again with an open-handed slap across the face
that swiveled her head.

Jessup grabbed Pepper's arm when he recoiled to strike
again. "You can kill her when we're done."

"I'll kill her right now if she doesn't tell me where the

whiskey is," said Pepper, wiping blood from his torn ear. "Whiskey? Where is it?" he demanded again.

Muriel turned her head and gestured out the front door. "In the shed." She lied, but if he took her that direction, she would get closer to Laura.

"Suppose you show me where," Pepper said, propelling her towards the door.

Intent on getting their share of this attractive woman, and any whiskey, the men inside followed Muriel and Pepper out the door. When they moved past the crumpled body of Laura, Muriel fought to go to her, but rough hands held her firmly and pushed her forward towards the first outbuilding.

At the door to the shed Pepper grabbed her blouse, ripped it open, and then shoved her towards Jessup. "There ya go boys. I'll see what they got in here."

Held by Jessup, Muriel struggled to cross her arms in front of her exposed chest. Men began arguing about who would have her first, and again she struggled to pull away. She felt Jessup's fingers dig into the flesh on her arm, holding her firmly. Muriel shook with fright, with her eyes fixed on Laura's body lying in the dirt yards away.

Leon's cheek slid on blood. He swiveled his head on the warm surface and looked around the room. He was alone. His lungs gurgled, he coughed, and blood filled his mouth. He pushed with his arms to raise his torso. Once he was halfway up, he allowed his right arm to collapse first and was able to roll once and come up against the leg of the cupboard. He reached up and pulled the drawer all the way out letting it fall on him, and his pistol fell free beside him.

He propelled himself along the floor by pushing with his knees and dragging himself forward with his one good arm. His useless hand dragged the pistol. He made his way across the living room towards the door. Outside, men argued among themselves, and he heard the clink of bits and the soft thud of horse hooves. He felt himself losing consciousness and lowered his head. He saw a long streak of blood on the floor behind him. A final effort put him at the doorway, holding his pistol.

Muriel's face showed no fear. She stood upright in the grasp of one of the men, her arms crossed in front of her chest, fists tucked under her chin. Her eyes stared at Laura's crumpled frame lying motionless in the dirt. The pistol felt heavy in Leon's hand. He pulled back the hammer and pushed his arm forward.

"I'll be looking for you on the other side my love. God forgive me."

Leon pulled the trigger and shot his wife.

Several gang members jumped for cover, not sure where the shot came from. Others pulled guns and fired at him, but he was a small target, only a head and an arm showing at the bottom of an open door. He made no effort to protect himself as bullets landed around him. He raised his pistol and fired again. The bullet struck Pepper in the belly as he rushed out the shed door. A bullet hit the edge of his neck and jerked his next shot off target. Splintered wood stung his face as bullets continued to hit the wood at the bottom of the door. Leon shot again and saw a horse collapse in the middle of the yard. His last shot dug a groove in the porch just a foot in front of the muzzle of his pistol. Leon's head sank to the floor, his vision failed, he took a final breath, and died.

CHAPTER 9

Veronica, Monte, and Courtney heard the shot.

"That was a gunshot." said Monte.

"You think Dad shot a coyote?" Courtney asked.

A moment later another shot cracked, this one more muffled than the first.

Monte raised the alarm. "This don't sound right."

"Let's go." Veronica ran for home, with Monte and Courtney right behind her.

They ran back to the top of the bluff and looked down, all of them standing on the highest rock. Horses and men crowded in front of the house. They saw their mother standing near the shed among the riders. A single pistol shot came from the house, and their mother dropped into the dirt.

"Mother!" Veronica screamed as an explosion of gunfire was directed towards the house. Monte and Courtney scrambled over the rounded top of the boulder to run down the trail to the house.

"No!" Veronica yelled to make herself heard over a roar of gunfire. She sprang forward and grabbed a brother in each hand and wrestled them down out of sight.

"Let go!" Courtney screamed back at her.

"We gotta think! We gotta think!" yelled Veronica. She looked at Monte, and saw him start to panic.

Both boys fought to get free from her.

"We've got to think! Stop! Stop it!" Veronica slapped Monte, who was struggling free of her grip as the shooting below stopped.

Veronica peered over the top of the rock, but this time showed only her eyes. Courtney and Monte slid up beside her.

Courtney saw one of the outlaws looking their way, pointing at them.

"He saw us."

Veronica jerked the boys backwards, out of sight from below. "Run," she said.

CHAPTER 10

Colin saw Muriel drop at the shot. Pulling his pistol, he searched for the shooter, but his view of the house was blocked by men and milling horses. Movement on the bluff above the house drew his eye. He saw two kids and a young woman fighting with each other.

"Up there," he shouted, pointing, but his voice went unnoticed in the roar of gunfire directed at Leon. A second later a panicked horse knocked him violently backwards as it fled the congested area. When the shooting stopped, he stood stiffly and held one shoulder gingerly. "Wardell?" he called.

"What?" Wardell was flushed with adrenaline after emptying his gun at Leon. He gave Colin scant attention and focused on rapidly slipping bullets back into his gun.

"I saw—" A spasm of pain from his shoulder choked off his sentence.

"Don't think you saw anything rolling around on the ground like that," said Wardell. "I'm the one that got him." Wardell looked around at the others who were all reloading pistols as well, to see if anyone disputed his brag. No one did, and no one seemed to care. Several gang members gathered around Pepper, who sat in the dirt holding his gut and examining the damage. Others made their way to the house, intent on looting.

Colin looked to the top of the bluff. "Never mind," he said in a lowered voice. Colin groaned as he stood. He ignored Wardell and fell in behind Grady and Jessup. The three of them walked towards the barn.

"Bunch of idiots we're riding with. Why don't we split off?" suggested Grady.

"We ought to send every last one of these pissants packing and go it alone," said Jessup, who'd turned his head to glare at Colin.

"Not yet. We need to find one more place where we can load up. I don't think we're gonna get much out of here," said Grady.

"Well let's hope we get some horses. Jessup gestured at the barn, then glanced backwards again. He curled a lip upwards and shook his head at Colin, then scanned the rest of the area to see what the others were doing.

Colin understood Jessup perfectly and didn't argue. Jessup was going to get first pick of any horses that might be in the barn. Colin knew tensions could explode within their ranks at any moment, and if they did, he was probably going to come out of it badly. He suddenly knew what he was going to do. He was going to leave this bunch now, and he was going to do it in style. Colin would keep his secret about what he had seen at the top of the bluff. He would go catch that woman, take his pleasure, then find some rough country to hole up in for a while. All he needed was feed for his horse and himself and, if he was really clever, a bottle.

Grady and Jessup entered the barn, and Colin was three steps behind. Four burlap sacks of grain were stacked on a bench to the right as they entered. There were also shoeing tools, horseshoe nails, and steel horseshoes. Saddles, harnesses, salt, blankets, bridles, and leather hides, all hung or organized neatly along the walls.

Grady grunted his approval and went over to the grain, making sure it was what he thought it was. "This is going to help."

"You ain't kidding. Don't see that stuff too often," said Jessup. He'd walked farther into the barn. Occupying four box stalls stood Leon's team of Morgan horses. Jessup moved down the row, looking into each stall. The mares eyed him from deep in the stalls. Stopping at the last one on the right, he stared for a moment, then drew his gun and pointed it at Grady and Colin.

"This one is mine," he said. "And I'll kill any man who wants to argue."

"Must be a good one," said Grady looking at the pistol. "Go ahead, take it."

Jessup twirled his gun and slipped it back into its holster. He grabbed a halter, opened the stall door, and entered Viking's stall.

"I need a horse," said Colin.

"You'll have to take it up with the fellas outside," said Grady, giving him minimal attention.

"Probably other people around. We ought to get moving," growled Jessup. "I don't think these two old people have been running this outfit by themselves." Jessup led the stallion out of the stall. He paused to admire the animal, and his smile broadened further as he appraised the well-shod feet.

"You get your paws on a nice horse, all of a sudden you feel like traveling?" Grady's head tilted sideways and bobbed up and down as he appraised the stallion. "That horse will get you all the way to Mexico and beyond, no doubt about it."

"I'm going take ten pounds of that grain and this horse. They can have everything else," said Jessup gesturing outside. Jessup knew his chances of hanging on to the stallion were better if he had him haltered and in hand before he went back outside. He tied Viking, pulled his pistol, ejected two spent shells, and replaced them with new ones. He glanced at Colin, who was leading a mare out of the stall. "You're on your own, far as I'm concerned," he said bluntly.

"No kidding," replied Colin in a soft voice.

Ignoring Colin, Jessup put ten pounds of grain into a bag and spoke to Grady. "The sooner I get my saddle on him the better," he said. "There's no women, probably no whiskey, and burning the last place sent up a smoke signal for everyone to see. Let's shoe the ones that need it, grab what there is, and put miles on."

"Might be wise," agreed Grady.

You gonna put the glom on one of them?" Jessup pointed at the mares.

"No. All I need is fresh shoes for my horse. And besides, I'd have to kill someone for one of them mares. I ain't in the mood." Grady raised his eyebrows at Jessup. He looked at the stallion and then gestured outside, where men's voices could be heard getting louder as they fought over the spoils.

"I'd like to shoot Wardell," said Jessup, blaming the Parson fire on the half-breed, and ignoring Grady's warning.

"How do you know it was him?"

"It was him all right," said Colin.

Jessup moved closer to the barn entrance and looked out at the sky. "Weather is comin'. Might be enough to cover our tracks, if it's got any strength to it," he added. Jessup drew his gun and spun the cylinder, assuring himself for a second time that it was fully loaded.

Grady looked west. "All right, I'm convinced. Let's git and let the storm cover our tracks. You go tell 'em the plan," he said poking his thumb towards the door. "I might just shoot that ornery snot myself," he added.

"You go tell 'em. I gotta get myself in the proper mood before I introduce 'em to my new horse," countered Jessup. He winked at Grady, then gave Colin another hard look. Holding a bag of grain and the lead rope in his left hand, Skinner waited for Grady to pass by him on his way back outside. Jessup took one deep breath, stepped in behind Grady, and followed him out, leading the stallion, his pistol clutched in his right hand.

CHAPTER 11

When Jessup and Grady went out the front door of the barn, Colin went to the far end and peeked out the back door. He eyeballed the trail that led up to the top of the bluff. He looked back at the mares and thought about what Grady had said. Might have to pass on keeping one of you, he thought, as he heard men running towards the barn. In seconds he could hear them arguing and cussing at each other over who would get one of the mares. Colin quietly pulled coils of lightweight hemp rope off a roll, cut off fifteen feet, and stuffed it into his coat. He left the barn, returned to his exhausted horse, picked up the reins and—unnoticed by the gang, preoccupied with their looting—he led the animal over the rim back down the trail they had just come up.

Colin was confident Grady and Jessup would persuade the gang to depart before the storm. He led his horse for more than an hour back down the trail towards the Parson ranch. On a rocky section, where it would be difficult to track him, he left the trail and began to backtrack in a wide arch. His confidence was high that when his absence was noted and suspicion rose among them, they would only follow his tracks a short way if at all before their instincts for self-preservation and the safety of the herd mentality would convince them to abandon him. After traveling completely off any trails most of the way back towards the house, Colin came upon a rich stand of grass. He gathered his coat from his saddle and turned his horse loose to graze. He made himself comfortable on a spot where he could see well in all directions. He scratched his chin, tucked a lock of greasy hair behind one ear, and smiled. He was only a quarter mile from the house, and none of them had any idea where he was.

Colin considered what options the two kids and that woman would have. He spoke softly so only his horse could hear him, his tone was matter-of-fact and sure. "You got two choices. You can go for help. You can hide and come back after dark. See what the damage was. See if anyone's still alive." Colin shifted his position and hunkered down lower, making himself more comfortable. "Maybe you could split up. Send one for help and two stay here." Colin thought about the house and barn and how clean and neat the place had been. How the parents, futile as it had been, had fought back, and he convinced himself of what the kids would do, and what he was going to do as well. He spoke out loud again. His voice was a bit louder, his tone higher. "You're going to go half a mile and hide, then come back at dark. You're going to see that everyone is gone, and then you are going to come down to the house and see what the damage is. It won't be too hard to find you."

Colin sat for several hours. A cold breeze chilled him. Finally, he stood. It was time. He adjusted his clothing and buttoned his coat, then caught his horse and moved off on foot, knowing the effort would warm him. He circled some thick timber and made his way back towards the limestone rim to a point west of the house. He tied his horse and climbed up on a point where he could remain hidden and observe the house from a safe distance. He watched until late in the afternoon before he was convinced the gang had, in fact, moved on for good. Again Colin led his weary horse and made his way on foot towards the bluff overlooking the house. He asked himself: If he was one of those kids where he would hide? He studied the ground under his feet, looking for tracks, but quickly gave up. The land was covered with rock or pine needles, and it had been tilled by goats, people, and stock. Tracking in these conditions was beyond his ability; this effort was going to have to come from the brain.

Walking into the forest a short distance, Colin found a low spot to tie his horse. He poured some grain onto the ground knowing it would keep his horse quiet for a time. Pulling the length of rope out of his coat, he cut it into three pieces and tucked them on either side of his belt, and then he began his hunt.

He walked slowly in half circles from one piece of cover to the next, taking all the time necessary to listen and watch ahead, to make sure no potential hiding place was approached or passed by. He studied the big trees from a distance in case they had climbed one. He watched the brush-filled areas for long stretches, looking for movement. He chose his angles with care, traveled on the roughest terrain, and constantly considered his quarry's options.

"They're scared. They'll want to see if any of their family are still alive. They're miles from anywhere. No horses. No one to help. They're gonna find a place to hole up. That's what they're gonna do all right," he whispered to himself, over and over.

Colin searched for two hours. At dusk, half a mile from the house, he came upon a deep narrow wash lined with

large boulders. The hair on his neck tingled. He could see
a good distance along the bottom of the wash, but a cutout
in the right bank made him pause to wait and listen. Nothing. He moved closer and stopped again. Nothing. He
crept closer, found a place against a bank to lean his weary
body, and told himself to be patient. By his foot lay a stout
three-foot-long branch. Colin picked it up and silently
whittled at the few remaining twigs along its length while
he listened. Nothing. He moved another twenty feet closer
to the cutout.

He heard someone cry out, and then a different voice,
but he couldn't make out the words. Holding the branch in
one hand, he drew his pistol with the other, then stepped
around the boulder and cornered the twins and Veronica in
their hiding place.

"You kids oughta learn to hide better."

Veronica jumped up, spread her arms, and positioned
her body between Colin and the boys. "Stay away from
us," she snapped.

"Shut your mouth," Colin spat back at her. He wiggled
the club at his side and admired the woman in front of
him. "You ain't no kid. My mistake." He shook his head,
sucked in air, and made a clicking sound. "You're going to
need to learn how to listen, missy."

With their backs up against the stone, Monte and
Courtney pulled Veronica backwards, closer to them.

"You leave us alone. You go to hell," Veronica yelled.

Colin sat down on a boulder blocking their exit and
put his pistol on his lap. He rested his short club against
his thigh, reached into his front shirt pocket, and pulled
out the makings for a cigarette. He shook the can holding
the tobacco. "Last one."

He poured what was left in the can onto a small sheet
of paper, then tossed the can. "I'm celebrating." With slow,

deliberate care, he expertly rolled the yellow paper around a pinch of tobacco.

"Go to hell," Veronica yelled at Colin. She started to move forward but thought better of it when Colin tucked the cigarette into one hand and grabbed the club.

"If they knew I had you"—Colin shook the club at Veronica—"we wouldn't be going to hell, but all hell would surely be breaking loose." He lit his cigarette, sucked the smoke deep into his lungs and examined Veronica. "Ain't a one of 'em seen anything like you in a long, long time. Probably ever."

A cold, steady breeze swept up the wash and caused Colin's cigarette to burn faster. He studied it and grimaced. "Dry as a bone," he muttered. He looked up out of the wash towards the west; a solid bank of storm clouds was building fast now. He would need shelter if he was going to enjoy raping this woman, and the only real shelter around was the ranch. He pulled in another lungful off the cigarette, then flicked what remained onto the ground. Could he afford a night there since the gang left, he asked himself. He would have comfort, and the woman, but probably no whiskey. Maybe she knew where some was hidden. He questioned his intuition. He could slip in there and stay for just the night, or at least until the storm broke. There was risk. Colin thought back to Jessup cursing Wardell over the fire. But what if he stayed in the barn and not the house? That would give him warning if someone were to come.

Colin stood and looked down at Veronica. He would threaten to kill the boys to make her do his bidding. She could probably provide food, even after the house had been looted, knowing it as well as she did. He would have shelter, food, warmth, and he would have his way with her. He chuckled, looked out at the approaching storm and thought about his former colleagues riding all night in the rain.

Colin stepped towards the kids, swung the club, whacked Courtney on the head, and watched him collapse into the crook of Veronica's arm.

CHAPTER 12

Too Tall kept up a steady run in between wagon ruts for a mile after leaving the Parson ranch. Hooves slammed onto the ground and lifted the rainwater lying an inch thick on the land. It splashed off his legs and chest with a rhythmic cadence until Skinner pulled him down to a slow trot for a short rocky incline. As they emerged at the top, Skinner could see in the diminishing light the recently trampled earth where the horse trail cut off from the rutted wagon road. This shortcut to Veronica's house was rougher but more than an hour shorter, and it was clear from the churned-up soil that the gang had used it. Too Tall veered left onto the trail and worked his way into the forest.

The cloud cover, rain, and heavy timber filled Skinner with dread about the pending darkness, and by the time they had covered another mile he could not see his hand in front of his face. He placed a hand on Too Tall's neck, "It's going to be up to you tonight."

When Too Tall's deliberate pace faltered, Skinner knew the big horse had gone off the trail, but he had no choice; he had to trust his horse to find the way. Too Tall lowered his head and took in the scent of the soil. When he turned with confidence and increased his pace, Skinner knew he was back on the trail. *It's going to take eight hours,* he thought.

Skinner's hat was clamped down tight, the front edge pulled low, and he kept his chin tucked to protect his face from low branches that swept over him in the dark with alarming suddenness. After an hour of travel, Too Tall made a hard right turn, and Skinner knew this switchback marked the beginning of a long incline covered in loose rock. Traveling this portion of the trail would consume considerable energy from Too Tall, and they were only a quarter of the way to the ranch. "Damn it all," he yelled out.

Too Tall sped up in response to Skinner's tone.

"Hell, I ain't mad at you. I'm mad at the world," he said to his horse. Haunted by the sight of Mr. Parson's burned body and his wife lying sprawled and naked, Skinner projected images about what might be waiting for him ahead, and he didn't slow his horse down. His imagination placed him at the packed earth area around Veronica's house. The gang was tormenting the family and fighting over the spoils. He pictured himself charging through the buildings, firing on the leaders, diving off Too Tall and rolling for cover. Then he was up and running forward, firing more shots, killing them one at a time. The first man to fall was wearing a stained black vest, the next a ragged brown coat. He felt his hands handling the rifle action with precision, loading bullet after bullet into the hot breach, and he never missed a shot. He saw them fall clutching fatal wounds, and all through the fight Veronica screamed in the background. He pictured himself achieving one heroic action after another as more gang members descended on him, and he made a mental note to have extra ammunition ready in his right-hand coat pocket.

Suddenly, though, his thoughts turned, his intellect took over, and he remembered Chaco's warning and he made a mental effort to try and get control of the tortured images swirling in his mind. Only a moment passed before anger, impatience, and anxiety began to consume him once more. Responding to his rigid body, Too Tall began floundering on the rocky trail and his struggles again broke through Skinner's tormented thoughts. He lifted the reins knowing he would soon be walking if he didn't. "Ease up."

Too Tall slowed from the foolhardy pace but continued to respond to his rider's urgency. When a foot rolled on a loose rock causing a misstep, Too Tall's body jerked hard as he compensated. Solid footing for one hoof sent three feet scrambling with stretch and speed to gain more ground. Any good portions of the trail were taken in powerful long strides at a wide-open, ground-covering trot. On very steep sections the big horse brought his hind feet under him and lunged upwards, clearing obstacles in one or more leaps. When they encountered deep washes with rocky bottoms Too Tall braked hard, dropped his head, and sniffed his way through, then scrambled on.

On occasion, Too Tall's quick bold moves in the dark came so suddenly and with such power that Skinner became unbalanced in the saddle. He cursed himself each time, but Too Tall took no notice and pushed on in the near total blackness. Skinner understood the message coming from his horse. He slid a hand onto Too Tall's neck and squeezed the rain-and-sweat-soaked neck. "I hear ya boy. I hear ya."

After another twenty minutes of travel, Too Tall broke out of the timber and onto a meadow. With no urging from Skinner the big horse increased the pace to a canter. His breathing punctuated the sound of rain hitting the grass with snorts and huge deep, inhales. This was the halfway point, and in this small clearing, for the first time in three hours Skinner could just make out the surface of the land. He seized the smooth terrain as an opportunity to pray. *Just in case that preacher was right,* he told himself, thinking back on his youth and church experience. He pinched the skin on the bridge of his nose and ducked his head. Cold rain pelted his neck and trickled down his spine. His mind couldn't focus, and before he could begin a coherent prayer, Too Tall's feet slid awkwardly on the wet grass as he approached the heavy timber and deadfall that lined the far side of the meadow. The rain, frustration, and the need to suddenly redouble his riding effort shortened Skinner's prayer. He tilted his head backwards and screamed out into the cold, wet darkness. "I swear to God I'm going to send you all to hell."

CHAPTER 13

Veronica reacted instantly when Colin hit Courtney. She aimed for his knee, swung her leg off the ground and kicked out hard. The bridge of her foot smacked into the side of Colin's knee with force.

"Whore!" Colin swore at Veronica as his leg buckled.

Veronica kicked out again, aiming for the same spot, and connected with Colin again. This time Colin fell to one knee.

Colin swung his club and hit Veronica a hard blow to her thigh.

Veronica yelped in pain and doubled over, grabbing her thigh as she fell to the ground. She saw him raise the club again, she pushed out with her feet and tried to slither further backwards, but the second blow arrived with just as much force. She screamed out again and ducked as the club was raised a third time, but now it was directed at Monte, who lunged at Colin. Veronica's high-pitched scream turned into a low growl of anger in the same breath. She tried to get up and defend her brother but was too late; the outlaw hit Monte, who fell back and landed squarely on her chest. Veronica fell backwards, holding her brother to her chest as he gagged for air.

"Want more?" Colin said. "Any of ya?"

Veronica's face was pulled into a tight grimace, but she didn't make a sound.

"What you gonna do, kid?" said Colin, looking down on Monte as he rolled off his sister.

Blood poured off his jaw, and he was obviously close to losing consciousness. He groaned and reached out and dragged Courtney, who was still unconscious, closer to him. Swinging his arm around his brother, he turned away from the outlaw and lowered his frame protectively over Courtney's head and chest.

Colin pulled the small coil of rope out of his belt and put his attention on Veronica. "Lay down on your belly and put your hands behind your back."

"I'll be damned if I will," answered Veronica.

Colin swung the club viciously against the rock next to him. The tip broke off and twirled away into the wash. "Lady, you don't do what I tell ya, I'll kill him." Colin set the jagged end of the club against Courtney ribs and applied pressure. "Get on your belly." Colin waited.

Veronica felt overwhelming anger building inside her as she lay face down and he tied her hands. She gritted her teeth and swore at him. When he pulled her feet up behind her and tied them, then connected the rope to her hands behind her back, it pushed her closer to the brink of panic.

"Go to hell," she growled and cursed at Colin over and over.

"Shut up, I'm warning you." Colin jabbed Veronica in the ribs with his club and silenced her.

Veronica struggled against the ropes binding her but remained silent and watched his every move as he hauled Courtney over to her and tied him in the same manner.

Colin passed the last length of rope over a boulder and

stretched it between their hands. When he pulled it tight it suspended both Courney and Veronica slightly, so that their hands and feet were above them and their faces looked at the ground. When he was done, he stood over Veronica. Tied the way she was she couldn't see his face, but she could see his limp as he moved. She had hurt him. His voice was low and not a hint of bluff could be construed from his cold tone.

"I'm gonna take this kid with me. When I come back, if I see you been trying to undo them ropes, I'll slit this one's throat right in front of ya. Don't even try to work 'em lose."

Moments later Veronica heard Monte and the outlaw leaving. She flexed her limbs against the ropes. They were tight, secure, tied with skill. She flexed again, and the rope binding her hands hurt. Her hands had already begun to swell. She could not think of an option. She wriggled and twisted as much as she could and tried to see as much as she could. Afraid the outlaw was still within hearing distance she waited a full minute before she called out. "Courtney. Courtney," she whispered. "Court, can you hear me?" Veronica rolled and tried to tug on the rope going over the rock, trying to get her unconscious brother's attention.

"Court, can you hear me?"

CHAPTER 14

Colin threw the still-wobbly Monte across the saddle, then worked his way back to the top of the bluff above the house and peered down. Not ready to accept that all was well, Colin left Monte and the horse and circled until he found the gang's tracks heading north. He used every bit of the remaining daylight following their trail, trying to assure himself that they had left him and did not intend to come back. When he could no longer see well enough in the darkness, he returned to the barn and threw Monte into a stall just as it began to rain. Then he returned to the wash and Veronica and Courtney. As weak as they both were from being tied in such an awkward manner, as well as from the beating he had given them, it took some time to get back to the barn. An hour after full dark the three of them arrived at the barn soaking wet and cold.

Colin felt good about his plan. He felt safer staying in the barn; it would give him some warning if someone came. He loosened the cinch on his horse but left it saddled and tied it by the back door, then put his full attention on Veronica.

"I'm gonna enjoy myself tonight. First time you do something I don't like, he's gonna die," he said pointing at

Courtney while staring at Veronica. "If he don't die on his own." Colin poked the toe of his boot under Courtney's armpit and rolled him over on his back; blood dripped off the side of his head. Colin pulled out his sheath knife and drove the tip into a board above Courtney. "I'll pull him right over here next to you and cut him up slow like." Colin bent over Veronica and spoke in a lower, cold voice. "I'll kill him real slow if you don't do like I want. I'll kill the other boy next." Colin paused, waiting for Veronica to reply, but she remained silent and did not look at him. "You're going to do exactly what I want, aren't ya?"

Veronica nodded her head with her eyes lowered.

"You know where there's any whiskey they might have missed?" Veronica didn't respond instantly, so Colin reached behind him and jerked the knife out of the board and limped closer to Courtney. "Answer me."

Veronica gestured with her eyes to a small cupboard high above the bench by the front door.

"You gotta be pulling my leg." Colin's limp was getting worse; he struggled to get up on the bench to reach the high cupboard. The heavily scratched glass flask contained an inch of liquid in the bottom.

Colin laughed hard, pulled the cork out, and shook the contents. It was a tease but better than nothing, and better than what those rats riding in the rain probably had. "Too good to be true." Colin chuckled. "My, my, my, that's good." He licked his lips and flapped his tongue up and down. He looked down on Veronica and stared, studying her response. He set the flask down and dragged Monte and Courtney into separate horse stalls and slammed both doors shut. Near where Veronica lay tied on the floor was a stack of saddle pads on a wooden platform. He took six and arranged them on the floor into a rectangle, then he made a chair that leaned against the front of a stall with the remaining saddle pads. He sat, reached for the flask again, admired the whiskey inside, and a long sigh emanated from his lungs. "Good stuff. Oh my, this is good stuff," he said. A tight smile curled in the corner of his mouth as he thought once again of his former colleagues enduring the rain somewhere to the north. He chuckled and admired Veronica from head to toe. He laughed and smacked his thigh with the palm of his hand. He reached for his knee where Veronica had kicked him and rubbed it for a few moments, still staring at Veronica. Then he took another pull off the bottle and very carefully replaced the cork and set it down beside him. His eyes swung back and forth from the bottle to Veronica. He pushed the bottle back to a more secure spot by the wall before leaning over Veronica and untying the rope binding her feet. He rolled her over until she lay face up on the center of the pads. Her hands were still tied. He put his shin across her neck, pinning her. He reached behind her and undid the rope binding her hands. "Don't do anything stupid now little lady." He pulled her hands back together in front of her body and retied them. Then he used the length of rope from Veronica's feet to connect her to the bottom of a partition post near the rectangle of saddle pads.

"Little lady, I don't like crying. Matter of fact, I don't like noise of any kind." Colin ripped her blouse open and studied her breasts as they rose and fell. His eye then moved to the bottle. He reached for it and sat down to enjoy his last swig.

Veronica's breathing came in gasps. It was clear how this was going to end if she couldn't find a way to defend herself. Veronica watched Colin raise the flask for the last remaining whiskey. "I have more." Veronica squeaked out the words.

"You got more whiskey? I doubt it. You a little liar too, huh?"

"I have more," Veronica offered again.

"Where?"

"It's hidden away, and I'm not going to tell you where unless you let me tend to my brothers." Veronica gestured at the stall where Colin had put Courtney.

"That ain't gonna happen." Colin stared hard at Veronica. "What else you got to bargain with?"

Veronica felt a shiver go through her. The man had shown his ability to read her mind. To know that she was trying to negotiate and prolong the inevitable. He knew what she was trying to do but he wanted to hear her out to see how he could profit from her knowledge of the ranch. She had a chance.

"Little lady, you better tell me what you got, fast."

"I can get more whiskey."

"Maybe—if the others didn't get it all."

"Let me tend to my brother first, then I'll get you some?"

"Nope, it's got to be the other way around. You get me the whiskey, and I won't go ahead and finish him off."

Veronica knew she could not ask again, but she had an opening. "Okay. Let me go get it."

"We'll go together. You show me where it is."

"No."

"You don't tell me no, little lady."

It was becoming clear that Colin liked whiskey more than he liked the prospect of having his way with her. "I'll go alone and bring it back. I won't leave my brothers."

Colin grabbed his knife and cut her leg loose but left her hands tied. "No, I'm going with ya. Now where is it?"

"It's up towards the outcrop over the house. There's a bench up there where we sat as a family in the evenings." Veronica hesitated and stammered through her lie.

Colin paused. His knee was swelling fast, and the thought of walking uphill was not in his plans. "All right, you go get it, but you better know that if you isn't back in five minutes, I'll start cutting them boys to pieces. You hear 'em screaming you better get here quick, 'cause they'll be enjoying their last breaths. Any questions?"

"I can't get there and back in five minutes. I need fifteen."

"You get ten and I'm starting now." Colin stared at her, then added. "You leave them hands tied too."

Veronica lunged for the front of the barn, and Colin did not stop her. Her leg hurt as well, but it was not going to slow her down. She fled out the door and raced for the house. Bursting through the door, she stepped on her mother's body. She stifled her scream and in the pitch dark reached for her mother and felt the cold skin on her bare arm. She sobbed in silence and kept moving. She found Laura next and wondered how she had been brought to the house. She found her dad last, his body discarded in a corner of the main room. Veronica couldn't stop to grieve; her brothers were still alive and by the slimmest of margins. If she kept going, she might be able to save them. She had a plan. She moved to the panel to the right of the fireplace and slid the false log back. Inside were whiskey glasses and several bottles of imported whiskey, all gone unnoticed by the others in Leon's secret spot.

Tears rolled down her cheeks as she recalled the times she heard her parents whispering in their room. Her father got amorous after drinking more than he should, and her mother would reject his overtures, mainly on the grounds that his whiskey-induced impairment made their intimacy difficult. It was embarrassing when she'd heard them talk like that, but she had listened on several occasions and understood what they were whispering about. She grabbed a bottle and then thought hard about how much she should take back. She filled a glass a quarter of the way up. This would be her first wager: An amount just short of enough. Make him get her to return for more.

The ruse worked, and Veronica made two more trips before Colin succumbed to the effects and lost his patience. When she entered the barn after her third trip to the house, Colin attacked her. Despite the increasing pain in his leg, he managed to pin her down and tie her leg once again. He ripped off her clothing, stepped back, and picked up the whiskey bottle she had brought with her on this last trip. He pulled the cork, lifted the neck of the bottle to his lips, and took a small sip, which he swirled around his mouth. Then he threw his head back to swallow the liquid in a gulp. Lowering the bottle, Colin looked at the label and raised an eyebrow. He squinted and examined the label on the bottle intently. His eyes swiveled left and downwards. He didn't look Veronica in the eye. He looked at her body as she twisted sideways to hide her nakedness. Then he swerved to the left and stumbled on his bad leg. "Damn good stuff," he said. He watched Veronica curl into a ball. He set the bottle down. "Damn good stuff all around."

Veronica looked away as Colin pulled off his boots and stripped off his filthy, stinking pants. Angry tears rolled across her cheeks, she yanked at the rope binding her hands. When he descended on her she kicked out and curled her legs away, grunting with effort. She rolled left, then right, she curled her legs up under her, she kicked again. The outlaw yelled a warning into her ear, following the warning with a vicious slap to the side of her head. Veronica's anger surged; she felt no pain from the blow, and she swore back at him. More slaps hit the side of her head, a fist slammed into her ribs, then a hard callused hand struck her jaw. She yelled out and fought harder. Another vicious blow landed against the side of her head. She heard Monte yell out, cussing at Colin to leave his sister alone. Suddenly she heard Courtney's voice as well, but his words were unintelligible.

Fear rose from her chest with a surge and poured into her brain. Her body responded to the mix of fear and anger. Every muscle became ridged as he wriggled on top of her. She kicked out again and threw him to the side. He hit her again and she felt the blackness coming over her. She panicked and forced herself to refocus; she understood her panic was born of desperation. *I can't lose consciousness,* she told herself. *I need to stay conscious, to stay with them.* Veronica's thoughts organized around a single concept. *My brothers. I'm the only chance they have.* Veronica fought for the three of them.

CHAPTER 15

As they entered their fifth hour of travel, Too Tall continued at a pace just short of reckless, but Skinner could feel his stride begin to shorten and less snap coming from the hind end. Hard work, miles, and a lack of food and water were taking a toll. Skinner rose up in the stirrups, riding on the balls of his feet, his calves pressed against the stirrup fenders, water-soaked leather reins hanging loose, for Skinner was merely a passenger.

Too Tall put on the brakes and brought his hind end under him. He braced his back legs while his front feet took quick nimble steps, and they slid thirty feet down a steep, muddy section of trail into a wide wash that was running with water. The big horse came to an abrupt stop and plunged his muzzle into the muddy liquid. Already soaked to the bone, Skinner dismounted and stood in the water by his horse's head. Water ran into both boots through holes along the edge of the soles. He allowed Too Tall to drink for thirty seconds, then he pulled his head up and led him up the opposite bank to a flat spot. He knew his horse wanted more, but he was too overheated to allow it. Skinner stood beside the big horse, shivering in his wet clothes, and warmed his hands against Too Tall's steaming wet hide. Hot air coming from the big horse's lungs drifted across his cold cheeks. "You're somethin' else Too Tall," he said. Skinner allowed Too Tall to drink again after a few minutes.

They were a mile from the ranch and had made the trip so much quicker than Skinner had predicted that he needed to reevaluate his next step. If he tied up here, out of earshot, he knew his horse would waste huge amounts of energy spinning and turning, worrying about being left alone. If he stopped closer to the ranch and went in on foot, Too Tall would whinny and blow his cover. Skinner threaded the reins through his hands and pondered his choices until a big wet head suddenly swung into the small of his back and shoved him down the trail.

"Okay. You're damn good company anyhow."

Stiff, sore muscles and wet pants clinging to his legs caused him to mount awkwardly, and they were three steps down the trail before he could shove a water-filled boot into the offside stirrup. To the west an unwelcome development appeared in the form of a star. He had been counting on the storm to cover his approach, and now it looked as though the weather was breaking.

"Damn."

When they were a quarter mile from the house, Skinner stopped to listen. Too Tall, having pushed hard to get there, pawed the ground in frustration, his shod hoof striking a rock and breaking the silence. Skinner let him forward before he could do it again but pulled him off the trail and began a slow circle to the east, looking for an alternative place to climb up through the limestone rim, away from the main trail. Once on top, Skinner stopped again, but this time he jiggled the reins, tensed in the saddle, and drew in a quick, heavy breath, communicating to Too Tall his nerves. The big horse brought his head up, gave a low snort, and began testing the air. Keeping his body stiff in the saddle Skinner placed a hand firmly on the crest of Too Tall's neck. "Attaboy," he whispered. Spooked by his rider, the big horse now placed his hooves with care upon the rain-soaked earth and tested the air incessantly. When the dark silhouette of the house finally appeared, it was much closer than Skinner had expected. Too Tall jerked to a stop and tested the air, then shied violently and pivoted back the way they had come. Skinner had to jerk the reins hard to check his horse and hold him in place. He swore in a whisper, "You bastards." Skinner didn't swear at his horse, he swore at what his horse had told him with absolute clarity. His horse had smelled death. Skinner slumped in the saddle, his lungs deflated, and a muscle in the back of his neck popped as his head tipped forward onto his chest. *Of course, there's nothing but death waiting. What the hell were you expecting,* he told himself. Skinner brought a cold, wet hand up and rubbed the back of his neck. He blinked his eyes repeatedly to help himself see better in the dark. After a full minute Too Tall twitched his ears and the tension in his body dropped. Skinner took off his slicker and dropped it in the mud. He drew his rifle from the scabbard beneath his leg and checked his load, then he arranged handfuls of bullets with all the tips forward into his right coat pocket. "One for each of them," he whispered.

Skinner nudged Too Tall forward just as the rain quit falling. Too Tall's hooves squishing in the mud was unbearably loud. "Easy," Skinner whispered. More stars began to emerge behind the retreating storm clouds. Skinner placed a hand on Too Tall's mane and pinched the horse's neck. "Easy boy." He kept tension on the reins, asking the horse for only one step at a time. In five minutes they covered fifteen yards towards the house. Skinner

made out the form of a dead horse lying in the center of the
packed earth between the buildings. "Easy boy," he hissed
again. He swirled his tongue around the inside of his
mouth, licked his lips, and swallowed. He strained to see
details. The chill that had gripped his body all night long
was gone, and beads of sweat trickled down his face. *It is
still too dark. Better not go any farther or you're going to
get shot. Check the corral,* he told himself.

Skinner retreated, skirted the buildings twenty yards
out, and made his way towards the small corral by the
barn. Both were empty, and the gates were open. He swore
under his breath, "I'll shoot everyone of you." This still
didn't mean there was no one there, but it probably meant
that the killers had five fresh horses.

It was too quiet, so Skinner retreated to a safe distance
once again. If anyone was still alive, his best chance to
help would be at dawn, still an hour away.

"Easy boy. Easy now. I'm gonna wait here until we
have some light." He stripped the saddle off Too Tall, led
him back down below the lip of the rim, and turned him
loose. Too Tall ambled away looking for grass. Skinner
had no need for his horse now and was confident the com-
bination of hunger, fatigue, and the dead horse would
keep Too Tall from returning any time soon.

To the west more stars indicated a clearing sky. Skinner
found a hidden spot in a cluster of small trees where he
could sit and watch the house. There was no movement, no
sound, nothing to suggest life, and he remained where he
was until the chirp of a hungry house finch brought him
slowly and stiffly to his feet. The finch was answered by
its mate, then an agitated cardinal chimed in, and soon bird
chatter came from all directions. Gray light began to grow.
Skinner drew in several deep breaths and lifted his rifle
and opened the trapdoor enough for his callused thumb to

feel the smooth shell casing sliding back. He closed it and lowered the hammer on the chambered round. He drew his pistol, pulled the hammer back two clicks, rotated the cylinder, and felt the heads of six shells slide against his thumb one more time.

His approach was directly from the woods, away from any paths, and he slunk from one piece of cover to the next, pausing at each one for minutes at a time. Fifteen yards from the main house, he held the trigger of his rifle back and set the hammer noiselessly. Sweat loosened his rain-soaked hat and it slid low over his eyes,

Crouching, Skinner crossed an open space and pressed his back against the logs at a corner of the house. Birds chattered with increasing vigor as the light began to build. He moved along the wall in a tight space between Muriel's flower garden and the front porch and paused to listen. When he stepped up on the porch it squeaked, so he kept moving on tiptoes to the front door. The door was wide open, so he didn't stop. He took one step inside and put his back against the wall to his left. It was darker inside; his eyes strained to see as they swept the room, looking for movement. When he looked along the wall to his right, his eye caught movement outside. With trouble behind and potential trouble inside, he choked off a gasp and took cover by taking two more steps farther inside and pressing his back tightly against the wall. His lungs pumped air trying to absorb adrenaline, he let his mouth fall open so he could breathe with no sound, and his thumb stayed hooked around the top of the hammer of his rifle. Nothing moved inside, so he tiptoed along the wall to the first window and took a quick peek outside. He could not identify what it was he had seen. He straightened and surveyed the room again. Stronger light began to fill the house.

Stretched out below Skinner's feet, lying side by side,

were three bodies. He swung his rifle downwards and nearly pulled the trigger, expecting the people at his feet to explode off their beds. *They're asleep right at my feet.* Something wasn't right; he smelled blood. He stood motionless, afraid to make a decision. His hat brim slid farther down his forehead as he stared. It was Leon, Muriel, and Laura. All of them had their hands folded across their chests in the classic repose of the dead. His lungs demanded huge amounts of air, and it was hard to keep his breathing quiet. He took another look out the window and saw Too Tall ready to skirt the dead horse and go to the barn. "Damn," he hissed. Too Tall had filled his belly while Skinner had waited for dawn. Now he wanted oats, and knowing where they were kept, had come for them.

Too Tall let out a snort twenty feet from the dead horse, and the noise carried all through the buildings. Immediately there was an answering whinny from the barn.

"You stupid fool," Skinner swore under his breath.

He'd made a major mistake letting Too Tall remain loose all that time. There was another horse here, and that meant trouble. He side stepped back along the wall to the front door and hunkered down on one knee with his shoulder braced on the door frame. He could not regulate his breathing, and his body shook.

Light reflected off Too Tall's wet hide just twenty yards away. The big horse stood focused on the barn door; the dead horse was to his side. He whinnied again, and this time the horse in the barn answered with more shrillness and volume. Three times they whinnied back and forth. Too Tall stomped his right foot, then his left, but did not move forward.

Skinner saw the barn door open a foot and a hat brim appeared at its edge, but he couldn't see the face beneath. He brought his eye within an inch of the rifle sights and trained the gun on the barn door. He continued to flick his gaze back towards the interior of the house. The rifle shook in his hands. He heard voices in the barn, but the chatter of birds was too strong for him to know what was said. His finger curled around the trigger. The sound of oats being shaken in a can came to him, and both horses whinnied simultaneously in response. The hat brim appeared briefly at the barn doors' edge; a gray, bearded jaw jutted forward beneath it. Skinner heard rustling and more voices. The barn door creaked farther open, and out stepped Veronica with a halter and a small can. Skinner's finger flicked forward away from the trigger. He watched her take tentative steps towards Too Tall.

"Too Tall. Come here, boy," she stammered.

She recognizes Too Tall. She knows I'm here, Skinner thought. He waited, not knowing what to do.

The pitch of her voice was high, she was obviously terrified, her steps were stiff and short, and she was barefoot. Her lower legs and feet were covered in mud. A faded red blanket was draped around her shoulders. She clutched the edges of the blanket, the can, and the halter awkwardly in front of her chest.

Veronica called out to Too Tall again, "Here boy, it's all right. Here boy. It's okay, boy." Skinner watched Too Tall step back, stiffen his frame, and snort his nerves at Veronica.

The horse inside the barn whinnied again.

Skinner saw Veronica's index finger point upwards. Why was she holding the can like that?

She took another step towards Too Tall, and Skinner saw her index finger curl and uncurl several times, then she pointed backwards with a thumb towards the barn, her hand motions all hidden from whoever was wearing the hat behind her.

Skinner saw the hat brim move just at the edge of the

door. His eyes moved back to Veronica, and he saw her legs wobble. He took a quick glance behind him at the interior of the house, then he drew in a deep breath and put the sights of the Springfield on the heavy plank lining the edge of the barn door, six inches back from the hat brim and one inch lower. He took another deep breath, held his body motionless, and as the air left his lungs pulled the trigger. The heavy bullet tore through the wood. The bullet and fragments of wood took most of Colin's head off, and his lifeless body cartwheeled into the mud.

Before the sound of the big gun dissipated Veronica collapsed on the ground screaming. Too Tall wheeled and bolted back over the lip of the rim, and frightened whinnies and hooves scrambling on a wooden floor came from the barn. Loading another shell into the breach, Skinner raced for the barn. He fell to his side and rolled on the ground in front of the barn doors. His finger jerked the trigger unintentionally, and he sent a wild bullet into the dark interior of the barn. This shot was louder as the sound waves pounded off the back walls of the barn's interior. He rolled once again and used the dead outlaw's body for cover, his hand groping for another shell in his pocket. He pulled one out and shoved it into the breach.

Veronica screamed behind him, "Don't shoot! Don't shoot!"

Skinner scrambled forward across the dead outlaw and in a crouch pressed his body up against the far side of the barn door. He swung his rifle back and forth, not knowing where trouble could come from next. "Are there any more?" he yelled

Veronica scrambled to her feet and the blanket fell away. "Don't shoot! Don't shoot!" she yelled. Naked, she rushed past him into the barn.

Skinner yelled out. "Are there any more? Are there any more?"

"No. It's just us," another voice yelled, barely audible over the whinnying of the horse inside.

Skinner recognized Courtney's voice, and he rolled forward so he could see farther into the barn. He saw Veronica drag a bound Courtney from one of the stalls. She left him in the middle of the floor and moved to the next stall. Despite his adrenaline-filled body, and all the fear and nerves, and despite having just shot a man, Skinner stared at Veronica. She tugged and tugged on the door, unconcerned by her lack of clothes. Skinner's heart sank. The door of the second stall opened a few inches but got hung up on a saddle pad. She yanked and yanked on the door with no success. She yelled out unintelligible words, and each time she tugged at the door she weakened. She dropped to the ground, and on her elbows and knees sobbed and gagged for air.

"No one else is here?" Skinner asked again, still poised by the barn door with his rifle held ready.

"No," Monte answered.

"How long have they been gone?"

"They all left yesterday, except for that one. They're gone."

Skinner moved inside, pulled off his wet coat, and draped it over Veronica. He jerked the door to the stall open, pulled Monte out, and untied the ropes on both boys. When he was done, he looked at Veronica, the whiteness of her body showing beneath his coat pulled his eye again, and he saw a huge dark bruise running from above her knee, up the side of her thigh, and across her hip. He reached for her, but she rejected his offer to help her and moved on her own to collect her clothes and dress. When she was fully clothed, she sat with her back against a wall, brought her knees up to her chest, ducked her head, and rocked back and forwards. Her shoulders and chest rose and fell rapidly with her sobs.

Monte, stiff and sore from having been bound so long, crawled over to his sister and leaned into her. Courtney rolled off his side and needed Skinner's help to stand. He moved over by his brother and sister and sat beside them as well. The boys stared at Skinner standing in front of them but didn't speak. Colin's skinny horse was pulling back against its halter rope by the back door of the barn. Unwilling to put up with the noise it was making, Skinner walked over to the horse. The knot tying the animal had been pulled so tight that Skinner pulled his knife and cut the rope. The animal fell backwards onto its haunches, then gathered itself and skittered out of the barn. Skinner pulled his hat off and squatted in front of the twins and Veronica.

"I'm so sorry," he said. "I should have gotten here sooner. I didn't have a . . ."

"He was going to kill us and take her this morning," said Courtney.

Monte raised his head. "You got here in time . . ."

"We need to be alone for a while Tom," said Courtney.

Standing up, Skinner looked down at Veronica, whose face remained hidden, down on her knees. "I'll be outside."

Skinner went over to the body of the dead outlaw, grabbed a wrist, and pulled him just out of sight from where Veronica and the boys sat. He went back to where the outlaw had fallen and kicked mud over the pool of blood that had gathered, then he picked up handfuls of mud and flung it against the barn to hide the blood-and bone-splattered walls. Tugging the outlaw once more, he dragged him to the smallest shed, heaved him inside, and slammed the door, then squatted by a pool of rainwater and washed the outlaw's blood off his hands. The calling of birds who'd fled the gunfire just minutes ago was already increasing as they vainly jostled to be first to receive handouts from the house. Skinner took off his hat, wiped his brow, then shoved two fingers into his mouth and whistled for Too Tall.

Too Tall failed to appear after a few minutes, so Skinner crossed over to the house to see what food and clothing he could find, and to look the house over. He took a short look at Leon, Muriel, and Laura's bodies and knew that Veronica had somehow found an opportunity to tend to them. He would hear the story of what happened later; it didn't matter now anyway. He went into the kitchen next, fired up the stove, and set a pot of water to heat. He took a careful look around and realized there was not a scrap of food to be had, but he did find a tin of tea. *That nasty cur probably sent her here for food during the night; that's how she tended to them,* he thought.

As he went through the house, he gathered fresh clothing for the three of them, which he bundled into a small throw rug. In Leon and Muriel's bedroom he was so startled by the sight of Pepper sitting in the bed that he threw the rug, pulled his pistol, and nearly fired a shot before it registered that the man was dead.

Pepper sat upright in the bed, surrounded by pillows, gut shot. Blood stained everything around him. One eye was squinted shut, the other remained wide open. His lower lip drooped, and his head was slightly to one side, eyes staring at his feet.

Skinner looked at the body. "Your friends will be joinin' ya soon enough," he growled.

He left Pepper where he was and returned to the kitchen.

Gathering mugs, the tea pot, and the clothes into one load, he returned to the barn.

"When you're ready, might be a good idea to get out of here, somewhere different," he said.

Veronica kept her face hidden and didn't respond. Monte and Courtney both looked at him.

"How did you know?" asked Courtney.

"Two days ago a courier came to the fort, warning us about 'em. I got here as fast as I could." At the end of his response, he saw Veronica begin to rock back and forth more rapidly. Skinner changed the subject. "Come on, let's get out of here. We can carry all this stuff with us. Let's go sit in the sun over by the big shed."

Veronica never met his eye, and no one spoke while he settled them in the sun and handed out mugs of hot tea. Words wouldn't work for any of them right now, so he left them and moved down the trail to look for his horse. Too Tall stood hip shot sound asleep on a flat spot not far away, and the outlaw's horse grazed nearby. Skinner went a little farther down the trail and with rocks arranged the letters *OK* for Chaco to see. Then he returned to the horses and found himself a place to lie down nearby. He had been up for two nights; his body was stiff and cold, his hands and face black with dirt and blood, he was emotionally spent, and only one thought swirled in his head. He knew the thought was selfish and filled him with guilt: *Would she ever trust a man again? Would she ever trust me?* he asked himself. *Especially after what happened and what I did.* He flopped backwards onto the ground, and the back of his head hit the wet grass with a thud. His body pressed against the earth as though he weighed twice as much as he did. The sun penetrated his wet, mud-caked clothes and warmed him. *I'll sleep until Chaco gets here,* he thought.

CHAPTER 16

At midmorning Skinner was awakened by the sounds of hooves coming up the trail. He rose, rubbed his eyes, and stumbled down the trail to meet the patrol well away from the house and barn. He walked up to Chaco and stood by his stirrup. The men behind shoved forward and brought their horses to a halt, all wanting to hear what would be said, and Skinner raised his voice so they could.

"Leon, Muriel, and Laura are dead. They're in the house. Veronica, Courtney, and Monte are alive, and they're in the bigger shed. I'm not sure how they ended up with just one of them, but he had them holed up in the barn. I killed him this morning."

A murmur rose among the men. This patrol had just crossed another line, now that their side had killed.

"I don't really know what-all happened. They're all in bad shape," Skinner said gesturing up towards the house. "Here's what we gotta get done: They managed to kill one of 'em, or else he got killed by his own men, I don't know. Either way, he's in the house, and we need to get him out. Greg, you and Vance haul him out of there and put him in the small shed. You'll find the one I shot already in there. Wrap them both up in something and nail the door shut.

Tell you right now: be ready for a grim task." Skinner moved halfway down the column of men as he spoke. "I don't want anyone near the other shed. They need privacy. There's not a scrap of food here for horses or us. Skeeter, you and Vance get a fire going and make a meal out of our kit. Boomer, you and Charlie quarter that dead horse and haul it out of here. Cut steaks if you want, then throw it over the side down there. I want it done quick and quiet, don't leave a trace of it for anyone to see." Skinner swung his arm towards the area he wanted the horse hauled too. "Sunny, get the clincher off my saddle, check every nail on every shoe. Victor, take up the trail, see what you can find out, but be back in four hours. Their trail's out behind the barn. Might be hard to follow after the rain; see if you can get the general direction. Wade, you wrangle. Get on the far side of the horses, we don't want them going anywhere. Rest of you, strip the tack and give 'em all a good rub-down. When you're done, push 'em over to that good grass. After you all get something in your bellies, rest. We'll be back in the saddle by midafternoon."

With tight-lipped grim expressions, the patrol dismounted as one, then moved towards their appointed tasks with haste that matched Skinner's speed in dishing out orders.

"Chaco, give me a hand will ya? We need to visit."

Chaco stripped the tack off his chestnut, dropped it on the ground where he stood, and followed Skinner. Before they went to work, Skinner inquired about the Parson boys.

"We never found them," answered Chaco. "Don't believe they were around."

"Did ya see my horse down there?" Skinner abruptly changed the subject.

"Yeah, he's packing it away. I'm surprised he didn't follow us in."

"How'd your horses do?"

"Only half dead," answered Chaco. "That black is the worst."

The two of them appraised the horses from afar. Chaco remained quiet, waiting for Skinner to speak.

Skinner pulled off his hat and began picking mud off the brim. "I got spooked in the dark last night. Made one sashay through while it was still raining, but that was pretty dumb. If they'd been around, they could have killed me easy. It wasn't until close to first light that I went into the house. Leon, Muriel, and Laura are laid out in there. I'm thinkin' that killer used the twins as a threat to make her do whatever he wanted. Probably sent her in there for food, and she had a chance to tend to them. I tell ya, Chaco, I never expected to find them like that. Anyway, I was in there, and Too Tall comes walking up looking for oats."

Skinner told Chaco the story from beginning to end. "I'm not sure how they're going to come through, Chaco. She's got that look in her eyes, the look . . ." Skinner found himself wordless, unable to express himself. "Like I said, I don't really know what happened before I got here. It's gonna be hard to be patient on that subject. I think I need . . ."

Skinner, still struggling to find words, was interrupted by the sound of Vance and Greg bursting out the front door of the house with the dead outlaw. They each held a wrist, and bent over with effort, they dragged Pepper through the mud.

Work ceased, everyone wanted to see the face of one of these outlaws, and Skinner did nothing to discourage them from going for a look.

As they gathered around the body, Charlie was the first to speak.

"Hell, he ain't what I expected."

"Just what the hell was you expecting?" asked Skeeter impatiently.

"I was expecting him to be bigger I guess. I don't know," said Charlie in a shaky voice.

"He looks mean as a snake," said Vance.

"Who do you think shot him?"

"Hell, Captain just told ya he doesn't know the story."

"He sure looks dead." Charlie regretted the comment right away.

"What the hell is that supposed to mean? Are you feeble-minded or something?" said Skeeter harshly.

"Sorry, you miserable back biter. I guess all these dead people I been seeing lately are getting to me," said Charlie, clenching his fists and staring at Skeeter.

Skeeter bristled, clenched his fists and started forward.

"Skeeter. Easy does it," said Boomer, stepping between them. "Keep your wits. We got people around who need us. Need us to be strong."

"Watch your mouth," said Skeeter, glaring at Charlie.

Skinner moved closer, his voice rising over the mumbling coming from the cluster of men. "That killer died hard. Just like the rest of them will when we catch 'em." The comment abruptly changed the topic, and Skinner kept talking. "Leon's family and the Parson family were friends to most of us, and I ain't waitin' for any input about how to handle this. My orders are to stay on 'em if we run across 'em, then send word back to the fort. I already done that. Now I intend to put a chase on 'em and see what happens. One thing everyone better get settled in your brains: This job has fallen to us, and no one will be even close to helpin' us before we finish it. They came into our country, and we're the ones that's gonna put a stop on 'em."

Greg was the first to speak. In his usual low, quiet voice he asked, "Captain, they got a day's head start. What if we don't catch 'em?"

"You don't have to worry about that. You'll be part of the escort taking those three back to the fort." He waited for anyone else to speak, but no one did.

"Wade, you'll be going with Greg as well."

"Yes sir!"

"Greg," said Skinner. "I'm puttin' you in charge 'cause you got the manners called for. It is going to be a hard job, a delicate job, takin' 'em back."

"Yes sir! I understand."

"Captain!" Boomer gestured towards the shed. They all looked. Veronica stood in the doorway, and Monte stood in the shadow of the doorway behind her, both of them watching Skinner and the patrol.

Skinner spoke softly. "Get this corpse into the shed with the other one now. Rest of you get back to work."

Trailed by Chaco, Skinner moved towards the mules to put some hustle in the food preparation. He wanted a hot meal for Veronica and the boys.

"I'm thinking we should let the horses get a bellyful, then get them all on the trail back to the fort as soon as we can," Skinner said to Chaco. "Send the worst-off horses with 'em."

"What about the mules?"

"Trade one out for that black horse. Keep two for our kit. The rest go back with Greg and Wade. That black can carry one of the boys. We'll go on three days' rations, saddle animals only. Willy can follow us with our kit on whatever mules we got left." Skinner gestured with his head in Veronica and the boys' direction. "All their saddles are still here."

"Brooks is probably back by now. They might meet up with reinforcements before they get back," said Chaco.

"If that Brickman can get out of his office they might. Nothing I can say or do about that, it's outta my control. But I ain't gonna consider anything reinforcements can do for us going forward. We're on our own."

Chaco nodded.

"Remind me to tell Greg to bypass the Parson ranch goin' back. I don't want them to see it." Skinner waved an arm in the direction of Veronica and the boys.

"Que mas quiere, compadre?" asked Chaco.

Skinner nodded at Chaco. "We're pretty much done for a while. Have 'em all rest as soon as possible." With a visibly shaking hand, Skinner gestured towards the shed. "I'll go tell 'em our plan."

"Tell them to stay with Maria when they get back."

"Okay. That sounds good I will. Thanks."

Skinner piled cold biscuits and jerked meat on a plate and headed for the shed. The flimsy door was closed. Skinner called out, "Veronica, it's me. I brought food." He tapped the bottom of the door with the toe of his boot. He had to wait a minute before the door opened, and it threw him off the businesslike demeanor he'd planned to use with them. He felt unwelcome, unsure of what words to use, when the door opened and Courtney waved him in.

Veronica and Monte sat with their backs against a wall. The rug Skinner had given them the previous night was draped across their legs. Skinner put the food down near them, then reached over and put a hand on Veronica's shoulder. "I'm sorry. I'm so sorry." Her face tilted up at him, and Skinner recoiled at her red eyes and drawn face. She looked different, almost like another person. He hesitated between words as he spoke, afraid of saying something wrong, or in the wrong manner. "I wanna send you all back to the fort. I'll have two of my men go with you. Chaco told me his wife would welcome you and put you up. If that's okay."

Veronica ducked her head.

"The rest of us are going to run these outlaws down. I'll need you to be ready to go in about two hours."

"Okay," said Veronica without looking up.

Skinner stood. "If you'll show me where, I'll have my men dig some graves."

"Not yet. I'll come outside and we can talk about that." said Veronica.

"I'll wait outside." Skinner rose and moved towards the door quickly to hide tears that had welled in his eyes with uncontrollable suddenness. He didn't look back when Veronica spoke to him again.

"Don't let anyone go into the house."

"Okay."

Skinner wiped his eyes and walked back towards the fire and his men.

"No one goes in the house," he barked. Then he abruptly changed directions and went around the side of the house to an area that blocked the breeze and collected the sun's warmth. He slumped down with his back against the base of a ponderosa pine on the edge of the rim. From his spot he could watch the shed and wait for Veronica to come out. The next thing he knew, Chaco was kicking his foot, waking him for the second time that morning.

"What's up?"

"Veronica and the boys just walked into the house."

Skinner sat up groggily. "Did she ask for me?"

"No. But she's doing something in there. You can hear her working."

Skinner looked up at the sun, trying to figure out how long he had slept. "Damn."

"Que pasa?" asked Chaco.

"We still have three graves to dig." Putting on his hat, Skinner looked towards Boomer, who was bringing him a cup of coffee. "Thanks Boomer. Let's give her some time. Is Victor back?"

"No."

"Fire." yelled Boomer. A roar of sound and a cloud of thick smoke emerged from the windows of the house. Everyone started forward. Flames burst through windows behind the smoke.

"Hold it right there," Skinner shouted above the roar of flames.

Veronica and the boys dashed out of the far side of the house several seconds later. They moved to the shed and stopped just outside the door. The three of them stood watching the house turn into an inferno. As the flames grew, everyone had to move back from the heat. Clouds of black smoke rose three hundred feet into the air before wind leveled it off and carried it to the southeast.

Skinner knew Veronica had used every drop of lantern oil they had for the house to burn so fast and hot. He watched them more than the fire and was glad to see tears rolling down Monte and Courtney's cheeks. Veronica's expression, however, remained drawn and unreadable.

Skinner saw Victor jog out of the trees beyond the house, east of the bluff.

"Why burn the house?" Victor asked Skinner.

"We didn't." Skinner didn't try to explain it. "What did you find out?"

Victor threw his hands into the air, frustrated by the smoke rising into the air, but gave his report. "They're new to the country."

"How so?"

"Going straight north."

"Is the trail hard to follow after all the rain?"

"No. There's a lot of them." Victor replied. "They're going straight north."

"They'll run right into Clear Creek soon." Skinner balled his fists and stared at Chaco and Victor with bloodshot eyes.

Clear Creek Canyon was a huge gash in the upper plateau, uncrossable by horse for most of its length. The canyon ran from east to west. To get past it, travelers had to go west to the mouth of the canyon, or east to its head.

"We got a chance. We got a fifty-fifty chance to shortcut 'em. We guess right, we can catch 'em," said Victor.

Skinner took off his hat and ran his fingers through his hair. He clamped it down again and pulled it tight over his forehead. "We gotta make a choice. Are they gonna turn east or west?"

"What if we get it wrong, Captain?" asked Boomer.

"We can follow 'em for a while and make our choice later on," said Chaco.

"That's what we're gonna do. Boomer. Gather the men. Wrangle the horses. Time to saddle up," said Skinner.

CHAPTER 17

The house continued to produce huge flames, and thick smoke drifted over Charlie as he followed the rest of the patrol to the top of the bluff behind the house. As ordered, each man had traveled afoot and led his horse to the summit to save them the effort of carrying a rider up the steep trail. As Charlie topped out, he saw an argument had broken out between Vance and Boomer, and his unease about the entire situation grew deeper. Charlie was sure the argument had something to do with their diminishing ranks. Brooks had been sent back to the fort yesterday. Now Greg and Wade were going back as an escort for Veronica and the boys. Willy was going to be behind, bringing the mules. The original twelve-man patrol had been reduced to eight, and it looked like there were twice that many outlaws. And these weren't just outlaws; these people were killers, the worst kind. There was no doubt, among any of them, that if they caught up to them, there would be a gunfight.

Charlie watched Skeeter, Sunny, and Victor, assemble near Vance and Boomer, all holding the reins to their horses, which stood around them in a wide circle that Charlie hadn't been made welcome to join. Chaco stood

to one side, ignoring the men; his focus was directed at
Skinner, who was still below them, down by the barn,
giving out final instructions to the escort. Charlie took a
deep breath, swallowed a wave of fear. He thought through
the events that had landed him in that spot and wondered
how he was going to handle himself going forward. He felt
Boomer's eyes on him, but he didn't look back. He just
listened to their conversation.

"I got a feeling the pace of this ride is gonna increase,"
said Vance, who was standing by Boomer. "This couldn't
be any more personal for him."

"He's hell-bent to chase down this gang and end it, no
matter what," said Willy. It was obvious Willy was torn
about his role to trail behind with three overloaded mules.

"Hell, any way you look at it, this is going to be a once-
in-a-lifetime ordeal," said Boomer as he watched Charlie,
who he knew was listening.

Vance made no effort to hide his nerves over what the
future might hold. His jaw was tight, his lips drawn downwards, he spoke fast and tripped over his words. "There's
gonna be a big fight if we catch 'em, ya know."

"You're nervous, ain't ya?" replied Boomer in a soft voice.

"Nope, I'm getting scared silly about my own hide all
of a sudden. We're outnumbered to beat hell." Vance tilted
his head Charlie's direction. "I ain't the only one either."

Boomer left the circle and moved up alongside his
horse to make a minor adjustment to his cinch. He looked
over his saddle at Charlie, again trying to read him, trying
to see if there was fear showing. But Charlie's face only
revealed that he was thinking hard. "One thing for sure:
horseflesh is going to decide the outcome," said Boomer
over his shoulder.

"You're goddamn right about that one." Vance looked
down at the hind leg of his horse, Mousy. After their

morning's rest, the leg had swollen slightly, but despite the injury from the first night out, he'd made the cut when Chaco went through the horses. "How you figure the captain is going to catch that stallion of Leon's? That stud has a lot of go in him. I bet whoever stole him is feeling pretty smug right now." Vance's voice was loud so no one else could interrupt him.

Charlie found the subject of the conversation incomprehensible and Vance's tone alarming. Which horse was the best was idiotic talk as far as he was concerned. Charlie wanted answers, assurance, or at least a gut feeling for how he was going to get through what was coming. Even more worrisome, he could sense that they had begun to fall apart as a unit.

"I think he's figuring on riding hard, coming up behind them, and letting 'em have it," said Skeeter. "If this thing does turn into a big chase, I'll tell you what—there's a couple of horses that could cover some country before it's over. Now that I think about it, I don't know two better horses than Too Tall and that stallion of Leon's. They call him Viking, I think."

"Viking, that's it. Yeah, you're sure right. Only Viking is fresh. Ours are half dead," said Vance.

"What the hell are you two getting at?" Willy asked.

"We were just speculating on what could be the horse race of the century," answered Vance quickly.

Charlie almost yelled at them in frustration as it became more and more apparent that he was totally subject to the decisions and actions of Skinner and might need to trust his safety to people like Vance. He had no confidence in any of them, and all they could do right now was talk about some vague idea of a horse race. Charlie wanted to run. He wanted to leave and return to the fort. But he was too late. The escort was leaving and he was atop the bluff with this group of idiots.

"You wish you was goin' with em'," said Skeeter to Vance, and gestured with his eyes at the escort preparing to take Veronica and the twins back to the fort.

"I wish Greg was going with us," answered Vance. "He's a good shot. He don't get nervous neither. Hell, there's only eight of us now. We must be chasin' twenty, maybe thirty of them rotten people. How'd they get that job anyway?" Vance jutted his chin downhill, towards Greg and Wade.

"Because he can handle 'em gentle. He won't do or say something stupid getting them back to the fort. Captain made a good choice. They're fragile as teacups. Rest of us would make a mess of that job." Boomer slapped Vance on the back. "Don't worry, I'm betting you ain't going to get shot," he said. Boomer walked over to stand by Charlie.

Charlie rolled his eyes at the continued flippancy and stupidity of the conversation; he stared down through the billowing smoke at Skinner and shook his head as Boomer moved up behind him.

After joining the military Charlie had questioned the command structure in minor ways but had always sort of understood that following orders without question was how the military kept order and made the whole organization work. But now, out here in the field, under pressure, with danger lurking and a leader consumed by rage and revenge, following orders had taken on a new magnitude. Charlie's jaw clenched, his heart pounded. and real fear began to build inside him. He'd been sent along to monitor the patrol's actions, and he wasn't monitoring anything. He was just getting hauled along for the ride, and it was getting more dangerous by the minute. *You're an darned idiot, Brickman,* he thought. As the craziness of the military's power structure descended on him, he suddenly didn't want to follow orders anymore. His body jerked violently when Boomer touched his arm.

"Easy does it, private," said Boomer.

Charlie concentrated on keeping his face unreadable, but he was reminded of Boomer's advice back at Stinking Springs: "Play the hand you're dealt," Boomer had told him. "You're smart, just keep quiet. It'll all work out, you'll see."

Charlie's eyes remained downhill, he watched Skinner speak with Wade and Greg. Then with Too Tall trailing along behind, he walked over and spoke to Veronica, Monte, and Courtney, who were sitting astride two of the patrol's pack mules and the black horse. Skinner rested a hand on the arm of each boy and said something brief. He approached Veronica but didn't reach up to her. More brief words were spoken, then Skinner took a couple of steps back. A moment later the escort disappeared from the lip of the rim heading back to Fort Verde.

"Keep your wits about ya, Charlie. It's all ya got now." Boomer spoke so only Charlie could hear him.

"Eight of us are chasing who knows how many. I hate this," Charlie replied in a hushed voice. "What the hell am I doing here? I don't have any experience with this." Charlie jutted his chin forward in Skinner's direction. "You and Skeeter told me at the Edge Camp I would see how they are if we get in a scrape. So far I ain't liking it."

"You scared?" Boomer moved closer to Charlie.

"Little bit. Don't know how I'll feel if we catch 'em."

Boomer saw Charlie's eyes were squinted, his chin was slightly ducked, and he kept moving his head from side to side in frustration.

"What else is eating you?"

"Don't like having to follow orders from someone as mad as him." Charlie again gestured down at Skinner.

"Welcome to the cavalry. We're always following orders

from madmen. Hell, you're just learning what all of us already know."

"Thought it would be different when I joined up."

"We all did."

"I don't like it. He's half mad, and Chaco's half Mexican, and I gotta do what they tell me even if it means I get killed doing it. How in the hell did I get myself into . . ."

Boomer shoved Charlie sideways. "Don't be bad-mouthing Chaco around me, pup, or you're going to lose the only friend you got in this group."

Charlie turned and faced Boomer about to push his point, but Boomer's tight face and clenched jaw silenced him.

"You got a lot to learn Charlie. Like I said a while back, it might help for you not to feel a need to comment on everything that comes into your brain. Might help you to watch and learn and keep your trap shut."

"What am I going to learn? How to get shot?"

"You're going to learn that it doesn't matter where you're from or who your parents are. You're going to learn that how a man handles himself when things go to hell in a handbasket is what counts. You need to shut up and pay attention. Got it?"

"Yeah. I got it."

"Good." Boomer slapped Charlie on the back.

Leading Too Tall by the reins, Skinner walked over the crest of the bluff with long powerful strides. His chin was up, his shoulders pulled back and squared, his hat was pulled down tight on his head. He moved like a man who'd acquired an unnatural surge of energy. The circle of men opened to accommodate him, as if they had been ordered to do so.

"Listen up: The horses and how we ride is gonna be all-important. We might have to do a lot of walkin', even runnin', at times. When we get into malapai we need to be at our best. If your horse goes lame, you're going to be on your own and will need to head back to the fort. We ain't stoppin' for nothing." Skinner's gaze swung from man to man as he spoke. "Got no idea when we're going to come on 'em. Tonight. Tomorrow. In five days. I don't know. But I do know this: These truly dangerous people rode into our country and we're not going to let them out. They all just made the biggest mistake they ever will."

Skinner threaded the reins through his hands and eye-balled the men through blood-red eyes. "The way I see it we have a tough job ahead, and I don't mean just hard ridin'. There ain't any way we're gonna end this without bullets in the air, and we need to be together on something right here right now because there won't be time later." Skinner took a step closer to them and lowered his voice to a growl. "What I'm tellin' ya is when we come on 'em, we have to be ready to kill 'em all."

No one spoke; most looked at their boots and shuffled their feet.

Boomer finally broke the tense silence. "I've had a bel-lyful of what they're all about, Captain. I don't think any of us can't do what needs doing."

A light murmur of agreement followed.

Skinner waited.

Chaco stood with his eyes shielded by his hat. His thumbs were hooked into his belt. Turns Good stood behind him, his head just inches from Chaco's shoulder.

Skinner looked in Chaco's direction, and the men turned their attention on him as well.

Chaco tilted back his head and nodded a couple of times. "I wish this job wasn't on our laps, but it is," he said. "Captain is right to bring it up. I never shot a man before, but soon I don't think I'm going to be able to say that again. If we get the drop on them, we better lay into them with no mercy, because if we don't, some of us are gonna die. These are killers to the core. We need to be ready to play rough."

"What if we don't catch 'em Captain?" said Vance in an upbeat, contrived voice.

Skinner didn't answer. He took another impatient step closer to the men, ignoring Vance, his face reddened. He was just about to explode on them.

Boomer raised his voice. "I hear ya, Captain. I'm ready to do what needs doing."

"Me too."

"Count on me, Captain."

Every man spoke, right on down the line.

Skinner nodded his head at each of them, then pulled Too Tall up close and let the big horse circle him. "Let's ride." Skinner vaulted into his saddle and turned northward.

"Mount up!" Chaco snapped out the order.

The storm had cooled the air and the day was the coldest yet since leaving the fort, which Skinner knew would help the horses travel with less overheating. He set a brisk pace, and the patrol snaked along behind him at a trot in single file, twisting through the trees and hopping over deadfall.

The men behind stood in their stirrups, holding their weight centered, and pushed tired mounts to keep up with the horse in front, and to keep pace with their Captain. Each man's mind was filled with questions regarding the rising danger of the mission, their Captain's motivations, and his resolute determination, and it was not easy to put these questions to rest. And even when they did there was no respite because one huge question about themselves filled the void. How would they handle themselves in a fight? No one talked. They just did as ordered: prepared themselves to kill and rode well.

The mind of the long-legged dun leading the patrol, however, was clear, and he understood his rider fully. Too Tall looked ahead and picked the smoothest terrain to travel over. When a long, narrow meadow opened up before him with a well-worn game trail running down the center of it, Too Tall gathered his weary frame, broke out of his trot, and stretched out into a ground-covering lope.

After an hour of uninterrupted hard travel in the ponderosa pine trees, the land dropped precipitously, and the vegetation changed abruptly to an area covered in cedar and juniper trees. They had arrived at a promontory, where a person could look over about forty square miles of land to the north. The spot was known to some of the locals; it had been used by horse thieves running south from Flagstaff in the past to watch for pursuit. It had acquired the name Horse Thief Bench.

Skinner called a halt just back from the edge of the promontory in the shelter of the trees. He watched his men slide stiffly out of the saddle and land on sore knees and hips, several groaned or swore as legs buckled, but no one dared voice a complaint.

Boomer gave out a few instructions, and the men loosened the cinch of their horses, pulled the bridles, then covered their horses steaming hind ends with their coats to help them avoid cooling out too quickly. Boomer walked through the horses and checked their condition. Vance's horse was the worst; it had wide cinch sores behind the front legs that had turned red and swollen.

"Center fire that cinch before we go," Boomer told him.

"What's that mean?" Vance looked worried. He knew he would be left behind if his horse failed, and he had no idea where he was. He supposed he could follow their tracks back, but it was a long way, and he had no confidence he could make it alone. Besides, he might run into that gang if they reversed direction for some reason.

Boomer showed him how to run the latigos on both sides up to the back D-ring on the saddle skirt and then back to the cinch ring, pulling the whole cinch backwards, away from the sores. "That comes from not grooming your horse well enough. You're lucky you ain't riding a McClellan. You wouldn't have as good a fix for them sores. Let me check it again before we leave."

"Don't tell the Captain, Boomer. I don't wanna get left behind."

"He won't leave you as long as that horse can move."

The men spread out and led their mounts to choice patches of grass, allowing each to graze unhindered by competition from another exhausted, foul-tempered horse.

Skeeter moved up by Vance. "I don't know where the hell we are, or where the hell we're going, but we're sure making good time," he said.

"Shut up," said Boomer, then he turned his back on the pair of them and went over to where Skinner, Chaco, and Victor stood on the promontory.

"They're sucked up in the flanks pretty good," said Boomer. "Got a lot of cinch sores. One wither sore on Charlie's horse."

"Is that right?" replied Skinner in a dismissive, pre-occupied tone. Sores could cause a horse to spend more energy compensating for discomfort, but the big concern for Skinner was his gamble, and the horses could endure the sores long enough to give his gamble a chance to work. Skinner studied the land below them. "We'll get to water soon. Give me the long eye, Chaco. What do you think?" asked Skinner as he stretched out the lens.

"Don't have a sense of it yet." Victor replied.

"You guys think they know the country?" asked Vance.

"I'm guessing no. They're still traveling straight north," answered Skinner as he snapped the long eye shut. "They're going to hit Clear Creek. I think we need to stay behind them until we find their campsite. It'll probably tell us a lot. We just gotta make sure they aren't still there."

"You think we're that close to them, Captain?" asked Boomer.

"I don't know, but they're traveling easy from the looks of it," said Skinner.

Victor spoke up. "The smoke from Leon's ranch made them nervous. They're putting on miles." Victor looked to Skinner for permission to speculate further and got it. "I think we'll find their next camp empty. They'll take rest stops on high points where they can watch their back trail. They're nervous, but not worried yet. I agree with you Captain, we should find the next camp."

Skinner hesitated before replying; he was approaching the end of his third day on little sleep, and he'd told himself to recheck every decision three times before giving out an order. Finally, he took a deep breath and announced to the gathering of men. "That's what we're gonna do. Boomer, you wait fifteen minutes and watch for movement out there after we bail off the ridge. Vance, you and Skeeter ride a close flank. Victor, follow the sign and we'll come along a mile behind. Hold your position at full dark until we join up with you. If we don't find their camp by then we'll push on and travel slow until midnight. It's gonna be malapai all the way from here. Move out."

They slipped off the ridge and halfway down, the sun disappeared below the horizon. At the bottom of the slope, they entered a pocket of cold air that had them all reaching for coats. The evenings were short at this time of year, and full dark wasn't far away.

As they traveled, the choices before Skinner were all about how to gain ground and not be seen first, and so he kept them in the heaviest cover instead of directly on the gang's trail.

At the far end of a huge expanse of flat land Victor met the patrol. He stood by his horse on a slight rise silhouetted against a dark sky, and Skinner sensed he had news.

Skinner waited for the men behind him to gather around Victor. Then he asked, "Whattya got?"

"They made a dry camp over there," said Victor.

The significance of the information was not lost on anyone.

"Which way did they head out this morning?" asked Skinner.

"North, but I only followed their trail for a few minutes."

"What's your take on when they started to travel?" asked Skinner.

Everyone was calculating and figuring on what they were hearing, wondering what the next decision would be. Vance and Skeeter rode out of the night to join the group from the flank position. A few horses raised their heads to check on who was coming in, but most just stood on numb legs, wishing the work would end.

"It was after sunup when they left their camp. We should go to the spring."

"Let's get there." Skinner wasted no time and led his men off into the night.

The crucial decision was almost upon them, and Skinner calculated. The gang had been unaware of the spring and made a dry camp, showing once again that they were unfamiliar with the country. If they remained on their present course, they would run straight up against Clear Creek Canyon close to its middle. Would they turn east or west when they hit the canyon? The right guess would present a clear opportunity to gamble on catching the gang by abandoning their trail and cutting the angle. The gamble was guessing which way they would turn.

The fact that he would be breaking another order of Brickman's also occurred to him. "Stay on them. Whatever you do, don't lose them. Leave us a big trail, send word back to us, and we'll come to help." He had already sent word, and the trail he'd left was well marked with dead bodies. That's as far as it went, though. Circumstances were developing that were giving him a chance to gain the upper hand, and he was going to go for it.

The darkness was a comfort as they made their way across a treeless area covered with malapai. Stars began making their appearance by the thousands. Skinner felt confident that after their dry camp, the gang's horses were probably going to smell the spring and take them to it. Leon's horses would pull hard for it, probably having been there before. How long they stayed at the spring was the all-important piece of the trail information now, as it would dictate the timing of his plan.

Skinner stopped and called for a dismount several miles from the spring. He and Victor would leave them to rest, scout ahead, and make sure no one was still around. They moved off into the dark and circled to the east, so their approach was from downwind. They paused and listened for minutes at a time to the sounds of the night as they approached the spring. Victor looked at Skinner. He raised a clenched hand, then opened his fingers quickly indicating he felt they were gone. They rode in closer and stopped once more just at the fringes of the spring's life-supporting reach. They could see the water reflected in the starlight that stretched twenty yards down the draw. The place was empty.

"You check the sign; I'll circle once and then ride back and get the others," said Skinner.

Victor went to work to find out as much as possible before the patrol came in and disturbed the area. Bent low to the ground, his hands felt the grass where the horses had rested. He took note of the number of manure piles and their odor. He picked manure up and felt the thickness of the dry outermost layer. He looked for spots where horses had bedded down and felt the bent grass. He added or subtracted time with each piece of input, and he only studied the sign left by the horses, knowing it would tell him everything he was going to find out. In the daylight he could have read the sign in seconds. In the dark it took him half an hour.

Skinner returned with the patrol. The men led the horses to the water and let them drink. Every man had his saddle off before a single horse pulled its muzzle from the water.

Skinner saw Charlie preparing to hobble his horse.

'No hobbles. They won't be goin' anywhere. Let 'em graze in comfort."

"What's your guess?" Skinner asked Victor.

"Half a day's ride ahead," he answered.

Skinner shook his head, confirming to himself the decision he would make. He looked at Victor in the dark. "Let's grab something to eat. Chaco, come here, will you?" Skinner questioned his own knowledge of the land and began to form a plan as he dug in his saddlebags for a hunk of jerked meat.

"Looks like they have six hours on us. You think we can cut 'em off?" Skinner opened the discussion and then bit off a big bite of meat and chewed rapidly.

"If we miss them, we won't have any horse flesh left," Chaco replied.

"It's going for broke, I know." Skinner put his hands on his cheeks and rubbed them. "If we miss them, we'll be fourteen hours behind. We'll have to change tactics and grind them down over a longer period."

Victor spoke up. "There's lots of malapai on the route they're taking."

"That's sure as hell in our favor to shortcut 'em," said Chaco.

"I think it's a good gamble," said Skinner. "What's your opinion on our timing?" He put the question to both of them.

"Let them get a bellyful. Then *vamanos*," said Chaco.

Victor nodded his head in agreement.

"Okay, here it is: Victor, I want you to follow their trail one hour and make sure they don't start drifting west or east on us. We'll follow in an hour. If they drift one way or the other, I might change my mind, but right now my guts tellin' me they're gonna go east." Skinner clenched his fists. "East or west?" He paused and waited for anyone to say something, but no one did. This would be his choice to make alone. "Might be hard to meet up out there. How you want to handle that?"

"I will be a lonely owl on a southern slope," said Victor with a smile.

"If we do miss, go for the head of the canyon," added Skinner. "I'm betting they'll go east."

"I won't miss," said Victor.

"If we're successful, we should see the dirty birds walking right at us by midmorning," said Skinner.

"I think it will work," said Victor.

"Maybe," said Skinner.

"Yo tambien," said Chaco.

Skinner and Chaco didn't say anything more. They watched Victor grab some food, fill a small canteen, and disappear into the night on foot. They would bring his horse along after the short rest.

Not a single horse was eating when the men went to catch them an hour after Victor's departure. Most stood in a cluster, standing hip shot, the others were lying down. Skeeter looked on as Vance walked right up to Mousy and put the halter on while the animal was lying down.

"He all right?" asked Skeeter.

"He's about done," answered Vance. "I'm going into a big fight on a played-out horse. I ain't liking this one bit."

"What the hell are we going to do if we miss 'em up there?" Skeeter asked.

"Whatever it is, we'll be slowing down," said Boomer.

"I ain't exactly thrilled about catching up with them," said Vance.

Skeeter didn't answer right away. "We'll be all right."

Vance continued, "It don't matter how ready we are. It ain't like these bums aren't going to shoot back. Did you see all the tracks we've been following? It looks like twenty-five or thirty of them to me."

"Just shut up, will ya?" answered Skeeter.

"Yeah sure," said Vance. He led his horse around the back of the herd and started swinging his lead rope. "Hup. Hup. Hup." Vance pushed the horses back towards the spring.

Chaco woke to Skinner kicking his boots.

"Hey, wake up. Time to go."

Chaco heard horses being brought in. "Sorry I slept, Tom."

"Don't ever say sorry to me again," replied Skinner over his shoulder.

As men pulled their gear together, grunts and moans could be heard as saddles plonked into place on sore-backed horses.

Skinner sized up Too Tall's attitude. "Hey, boy," said Skinner. Too Tall looked toward the familiar voice. His ears twitched back and forth a couple of times.

As Skinner lifted the saddle in place, Too Tall pawed the ground a couple of times, but Skinner could tell it was more from habit than real eagerness. Skinner patted him affectionately, then tightened his cinch and stood waiting for the rest of the men to get ready. He stroked his horse's neck and spoke to him in a whisper. "Keep your head low. Don't want to lose you too. You're the only thing I can count on right now."

He turned away from Too Tall and saw Chaco moving towards him leading Turns Good and abruptly felt a sense of shame sweep over him. "A good friend and a good horse, that's what I got."

"What?" answered Chaco.

"Nothing." Skinner reached into his saddlebags and handed Chaco a chunk of dried meat. "Here." The two of them led their horses towards the men.

"Make sure you're full on water, ordered Skinner. "Everyone lead your horse until I give the order to mount up. We gotta let 'em loosen up before we ride."

Skeeter led his horse up near Chaco and Skinner. "He ain't too happy to feel that saddle again."

"You won't be either," replied Chaco.

Skeeter chuckled. "You're right about that. But I'm sure glad I ain't one of these horses."

The malapai thickened just beyond the spring, and men and horses stumbled stiffly through the rock for the first quarter mile. Small clouds moved above them across a moonless starlit sky. Silence reigned until Skinner gave the order to mount. Within minutes kicks to the sides of the horses began to get harder and more frustrated in their delivery. Some used the ends of the reins to whip their horse's hind ends, pushing them forward, keeping the gap closed between themselves and Too Tall at the head of the column, who was once again pushing the pace, pushing northward into the night.

Skinner could feel the attitude of man and horse behind him without having to turn around. After half an hour he ordered them to get off and lead their mounts again. Men and horses stumbled through the malapai, through the dark, across a huge expanse of land. After an hour and a half of travel, a meadow thick with grass offered a brief respite from the malapai and Skinner ordered a halt to allow the horses to graze.

"Everyone quiet. Listen for a lonely owl."

After a ten-minute rest they mounted and continued on, stopping occasionally to listen. Suddenly they all heard a mournful sound coming from up ahead.

"Qué es eso?" asked Chaco.

"It's Victor trying to scare every bad guy in the country away. Answer him, Boomer," said Skinner.

Boomer cupped his hands together and hooted back.

Ten minutes later Victor joined them out of the darkness. He held both his thumbs pointed straight up. He took his horse from Boomer, swung aboard, and moved up between Skinner and Chaco. Skinner immediately led off.

"What the hell was that noise supposed to be Victor?" asked Chaco.

"I'm not too good at that, huh?" answered Victor.

"They still going north?" Skinner asked.

"Like an arrow, only slowly," said Victor.

"How's that?" asked Skinner.

"They're strung out. Some horses are worn, some are fresh. The ones in front are stopping to study their back trail while the others catch up," Victor replied.

"How in the hell did you figure that out in the dark?"

"Where they waited the ground is covered in tracks and cigarettes."

"Whatcha think?" asked Skinner.

"They'll hit the canyon near the narrows. I think they will go east."

"Me too," said Chaco.

"We can only hope," said Skinner. "Cause that's the way we're cuttin'."

Skinner kept running through different scenarios. It was obvious now that this bunch wasn't familiar with the country. This new information and the image of the gang hitting the canyon near the narrows helped him to believe the patrol was taking a calculated gamble that was going to work. Victor's news that they were traveling easy boosted the chances of beating them. Skinner made up his mind to increase the pace. The worst possible thing he could do right now was be late.

Turning his head around, Skinner checked that everyone was lined out and still nose to tail, then he steered Too Tall slightly to the east and barked out an order to his men. "Trot!" Skinner rose in his stirrups as Too Tall lifted into a trot. He strained to look ahead in the dark, trying to pick the best possible route. They traveled steadily for three hours when Skinner heard a commotion behind him. He pulled Too Tall up and turned back. Vance's horse, Mouse, had balked and was now down on his side. "Get him up," Skinner ordered.

Vance jerked the reins pulling Mouse's head off the ground. He clucked and swore at the animal, but it wouldn't get up. "He's done, Captain."

Skinner swung down and pulled his sheath knife. He gripped the blade so only a half inch of the tip protruded beyond his fingers. With a quick motion he kicked the rear end of Vance's horse then stabbed it in the hip with the tip of the knife. The horse lurched to its feet. "Chaco get behind this horse, use your whip, and keep him moving. Everyone walk your horse." Skinner led off without another word.

An hour passed before the second horse went down and refused to move. Boomer used Skinner's technique to get the animal to move before Skinner even knew there was a problem, but the pace had slowed, and everyone was using the ends of their reins to whip the exhausted horses ahead of them. Low voices could be heard as the men cussed at the animals, and slap after slap of reins coming down on horses' rear ends could be heard all along the string. The whole herd had begun to quit on them just as a hint of light began to show in the east, mourning doves began calling, and Skinner felt adrenaline creep into his system.

Thirty minutes later the patrol, stumbling along afoot and tugging their horses by the reins, entered a dense ponderosa pine tree forest. Skinner stopped. The head of Clear Creek Canyon was one hundred yards beyond them.

"Rest. I'll be back. Victor mount up come with me." Skinner stepped aboard Too Tall and left the patrol.

"My horse is done. I'll run." Victor called after Skinner.

Skinner led off for the head of the canyon with Victor jogging along behind. He went straight to the canyon rim and scouted for tracks.

"No tracks, Captain," said Victor, moving up beside him breathing hard.

"We beat 'em to this point." Skinner looked left and right at the canyon. To his right the steep sides of the canyon tapered off. To his left the canyon sides cut by rushing water steepened abruptly and were uncrossable by horse. "Let's get back to the men," Skinner said. A huge sense of relief ran through him, but he remained nervous, and with Victor trailing him he made plan after plan in his head. He questioned each, then altered it. He planned for contingencies, figuring what he would do if things went wrong. How would he handle it if one of his men got shot or wounded? Where would he set the ambush? What if the gang got into cover and he ended up with a pitched battle going on? What precautions could he take to increase the advantage? One thought became paramount: He had to get his exhausted men fired up for the job. He had to make them realize the importance of pressing home the attack once it started.

They still had one more short ride before they could be absolutely sure they had beaten the gang to the crossing. Ten more minutes down the canyon was a place the outlaws could cross, but it was rough, and most travelers this close to the head of the canyon usually went all the way around.

Skinner felt sweat form under his hat brim as he rode up to the men. "We beat 'em to this point. I want it all quiet. We could get into them any time now." Skinner stood Too Tall sideways to them. When he had all of their attention, he tickled Too Tall with his offside spur and asked him to move out, but he checked the horse with the reins. Too Tall rose up on tired legs and presented an alert attitude. Skinner sat bolt upright in the saddle. He reached down and pulled his rifle from his scabbard. Too Tall pranced in place at the sight of the rifle. Skinner let the butt of his rifle rest on his thigh and swung Too Tall closer to the men.

"Here it comes boys. I can feel it. We're going to do some killin' before this day is over, and I'd just as soon that don't include any of us. So stay sharp and listen to orders. There's one spot where riders can cross, a few more minutes down the canyon. We're going just beyond that and set up an ambush. What I'm worried about right now is ridin' into them as we make our way there. Victor and I will go out five minutes in front. If we run into them, we'll retreat back to you no matter if they see us or not. If you see us comin' tie your horses, advance fifty yards, take cover, and wait for my order to fire. If we don't run into them, keep goin' until you catch up with me. Your horses only gotta go another quarter mile. Go to the whip. Get it done, but no talking. When it comes time, remember who we're dealin' with. Any hesitation might get us killed!" Skinner paused, letting that thought sink in. "Mount. Draw your weapons, check your loads! Skeeter, Boomer, ride a close flank!" Skinner gestured away from the canyon and Boomer and Skeeter moved off forty yards. Skinner nodded at Chaco. "Get 'em there Chaco. Victor, can you get your horse to stay with me?"

"No."

"Charlie, drag that mangy cuss with you; Victor's gonna go on foot." Skinner rolled Too Tall towards the west, down canyon, and moved off at a fast walk, with Victor jogging along beside him.

Victor studied the ground as they moved across the forest floor, and Skinner watched the area out ahead. As the timber which had been providing cover for them thinned, they slowed down and made their way warily along the edge of the canyon to the final spot where horses could cross. Here the canyon suddenly spread wider, and its walls sloped more gently; a faint rocky game trail led into it. Still no tracks. They'd made it. They had beaten them.

"Good job, boss," said Victor. He looked at Skinner with a broad smile spread across his face.

The man loves a fight, thought Skinner, as he drew in

a long breath. "Okay let's move on a little further. I think I know the place we're looking for," he said.

The two of them moved along twenty yards out from the edge of the canyon. After a few minutes of travel, a large clearing showed itself through the trees ahead.

"This is it. We'll stop here and set up in the trees. The only way we'll miss them is if they turned west yesterday or they go back inland, and they ain't going to do that," said Skinner.

Victor shook his head. "No, they won't. We got 'em," he said.

"You go down the trail twenty minutes past the far side of the clearing and watch for 'em. I'll get everyone set up right over there and we'll try to pin 'em against the canyon when they show. Don't waste any time gettin' back here when you spot 'em." Victor turned to go, but Skinner spoke to him again. "Hey."

"Yeah."

"You've done a damn good job so far. I want you to know that."

"You did too," said Victor. Then he raced into the woods, well back from the canyon edge to avoid the clearing.

Skinner retreated a hundred yards back the way he had just come, towards his men. He saw Chaco and the patrol come angling through the trees. Skeeter and Boomer saw him, and they immediately left their flank position and rejoined the patrol.

"My God, how in the hell does he know they're coming here?" Skeeter whispered at Boomer. The clearing in front looked very similar to about a dozen others they had ridden through since daylight that morning.

"It's a gamble. You heard him say that. He figures they're

going to ride the edge of the canyon looking for a place to cross," answered Boomer in a hushed voice.

"I hope he's right because we're going to be the hardest riding bunch of jackasses you ever saw if he's wrong," whispered Vance, who had moved up to hear what they were saying.

"Shut up, Vance," said Boomer.

"Yeah, shut the hell up, Vance," hissed Skeeter. "The way my skin's a crawling, I think he's probably right."

They all fell silent when they saw Chaco glaring at them.

Skinner rode up and didn't say a word; he just waved them to follow him the way he had just come. Just short of the clearing and out of sight of anyone who might come from the other side he ordered them to tie their horses. "Good tight knots on every horse. Grab ammo belts, canteens, and something to chew on. Now. Hurry." Skinner hissed out the order, and when the last man assembled, he led the way on foot back to the trees near the very edge of the clearing

"Chaco, you'll set up right here for the ambush," Skinner pointed to a big log which would be the spot nearest to the canyon edge. "But until we hear from Victor, I want you to get closer to the clearing and watch for him. If he's comin' back, that means they're on their way."

"Got it," said Chaco.

"Rest of you start building some cover right here. Hurry. Hurry. I want Skeeter on the far end there. Boomer you're next to him right here." These two were the best shots, and Skinner wanted them to anchor the flank and keep the outlaws pinned against the canyons edge.

They moved a couple of logs around but were careful not to disrupt the ground too much. Hunched over, Skinner

walked back and forth to check and make minor adjustments to their fortifications and cover. As he walked by
each man, he told them what he wanted and expected.

"Skeeter, Boomer, if things go wrong, don't let 'em go
south. Shoot like hell. Whatever it takes. We gotta keep
them pinned against the canyon. Skeeter, your man is the
farthest to the left. Boomer, yours is second from the left,
then both of you aim for the third. I'll give the order to
shoot."

"Yes sir, Captain," they said at the same time, in low
serious voices.

Skeeter whispered, "This is unbelievable, Captain."

"Good luck."

Skinner moved to the next man, Sunny, who was
hunkered down behind the end of a log. He looked as if he
expected the fight to come in the next ten seconds.

"How you doing, Sunny?" he asked.

"Nervous." Sunny was always a little uptight, but
Skinner saw his eyes blinking rapidly and he looked like
he was going to bite his lower lip off. He didn't look up at
Skinner. Instead, he was watching the clearing, ready to
open up with his rifle any second.

"Steady, Sunny." Skinner lowered his voice. "You're
moving so much they'll spot you a mile off. Steady now."

"Yes sir." Sunny looked up. "Ok thanks, sir. I will."

Skinner tossed Sunny a chunk of the dried meat. "Here,
chew on that. It could be a while. When they come, your
man is the fifth from the left. Go for the man on his right
next. Keep shootin'."

"Don't worry about that, Captain. I'll be the shootinest
son of a gun you ever saw," said Sunny, stuffing the meat
into his mouth. He gripped his rifle hard with both hands.

Skinner kept moving along his ambush line.

Vance looked up at him from his spot behind a tree. He

sat with his back against the tree and his rifle between his knees in hands gripping the barrel of his rifle so tightly they had turned white.

"Vance, you're going to be all right. We got 'em in a bad situation."

Vance didn't answer.

"Vance, can I count on you?" Skinner demanded a response from him.

"How many of 'em you think there are, Captain?" he asked.

Skinner took a step towards him and slapped him across the face. Then he grabbed him by the shirt collar and pulled him up close.

The rest of the men watched, all wondering if during what could be the final minutes before a battle their captain was using the right technique to bring about a scared man.

Again, Skinner asked, "Vance, can I count on you?"

Vance took a second and then started to speak, but it was too slow for Skinner. He slapped him on the other cheek, harder this time.

"Can I count on you?"

"Yeah, yeah, I'm sorry. I'm scared is all." Vance let it out.

"We're all scared. But it's too late. We're committed. We're goin' to fight." Skinner slapped him again, and this time he got the response he wanted.

"All right. You can count on me," snapped Vance. Anger had crept into his voice.

"Hunker down, Vance. You're going to survive this." Skinner dropped his voice to a whisper but kept his eyes on Vance. "Your man is the sixth from the left. After you shoot, I want you to start taking out horses. We'll put 'em afoot that way at the very least."

"Yes sir." Vance shook his head. One hand rubbed his

face as he turned and got behind his cover. He purposefully
avoided the looks coming from the other men.

"Which man is yours?" Skinner pressed him.

"Sixth from the left, sir."

"Then what?"

"Start shootin' horses."

Skinner moved on. "Charlie your man is seventh from
the left. Got it?"

Charlie nodded.

"Remember, aim for a button, not the shirt. Got it?"

"Yes sir." Charlie bobbed his head up and down vigorously, wiggled down deeper in his position, and looked
down the barrel of his rifle. He wanted no part of what
Vance had just endured.

"This is it, boys. We need to fight or we are going to be
in trouble. Focus. Aim for a button, not the shirt."

Skinner adjusted a log at Charlie's spot to give him
better cover. When he was done, he took up a position
near where Chaco would be and waited. If a soldier moved
his position to relieve a stiff muscle, he got a glare from
Skinner.

Only twenty minutes passed before Chaco stood and
moved towards them, waving his arm. A moment later
they saw Victor streak out of the trees in a dead run on
the far side of the clearing. His path took him over the
roughest terrain, where horses wouldn't travel, so his
tracks would not be present in the grass.

Skinner's voice rose. "Steady boys. Wait for my signal."

Chaco shook his head in disbelief that they had pulled
this off as he dropped into position. Victor was now
halfway across the clearing. He ran with an urgency in his
pace that had Skinner thinking hard. Everyone was quiet.
Skinner glanced at Vance and saw he was ready as he waited
for Victor to pound up the last few yards towards him.

With his breath coming in gasps, Victor spoke for all of them to hear. "They're coming right at us. They'll be here in ten minutes. The problem is, they're strung out."

"How far apart?" Skinner barked.

"As wide as the clearing."

"Are they in groups or are they all strung out?"

"Two of them are way out front. The rest are in twos and threes.

From his position, Chaco would be the first to spot movement. He watched the trees across the clearing, waiting for Skinner's order.

The other men's eyes moved around, looking first at each other, then at Skinner, then the clearing.

"We're going for it." Skinner announced. "Victor circle back into the trees and shoot any that don't make the clearing after we open up."

Victor bolted away from the canyon, entered a thick stand of trees to the left of the patrol, and took cover.

"We'll let the front two come right on top of us and wait for the main bunch to appear. On my signal, everyone take the target you've been assigned as best you can, left to right. It's going to be a longer shot for everyone so aim well. I'll fire on the two up front." Skinner reached out and bent back a pine branch. Pulling his knife, he viciously cut it off then tossed it to Sunny, whose position was the most visible up close. "Put that in front of you." Skinner looked to Chaco who sat unmoving, concentrating on the far edge of the clearing. "Hats off. Hunker down. Get ready to fight."

Skinner didn't say it to the men, but his plan was that if they were spotted before the main bunch appeared they would take out the ones in front and push the rest back the way they had come, back into the malapai. From there they would take it one step at a time. Skinner swore under his breath. "Damn lowlifes." They were about to ruin his whole plan and only by blind-ass luck. If they weren't strung out, they would have had them. Quietly, Skinner checked his load for the third time. He looked at the men. Then across the clearing. He drew in a deep breath and waited. They all waited, full of adrenalin, bodies unmoving, guns cocked, ready.

The whistle from Chaco could barely be heard. Two riders appeared, their horses walking past the last few trees and into the clearing. Skinner could tell the second horse was Viking. His teeth ground together.

The two horses stopped, their riders looking at the clearing. Skinner felt his body sway a half inch further behind the tree. The riders moved forward twenty yards and stopped again. The rest were nowhere to be seen.

Chaco watched the riders. He crossed himself, his lips mouthed a silent prayer.

The man on Viking trotted over to the edge of the canyon, looking for a place to cross. Finding it still impassable, he rejoined his partner and they continued on. They were halfway across, moving straight at the patrol, when Skinner saw movement in the trees behind them. Four more riders emerged out of the trees, and then others could be seen behind them. The sound of the first two horse's feet clicking against rocks was heard by all of them. Then they got a break. For no other reason than to avoid a patch of rough rocks, the front two riders turned slightly away from the patrol towards the canyon. This detour added a few precious seconds for them to bunch together. Skinner looked at where he thought they would be when it was time to fire on the others. He swore as he saw that his field of fire would be blocked by trees. They were only yards away now. *How can they not see us?*

thought Skinner. The rest of the gang was exposed in the clearing. It was time to open up. The two in front disappeared into the trees almost on top of them.

"Fire!" Skinner let out the single word.

A tremendous roar of gunfire erupted to his left. Skinner tried to get a shot at the two men in front. He got a glimpse of them sooner and they moved faster than he expected, being so close. He fired a quick shot and then fed another round into his gun. A second volley roared on his left. Out in the meadow, returned shots came at them. Heavy-caliber bullets thumped into trees and logs, others hit rocks and whined in the air over their heads.

One of Skinner's men screamed, "I'm hit! *I'm hit!*"

Out in the meadow a horse whinnied in pain, others galloped riderless back the way they had come. The volume of shots going back and forth continued to escalate as both groups tried to overwhelm the other with sheer firepower. Skinner looked for another opportunity to fire again on the two advance riders, but they were past them and running, and his field of fire was blocked by more trees. He looked at the meadow for a target. Two horses were down and had several men behind each one, shooting across the saddle. Skinner didn't count, but there were bodies everywhere. Several more horses bolted back towards the trees they had just come out from. Only one was being ridden, the rider slumped in the saddle. Another was hopping on three legs, blood streaming down its shoulder, neighing in fright. A bullet slammed into the tree by Skinner's head, causing him to duck. Another roar of gunfire came from his left. One man crawled for the cover of the downed horses, then he jerked with the impact of a bullet and quit moving. Now only the occasional shot came from the meadow, and it was followed by massive shooting from Skinner's left.

"Skeeter, let's flank the ones behind the horses!" yelled Boomer.

"You got it. Cover us!" Skeeter yelled back.

Gunfire rolled on and on as each took quick turns helping to pin down the men behind the dead horses. Skeeter and Boomer took off at a dead run to the left and then dived behind a big log.

Chaco had quit firing and was holding on a spot where he knew a man would appear over the top of the horse to shoot. Three seconds passed, then his target appeared. Squeezing off the shot, Chaco saw him rock violently backwards. Two of the outlaws had managed to get into the trees down below the patrol. They were the most dangerous at this point because they had good cover and a good angle to shoot from.

"Leave 'em be for now! Stay down, they're waiting for you to show yourself!" Chaco yelled as he heard Sunny, spurred on by the actions of Skeeter and Boomer, start to talk about a move of his own. "One at a time. That's the way I want it!"

Skinner looked at Chaco, just in front of him. "Chaco finish it."

Chaco rolled onto his back so he was completely under cover and looked at Skinner, wanting more information.

"I'm going after the other two. Finish here and wait for me. Vance is hurt. There's one that made the trees, but wounded."

Shots boomed far to the left in a new spot. Skinner and Chaco both flinched then looked to see the ones behind the horses roll out dead. Boomer and Skeeter had taken them out.

"Go slow on the ones down there." Skinner gestured to the two gang members below the lip of the canyon. "Be

careful of any tricks from the ones lying dead out there."
Skinner raised his fist and shook it.

"You too," said Chaco.

Skinner ran for the hump between himself and where
the horses had been tied. He was surprised he had only
fired one shot during the ambush. His role was to shoot in
the direction of any problems, but the patrol had done so
well that there was little he'd had to do. The first volley
had killed at least six of the gang and then a couple more
had been hit in the second round. Boomer and Skeeter had
done well flanking those behind the horses. Chaco could
handle it from here.

Already agitated by the gunfire, the horses pulled
back on their lead ropes when Skinner came running over
the hump.

"Whoa! Whoa!"

Skinner stopped at the closest horse, Sunny's compact
bay, and jerked the cinch tight. He pulled him over to Too
Tall and jerked his cinch tight as well. Grabbing Too Tall's
reins he took a double wrap around one hand then grabbed
the mane on Sunny's horse and swung into the saddle.
Skinner's legs dangled six inches below where Sunny's
stirrups hung. Not bothering to use them, he dug his spurs
into the bay's flanks. With Too Tall running beside him,
they ran for the head of the canyon.

Sunny's horse, frightened by the gunfire and Skinner's
punishing spur, ran hard, but his endurance had been left
behind on the long ride, and in less than a quarter mile
its weary legs began to fail. Skinner yanked on Too Tall's
reins and pulled the big horse up alongside of him. He
leaned over and grabbed the pommel of his own saddle.
With one hand holding his rifle he heaved himself onto
Too Tall and abandoned the bay without a backward
glance. Too Tall braced for the weight of a rider but didn't

slow down. In a steady gallop, Too Tall carried Skinner past the head of the canyon. Too Tall's lungs worked hard, and Skinner could hear the air coming from his nostrils in labored bursts. Skinner cussed the men in front of him, calling them every foul name he could think of, knowing if he didn't see them soon, he would have to accept that they might get away. Too Tall looked to the left.

"There they are." Skinner spoke to his horse and slowed to a canter matching their pace. Skinner pulled the hammer back on the Spencer and looked for an opportunity to take a shot. The trees thinned out. Skinner hauled Too Tall to a rough stop, swung his right leg over the front of the saddle and dropped to the ground. He took a deep breath, leveled the rifle, and fired at the closest man. The man jerked in the saddle, but he stayed mounted, and the pair kicked their horses back into a full run. Skinner leapt back into the saddle, and Too Tall took off once again.

The two outlaws turned left, heading for thicker timber and a low hill. If he lost sight of them on the far side of the hill, he'd have to back off, as they could bail off their horses and lay for him in seconds. The chase had turned into a race.

"Git" he yelled at his horse, and spurred him on, asking for more. Too Tall responded, but this time the increase in speed didn't come with the instant surge that it would have if he'd been fresh. But the will to please remained. His strides were labored but continued to lengthen. Hooves pounding the soil, the big lined-back dun hurled himself up the slope and kept the two riders ahead in sight, and in that moment, despite the fear, and the fight, and having left his men behind, Skinner knew he would never ride a better horse.

They came over the top of the hill, just able to see the hats of the men above its crest. He saw them haul their horses to a stop, and the man on the red roan bailed off, rifle in hand. The man on Viking remained mounted. Too Tall was in a full, belly-to-the-ground run, when all three men fired their guns just yards apart.

Too Tall's legs went out from under him, he crashed headfirst onto the ground and somersaulted twice. Skinner fell to the right; his rifle was jerked from his grip when he hit the ground. He rolled over twice and clawed at the pistol in his holster. The two men shot at him again. Skinner fired his pistol and saw the man on the ground spin and fling his rifle into the air. The man on Viking shot once more, then yanked Viking around and raced for the trees.

Skinner felt a burn under his arm, but he paid it no mind and kept his pistol trained on the man in front of him. He stood slowly; his hands and body shook. Too Tall lay fifteen feet to his left, his sides heaved with the effort to fill his lungs. Gun smoke drifted over them all.

The outlaw was down on his side. His hand still clenched the reins to his horse. Beyond him Skinner could see Viking running north. His mind told him to grab his rifle off the forest floor and take a shot, but he made no move.

Grady was bleeding badly when he finally rolled over to a sitting position. He looked at Skinner and grimaced. "You got me good." He let go of the reins. The red roan stumbled a few steps down hill then stopped. Behind them, at the ambush site, the sound of sporadic gunfire continued.

Skinner didn't answer. Urgency threatened to overwhelm him. He wanted to go to his horse, and this man in front of him was holding him up. Too Tall, being on his side, could not get the air he needed after that big run, and his breathing was labored, ragged, desperate.

Too Tall attempted to rise. He got his neck off the ground, but his front legs floundered. When he fell back, his head hit the ground with a thud. Skinner took an involuntary step towards him, then checked himself. "Who in the hell are you people?" he asked.

Grady looked down at the huge wound in his thigh and sucked in a painful breath.

"Who in the hell are you?" Skinner asked again.

Grady chuckled, until a spasm choked it away. He spoke through the pain, the thought too important for him to let it go. He raised his head and his eyes looked straight at Skinner. "You mean you don't know? Why hell, we're famous. We're"—Grady bit his lip before he could spit it out—"the last of the worst."

Too Tall lifted his head, his nose hovered over his fore-leg to examine the damage.

"The last of the worst?" Skinner winced. His face was rigid, eyes unblinking.

Grady nodded his head. "That's right."

"You got that right," said Skinner. He waited.

Grady swung his head and looked at his horse. He looked out into the forest and briefly tilted his cheek to feel the sun's warmth. He brought his gaze back and faced Skinner. "My horse. He's the best one I ever rode. I want you to have him." Grady gestured at Too Tall. He raised his hand and scratched his jaw. "Okay, I'm ready," he said.

Skinner pulled the trigger. The bullet tore through Grady's breastbone and exited through his spine, and a stream of blood and bone arched onto the forest floor ahead of his body, which cartwheeled backwards and lay motionless.

The red roan took one step at the shot. Too Tall flinched.

The gunfire back at the ambush site had stopped. The labored breathing of the horses was the only sound. Too Tall slid his neck along the ground and looked at Skinner. A shiver started in the big horse's shoulder and ran along the ribs and back into the flanks. Skinner dropped his

pistol at his side, moved over to his horse, and flopped
down near his head. He reached out and stroked Too Tall's
neck behind the ear, and for the first time noticed the blood
covering his own arm.

"Hey, buddy, I thought I told you to watch yourself."
Skinner looked at Too Tall's leg.

Too Tall lifted his head just off the ground, moving it
closer to Skinner. The edges of his nostrils fluttered with a
shallow gulp of air. The eye pinched closed then opened
with each of his last three breaths.

Skinner stroked Too Tall a couple more times while he
stared at the terrible wound and the tremendous amount
of blood that had soaked into the carpet of pine needles.
His horse had bled out from a bullet wound above the
front knee.

Skinner was emotionally spent, and he made no effort
to stop the tears that rolled down his cheeks. He looked
over the scene around him. The red roan had begun to
regain control of its breathing but appeared in bad shape.
Skinner was sure that its muscles had tied up.

The outlaw had been hit in the hip and forearm by his
Spencer and shot through the chest with the pistol at close
range. His bloodied carcass lay flat in the grass, facedown, arms and legs spread. Skinner lifted his arm and
opened his shirt. A bullet had ripped the skin near his
armpit, and it dripped blood. He took a look in the direction of the man who got away, who was on Viking, a fresh
horse, Veronica's horse, running north. The forest was
quiet, not a sound. A slight breeze blew against his cheek
as though nothing had just happened.

The red roan didn't move when he approached. Skinner
picked up the reins and tried to lead the animal. It took a
step with its front legs, but the back legs remained still. As
he'd suspected, the horse's muscles had tied up. He would

have to walk back to his men. He pulled the outlaw's bridle and saddle off and left the roan loose.

Skinner picked up his Spencer then knelt by Too Tall and stroked the warm body. "I'm gonna miss you," he said. He rose to go, but his feet didn't budge. He couldn't leave so quickly. Bending down once again, he straightened the damaged leg. Then he ran his fingers through the thick mane and forelock. "Yeah, I'm gonna' miss you. Gonna miss you bad." He tugged Too Tall's ear gently, then in a fast walk, started back to his men.

In minutes he saw Chaco and Skeeter riding towards him.

"You all right?" Chaco asked when he saw Skinner's bloodied shirt.

"Yeah. It's already stopped bleeding."

"Too Tall?"

Skinner pointed over his shoulder with his thumb. "He's dead." Skinner continued before Chaco could respond. "One got away. I killed the other."

"The way the gunshots were spaced, made me real nervous for ya." Chaco paused, then gestured with his thumb back toward the ambush site. "The two that got into cover below us gave up. All the rest are dead. Boomer got hit by a ricochet. He's in trouble. Vance got a face full of splinters, but he's all right. The rest of them are fine." Chaco was going to tell him that they had to shoot a lot of horses that had taken bullets but decided against it.

"What about the one that made the trees?" asked Skinner.

"He only made it a mile before he died," said Skeeter.

"It's over for now." Skinner looked around him, dazed and confused for just a second. "You say two gave up?"

"Yeah. You all right, Captain?" Skeeter leaned down off his horse and looked Skinner in the eye.

"Just got dizzy for a second is all. Let's get back to the

clearing, see what we can find out about the one that got away from them two." Skinner started to move off.

Skeeter vaulted off his horse and held the reins out for Skinner. "Here Captain, you ride."

Skinner acknowledged Skeeter with a nod of his head. When he swung his leg over the saddle he grunted with pain and felt his wound start to bleed harder. He looked down at the blood soaking into his shirt and running down his side but did nothing about it.

Chaco slipped off his horse. "Better let me have a look." Chaco reached up and pulled Skinner's shirt open as he sat Skeeter's horse. "Lift your arm up." He pressed his finger against Skinner's ribs above the oozing blood and lifted the skin, stretching open the wound. "I don't think it touched any bone. Just skin and meat. Let's get back to the men. I'll clean it up back there, take a better look."

"Boomer's in trouble?" Skinner asked Chaco as they walked off.

"Yeah. It's bad."

The three of them approached camp under the fixed gaze of everyone. In a shady spot out of the sun's warmth sat two bound outlaws. Beyond them Boomer and Vance had been made comfortable near the center of a campsite. A fire was burning, and Sunny was doing double duty as cook and nurse. Three back straps, cut from dead horses, lay across a rock, and Charlie, sure to be seen working, was cutting off steaks and skewering them on branches, preparing to cook a meal.

"You all right, Captain?" Sunny was the first to speak.

"Think so. You better take a look when you're ready." Skinner eased off his horse and handed the reins to Skeeter.

"Come over here, Captain," said Sunny.

Skinner moved over to Boomer and Vance. He took in the pale yellowish skin color of Boomer's cheeks and forehead. Skinner quickly ducked his head so his hat brim would conceal the expression his gut reaction had created. He swiveled his head and looked towards Vance. His face was swollen and painful looking, and small streaks of blood ran downwards from each spot where Sunny had pulled splinters. Skinner inhaled sharply and then knelt down at Boomer's knee.

"I'm in some trouble, Captain."

"We're gonna get you through this, Boomer."

Sunny took a step sideways to allow Chaco, Skeeter, and Vance to move into a circle around the two men as they spoke. Chaco took a knee at Skinner's side. Charlie moved in close as well.

"I don't think so, Captain. I can feel things churning." Boomer put a hand over his belly. "Don't feel fixable."

"You're gonna make it."

"I laid into 'em. Just like you told me too. Shot nine times before they got me. Damn thing must have hit a rock under that log." Boomer's chin dropped; he pulled the bandage away from his stomach. "It come right under. Got me."

Skinner saw the bruised area and small hole just left of Boomer's belly button. Skinner gently rolled Boomer sideways so he could see the exit wound. Bright red blood oozed at a jagged opening that was smaller than Skinner had anticipated. He looked up at Boomer's face and saw his color change from yellow to white. Skinner's stomach rolled. "Of all the people, Boomer, why you?" Skinner growled.

"I'm not that lucky, Captain. Never have been." Boomer coughed. "Better me than any of you." Boomer smiled then gestured at Skinner's wound. "You better let Sunny doctor you up."

Skinner pulled his shirt up and showed Boomer his wound. "Mine's not as bad."

"That's good, Captain. Woulda been a damn shame for scum like that to . . . get us both."

"I'm gonna sit here beside you, let Sunny work on us." Skinner slumped onto the earth by Boomer and leaned up against the log. He pulled his hat off and placed it beside him.

Boomer coughed, and everyone heard the gurgle come from deep in his chest. "I feel more sorry for you than for me," said Boomer, turning his head to look at Skinner. "That's why I know I'm dying."

"What the hell, Boomer," answered Skinner.

"It don't matter. We got 'em. They're going to cut your balls off when you get back. You broke orders and lost a man."

Boomer smiled, and Skinner saw blood lining the spaces of his teeth.

"You're a hard ridin' man, Captain. I got no regrets being a part of this. Except for the dying part." Boomer would have slumped sideways onto Skinner, but Chaco caught him and held him. "My minds moving fast. I guess I'm about to find out the big secret."

"What secret, Boomer?"

"If there's somethin' on the other side. I'm still thinking there ain't."

A wrinkle on Boomer's shirt near the collar folded and unfolded as his chest rose and fell. A small amount of blood trickled out of his mouth and slid down his chin. "It's okay if there ain't."

"Oh no. Oh no, Boomer." Skinner wriggled around and put his hand on Boomer's shoulder, their faces only inches apart. "I shoulda . . ."

"I'm not scared. Either way. I ain't scared."

Skinner kept his face near Boomer's for a full minute before he reached up and closed the soldier's eyes. He stood, put his hat back on, and faced everyone around him. His shirt was open, and blood was smeared across his stomach and chest. Blood had soaked into the top edge of his pants. His bright red eyes glowed above an unshaven face filthy with a mix of blood, horsehair, sweat, and dirt. Two short streaks of clean skin snaked away from the corners of his eyes.

"Captain?" Sunny took a step towards him, but Skinner's appearance stopped him.

"Assemble everyone." Skinner shook his head in the direction of the clearing where Victor and two others were still working, piling the outlaws' tack and weapons near a dead horse.

Sunny cupped his hands and yelled into the clearing, "Assemble. Now."

Moments later Victor came walking into camp, eyeballing Skinner.

Skinner shook his head. "One got away. He's riding a fresh horse and running like hell."

Skinner gestured towards where the prisoners sat. "Charlie, you and Victor pick out the meanest of them two and bring him over here. I want to find out what I can about the one that got away."

Charlie wanted to ask how he should determine who was the meanest one, but Boomer's words of warning and advice to him yesterday took hold, and he stifled the impulse.

Skinner continued, "I got a good look at him; let's see if we can get a name and a direction."

Moments later Ricky was dragged over to where Skinner waited. He was tied at the feet and the knees, and with his hands behind his back. Charlie dumped him in a heap near Skinner.

Ricky struggled to a sitting position. Through squinted eyes he peered up at Skinner. The fire popped and coals tumbled across the ground.

Skinner, sensing that Ricky was about to open his mouth, took a step and booted him on the side of his head, knocking him backwards. "Who was the one riding the stallion?"

"Why should I tell you murdering dogs?" Ricky spit at Skinner.

"If you don't, I'm going to burn you alive." Skinner kicked him in the ribs.

Ricky rolled over. "I heard him. You're in trouble already. I don't think you're going to do nothing of the kind."

Skinner grabbed Ricky's bound feet with one hand, dragged him closer to the fire, and with a heave he flopped the man's torso across the flames.

Ricky struggled hard, but bound and with his legs held up by Skinner, he couldn't get himself off the flames. Ricky twisted back and forth and smothered the flames, but a thick mat of coals held in place by a circle of rocks remained, and he began to scream.

Chaco moved up by Skinner, grabbed his elbow, and in a low firm voice said, "Tom, let me have him."

Skeeter watched Charlie stare at their captain with an open mouth and wide eyes.

"Captain, let me have him. I'll get it out of him," Chaco grabbed Skinner around the waist and pulled both men away from the fire.

"I wanna know his name and where you were going," Skinner yelled at Ricky.

"I'm not telling you anything," said Ricky as he flopped around in the dirt trying to rid his clothing of coals.

The other outlaw, back in the shade, yelled out, "I won't forget what I'm seeing. You can count on that. I won't forget."

Breaking free of Chaco's grip, Skinner heaved Ricky back onto the fire pit and fell on top of him, pinning him hard against the coals.

"His name is Jessup. Jessup Henry."

Skinner held him. "Where's he headed?"

"We was going to Mexico. Don't know where he's going now."

Chaco grabbed Skinner around the waist with both arms and heaved both of them back from the fire again. "Tom. Tom. It's done." Chaco fell on top of Skinner and remained on him until he felt Skinner's muscles relax, then he hauled him upright and pushed him out of camp and into the forest.

CHAPTER 18

Charlie watched Chaco depart, pushing the captain ahead of him. Despite being surrounded by the men of the patrol, with Chaco and Skinner's departure, he couldn't stop the feeling of isolation sweeping over him. The outlaw lay by his feet, his clothes smoldering in several spots. He continued to yelp and holler for help and roll around, trying to rid himself of coals. Charlie's gaze fell on Boomer's motionless body still leaning against the log.

"Help me, goddamn it!" Ricky began to writhe with renewed vigor.

Charlie ignored the outlaw, stepped over him, and knelt by Boomer. He fastened the buttons on Boomer's coat and then grabbed handfuls of the coat up by the shoulders and dragged him away from the log so he could lay him flat on the ground. He folded Boomer's arms across his chest and then flopped into the dirt by his side with his back turned on the men.

"Hey, Sunny, did he mess his britches?" asked Vance, trying to make light of the situation. "Goddamn that was funny."

"Shut up, Vance. Shut up right now," said Sunny.

"You shut up. You ain't my boss. Captain is saying and doing all kinds of things that ain't right and you know it."

"Shut the hell up before I come over there and beat the tar out of ya."

"The captain's already come apart. Now you too."

"Shut up."

Ricky yelled out for help. Smoke poured off his clothes. Charlie's mind couldn't absorb all that was transpiring. *Everyone's coming apart. We're days away from anywhere, surrounded by dead bodies.* Charlie rested a hand on Boomer's chest and took a look into the forest after Skinner and Chaco. He shook his head hard, then stood and returned to the slab of horse meat, grabbing the knife and hacking away at it. The knife clinked against the stone every time he missed, and small hunks of meat fell into the dirt at his feet. Skeeter's low voice snarled with anger behind him. Charlie froze in place, one hand gripped the backstrap, the other a knife.

"You're making a mess of our food and you're letting him burn at the same time," said Skeeter.

Charlie felt Skeeter move closer and stand over the outlaw. Smoke now poured off his clothes. "Boomer was the best. The best one of us, and you killed him. I guess burnin' ain't too harsh for someone like you." Skeeter turned towards Charlie but before he could open his mouth again, Charlie spun and rushed at the outlaw. He knocked Skeeter backwards then struck out at the outlaw's face. His first blow glanced harmlessly off the side of his head. He brought his knee forward and slammed it against the outlaw's ribs three times. He punched with both fists, hitting the outlaw with abandon. He landed ten solid blows into the outlaw's face, before he felt hands pulling him back.

Ricky lay in the dirt nearly unconscious. His bloodied

mouth hung open, his lips and teeth oozed blood. Smoke still drifted off his clothes and into Charlie's face. Charlie struggled out of Skeeter and Vance's grip. He saw the men all watching him. He looked up at Skeeter, and saw his face pinched into a tight-lipped smirk.

"We'll be back at the fort in a few days. Guess you won't be mouthin' off about nothing now. You won't be mouthing off about what a bunch of ill-disciplined heartless idiots we are, will ya?" Skeeter pointed at the cuts on the outlaw's face. "Them don't look like wounds someone would get in a shootout, do they?" Skeeter pointed at the burnt clothing on Ricky, still smoking. "Nope. Them don't look like church clothes either, do they?" He motioned with his arm and hand at Sunny and Victor, who stood to the right of him. Vance was on his left. They all stared at Charlie. "Got a lot of witnesses too."

Skeeter reached down and brushed the coals out of the outlaws clothing, then dragged him back to where the other outlaw sat. "Don't let me hear a sound out of either one of you," he said in a loud voice. "Or I'll turn him loose again." Skeeter jerked a thumb over his shoulder in Charlie's direction.

Charlie stumbled out of camp in the opposite direction Chaco and Skinner had gone.

CHAPTER 19

Chaco had been dishing out orders from the moment he'd woken. Skinner lay in his bedroll like a dead man, and Chaco had every intention of having every need attended too long before Skinner stirred. He was going to take over every aspect of the return trip he could and keep Skinner from having to deal with anything that might pull him out of character again. Chaco had also taken Skeeter aside and had told him he needed to do more, take on more responsibilities, and Skeeter had rallied. The two of them had relieved the sentry long before sunrise and had been working hard hauling water, digging a grave for Boomer, bringing in firewood, and preparing a breakfast. Their supplies had been bolstered with the arrival of Willy and the mules late last night.

"Okay, Skeeter, wake 'em up."

"How about the Capt'n?"

"Leave him be."

It was still dark when the sound of horses approaching the campsite had soldiers rolling out of their blankets to grab halters. Skeeter was at the back of the herd, mounted on Boomer's black-faced blue roan. He rode right up to the

fire and looked straight at Skinner, who had woken and
watched the horses approach.

"I figured Boomer wouldn't mind if I rode his horse.
He's a lot smoother than mine. Might be easier to keep my
false teeth from rattling so much. You got a preference,
Captain? You can ride this one if you want."

"I'll ride the bay with the star," said Skinner, pointing.
"They called her Maggie."

Chaco shook his head and took a quiet, deep breath in
response to Skinner's use of the past tense. *It's going to be
a long ride home,* he thought. "Skeeter, you're in charge.
Lead the horses up the head of the canyon, and water 'em.
The captain and I will meet you up there; we gotta go get
his saddle.

To avoid having Skinner aggravate his wound, Chaco
dropped to one knee and let Skinner stand on his thigh to
mount Maggie bareback. Chaco shook his head in antici-
pation of what would happen next. Having ridden so many
miles beside Skinner and Too Tall, Chaco knew he would
be taller in the saddle when they rode side by side. It un-
nerved him. Chaco remained quiet as they picked their
way across the forest floor. After a few minutes he decided
it would be easier for them to travel single file, and he
swung in behind Skinner.

Skinner allowed the mare to choose her own path, and
she set out in earnest. Skinner knew she was looking to
find her companions that all lay dead out in the meadow
behind them. Her gait was pleasant, familiar, and he decided he would ride her all the way home. There was no
talk between him and Chaco, and his gaze remained forward. His eye was pulled down to the earth, pulled by the
tracks of an old friend. The muddy gouges had been made
with power and could be easily seen in the dim light. They

went on and on. It was too much. Skinner's hand wiped away the first tear, but more followed, he couldn't hold them back, and he was thankful Chaco had decided to fall in behind him.

At an easy walk it took fifteen minutes for them to arrive at the top. Skinner sensed Chaco studying the tracks behind him. When they topped out and could see Too Tall and Grady lying in the grass ahead, Skinner pulled up. The red roan was gone. Skinner turned the mare to face Chaco and the slope behind.

"I was way back by the gully when they started up the slope." Skinner wanted Chaco to understand what Too Tall had done.

"I had to keep them in sight, or they could have laid for me. Skinner pulled off his hat and swept his hair back. "Ol' Too Tall. He was flying, Chaco," added Skinner after a moment. "He saved me with that run."

Chaco looked the scene over. "Been bouncing along behind you two a long time. He was a traveling devil, I'll say that. You may never have a better one."

Skinner's head involuntarily jerked up and down. "Yup. You're right about that."

The two of them sat on their horses for several minutes, letting the sun warm them.

Chaco broke the silence. "Boomer was right. This is going to go bad when we get back."

"Yup." Skinner looked into the forest where Jessup had gotten away. "Makes me think I should cut out now, find him and kill him. Could take a while. But it don't matter, I'm done for with the cavalry."

Chaco took his hat off, set it down on the front of his saddle, and rubbed his face with both hands. His long, callused fingers moved behind his head and massaged his neck muscles. He adjusted his shirt collar higher, waiting for Skinner to continue.

"I didn't have a fresh horse, or I guess I would be long gone already, putting a chase on him. If it wasn't for all of you . . ." Skinner looked Chaco's way and then gestured back towards the ambush site.

"I know."

Skinner looked towards Grady and Too Tall. "There's something else." He pushed out his chin in Grady's direction.

"What, Tom?"

"He was done, had a bullet in the hip, but he'd a probably lived. I killed him. It wasn't no accident. It was murder, Chaco."

Chaco nudged Turns Good up close to Skinner.

Skinner stared at his friend and waited for a reply.

"No one's ever going to know that but me," said Chaco. "Far as I'm concerned you killed him on the run. Got it?"

Skinner looked away. "First a kid, then that one back at the ranch. Now this vermin. That's three lives I've taken. Never saw any of 'em coming."

"That's the reason you shouldn't beat yourself up about it. None of them was something you was lookin' to do, Tom."

"I'm lookin' to do one now. All I wanna do is finish the job." Skinner's jaw clenched, the corners of his lips turned down, he hunched his shoulders and leaned forward, his hands resting on the mare's neck, his legs hanging loose over her ribs.

Chaco kept talking. "Stay in your head. Don't be thinking with your heart right now."

"Hell." Skinner's chin went down on his chest. "I'm

damaged goods, Chaco. Everything's squished together so tight inside, there's no separation."

"I got a plan," said Chaco.

"Yeah?"

"We got a long ride home. Have the men trail the two of us. Make them ride a quarter mile behind us. We gotta talk. We gotta talk a lot. We gotta talk the whole way." Chaco jerked his head backwards towards camp and the men. "They ride a quarter mile back the whole way. All right?"

"Whatever you talk me into better include me getting after that one that got away first opportunity that comes along. I'm gonna kill him too."

"Use your head. Don't let anger guide your thinkin' right now." Chaco swung off his horse.

"It ain't comin' from my heart or my head. My mind's working from a place I ain't familiar with." Skinner swung his leg forward over the mare's neck and slipped down as well.

"Don't go to that place, Tom. Stay strong."

"It's all I got right now."

"No, it ain't. You got a bunch of men back there that look at you like a hero. You got three people back at the fort that won't even begin to heal until they see you again." Chaco reached over and gave Skinner a hard shove. "You pull yourself back from that kind of thinkin'. You hear me?"

Skinner pulled up his shirt. The shove had started another trickle of blood running down his side and soaking into the hem at the top of his pants. "I'm damaged goods." He brushed a hand across his ribs and swiped up the blood, then began massaging the red fluid into the palms of his hands.

"There's all kinds of people need you to stay strong Tom. You hear me?" Chaco's voice was shriller.

"Yeah. Sure."

Chaco grabbed Skinner's elbow and steered him towards his horse lying in the wet, bloodstained grass. "We got work to do. Come on let's get your saddle off Too Tall."

CHAPTER 20

Three and a half days had passed since Veronica had set the house on fire, and when the patrol crested the rise above the barn, one small tendril of smoke still rose from a corner log. Skinner drew in a deep breath of relief when he saw that the house was completely burned. He'd worried that there was not enough fuel to burn the bodies fully and he would have had the difficult and unpleasant task of finishing the job Veronica had started. It looked as though his worries were for naught, but it still needed closer examination. As the mare carried him down the familiar trail above the house, he felt her gait change from homeward-bound eagerness to one full of hesitation. Her attitude passed to the rest of the bunch; heads came up, and ears pricked forward as they carried the men down to the packed earth surrounding the barn, sheds, and remains of the house. Skinner led the patrol, the prisoners, and five extra horses loaded down with confiscated saddles and weapons, past the house to the pasture below.

"Skeeter, take charge of setting up camp. Chaco and I are going to go have a look around while it's still light."

"Yes sir."

Skinner was going to make a suggestion on what to do

with the prisoners, but he saw Victor already untying the
rope that went from ankle to ankle under the horse. The two
prisoners were grim faced with pain, having been tied for
over forty-eight hours with leather reins. They'd complained often during the ride, but now at the scene of the
crime and in Victor's presence, they remained silent.

Skinner and Chaco stripped the saddles and bridles
from their horses, put hobbles on, and turned them loose.
On the way out, riding had been done with bodies primed
for adventure, but the journey home was different. Trouble
loomed, and saddle time had become doubly arduous.
Everyone complained openly and walked stiffly on wooden
legs as they tended to their mounts.

"Feel like I been pounding railroad spikes all day," said
Chaco.

"Me too."

At the shed, they stopped. Chaco stood back a couple
of steps as Skinner let the door swing open, both of them
expecting a foul odor to drift out.

"Got any ideas as to what we should do with them?"

The bodies weren't as bad as they were expecting. No
critters had bothered them, and the cool weather had kept
them from spoiling too much. Still, even wrapped in blankets, they were obviously stiff and bloated. An awful,
pungent, odor floated out with increasing strength.

"I hate to have them anywhere near this place," said
Chaco, gesturing with a nod of his head towards the house.
Like Skinner, he lifted his arm and buried his nose in the
crook of his elbow.

"I know what you mean. I guess I'll drag them out into
the forest and bury them somewhere," said Skinner. "Let's
wait until morning. Ain't in the mood for the job right now."

"Me either."

With the house burned, the barn loomed larger in the

setting, and Skinner and Chaco made their way to it. Inside, stored in various places, all the tools of the ranch, including a light buckboard, Leon's custom wagon, and a valuable harness remained neatly in place.

"We don't have the horses to get both these outfits out of here, which means somebody is going to have to come back." Skinner started to think out loud. "Unless we can exchange some horses when we meet up with Brooks and reinforcements. We could have some of them come up for it. Why the hell they're not already here is amazing to me."

"If we load all the crap the extra horses are carrying in the wagon right now, that would work." Chaco pushed that idea. He didn't want Skinner to think he had to go back with the wagons. The wagon road took longer than the trail they came up on to get back to the fort, and Veronica and Skinner needed to talk.

The two of them moved to the house and walked with trepidation through the thick ash to where Leon, Muriel, and Laura had been. They were glad to see that there was nothing left. It was clear now that the rustling they had heard when Veronica was in the house was her putting anything that would burn around her parents and her sister, and she'd done a more than adequate job. Only one area had withstood the flames to any degree, and that was the back of the house where the seep was. There, some of the walls soaked by humidity from the seep hadn't burned. A piece of wall stuck out on either side of the seep, and a ragged piece of roof attached to the rock behind remained.

Skinner waded through the ashes that came up to his ankles in places, passing the cookstove, and made his way towards the seep. The seep continued to run, and the unused water had cut a miniature canyon through the ash to the edge of the house foundation before running off into the woods behind. A heat-blackened water dipper hung on the left wall. Next to it was a small pencil drawing of a jaguar lying on an outcrop of rock somewhere on the Mogollon Rim. It was signed Leon Sharp and dated October 1880. The side of the wooden frame was charred, but the drawing behind thick glass had somehow survived. Skinner took it carefully off the wall and wiped the glass across his shirt front. The jaguar was accurately done and depicted the animal lying in the grass. The tip of its tail curled around a large stone. Its expression was calm, and Skinner imagined the tip of its tail flicking up and down as it looked for prey below. He wondered if Leon had come across such a scene, since jaguars, as far as Skinner knew, had been all but shot out long ago. If he had, he'd never mentioned it. Skinner tucked the drawing under his arm.

Chaco took off his hat and wadded up the brim with his filthy hands. "Tom, I'll go tell the men the plan. Why don't you pull a couple of thick boards off the barn, and when I come back, we can carve these people a marker."

"Sounds good. Get yourself something to eat while you're down there. I'm gonna keep looking around."

Skinner watched Chaco's back as he shuffled away though the ash, and he couldn't help thinking about how steady Chaco had been all this time. Skinner almost called out to stop him and acknowledge his support, but this wasn't the time or the place, and he let him go. He looked down at his feet, kicked at the ashes, and watched a small amount float away to land somewhere unknown on this beautiful landscape. He understood why Veronica had elected to burn the house. The cookstove caught his eye, and he was reminded of the many burnt-out houses from the Apache wars he had seen. Virtually everyone had a cookstove remaining behind, undamaged in burnt rubble. He was tempted to have his men pluck it from the ashes and load into the buckboard now, but he knew everyone was exhausted, and he quickly decided not to. Perhaps someone would take it and put it back to use in time.

Skinner walked back to the barn. Inside, on top of a partition, were two thick, hand-hewn boards. Grabbing a pry bar, Skinner pulled them off. Crossing one across the top of the other, he pounded a couple of long spikes all the way through and bent them over on the backside. With a hammer and a chisel, he began to carve on the cross, not waiting for Chaco to return.

He listed their names but left a space open for their dates of birth, as he didn't know any of them. The date of their death, January 3, 1890. Skinner thought hard about what he could say in their memory. Finally, he realized he wasn't the one to do it and left another spot blank.

When Chaco returned, they set the cross deep in the ground between the edge of the rim and where the house had been. Chaco knelt in front of the cross and said a prayer in Spanish.

"I think I finally figured out why you speak Spanish when things get serious."

"Oh?"

"Spanish is more eloquent than English."

"What's eloquent mean?"

"It means better. It's a better language when you want to say somethin' serious. Somethin' meaningful. Like you just did."

"You didn't even understand what I said."

"What did you say, Chaco?"

"I said you and I are unsure if there is a God out there. I said we hoped there was, and if there was, and he was listening, we could sure use some help to put everything back together as best we could, for Veronica and the twins. I told him this family's belief in God didn't need testing. I told him he'd made a mistake."

"What else?"

"I told him my friend was being strong, and I asked him to keep you that way." Chaco gestured at the cross. "I told the three of them we hoped to see them on the other side."

"I understood you just fine Chaco," replied Skinner.

"You okay?"

"She didn't say a thing when she left, just stared straight ahead. I think she's done with me. Probably done with men for life. She's like me: damaged goods."

"She needs time. So do you, Tom."

"I don't know about that. People who go through what she did . . . they change. Especially after what I did up at the hunting camp."

"You going to tell me what you did?"

"It don't matter now anyhow."

Chaco pushed up against Skinner. "Don't go there, Tom. Stay away from that dark thinking you've been doing. It's gonna eat you alive. You hear me?"

"I just can't stop my head from rehashing two thoughts."

"Well one of your thoughts is okay, and the other isn't."

"You know what's eatin' me, do ya?"

"Hell yes, I know. You want to see her just one more time, and that's good."

"What else?"

"You want to finish the job, and that's the thought that don't sit right. You gotta let someone else take care of that. Even if you could find him, it won't help if you go off half-cocked and kill that murdering devil. It won't make anything better. I'm telling you, it won't."

CHAPTER 21

While dinner was being prepared, Al Resendez slipped out the screen door onto the porch, pursuing his padded chair. Low grunts emanated from his throat as he settled in and pulled a worn serape over his skinny old legs. Callused bony fingers reached inside his sheepskin coat and grabbed a small flask, which he shook to assure himself it was full. He unscrewed the cap, took a sip, and let out a long sigh, but his eyes lingered on the flask and its contents. Conscience fought desire in a familiar ritual. Every sip meant there was less to sell, and Al loved both money and whiskey. While paying heed to his conscience, movement to the northeast caught his eye.

A lone rider coming down the hill appeared briefly from behind big manzanita bushes. The trail they were on was well used, and Al had no reason to expect trouble. Living this close to Prescott, he got a lot of people riding by; mostly it was mule and burro pack trains moving supplies out to the mines at Jerome. He survived here because of the strategic location of his water supply. For the packers and their animals, and everyone else who traveled this route, it was a perfect stop. It wasn't only water to be had; he also kept a good supply of mescal, whiskey, and food on hand. The packers often wanted a few warm-up nips to get ready to hit town, and at times they needed a bit of the same for medicinal reasons on the way back.

The way this horse and rider were moving, however, triggered Al's instinct for trouble. There was something unnatural in their movement. He reached for the double-barrel shotgun leaning against the wall behind him and placed it across his lap. His suspicious nature and a willingness to point a gun at people had helped him defend this watering hole for a long time. Al studied them. He decided it was the rein hand that bothered him. It was unsure, yet he could see they had traveled a long way. The hair on his neck rose.

"Hijo de la madre. No quiero eso ahora," he whispered.

This visitor, who was still a hundred yards off, was ruining Al's evening. He rubbed the stubble on his jaw and continued to study the pair. The horse had been ridden hard, its hide dirty with sweat and dust, yet it came off the hill in a ground-covering walk, the front legs reaching out, crunching the loose rock. *This is a horse of quality*, thought Al. One hand began to shake, adrenaline began replacing the whiskey in his old veins. The rider was running to something or from something, and Al's intuition was telling him it was the latter. His fingers crept towards the triggers and hammers of the shotgun. On the last bend it came to him: the horse and rider had no rapport. Al now understood this was a stolen horse.

At the bottom of the hill the trail changed from loose rock to chalky soil. Dust swirled underneath and gently out behind the horse as it headed straight at him. His eyes caught the stranger's and they met. He lifted a hand in a wave, and the rider returned it. The horse veered towards the water trough, but the rider angrily held it straight. Al knew that the horse had been here before, but not the rider. The man was well armed: two pistols and a rifle. Al felt his body tense. *This is a real bandit.* Again, the horse pulled in the direction of the water, and the rider, who could now see the trough, let it turn this time and asked for permission with a gesture of his hand.

Al gestured back, waving him on. "The water is for everyone," he said.

As the horse turned, Al could see the long curly mane, the outline of the Morgan jaw, the deep girth and strikingly perfect confirmation. *Madre de Dios. That's Leon's stallion, Viking.* Al knew Leon; he was a regular on this trail, he would never have sold the horse. He had been bringing that horse to Prescott for years and had turned down every outrageous offer made for the animal. *I need to capture this bandit,* he told himself. *There has to be a reward out for this hijo de la. . . . Don't be afraid old man, this is opportunity,* he lectured to himself.

Viking's head came up, muzzle dripping.

"Tengo comida." Al set the bait.

"Is that right? I bet it ain't free like the water," said Jessup.

Al could feel his hand shaking at twice the speed of his pounding heart. The reward was probably huge though. He was sure he could get twenty dollars from Leon just for returning the horse.

"That is correct, *amigo.*" Intentionally, Al waited until the man was looking directly at him, and then he took a drink from his flask.

"I suppose you got whiskey and food for sale?"

"A meal and bottle. *Si amigo.*"

Viking lowered his head for another drink.

Al's wife crept to the window for a peek at the stranger. She sensed the danger as well.

"How long from here to Prescott?"

"Three hours." Al stretched the actual time.

"I'll take a bottle of whiskey and a meal wrapped up to go with me."

"Mi amor, dos tamales para llevar, también una botella." Al called back to his wife.

The door opened a crack right behind him. His wife spoke to him in a whisper. Al nodded ever so slightly, his trembling thumb tapping the hammers of the shotgun.

As Viking lifted his head, the outlaw yanked on the reins and headed over to the porch.

Al's wife was quickly wrapping a meal up in old newsprint.

"Two dollars, *señor*." Al moved the barrel of the shotgun slightly to cover the bandit's approach and drew back the hammers.

Jessup counted coins as he walked over, leading the stallion. He looked up at Al ready to hand him the money, but Al made no move. He gestured with his eyes and the shotgun for the man to put the money on the railing of the small porch.

As their eyes met, Al spoke, "One has to be careful living so far from town."

"Especially when the price of food is so high."

"Exactamente, señor."

"You live here alone?"

"We have our animals and many, many visitors."

Jessup looked at the shotgun and saw his hand shaking. "Why you so nervous?" he asked.

"You might not like the food, *señor*," replied Al.

"Well, if I were you, I would relax. You might pull them triggers by accident."

"Si, señor."

Tense seconds passed as they waited for Al's wife. Finally, she appeared with the food and whiskey. Being careful to not get between the muzzle of the shotgun and the bandit, she placed the bottle and package on the rail, scooped up the coins, and moved quickly back into the house.

"You two are makin' me nervous," said the man as he backed to his horse. Tucking the bottle away into his gear, he mounted, and as he gathered the reins stared down on Al.

"Hasta pronto, amigo," said Al.

"I don't speak much Mexican but don't call me *amigo*," said Jessup. He yanked on the stallion's mouth and turned away from the porch.

"Si, señor," Al said quietly. He could hear the outlaw chuckling to himself as he rode off.

Al's eyes remained fixed on the trail where the bandit had disappeared. His hand shook violently as he brought the flask up to his lips for a guiltless drink. "You are right . . . you no *mi amigo* . . . you are, you are . . . a gift from God, *cabrón*." After a few moments he rose, walked inside, took a glance at the kitchen counter, and then hugged his wife. *"Eres magnifico, mi amor."*

His wife didn't respond, but it was clear she didn't share his absolute confidence in their plan. Al shrugged off his coat, put on a few more layers of clothing, then shoved a pistol behind his belt before putting the coat back on.

"Voy a regresar en dos horas, mi amor," he said.

"Cuidado," his wife called after him.

Al saddled his old mare, Chula, and headed down the trail, studying tracks. In five minutes, he saw the newsprint lying on the trail. After another half hour of travel, he

turned off the trail at a familiar spot and rode up on a ridge
to gain a broader view. The land here was more open than
where his little rancho sat, and he soon spotted movement.
Viking, trailing the reins and without a rider, was grazing
but still moving slowly in the direction of Prescott. There
was no sign of the bandit. After two quick sips from his
flask, Al kicked Chula into a fast trot down a well-worn
goat trail and set out after the stallion. He would have to
circle and come at him from the Prescott side, or he would
not be able to catch him. Forty minutes later he finally
emerged back on the main trail, ahead of the stallion. His
relief was double, as there would be no long trip chasing
a horse heading to familiar territory, and he could stop
trotting. *Oh my God, I am too old and drunk for such rough
riding,* he thought. He made a mental note to slow down
his consumption as he headed down the trail.

   "Calmate, mi amigo," said Al as he stepped down from
his horse. *"Calmate, calmate . . ."* Al radiated good nature
and was able to catch the stallion easily. Leading Viking,
he started for home. In less than ten minutes they came
across the unconscious body of the man, curled up like a
baby clutching his stomach. A broken bottle lay off to the
side. Al was slightly alarmed by his contorted position and
hoped his wife hadn't put too much in the food. Deadly
nightshade could kill a man with ease. Drawing his pistol
before stepping down, Al cautiously approached the
bandit. He picked up a fist-size rock and hurled it against the
bandit's ribs. Nothing. "I no nervous now, *cabrón*," he said.
Then he knelt and began searching the bandit's pockets
and gear. Sixty-three dollars, two pistols, an 1863 Win-
chester repeating rifle, thirty-one rounds of ammunition, a
Bible, his saddle, and the potential rewards. This was life-
changing money if the bandit did not die and complicate
the matter. Al's scrawny hand reached for the bandit's

wrist. His pulse was strong and Al's adrenaline surged. The bandit might wake before he could get him home and tie him securely for the long trip to Prescott. *"Ay Dios mio,"* Al shouted. He stood quickly and hauled the bandit into a sitting position.

It took a bit of grunting and wrestling to get the bandit over his shoulder, and Al was breathing hard as he approached the stallion. With a big heave he tried to flop the man across the saddle. Viking calmly stepped away, and the bandit hit the ground hard. *That would hurt if he were awake*, Al thought, and a high-spirited laughter took hold of him while his hand went for the flask, which he shook to gauge the amount left. He decided he could afford to rest for a bit; his wife would not worry too much if it took three hours for him to arrive home. Al made the decision to switch the saddles and eventually he managed to load the bandit onto Chula. Stepping up on Viking, his mood soared. He'd just captured a dangerous bandit and was heading home riding one of the best horses in the territory. He would take them both to Prescott the next day and collect all the money. Al looked up into the sky; small fast-moving clouds momentarily obscured the stars that made their presence known as full dark approached. *"Gracias,"* he said in a loud voice.

Al arrived home drunk but utterly elated.

"Mi amor, venga!" Al bellowed for his wife. *"Mire que tengo!* Swaying wildly in the saddle, one hand holding the reins and one hand holding his flask, he reached both arms skyward and made his toast to God.

"Gracias a ti, somos ricos."

CHAPTER 22

The next day Skinner had his men up and moving early. There was no hint of light as he began issuing orders. One crew carried all the confiscated tack and weapons up to the barn with him, another crew brought in the horses. In twenty minutes, everything of value that belonged to the Sharp family had been loaded into the wagon. The outlaws' saddles, tack, and weapons were loaded in the smaller buckboard along with Pepper's and Colin's bodies, which Skinner had decided to haul out instead of burying nearby. Both loads had then been covered with tarps and securely strapped down. Every man was summoned to roll the loaded wagons one at a time into the barn, where they would remain until someone could come for them.

After a meager breakfast and coffee, the men mounted stiffly and began the journey to the Parson ranch. Skinner had calculated that the possibility was high they could meet reinforcements at any time coming to their aid. He rode in silence at the head of the patrol wondering who he would run into first. The thought of turning a corner and seeing Brickman at the head of a column was maddening. By midafternoon, as the patrol approached the Parsons ranch, Skinner had worked himself up into a foul, confrontational mood.

"Where the hell are they?" Skinner asked Chaco.

"Can't believe we haven't run into 'em."

Finally, on the last bend in the trail, they saw Brooks standing by his horse, staring at them. The reinforcement party was behind him, dismounting near the burnt-out house, preparing to take a break. Both groups had arrived at the same time. Horses from each group whinnied back and forth as Skinner led his string of weary men towards the reinforcement party and Brooks.

"Hello, Brooks," said Skinner as he dismounted.

"Captain."

Skinner waved all his men off their horses.

"Who's in charge?"

"Kelly Saunders."

Skinner pulled his saddle off and dropped it on the ground next to the mare. His manner was as good as a direct order for the others to do the same. "What can you tell me?"

"Brickman went south from the Edge Camp. He went to meet up with General Miles, who is on his way north, out of the valley," said Brooks.

"You gotta be kiddin'."

"No."

"What's General Miles's plan? You know how far south they are?"

"I think they're pretty close."

"Pretty close to what?"

"They might make the Edge Camp tonight or tomorrow."

"What else?"

"Brickman put word out all over the place that them outlaws are in the country. He sent riders in every direction warning people."

"What else?"

"Don't know much more. Saunders does."

Skinner eyeballed the new men and horses, evaluating their strength. He looked for familiar faces.

"We all camped at the Edge last night," said Brooks. Uncharacteristically he added, "Veronica and the boys have been at the fort for several days now."

Skinner nodded. "Help Victor, will ya?"

Brooks moved off to visit with Victor, who was unloading the prisoners.

Skinner saw Kelly Saunders hustling towards him, and he quickly exchanged a knowing look with Chaco. Kelly was a junior officer, and that meant Skinner would remain in charge. Sweeny, the only other officer at Fort Verde of equal rank to Skinner, was probably still out beating the trails around Flagstaff. If Brickman had gone south, Kelly Saunders was the only choice left to bring reinforcements.

"Captain Skinner?" Kelly was supremely aware of the difference between his fresh-faced men and horses compared to Skinner's, who were dirty, bloodied, and gaunt. He saluted crisply.

"Kelly, how the hell are ya?" Skinner had been ready to confront Brickman, and with only Kelly to deal with, his ugly demeanor lightened. Skinner saluted back with considerably less precision.

"We're fine."

"How many of you are there?"

"There's ten of us all together."

"You have just the two pack mules?" Skinner was looking over Kelly's group again.

"Yes sir."

"There are three boys that belonged to this family who are missing. Have you seen anyone?"

"No sir. As far as I know no one has been here since you

left except Veronica and the escort. Greg told me she'd insisted to come here despite your orders."

"What do you mean?" Skinner had given Greg strict orders to bypass the Parson ranch.

"He says they stopped out that way, and she and one other walked over here." Kelly paused. "She wanted to pay her respects is what he told me, so he let her. He told me about it right after he arrived at the fort. I think he figured you was going to be pretty upset."

She didn't take no for an answer, thought Skinner.

"What's Brickman's plan?"

"He told me he would be joining up with General Miles. He said he would tell him the news in person. He ordered me to follow your trail and give support. . . ." Kelly paused, ducked his chin, and then added, "When I caught up with you, I was to send word to him with an update. Keep him informed of what was going on as best I could."

"Sounds familiar. Brooks said he'd been sending word out the gang was in the area. Is that right?"

"Yeah. He sent riders all over the place with orders to spread the word. The fort's about empty, but there's cavalry coming from all over the place. Like I said General Miles is working his way north. He must have found out this gang was coming this way even before you ran into them. Lot of men are on the move over this one."

"All right, you caught up with me. I suggest you send Brooks to catch up with Brickman right now."

"What happened, Captain?" Kelly blurted out the question.

"We caught 'em on the east end of Clear Creek. Damn near the head of the canyon. We engaged them. We took two prisoners and killed all the rest except for one that got away. Boomer got killed in the fight."

"Boomer's dead?"

"Yeah, he's dead."

"I wasn't expecting anything like that. What happened?"

"Got shot is what happened," said Skinner angrily. "He died hard."

"Oh my god." Kelly pulled off his hat. "How many were there, Captain?"

"Sixteen."

"Good lord, captain. This is big news."

"One got away, but I can recognize him. I'll give Brooks a written description he can take to Brickman."

The men from each patrol had converged on each other. Questions and answers flowed. Lots of glances from Kelly's patrol were directed at Skinner and Chaco.

"Listen up!" Skinner's voice rose over the talk, "Which one of you is the cook in this outfit?"

Two men stepped forward.

"I want you to lay out the best meal you have for us." Skinner pointed at four of Kelly's men. "You four take charge of the prisoners, put 'em right there in the middle of everything. Don't leave 'em alone for a second. The rest of you give our horses a rubdown, then get 'em on grass." Looking to his right down the row of his men and horses he said, "You fellas take a break; do what you want."

Kelly could see Skinner's anger rising fast. "We'll take care of everything, Captain," Kelly blurted out.

"Thanks, Kelly. Put some hustle into your cooks will ya? We're hungry."

"Yes sir."

"As soon as I get a report written for Brooks, I'm sending him on the double to find General Miles. When he leaves, double the guard on them prisoners and tell 'em that if they so much as look the opposite direction of them two, I'll bust their noses into the back of their skulls. Any of ya got something I can write with?"

"Yes sir." Kelly hustled to his horse and pulled a small leather binder from a saddlebag and brought it back to Skinner.

Skinner sat down and wrote out a short report as well as a description of the outlaw called Jessup Henry. He folded the paper and handed the note to Kelly. "Get Brooks on the trail now." Skinner left Kelly and motioned for Chaco to follow him. "Chaco, let's take a walk."

They walked down the slope to where Chaco and the patrol had buried the Parsons and their hired hand when Skinner had left them. Skinner walked right up to the graves. At the head of every grave was a lichen-covered rock and nestled against each was a small arrangement of twigs, grass, and pinecones. The arrangements were delicate and thoughtfully done. Skinner and Chaco took off their hats.

"Glad you got them buried Chaco. Can you imagine them seeing them like we did?"

"Would have been bad for sure."

"I'm taking that as a good sign, Chaco. There's no flowers around, but she wanted to do something for them."

"You're right, it's a good sign."

"You think it was a mistake to build that cross on the rim?"

"No. I think she will appreciate it."

"You know what Leon was always saying to his kids?"

Chaco shook his head and looked at Skinner.

"He told them a lot of times when I was around. 'It's a great life if you don't weaken.' I must have heard him say it twenty times."

Chaco put his hat back on but didn't make any motion to leave.

"Hey." Skinner clamped his hat back on as well and faced Chaco.

"What."

"I may have been out front, but you're the one that kept us . . . kept us from coming apart."

"It's a good bunch we've been riding with. They never quit on us."

"You're damn right. I gotta make sure that the trouble lands on me and not on them or you when we get back to the fort. I just gotta convince everyone to tell the truth now. Thought it was gonna be the other way around."

Chaco chuckled. "The one time we get in real big trouble and telling the truth is the best way through it."

"The one time I'm gettin' in trouble. You've been followin' orders and gettin' the job done, Chaco. That's what I'm gonna tell 'em, and so are you. We stick to that, they can't do anything' to ya."

"We didn't need to compromise Charlie after all."

"Whatcha mean?"

"Skeeter told me he got the job done on Charlie."

"You gotta be jokin' me." Skinner shook his head absorbing the news and how it would figure in his plan with Brickman and the general. "That's just typical. I guess it don't matter what he says anymore. One way or the other, he's out of the story." Skinner moved away several steps and stared into the woods, in the direction of the fort. "I just want to see her one more time, Chaco. One more time before all the guano starts to slide downhill. I'm thinkin' the smart thing to do is beat Brickman and the general to the fort."

"Boomer was right. You are a hard riding man." Chaco lifted his arms above his head and stretched, trying to relieve his saddle-sore muscles. "Can't you think of any way to handle problems besides riding farther faster?"

"I just gotta see her one more time, Chaco."

"I know."

Skinner gestured at the arrangements Veronica had put on the graves. "She had it the worst and look what she's done. I guess I oughta rise to her example."

"She's a strong woman, Tom. It's going to take some time, but she ain't going to quit on ya."

"I think she already has."

"I doubt it. One thing she knows for sure is that you came running."

"She got raped, Chaco."

"You think she blames that on you? I thought you was smart. You're an idiot."

"Chaco, when I went up to the hunting camp, I went too far with her, if you get my meanin'. And now this. She's gotta be done with men. With me."

"What the hell did you do?"

"I just didn't stop soon enough. We was kissin' and carryin' on, and I went too far."

"Did you force her to do something?"

"No. It wasn't like that. I just didn't stop kissin' and some other stuff right when she wanted me to stop. I just kinda lost myself for a minute, and she got really mad."

"You two are tied together for life. Whatever happens."

Skinner changed the subject. "I'm going to get hammered. I broke orders and lost a man. You shoulda seen Kelly's face when I told him Boomer got killed."

"Cavalry ain't like it used to be, anyway. It's just hard work for lousy pay and one stupid ass after another ordering us around."

"You're right, I am an idiot. A stupid idiot. But I'm gonna find that killer and end this."

"There you go again. No. You're gonna let someone else do that."

"Can't count on it gettin' done."

"Someone will get him. Quit with that failed thinking."

"You're wrong there, Chaco. The thought of finishin' the job is what's keepin' me sane."

Chaco changed the subject. "We leaving at first light?"

"I'm thinking Brickman and General Miles will be somewhere close, heading north anyway. We gotta beat them to the fort. We'll be leaving tonight."

"Hijo de la . . ." Chaco turned on stiff legs and walked back to the men.

CHAPTER 23

Skinner and Chaco remained patient through the grumbling. It was almost universal that not a single soldier wanted to ride any farther, but when the last mule was packed, they both began to push hard for everyone to mount and head down the trial. Skinner took the lead and never looked back. By full dark they arrived at the edge of the forest and began the descent of the long malapai-strewn ridge to Stinking Springs. The starlit views to the west and south stretched out forever, and the far horizons were just a dark blur. Skinner let the bay mare watch the trail, and he kept his eyes on the deserts spread out to the south, looking for fires.

The trip down the ridge was slow, men cursed and stumbled as they led the horses over the worst parts. Stinking Springs was only another hour down the trail when Skinner spotted the fires. Skinner pulled the mare to a halt.

"You see 'em?" he asked.

"Yeah," replied Chaco.

"Big group, if you ask me. Looks like more than a dozen fires." Skinner stepped down and dropped his reins. "Break out that long eye will ya?"

Chaco, already digging in his saddlebags pulled out the telescope. "Here."

Skinner lay down and rested the telescope on a rock. "It's them. For sure."

"Kelly was right. This is bigger than I thought it would be. They're closer too."

General Nelson A. Miles, one of the most famous generals in uniform, was heading north, and both Skinner and Chaco knew instinctively that his most immediate objective was to catch up with Skinner and find out what he had to report. Miles had fought in the Civil War and in dozens of Indian battles across the West. He was widely credited with subduing Chief Joseph of the Nez Perce, and he'd accomplished the end of Geronimo's reign of terror, and now he was camped just half a day's ride south of the Edge Camp

"Feels ominous, Chaco."

"Sure does."

Skinner stood and walked over to his horse.

Chaco staggered along behind him and both men started moving downhill on foot, leading the horses.

"We should make it to the Edge Camp before them. Might be close. Depends on how fast they move in the morning."

"I got this sudden feeling we'll be moving faster." Chaco shook his head.

"You're sure right about that."

"You got a plan? 'Cause most of our horses won't tolerate any more hard riding. I doubt we can beat them to the Edge Camp if the general leaves ahead of the pack train."

"Yeah, I got a plan."

* * *

At Stinking Springs Skinner and Chaco both took another long look with the telescope at the general's camp. Kelly Saunders joined them.

"Whatcha think?"

"It's them all right," said Kelly, trying to get a better image with the long eye at night.

Skinner yelled out an order at the men behind them. "There ain't much grass. I want every man to spread out. Feed you horses on the end of your leads. Make sure they have a bellyful before you come back to camp. Water them and then get some shut-eye." Skinner lowered his voice and spoke directly to Kelly and Chaco. "Kelly, our horses are worn out. I'm going to have you bring our horses along slow. My patrol is gonna switch out with you. You and your men will need to nurse them home. We'll be leaving ahead of ya. I'll stick with that mare I'm ridin', but the rest are gonna be up to you to get back to the fort."

"Are you going to try and catch up with the general?"

"Yeah. We'll leave three hours before sunup. Have your crew take 'em out for another feed an hour before that. No loose horses, keep 'em all on lead lines and ready to go when I call for 'em."

Chaco grabbed Kelly's shirt sleeve and tugged him closer. "I want you to take personal care of Turns Good. Don't make any mistake with him."

"Okay, I will. You really think you got to go that early?"

Skinner didn't answer and walked towards his men to deliver the news.

Chaco trailed along, leaving Kelly on his own. "I was right. You solve problems by riding farther and faster than everyone else." Chaco grumbled.

"We'll be at the fort after midnight tomorrow," said Skinner. "No way they can beat us."

"If I don't break in half we might."

CHAPTER 24

The sun was midway across the sky when the men of the patrol slid out of the saddle and let their horses drink from the Verde River south of Edge Camp. The horses had built a strong thirst after the foul-tasting water at Stinking Springs, and they noisily slurped the fresh water over their bits. Soldiers twisted themselves left and right and stretched and stomped their legs, trying to get blood moving over sore bodies. They watched Skinner as he walked stiffly up to the summit of a small hill with the long eye in his hand and wondered how long a rest he would allow them. Only seconds passed before he turned and hustled back to them.

"They're right behind us. Two dust clouds now. The one out front must be the general. They have two flags flying. The other's gotta be the pack train"

"Right behind us?" Eyes wide, Chaco stared at Skinner.

"Yeah. I'm figurin' they heard Brooks's report and started earlier than normal. Hell, we just beat 'em. They're comin' on the double."

"Mount up." Skinner barked out the order and swung the patrol north along the Verde and headed for the Edge Camp. With relatively fresh horses Skinner traveled at a steady trot. Every short break they took was in a spot where they could watch the dust clouds behind. Only one dust cloud was evident at the last stop they made before they would arrive at the Edge Camp, and it was much farther behind now.

"We gained ground," said Skinner.

"I think I left my ass back there for them to find." Chaco slid out of the saddle painfully, as did everyone else.

Skinner watched Charlie step down and wince with pain. He hobbled over to a rock, sat down, and rubbed his legs, having learned from the others how much massage could help during breaks.

"The horses are good; we'll make the Edge Camp easy. We'll take a short break there, and we'll make the fort after midnight." Skinner spoke as he watched his saddle-sore men rest. None of them responded, but they all looked his way and made no effort to hide their miserable expressions.

The sun was low when Skinner led the patrol through the thick stands of cottonwoods and sycamores just minutes away from the Edge Camp, and it wasn't until the last minute that he saw the camp was occupied. A sentry challenged them. "Who goes there?" a voice yelled out at them.

"Chaco, come here fast."

"Who the hell is this? You think this is the general and all we been chased by is the pack train?"

"I don't know. Hope not, 'cause this is going to blow our plan."

"Looks like a big group. No way there is going to be room for the ones behind and us."

"Who goes there?" the voice yelled out again. "Answer now."

"What the hell are we going to do?" Chaco hesitated and looked to Skinner.

"Go ahead answer him. Tell him the truth. Remember, all we gotta do is tell the truth."

Chaco cupped his hands and hooted back. "Patrol out of Fort Verde. Captain Tom Skinner in command."

No one answered back, but they could hear horses moving and orders being given. Skinner leaned over and whispered to Chaco, "Don't worry, I got a plan."

"Yeah, what the hell is it this time?"

"This is a big group. We got a lot more behind us comin' in too. If I don't get detained, I'll tell 'em that we'll camp across the river, up around the bend, to make room for whoever's comin' behind us. We'll just sneak out first opportunity."

"Damn." Chaco's chin dropped to his chest. He was exhausted but couldn't suppress his smile. "You just don't quit do ya?"

"Quit what?"

Three horses surged across the river and approached them at a fast trot. "Captain Skinner, I'm Lieutenant Moore out of Fort Lowell."

Skinner saw the lieutenant was good with horses and sharp; he sensed the man was used to dealing with weighty matters, which tore at his confidence. "Lieutenant." Skinner saluted.

"Captain Skinner. We are an advance party for General Miles, who is approaching from the south. It is our understanding that you got on the trail of this gang. What do you have to report?" The lieutenant waited.

"We caught the gang on Clear Creek Canyon. We engaged them. Killed thirteen of them, one escaped. We have two prisoners."

Moore's gaze swept over the men and horses of the patrol. He brought his eyes back to Skinner, waiting for more information.

"We had one casualty. He was killed in the fight. We have one wounded."

"What's the name of the wounded man? How bad is it?"

"Private Vance Brewer. A bullet gave him a face full of splinters. His face is a mess."

"What's the name and rank of your casualty?"

"His name was Boomer Dinning. Corporal Boomer Dinning."

"You look wounded too, Captain." Moore pointed at the blood on Skinner's shirt between the lapels of his open coat.

"Yeah, me too." Skinner had been right. This was an experienced officer; he wasn't missing anything.

"Lieutenant, we been tied for days now, my hands are coming off, these murdering heathens . . ." Ricky yelled from behind in the dark. Someone slapped him and cut off his outburst.

Before Moore could respond, Skinner barked an order. "Skeeter, tend to them prisoners." Moore snapped his fingers at the two soldiers beside him and pointed towards the prisoners. The men kicked their horses forward.

"Captain, I'm going to have these men help guard those prisoners. As soon as we cross the river, I will take them off your hands. I'm under direct orders from General Miles to capture, kill, or detain any members of that gang. Can anyone describe the one that got away?"

"I can. He's riding a well-known horse too."

"General Miles should be arriving tonight or tomorrow. We're expecting him at any time."

"They made camp last night out in the desert, just before the narrows. We have been seeing their dust all day. They'll be here tonight."

Moore grunted and was about to speak but Skinner cut

him off. "Lot of horses comin' in behind us. How about we camp upriver and make some room for the general?"

Vance sat his horse just behind Skinner. "Captain, I thought we was . . ."

"Private, do I want you to talk right now?" Skinner shot a vicious look towards Vance.

"No sir."

"Then keep your mouth shut."

"Yes sir." Vance's voice slunk down to a whisper.

"That'll be fine. Camp where you wish." Moore raised his eyebrows. "Looks like you could all use a break. Take a minute to line out your men, Captain. Then you can all follow me. We worked out a route where you won't get wet crossing the river."

"Thank you, Lieutenant." Skinner looked over his shoulder at Chaco and rolled his eyes hard, then winked. "Chaco, around that bend is a flat place we could camp, and we won't be in the way for the general. Go ahead and set camp. Vance and I will be along shortly."

"Yes sir."

Skinner and Vance rode along behind Moore, and Skinner's anger, triggered by thoughts of Too Tall as he trailed the lieutenant across the river, began to rise. He wanted to get away from Moore and get moving before General Miles arrived. The only thing in his favor right now was that Moore had said, "camp where you wish," and every one of his men had heard him say it. Skinner wished to camp at the fort.

"We have a medical officer with us. You're in luck," said Moore over his shoulder. "He can take a look at you both. He's slow but pretty good at his work"

Skinner swore under his breath, worried that whoever tended to them would take a long time and allow the general and Brickman to roll into camp. "I'm fine, Lieutenant. Vance can tough it out until morning."

"It's no problem, we'll get him to tend to you both, and while he's working on you, I'll get your description of the one outlaw that got away. I can send out riders tonight." Moore's horse walked out of the river and up into the Edge Camp.

An hour later Skinner and Vance left Moore's camp. The doctor had cleaned and disinfected their wounds, and Skinner had given out descriptions of Jessup and Viking. The prisoners had been put under guard in Moore's camp and, more importantly, Brickman and General Miles had not arrived.

"What the hell?" Vance uttered as he rounded a hill. All the horses were still saddled. Chaco stood in front of the men holding the reins to his horse. Everyone behind held their horses as well.

"Dust is close, Captain. They're almost here." Chaco gestured to the south.

"Sure as hell are."

"Let's ride." Chaco swung into the saddle.

"You got that right." Skinner never stopped. He guided Maggie right past Charlie, who watched him with his jaw wide open from the edge of the group. Skinner tipped his hat at him as he passed.

"No talking. Single file. Mount up," said Chaco in a low voice.

A quick rustle of squeaky tack and shuffling hooves was the only sound as a column of horses and saddle-sore men stumbled along behind Chaco and Skinner.

CHAPTER 25

It was midnight when Skinner and the patrol rounded the last hill and could see the fort. Weak lantern light glowed from three windows; the rest of the fort was asleep. Two dogs sounded the alarm in unison and within seconds a pack of dogs woke the fort. Shrieks could be heard passing from one building to the next as their identity became known. More lanterns were lit, and soon the parade ground glowed in pale light.

Skinner looked over his shoulder at the men behind him. He lifted the reins, shortened the steps of the bay mare, and barked out an order. In a tight column of twos, they entered the parade ground among a swirl of happy faces, almost all of which belonged to women. The fort was devoid of soldiers.

Skinner's legs felt empty of blood, and getting out of the saddle was the only thing that would make them feel better, but he lingered astride the mare and looked for Veronica or the twins, who had not made an appearance. Finally, he stepped down last. He landed with a thud and groaned when his legs threatened to buckle under him. Skinner shook them and waited for some sensation to return. When he looked over the top of his saddle, he saw

Veronica standing in front of Chaco and Maria's small house, clutching Monte to her side with one hand and holding a lantern in the other. Skinner raised his hand, but only Monte waved back. He saw Chaco rush to his wife and hold her in a tight embrace. Skinner shook himself, stretched out his legs again, and watched as his men, all equally stiff with fatigue and saddle soreness, began to strip their saddles. A hand appeared under Maggie's neck and grabbed the reins. It was Monte.

"I'll hold her for you."

"Hi, Monte."

"Hi."

Monte held his eyes wide open and stared at Skinner. His head was tilted slightly, one corner of his mouth was pinched upwards.

"We caught them, Monte. We caught 'em up near the head of Clear Creek canyon. One got away. He was riding Viking. He's on the run somewhere. Three of your mares got killed. This one carried me all the way out. Too Tall got killed also."

Monte's chin bobbed up and down above his chest.

"We killed all the rest except for two that gave up. They're under guard with a Lieutenant Moore at the Edge Camp." Skinner stripped his saddle while he talked. Holding it in his arms, he looked down on Monte clutching the reins. Monte's head was down, and he didn't respond to Skinner's news. "Let's put her in that small pen. What do you say we let her roll and eat for a few minutes, and then we can come back and clean her up?"

Monte nodded and said, "Thanks for bringing her back."

"You bet." A lump swelled in Skinner's throat. "How did you get along with that mule?" he asked.

"They're a lot different than horses," said Monte.

"You mean the way they walk?"

"Yeah, and the way they buck, too." Monte's chin came up.

"He tried to buck you off?" Skinner raised an eyebrow.

"He tried. Right in the worst part of the trail too. I showed him who was boss though. I never let him get going. You taught me that, remember?"

"Yeah, I remember. That was a good day." Skinner cleared his throat. "I wish I could have gotten there sooner, Monte. I'm sorry."

Tears welled in Monte's eyes, and Skinner could see them easily even in the dim light. He looked at Skinner unashamed. "Everyone's talking about how you broke orders."

"I tell you what, I'll come see you, Courtney, and Veronica in a little while."

Monte nodded. "Okay," he said, adding, "I'm sorry about Too Tall."

Skinner reached out and put his arm around Monte's shoulders. "How old are you now?"

"Twelve."

"A twelve-year-old kid acting like a full-grown man."

"What?"

"Don't have time to explain myself right now."

Monte shook his head and led the mare off. He stopped and looked back at Skinner. "I'm glad you caught 'em."

"Me too."

"Are the two you caught, the ones still alive, going to be coming here?"

"Yep. They'll come in tomorrow with General Miles."

"I don't want my sister to see them. Or my brother. Can you make sure they don't?"

"Yeah, I can do that for ya. I can sure do that."

Skinner entered the long narrow shed row lit by several lanterns. His men were moving in and out, putting things away fast, anxious to get the job done. He pushed his way to the far end and put his saddle on its rack, then walked to his quarters and shut the door. Despite the doctor's efforts at the Edge Camp his shirt was stuck to his skin with blood in a couple of places, and he winced as he peeled it off. The side of his pants below his wound was stiff with blood as well. His washstand pitcher was only half full, so he only cleaned up his face and hands, then pulled clean clothes over his bloodied body and clamped his hat back on top of his dirty hair. Skinner looked into a small mirror hanging on the back of the door. The stubble on his chin still looked dirty despite the washing, and his eyes burned red. He shrugged his shoulders and walked out.

Outside Skinner caught sight of Chaco watching for him from the porch of his house. Skinner stumbled over and walked up on the porch and waited. Chaco nodded at him, went inside, and a moment later Veronica walked out. She looked exhausted, her skin was pale, and her appearance startled him. His arms shook as he reached out for her. Veronica folded her hands, turned her head to the side, and leaned into him. Her frame felt stiff and thin and cold.

Chaco and Maria stood inside the open door.

Veronica stood in Skinner's embrace until she noticed blood seeping into his clean shirt. "You're hurt," she said, and placed a hand over the bloodstain.

"I'll be fine."

"It's all over the fort that you broke orders."

"That's sure enough true, Veronica. I was just too late. I was ordered south, but I couldn't go 'til I knew you was safe."

Skinner felt her palm press against his wound, but she didn't reply. He hugged her tighter.

"What's going to happen to you?" Her voice a whisper.

"I'll be fine."

She asked again with more emphasis, "What's going to happen to you, Tom?"

"Don't know yet, but it's going to be serious. Boomer getting killed made it a lot more complicated."

Veronica pulled away and looked up at him, tears rolling down her cheeks.

"Veronica, I made a mistake. I should have insisted on coming your direction. It's just that Brickman . . ."

Veronica looked towards Brickman's office. Abruptly she pushed past Chaco and Maria and fled into the back of the house before Skinner finished talking.

Skinner laced his fingers together and rested them on top of his hat with his elbows turned out. He paced back and forth across the small porch.

"Madre de Dios," Maria walked after Veronica into the back room.

"Maria, wait. Would you take something to her for me?"

"Of course. *Que es?*"

"I'll be right back." Skinner ran back to the shed row, to his saddlebags, and pulled out the picture of the jaguar. He wrapped it in a piece of burlap and tied a string around the bundle and returned to Chaco's house.

"It's a picture her father drew," he said, holding it out for Maria.

Maria started to cry. "It will help," she said.

Skinner returned to his barrack and sat on a bench inside the door, resisting an impulse to get a horse and get out of the fort altogether, get back on that outlaw's trail. *She just can't take any more bad news,* he thought.

The air felt suddenly cold inside. He reached for his coat and then looked behind his shelf for a bottle but found nothing. He rammed his hands into his pockets, leaned his head against the wall, and thought about how good a slug of whiskey would taste at that moment.

Chaco slammed open the door and walked in, "Hey, *cabrón*."

"Yeah?"

Chaco reached inside his coat and pulled out a half-full bottle of whiskey. Skinner grabbed it, pulled the cork, and took a long pull. "You're reading my mind. *Gracias*."

"De nada."

There was a knock on the doorjamb. Sunny appeared in the doorway with Vance standing behind him. Then Greg appeared with Victor. Both squeezed in and neither bothered to close the door behind them. Willy Klingbell and Skeeter came in next.

"Scoot over, fat one." Skeeter shoved his rear end down between Victor and Sunny on a crowded bench just as Wade made his appearance.

The whiskey bottle passed from man to man, and each took a healthy pull of the brown liquid.

"Close that door, will ya? I'm cold," said Sunny. Greg gave the door a shove, but it stopped halfway. A dirty hand grasped the edge. Charlie took a step inside and eyeballed the room with weary, bloodshot eyes.

Skeeter quickly lowered the bottle from his lips. "What the hell are you doing here?"

"Shut up, Skeeter." Chaco cut him off.

Charlie felt every eye on him. He took a deep breath and raised his shoulders. "I'm here . . . because this is where I want to be."

A brief silence ensued, then a hand reached out and grabbed Charlie's shirt sleeve and yanked him inside. The door slammed shut behind him, blocking out the cold. The knuckles of another hand from the opposite side of the tight space slammed into Charlie's chest holding a bottle. Snickers, chuckles, and a few elbows bumped ribs. Light laughter, mumbling, and lots of cuss words followed. Then Skeeter asked a question.

"What we gonna do for Charlie? He beat the snot out of that outlaw. I figure that's a loose end we gotta tidy up."

Chaco leaned forward, "We're all going to say we don't know what happened. That lily-livered fool must have gotten into a fight before we laid into them."

Everyone laughed and hooted, and Skeeter slammed a bottle into Charlie's chest again.

Skinner raised his voice over them. "Well fellas, Miles and Brickman will be here tomorrow, and I'm gonna get hammered on account of Boomer. I ain't gonna fight it. Don't want any of you to either. What's done is done. There's not a secret to be kept. Best thing for everyone is to just tell it like it was."

Charlie felt Skeeter's elbow jab into his ribs. "We got one secret."

"What the hell, Captain?" said Vance. "This just ain't right."

"It sure isn't." murmured Chaco.

"Best for everyone but you, Capt'n." Skeeter said.

"Like I said, I'm gonna get hammered anyway. Far as I'm concerned all of you followed orders. You followed orders and that's it." Skinner grabbed a bottle, took a slug, and waited for them all to calm down a bit. "I want to tell you all something while we got the chance. There was a time out there that I ain't gonna forget. It was when we were talkin' up on the bluff above the house." Skinner paused. The men grew silent. "We came together as a unit. We were cavalry, the best cavalry. Do you remember how we traveled after that? I think I issued ten simple orders for almost twenty-four hours. Hardly any." Skinner talked slowly, emphasizing every word for the group of silent men. "Everyone of ya knew his job. Everyone got the best from his horse. Then . . . when we met up with Victor, so slick out in the dark like that, I knew we were going to get to 'em. We were cavalry and no one was gettin' away from us." Holding the bottle by the neck Skinner stuck his arm out into the middle of the cluster of men. He took a swig and passed it on.

Skeeter groaned as the last slug from the bottle hit the back of his throat. "I got two of them devils when Boomer and I flanked 'em . . ." He flipped the empty bottle onto the floor among their feet with a twist of his wrist and scowled at it as it spun to a stop.

Sunny elbowed Skeeter. He slowly reached into his coat and pulled out a half-full bottle. With everyone's attention on him, he shook his half full bottle and looked around the circle. Then his lips stretched into a huge grin. His red eyes lit up like he'd just won a horse race. He reached inside his coat with his other hand and pulled out a second half-full bottle. Cheers erupted all around, and the bottles got passed.

"What else, Captain?" Skeeter motioned for everyone to be quiet.

Skinner leaned forward and put his elbows on his knees. "When we finally got to the canyon and there were no tracks, I couldn't believe what we had done. That's about as good as it gets." Skinner smiled at Sunny and Skeeter. His gaze swept the group. "We laid into that bunch, never gave away the upper hand. It was good. It was damn good soldiering. I figure . . . it doesn't get any better." Skinner grabbed one of the bottles. "Let's all take a drink to Boomer. All talk stopped as the bottles made another round, and once again the brown liquid was disappearing fast. Chaco was the last to drink. He shook the bottle; only a small swig was left. He held it up.

"Boomer was a good man." Chaco drank the last swig and tossed the bottle onto the floor; his head swung backwards and thumped against the wall. No one spoke until Greg reached into his coat and pulled out another three-quarter-full bottle. Everyone laughed except Skinner. He reached over and yanked the bottle from Greg's hand and nearly fell.

"When Boomer was setting there dying, he was thinkin' about me, worried about me. I ain't never going to get that thought out of my mind. Can't think of another example that beats it for . . . guts," said Skinner. He tipped the bottle upwards, and bubbles flowed freely up the neck of the bottle.

No one spoke, everyone waited in silence.

Skinner wiped a sleeve across both eyes and looked around the room at each man. Then he inhaled loudly through his nose and drew his shoulders back. "When I took off after those two that slipped through, I never worried. I remember being mad at myself for tellin' you to watch out for tricks from those men behind the horse." He nudged Chaco with his arm as he spoke. "I knew you wouldn't make mistakes. That was my nerves talkin'."

Chaco nodded his head.

"The way things are these days, well hell . . ." Skinner let this thought go unsaid; it was depressing. Skinner stood slowly and tilted his hat back a touch. "Anyway, I got this firm conviction in my head that what we just finished was a fine example of what it means to be cavalry. I won't forget any of ya."

Skinner's toast changed the mood considerably. The consumption of whiskey slowed, and men just took sips, nursing and sharing the last little bit that remained. Crammed into the small space and with increasingly slurred speech, they discussed, bragged, and purely for the sake of accuracy, argued, over every detail of the last seven days as Skinner listened. No one mentioned Brickman or what the morning would bring.

It was somewhere close to dawn when the effects of whiskey, the call of lovers for some, and fatigue pulled them to warm, padded beds.

CHAPTER 26

Unable to sleep, and frustrated with lying in bed, Veronica rose, wrapped a gray wool blanket around her, and went into the kitchen. She lit the fire and put a pot of water on, then leaned against the stove as it warmed. When the stove got too hot, she shifted the blanket higher around her shoulders, turned and stared down at the pot to watch it come to a boil. She added coffee grounds, sniffed the brew, and the aroma once again brought on painful memories. *Everything brings on a painful memory,* she thought. Veronica heard the roosters begin their early morning ritual. She filled a mug and went outside onto the porch. A crescent moon was low on the western horizon, and the starlight was beginning to fade. She sat down, and then her eye caught movement at the round corral. A young horse trotted along the rails, and moving behind it was a familiar hat shape. She froze, not wanting him to know she was there.

She watched Skinner and the horse come together. The young horse tossed its head. Skinner asked the horse to step forward. The horse sought distance. Although she could not make out the words, she could hear his soothing tone as he spoke. She put her lips to the hot edge of the mug with care, but the metal was too hot, and she couldn't drink. She blew on the liquid and let the steam mingle with her first tears of the day.

Suddenly she felt like an intruder invading another person's privacy. She stiffened and told herself to go back inside, but she didn't. She watched his actions and the young horse's response. The horse held its nose tucked, ears forward. Skinner ceded ground, and the horse moved off the rail. He closed ground, and the yearling swung back to the rails. He pushed the young animal around the pen, laps of give and take, gesture and reward. They moved in a deliberate, unaltered rhythm, a mutually understood pace. The young horse's confidence grew. Veronica took a sip from her mug. *He's talking to the thing he knows best, he's trying to sooth his own mind,* she thought, and she felt like more of an intruder than ever. She watched him move away from the horse and reach under the rails for a halter. The horse stood and faced him, clearly perturbed by the interruption. It let out a light snort and stomped a front foot.

"Easy girl, easy now. You're okay," he said.

But he didn't go back to the filly right away. He leaned against his forearms on the rail, his head looked to the ground, and the back of a palm swept across each eye. After a moment he tossed the halter onto the ground, turned back, and faced the filly. He stroked her neck and ran his hand along the length of her body. He moved behind her and up along her far side. The filly swung her head into his chest with her ears held forward and took in his scent. His voice was louder when he pushed the filly's head gently back, and she heard every word.

"That's enough for now. My mind's on someone else."

Veronica's heartbeat thumped against her chest, a tingle ran down the length of her forearms, and she drew in a full, smooth breath. She watched him climb up and sit on the top rail to look east at the rising light. His callused hand swept through his hair, the other clutched the brim of his hat down on one knee. His head tilted forward until his chin was down by his chest. Words her parents had spoken repeatedly came to her. *It's a great life if you don't weaken.* She whispered to herself, "If I don't weaken."

CHAPTER 27

Skinner sat on the rails silently verbalizing what he would say to Veronica that morning. He dismissed everything he thought of as inadequate, poorly phrased, or stupid, and his frustration grew until the crowing of a rooster broke his thoughts. Skinner jumped down, left the round pen, and headed for his quarters in search of pen and paper. He wanted to have his report written before Brickman and Miles arrived.

The sun was half an hour above the horizon by the time he was done. The whiskey and writing had taken a toll, and the need for sleep overwhelmed him. He stretched from his desk, looked at his bed, and went to it with the intention of sleeping for an hour.

Chaco woke him four hours later. "Hey, Tom, you better get your ass up if you want to keep the general happy. He's looking for ya. Told me he's leaving for Prescott and that you're his new cook."

"Bull."

"I wouldn't josh with you; you're my favorite turd."

"Besa mi culo, cabrón." Skinner rubbed the sleep away and sat up. "What time is it?"

Chaco's voice lowered. "Closing in on noon. There's dust to the south. Lots of it."

"How far out?"

"An hour maybe. They're coming."

Maria burst in on them with a pot of coffee.

"Tom, I spoke to Veronica." Maria paused. "Veronica is a strong woman, and you need to tell her that she fought for her brothers and saved them. It will help her to heal. She feels the guilt."

"Guilt?"

"I can't explain it either, but that's the way she feels. Tell her, Tom."

Skinner took a deep breath. "I will."

"I would like to turn Brickman into a steer." Maria handed Chaco his cup and then reached for Skinner's, in its usual spot. She turned it over and banged it upside down, then filled it quickly, spilling some over the brim. She handed the overflowing mug to Skinner. *"Ay Dios mio,"* she said, and started to cry.

Chaco embraced his wife, whispered into her ear, and turned her back towards their house.

"Maria." Skinner shook his head to wake himself, then he stood stiffly with his coffee cup in hand and stretched his spine. "I don't know what's going to happen, but they ain't gonna hang me."

Maria nodded but remained in a state of extreme unhappiness. "Tom, wherever you go, whatever happens, take them with you. God wants it that way."

"I don't know how to say what's on my mind. I need to find out what's going to happen first. I need to meet with Brickman and the general."

"It won't hurt anything for her to know how you feel. Tell them. Tell them today." Maria slapped the palm of her hand against the wall. "Tom, you need to know that

Veronica did not get raped. She used her wits. She got that stinking piece of garbage drunk on imported whiskey, not weak swill. He violated her but could not rape her. She was too clever. Too tough. She saved those boys too. She is such a strong woman." Maria grabbed Skinner's shirt and pulled herself face to face. "Tom, you don't want to let a woman like her drift away." Maria stood abruptly and swept a lock of hair back over her head. She had said her piece.

"I'm listening to you, Maria," Skinner replied.

"I hate this place now. I want to leave." Maria started cursing in Spanish.

Chaco pulled Maria to him and put an arm around her shoulders stifling the outburst. "She's right, Tom. Talk to her now, before they get here. I don't think you're going to get another chance."

Maria began cursing louder, and Chaco gently pushed her out.

"The years go quickly, don't they?" said Skinner.

"They slow down a lot without a friend," said Chaco. He put his rough, scarred hand out and gripped Skinner's.

"Chaco, I want to make sure that Veronica and the twins don't lay eyes on them two prisoners when they get here. So I'll be out front when they arrive." Skinner picked up his report. "I need a couple of favors in the meantime. Will you do inventory and add it to this report? Turn 'em both in when they get here." Skinner handed the papers to Chaco.

"Sure will," said Chaco, keeping his eyes on his friend. "One last piece of advice before you go, then I'm done. For a while, anyway." Chaco smiled. "Don't hold back over there. Say what's in your heart."

"Got nothing to lose, that's for sure." Skinner turned to go, then stopped, a tired and hungover smile spread across his face. "Turn him into a steer?" he said. "No wonder you behave so well around her."

Chaco didn't laugh. "Don't hold back Tom."

"Okay." Skinner stepped towards the door. "Thanks Chaco. Thanks for everything."

CHAPTER 28

Chaco began counting tack, equipment, bullets, and weapons, and making notes on everything the patrol had piled into the shed row the previous night. He took his time, wanting to get it done well so Brickman couldn't find fault. Then he sat down and read Skinner's report. It kept mainly to itinerary, personnel, and decisions made after they picked up the trail of the outlaws. It also made frequent reference to him and his role. It was detailed and accurate. Skinner took full responsibility for breaking a direct and written order. At the bottom of the page there was an addendum. Chaco read it three times.

> *General Nelson A. Miles,*
>
> *I would like to request that my sergeant, Chaco Velez, be considered for a promotion. His role in this last mission was critical to our success as outlined above. He is well respected by all who know him. He is a capable leader, and in the five years he and I have served together, he has never faltered in the performance of his duties. Not once.*
>
> > *Respectfully submitted,*
> > *Captain Tom Skinner*
> > *Fort Verde, Arizona Territory*

CHAPTER 29

Skinner looked south and saw the dust hovering over the land. He guessed they would arrive in half an hour, so he made his way directly to Chaco's house. Veronica came out onto the porch to greet him as he arrived. She reached for him, gave him a hug, and leaned her head against his shoulder.

"Morning."

"Morning. You look tired," Skinner said, pushing her back.

Taking his hand Veronica pulled him toward the bench at the edge of the porch. "Sit with me for a while?" she asked.

"They're coming."

"I know."

Veronica kept a tight hold on Skinner's hand and pressed her shoulder against his. They both looked south and watched the dust. Neither spoke, but it didn't seem to matter. Their shoulders were pressed together, and they held each other's hand, Veronica's fingers curled around the bottom of his palm.

The sound of pounding hooves approaching the fort from the west interrupted the moment. "What now?" said

Skinner. A lathered horse and rider came galloping onto the parade ground and pulled up short in front of Brickman's office.

The rider vaulted off his horse and shouted. "Where's Colonel Brickman?"

"What's going on?" Skinner shouted back at the rider.

"I got news for him. I was told Colonel Brickman and maybe General Miles would be here." The man tugged his horse closer. "I have never seen a real general before."

"What news?"

"We got word to be on the lookout for outlaws coming from the Mogollon country. Some lowlife just murdered 'ol man Resendez with a knife right outside the jail in Prescott. He grabbed a gun then shot Deputy Porter too. Before anyone had a chance to do anything he took off running right down Gurley Street, riding a horse that lots of folks say belonged to one of them ranchers up on the Mogollon. We're thinking it might be one of them outlaws."

Skinner moved forward. "What's the description of the horse?"

"I don't know what it looked like, but I was told it was a stud horse called Viking. All I can tell ya is they lost his trail on Yarnell Hill. He's a killer. He killed two people right in front of the jail like I told ya. He might be one of 'em."

Skinner pulled Veronica to her feet. He let go of her hand, took off his hat and swept his hair back, then clamped it on tight. "Veronica, will you come with me when I get back? You and the boys?" he said.

"Get back from where?" Veronica rose in alarm.

"Veronica, I'm in love with you." Skinner wrapped his arms around her and held her tight. "I'm done being a soldier. I don't want to be a part of it anymore."

"Where are you going?"

"I'm gonna go get your horse back."

"Don't Tom. Let someone else do it." Veronica's fingers grabbed the front of Skinner's shirt. "I don't want you to go."

Skinner looked over her shoulder at the dust. It was closer, higher in the air. "When I get back, I want to take you and the boys to a place north of here. We can build a house on a bluff overlooking the creek. It's about the prettiest place I've ever seen. I'm thinking we could start an orchard an . . ."

"Don't go, Tom."

"Will you come with me?" Skinner pulled her closer, trying to get an answer.

"Where's Chaco?" Veronica looked for help and clutched Skinner's shirt in her hand, holding him.

Skinner pushed Veronica's head back and pressed his lips gently against her cheek. "You can count on me coming back," he said. He kissed her cheek again, looked at her at arm's length. She held her lips drawn tightly against her teeth and her temples twitched. "I'll be back," he said. "Count on it."

Skinner jerked loose of Veronica's hold, spun around, jumped off the porch, and ran towards Muggs' quarters. He pounded on the door.

"What?"

"Get out of bed you drunken louse."

"No."

Skinner busted inside and saw Muggs looking up at him from his bed. Empty bottles and filthy clothes covered the floor. "I need three fresh-shod horses."

"Why is everyone in such a damn hurry around here?"

"What have you got, Muggs? Get out of bed."

Muggs sat up, put his feet on the floor, and mumbled, "I got a good gray horse. I ain't givin' him away, I can tell you that right now. I got shoes on the sorrel you was working on just before you left. He kept bucking everyone off, so Brickman let him go. He's mine. I got a bill of sale on him. I have a couple of others I put fresh iron on in the last week. Rest of 'em I can't call fresh shod."

"Bring 'em up to the corral, will ya? I'll pick out three and pay you cash.

"What the hell's happening? Hell, you just got back."

"Go get 'em. I'll meet you in ten minutes. Hurry."

Skinner was out the door before Muggs could complain further.

Skinner saw Chaco walking across the parade ground towards Brickman's office with his report in his hand. He ducked behind Muggs's small shack and ran for the shed row. He tied his bridle to his saddle then hefted the saddle onto his hip. He grabbed his saddle pad and rifle in his other hand and took the whole pile in one trip to the back door of the main kitchen, where he stuffed dried salt pork and biscuits into a sack. Loaded down to the point where it was hard to move fast, he took another route below the barracks to the corrals that allowed him to avoid the parade grounds. He met Muggs and a group of seven horses at the corral gate. Skinner slammed the gate shut and appraised the animals. The gray and the sorrel stood out from the others as put together the best.

"I'll take the gray, the sorrel, and that skinny black. How much you want?"

"You're sure in a hurry. What's happening?"

"I got one more bandit to chase down, and he's got a hell of lead. Help me out, I gotta' get moving." Skinner caught the gray. He grabbed another halter and cornered the skinny black. The dust raised by the general's column was thick, close, just minutes away. He kept his eye out for Chaco as well.

"Let someone else go. . . ."

"Muggs, you going to help me, or do I need to bust your ass?"

"Okay, Tom." Muggs backed off and began adding numbers out loud. "The gray is thirty. The sorrel bucks, but I want thirty for him too." Muggs looked at Skinner expecting an argument. "You can have the black for twenty-five."

Skinner held out a wad of money. "This is all I got. I'll pay you the rest later."

Muggs grabbed it. "You're coming back, right?"

The sorrel rushed by Skinner, trying to avoid being caught. Skinner jumped forward and slung both his arms around the sorrel's neck, and in a cloud of dust hauled him down. He got the halter on and tied him to a post. With all three caught, Skinner grabbed his canteen and handed it to Muggs. "Fill this for me?"

"Yeah sure. You being sent, Captain? This don't feel right."

"What don't feel right?"

"You just got back. I thought you was going to be in trouble. That's what everyone been saying. What the hell is going on?"

"Fill that canteen and don't worry about it."

Muggs dipped the canteen in the trough and watched Skinner manhandle the nervous black into being saddled fast.

"You might see this horse again soon if he comes back of his own accord. You can have him back if he does."

Muggs watched Skinner neck rope the other two horses. "You're gonna run hard."

Skinner tied the canteen to his saddle horn, jerked his cinch tight, then swung into the saddle and spun the black around. "Hand me that lead rope."

Muggs pulled the gray and the sorrel over to Skinner.

Skinner looked back at the parade ground; the dust was just around the corner. Chaco stepped off the porch of his house and looked south towards the general's column. "You know what, I don't need this." Skinner untied his pistol belt and handed it down to Muggs. "Give it to Chaco, will ya?" Skinner made a last check. Pockets full of food and ammo, a full canteen, rifle tied securely in a scabbard under his leg, and three fresh-shod horses. He was ready.

"Open the gate. Now. Hurry."

"All right, Captain."

Skinner stabbed the skinny black with his spurs and yanked the lead rope holding the gray and the sorrel. The gray bolted forward, and Skinner had to spur the skinny black hard to stay in front. The horses broke into a run three abreast. Forty yards out Skinner hauled them all down to a trot to negotiate a deep, narrow wash. The three horses crowded together on the edge and then slid to the bottom. Skinner spurred the skinny black and cursed at all of them as he urged them up the far side. The sorrel tripped in the thick soil on the far bank and pulled hard on its rope tied to the gray's neck. The gray was pulled backwards. With his arm now stretched past the skinny black's hind end, Skinner held on and encouraged the gray and sorrel with a clicking sound. He busted out onto the top of the opposite bank and took a quick look back at the fort, wondering if Chaco had seen him leave. The only people he could see were Muggs standing by the gate looking in his direction, and behind him, a flag bearer and the first soldiers of the generals' column entering the far end of the parade ground. Skinner skirted a thick stand of creosote to hide himself from the general's column and rode out of sight. Then he turned the three horses west towards Yarnell Hill, a hundred miles away.

CHAPTER 30

Maria and Chaco watched two of General Miles's troopers walk directly towards them from Brickman's office.

Chaco quietly reached for Maria's hand. "I'm going to falter now if I don't think of something."

"No, you won't." Maria moved closer to Chaco. They waited, standing hip to hip, as the troopers approached.

"He said I have never faltered." Chaco sighed and gripped Maria's hand harder. "I would have stopped him if I had known. We had a plan. Now I don't know." Chaco drew in another deep breath. "Desertion—you either did it or you didn't. There's no way around it. He's in real trouble now."

Maria squeezed Chaco's hand hard. "Think of something, *mi amor,*" she whispered when the two troopers were just yards away.

Under escort Chaco shuffled across the parade ground. His arms and neck tingled, and he started to sweat. He entered the office and saluted Lieutenant Moore, General Miles, and Brickman. Moore wasted no time questioning him. "Where's he headed, Sergeant?"

"He told Muggs he was going after that last outlaw, Lieutenant. He's going to finish the job."

"That outlaw is a hundred miles off and running. How the hell does he think he's going to catch him?" said Lieutenant Moore.

"He'll get him."

"I'm not so sure about that, Sergeant." Moore faced the general, who grunted approval of Lieutenant Moore's statement.

"Gentlemen, let's come up with a strategy. We need to find this outlaw. We need to get more men into the field. One deserter chasing him from here isn't going to get the job done."

"General, sir, may I speak, sir?" Chaco stammered.

"Go ahead, Sergeant."

Chaco's mouth moved but no sound came out. He stammered for a moment then finally blurted out a response. "Captain Skinner did not desert. Captain Skinner is following orders."

Colonel Brickman scoffed, stood abruptly, and started to speak, but he was stopped by General Miles's outstretched arm and palm directed towards him.

"Sergeant?" General Miles inquired.

"Sir. General. Sir." Chaco's voice rose to a level that was uncomfortably loud. "Captain Skinner is following orders. He was ordered to stay on them, not lose them no matter what." Chaco started to speak faster. "He was ordered verbally and in writing to stay on them, to not lose them if we came across them. Sir." Chaco nearly saluted but managed to pull his arm back down at the last moment.

Colonel Brickman yelled at Chaco. "What kind of stunt are you trying to pull now, Sergeant? Those orders are finished once you get back here. What the hell are you . . ."

"Colonel, please, please." Again, General Miles stretched

out his arm and put his palm in Colonel Brickman's face. "Colonel Brickman, is the bad blood between you and your men so thick that you can't for a minute recognize what these men have just accomplished?"

Colonel Brickman held his thoughts in check to absorb the huge change of direction the conversation had just taken.

"This patrol just helped avert what could quite possibly have turned into a huge problem with Mexico. That's where this gang was headed. Mexico, Colonel. We cannot afford a mistake with Mexico right now." General Miles paused and gathered his thoughts. "Not only that, what they did was damn fine soldiering, under pressure, and outmanned." General Miles kept Colonel Brickman off-balance. "Colonel, did you order him to stay on these outlaws no matter what?"

"Yes, General." Brickman had enough sense to keep his answer short and uncomplicated. "But in no way did that mean for Captain Skinner to take matters into his own hands once he'd returned to the fort."

"Why not? He received word regarding one of these outlaws' whereabouts. Did you order him to quit the mission when he got back?"

"No sir. But I did not . . ."

"Enough, Colonel. Consider this issue of desertion resolved. Where were we?" General Miles drew in a breath through pursed lip. "As I was saying, one soldier chasing this outlaw by himself is not going to get the job done. We need to end this. Thoughts, gentlemen?"

Chaco stepped forward. "Lieutenant. General. I don't think you understand what's happening here."

"Excuse me, Sergeant?" The general's spine straightened, and his shoulders drew backwards. His eyes opened wide and pushed scraggly eyebrows to an impossible height. He waited patiently, ready to give the small soldier standing in front of him all the time he needed to bring clarity to the discussion.

Chaco swept off his hat and clutched it in front of his belt. His hands squeezed the hat into a ball as he worked to find words. Chaco took a step forward. "Let me put it another way, General. If I was that outlaw and I knew I only had a hundred-mile head start on Captain Tom Skinner, I guess I'd sacrifice a couple of minutes to sharpen my spurs."

CHAPTER 31

The skinny black snorted and blew snot out its nose half a mile from the fort. The gray and the sorrel began snorting as well. Skinner hauled them down to a walk and let them refill their lungs and clear their windpipes. Two minutes passed before he lifted them back to a brisk trot. During the first hour they covered eight miles. Skinner worked them in a routine: ten minutes at a walk followed by twenty minutes of trotting. On smooth sections Skinner picked up the pace to a lope. Two hours passed before he arrived at a known watering hole. The gray and the sorrel, despite not being in top shape, still traveled on a loose lead. He allowed the horses to drink their fill and gave them ten minutes of rest before he climbed back aboard the skinny black and put them back on the trail. At the end of four hours of travel the skinny black took a leg-weary step and nearly fell. Skinner jabbed a spur into its side, cursed it, and pushed it on.

Ahead loomed the huge rock-strewn slopes that rose out of the Verde Valley and up onto the Prescott plateau. Near the base of the first foothill a grove of leafless cotton-wood trees and a second watering hole waited. Skinner walked the last quarter mile, cooling the heavily sweated horses down before they drank. They crowded together and drank noisily, their noses clustered together in the small puddle that remained. While they filled dry bellies, Skinner stripped his saddle, bridle, and pad, and dropped it on the ground. The sorrel was tired but still had the energy to keep a wary eye on what this human was doing, and it made Skinner's decision about which one to ride next easy. The sorrel, being barely broke, would waste energy learning how to carry a rider in the rougher uphill sections ahead, so he pulled the halter off the skinny black and put it on the gray. He swung his saddle up, adjusted the girth and pulled the latigo to a precise tension. He adjusted his bridle as well for the bigger-headed gray, then stepped aboard, scooped up the lead to the sorrel, and walked off, leaving the skinny black loose. Yards from the water hole a faint game trail led uphill, and Skinner began working his way to the top. He never looked back to see how far the skinny black followed them. He topped out on the Prescott plateau two hours later.

After three rotations of walking and trotting, the loose rock tapered off and the terrain changed to a light-brown, sandy soil. Skinner pushed the gray and the sorrel into a lope. Across the flat valley Skinner saw the mountain he and Chaco had come down as children so many years ago. The corners of his mouth turned down, and he urged the two horses on.

Most of the way up onto the Prescott plateau Skinner had been consumed with thoughts about Veronica and how she would come out of this ordeal. But as the miles fell behind, and his fatigued and sore body complained at an intolerable level, he found it easier to dwell on other fierce subjects. What was Chaco thinking about his choice to chase this killer down, his choice to go AWOL, and how many more miles did the horse beneath him have left? More miles passed, and Skinner's thoughts grew darker with each one. His body felt like it was tearing into half-chewed pieces of meat. His bones ached and sent sharp shivers of pain into his frame. He pictured Too Tall dying beside him, he remembered the way the outlaw had flipped backwards when he shot him at close range, how the blood had spurted out of his chest. He remembered how he'd held the other outlaw on the fire, and Chaco pulling him back. He conjured up one scenario after another about cornering this outlaw named Jessup Henry and getting Viking back, subjects that helped him endure the pain.

Skinner's teeth clenched and he shook his head violently. He looked at the sorrel trotting beside him and studied how the gelding placed its hooves and moved its legs. The stride was shortened, the hooves barely cleared the tops of each obstacle. It was tired and still didn't know how to carry a rider; the horse held no promise of being able to carry him well. Skinner stood in the stirrups. The small of his back ached violently, and the inside of his legs had chafed raw against the saddle fenders. An image of the outlaw and Viking fleeing up a desert hill distracted him from pain once again. He pictured himself bailing off his horse and taking a careful shot with the sights held on the outlaw's head, so if he missed by a little, he would not hit the stallion. His left hand hurt from squeezing the reins so hard, the gray's nostrils vibrated with each breath, the sorrel tugged hard on the lead in his hand.

Skinner hauled them both to a stop. When he switched his saddle from the gray to the sorrel, it stood like an old ranch horse resigned to another day of work. With the gray back on the neck rope, he used the ends of his reins to whip the exhausted sorrel into a rough, exhausted trot. Nine hours had passed since he'd left Fort Verde, and Yarnell Hill was still another three hours away. The sun had dropped below the mountain ahead long ago, and the air at this higher elevation was cold. Even though the cooler air would help the horses Skinner knew the sorrel would not last long, and the risk of it taking a bad step in the dark and falling was high. Skinner kept its neck curved and spine rounded with tireless spurring and whipping, but he knew the horse was ready to collapse. He ground his teeth and thought of Too Tall, who could have run all three of these horses into the ground. Skinner cursed and spurred the sorrel, but he got no response. He pulled them to a stop, stepped down, and led the exhausted horses on foot.

Well past midnight under a crescent moon slowly descending onto the western horizon, Skinner was again riding the gray and leading the sorrel. At a tiny creek near the northern tip of a long dry ridge that ran south from Prescott into the desert, they stopped. Skinner stripped his saddle and gave both horses several rubdowns with his hands. Each horse drank heavily at the creek, then rested on widespread legs, without the energy to eat. It was a bad sign that they didn't eat; it told him these two horses were done for and wouldn't be any good again for days. Skinner didn't bother to tie them, letting them remain loose, then he lay down near them and slept.

Skinner woke four hours later, gave the horses another rubdown, then saddled the gray. He led the two horses on foot until they had loosened their muscles as much as they ever would. When the light began to rise, he climbed aboard the gray and followed the tiny stream along the rounded end of the ridge. Prescott was forty miles north, and the bottom of Yarnell Hill was a mile to the west. He would be there in minutes.

A tiny settlement had formed at the base of this infamous incline that led from the low saguaro- and cactus-covered desert to the higher timbered area around Prescott. Nearly every foot of the climb from the southern deserts to the forested area near Prescott was accomplished on Yarnell Hill. Despite its long, difficult grade, it remained the preferred route for freighters coming from the south. Heavy wagons had to be pulled by double teams up the long switchbacks, and it could take an entire day to get one wagon to the top. The settlement at the base consisted of a cluster of several families' homes and outbuildings. These hard-living families provided corrals, spare parts, water, horses, mules, tools, whiskey, and food to the freighters.

A pack of dogs and several geese announced his arrival with a chorus of barks and honking. Men and women paused from their morning chores and watched him approach from the east.

A shirtless man with sunburned skin and a stark-white beard straightened from his work prying the iron off a busted wagon wheel.

Skinner introduced himself as Captain Skinner and explained his purpose.

"Ty Lahoe is my name. We heard about that outlaw. Quite a few looking to get him. Been people coming through for two days now."

"I take it none of you've seen him."

"That's right, mister. He would be ducking for good cover, I reckon, after killing two men right in front of the jailhouse. His trail was lost in the tracks on the hill."

"You have any horses to trade?"

"Trade for what? Them two?"

"Yep."

"They look pretty much used up. Used up for good."

"They're good horses. They'll come around. What you got?"

"I got one horse for sale. Nine-year-old mare. She's gentle and a fair traveler. I'll trade her for the both of them." Ty pulled at the scruffy beard wrapped around his jaw and stared at Skinner. "It ain't easy getting horses out here."

"I'm looking for two."

"She's the only one I got, unless you want a mule."

"I don't like mules."

"Why not?"

"Anyone else got a horse for sale?"

"Nope."

"Okay, I'll take the trade. You got a deal."

"You sure you're in the army, mister?" said Ty, looking at Skinner's patched and faded cavalry clothes. "You look madder than hell to me."

"Tired is all."

"You look tired all right. Look like you're going round the bend too."

"Where's your horse?"

"We can feed ya. You can take a break . . ."

"No thanks. Where's your horse?"

The mare stood in the far corner of a corral, as far from a group of big, tough mules as she could get. She was a dark buckskin with a small head and finely tapered legs. She watched Skinner as he approached and kept an eye on the mules behind her at the same time. Skinner hid the pleasure in his face from Ty. *She's on the small size, but she's alert,* he thought. *If she's sound, this could be a piece of luck.*

"She's small for my liking. But like I said, it ain't easy getting horses out here." Ty began bolstering his case on the two-for-one trade.

"She small all right, and she's unshod. How about you throw in some food and four shoes, make me feel better about the trade?" Skinner had to chase the mare for a minute or two before he could get the halter on her. *Good horses are always hard to catch,* he thought. He led her out of the corral to a post near the gray and sorrel.

"Don't have any shoes right now. But she's got good feet; she'll hold up for a while, dry as it is."

"You got nails?"

"Yeah, I got lots of them." Ty looked at Skinner.

"If you let me use your tools, I'll pull the shoes off that sorrel and put 'em on her. We got a deal?"

"Sounds good. It's fair." Ty turned and left Skinner to fetch the nails, tools, and food.

Killing time while he waited, Skinner filled his canteen, drank it dry then filled it again. He took his saddle pad and flopped it over a rail. Using his sheath knife, he scraped the sweat and dirt and horsehair off the bottom as best he could. Ty returned with a bucket of tools, a stack of tortillas in a white cotton bag, and some jerked beef, which Skinner added to his kit. While Ty pestered him for news which he mostly couldn't provide, Skinner pulled the shoes from the sorrel and placed them against the bottom of the mare's feet.

"Too big. I need a half inch cut off the ends of each one. Can you do that for me while I trim her up?"

Once again Ty departed for one of his sheds.

The mare stood patiently as Skinner nipped the hoof

walls and flattened the soles with a dull rasp. Behind him in one of the sheds he could hear the back-and-forth sound of Ty cutting the shoes with a hacksaw. Skinner tried to work fast, but his body was so sore, and bending over hurt his wound. He had barely finished before Ty, who had a more time-consuming job of modifying the shoes, returned. Skinner pulled a chunk of flat steel out of the bucket and hammered the shoes flat against its surface. A little more hammering and he had them shaped to a good fit and nailed them onto the mare's hooves. Skinner drove high nails on each hoof, clinched them, and then rasped off a little more hoof wall from the toe. He finished the last foot, straightened with a groan, and had to put a hand on the mare's wither to hold himself.

"You sure you're all right?" asked Ty. "Maybe you should stay the night. Get a fresh start in the morning."

"I told ya. Tired and sore is all."

Ty shook his head but didn't push. The way Skinner's voice had growled when he dismissed his concern was more than enough for him to know nothing he said or did was going to alter this man's plan.

Skinner swung his saddle onto the mare and adjusted the girth. He shortened his bridle straps and the curb chain and checked the saddle strings securing his saddlebags and rifle. He picked up the reins and led the mare away from the fence.

Shoeing the mare had aggravated both his saddle-sore body and his wound to a huge degree. "She ain't gonna buck with me, right?" he said through gritted teeth.

"Shouldn't." Ty stood back as Skinner mounted.

The mare took a few nervous steps, adjusting herself to Skinner's weight, but nothing more.

"What's her name?" Skinner asked.

"She ain't got one, far as I know."

"Well, I suppose I'll figure one out for her before too long. Thanks for the help." Skinner spoke over his shoulder as he turned the mare and headed west, into the desert, away from the heavily trafficked sections beyond the base of Yarnell Hill. *I gotta' make some big loops out away from the hill, see if I can find some sign. What else can I do?* he thought.

The mare's energetic stride and smooth gaits came as a huge surprise. Skinner reached forward and stroked the mare's neck, but he knew he had to learn more about her, he had to find out what she was capable of, before he could decide how to travel. He let the mare move out at a fast walk. A mile out from the corrals he headed up a long ridge and threaded his way between creosote bushes, ocotillo and stands of cholla. At the high point of the ridge, he stopped and looked over a vast expanse of desert that spread west and south. Behind him he could see the endless switchbacks of the wagon road leading up Yarnell Hill. The slope on the far side of the ridge was steeper than what he had ridden up. He nudged the mare forward but gave her no direction, letting her decide how to descend the steep slope so he could get a feel for her mind.

The buckskin mare snorted, pricked her ears forward, lowered her head, and angled off the ridge, selecting the first section of land devoid of cactus, even though it was steep. She set her center of gravity back and used her hind feet to do most of the braking as they slid down. At the bottom of the slope Skinner urged her into a trot and kept her moving until sweat broke out lightly across her shoulders, then he slowed her down to a walk. By moving her back and forth between trotting and walking and watching how quickly she began to sweat, Skinner could evaluate her condition.

"You got some spunk. You handle yourself pretty good," he said.

Skinner reached forward and slid his hand along the length of her neck, He looked down at the sweat on her shoulders and forced his mind to quit thinking about his pain and discomfort. He had to concentrate on forming a new approach to catch up with Viking and an outlaw named Jessup Henry, and so much depended on this mare.

"I'm figurin' you can travel quite a ways if I ain't too hard on ya."

Skinner thought back on Ty's comment about the mare being on the small side for his liking and chuckled. He'd only known one really good big horse. But he'd known all sorts of good little horses, and for the first time since leaving the fort, his confidence grew.

Skinner considered Viking's condition as well. Five days had passed since the ambush at the head of Clear Creek Canyon, and Viking had traveled to Yarnell Hill and beyond in that time. Viking was a tough and well-conditioned horse, but Skinner knew that after the killings in Prescott the outlaw would need to stay hidden and keep the horse close by at all times, and that meant the stallion might not be getting as much feed as it deserved. Viking was probably worn thin at this point, and he had undoubtedly suffered a period of extremely hard use when the outlaw fled from Prescott. Viking had one other huge problem that was in Skinner's favor as well: Viking was a breeding stallion, and despite Leon's constant claims about his stallion's endurance and toughness, Skinner knew Viking burned energy anticipating breeding a mare at the end of every trail, and that virtually all horses with similar nervous energy became worse when not in the company of other horses.

With every consideration taken into account, Skinner changed his tactic. There would be no more big runs now. He would ride the outlaw down with sheer saddle time. He would travel each day at a pace the mare could sustain for weeks, if necessary—a pace dictated by the mare's ability to maintain her weight and soundness.

Over and over Skinner considered the outlaw's choices. He put himself in the outlaw's place, and considered what options remained available to him. He remembered holding the captured outlaw on the fire after the ambush and hearing him say they had all intended to go to Mexico. Skinner reached forward and slid his hand along the mare's neck again. "Okay, little mare. You talk to me, you hear?" Skinner eased his body into a new position in the saddle and looked ahead. The area was flat, the horizon close. He watched the land surface, looked for tracks, and shared his thoughts out loud with the mare. "The man we're chasing needs water, needs to stay off any main trails. He won't go north back towards Prescott or east towards the Mogollon." The mare twisted an ear backwards. "South or west are his only options." Skinner looked west. The mare turned her gaze west as well, but both her ears drew halfway back, and she jerked the bit towards the south. "I agree with ya. Lot of dry desert that away. If I was him, I'd be heading to Mexico. You want to go to Mexico little mare?" he said. Skinner knew that if he allowed the mare to get used to his tone, and to him, at her own pace, if he didn't interfere with her summation of him, they would develop a rapport, and he would be better positioned to get every mile he could from her. Skinner gathered the reins, lifted her pace to a jog trot, reached forward and stroked her neck again. "Grass is good down there this time of year, is what they tell me."

The mare felt the tilt of the bit in her mouth alter. She tucked her nose and gathered herself, and her rider's frame softened in the saddle as a consequence. The mare reached a little farther forward with her hind legs, her front hooves rolled lightly off the earth, she rounded her spine, and began to prance. Her rider didn't restrain or encourage her moment of self-indulgence, and she soon understood his concern lay elsewhere. She settled, her eyes swept left and right looking for predators, her nostrils flared, and she took in the scents coming off the land with earnest. She felt the tilt of the bit in her mouth relax and heard her rider take a long, deep, satisfied breath. The mare understood his approval of her actions had grown. She placed her feet with sureness, her gate became rhythmic, workman-like, effortless; her focus remained forward and sustained. Her rider leaned forward and slid his hand down the length of her neck and the mare's composure dropped to a natural level, where she could concentrate on work and danger. Rarely did she flick an ear back towards her rider anymore. She was braced for the journey.

"That a way, Little Mare," said her rider in an easy tone.

Skinner kept heading southwest for two hours and saw no sign. He guided Little Mare to the crest of a round-topped knob and looked the land over before continuing in a more southerly direction. South, then east, then west, he moved across the desert, cutting for sign in huge loops. Saguaros, creosote bushes, barrel cactus, and cholla grew out of the light-gray gravel. Tracks could be hard to spot in this landscape and Skinner strained to stay focused through his fatigue. If he crossed any sign without seeing them, it could mean the outlaw would gain ground. By late afternoon he was only fifteen miles south of Yarnell

Hill, but he'd covered twenty miles looking for sign. The ground was so hard, he could barely see his own tracks behind him, and he began to question his tactics. Frustrated and angry, he stopped and stepped down to take a break. He took a long drink from his canteen, looked at Little Mare's freshly shod feet and wondered how Viking's shoes were holding up. This desert gravel was hard on horses' feet and was one of the reasons the wagon road coming out of the valley was far to the east, where the conditions were less abrasive. He moved off on foot to stretch his legs and keep himself awake.

Two hours of daylight remained; the sun was just above the horizon when the Little Mare pulled to the right. Having never been in this country Skinner was unfamiliar with any water sources, but he felt sure the mare had smelled water or knew where some was. He mounted and gave Little Mare her head. She turned southeast and walked out with purpose. The sun dropped below the horizon and the light was about gone when Skinner saw a low spot ahead and the tops of a dozen palo verde trees. The mare poked her head forward, content that water was close, and traveled on. Skinner lurched forward in the saddle when Little Mare stopped abruptly and dropped her nose to the ground. With her nostrils just inches from the ground, she took in a series of quick breaths.

Skinner stepped down. In the low light and on the hard surface he could not see tracks, but he knew Little Mare had detected a scent that she'd taken great interest in. He swore. "Too dark, damn it."

The buckskin mare, satisfied with her investigation, pulled at the reins and tugged him toward the grove of trees.

"Easy now. Woah, Little Mare." Skinner kept his horse still.

Skinner had no idea what she smelled, but his hunch was that it was another horse. He looked for manure piles but found none. He felt for a wet spot from urine, but the ground surface was too warm. Giving up, he pulled his rifle from the scabbard, mounted, and let the mare move forward. He shook his head vigorously, waking himself up, preparing to meet anyone or anything that might still be in the depression ahead. They entered the treed area and angled towards the thickest concentration. Skinner's eyes searched every shadow. He concentrated on Little Mare's reactions as well, knowing she would detect a presence long before he could.

Driven by thirst, Little Mare sniffed her way forward. She stopped once and tested the air, then she relaxed, walked forward, and put her head down to drink at the edge of a small spring.

Skinner stepped off and waited for his horse to get all the water she wanted. When she'd had her fill, he stripped his gear, and then used the saddle and pad to make a comfortable place to sleep. Without hobbles or any way to keep the mare close, Skinner let the mare eat while holding the end of her halter rope until she went to water for a second time. Then he tied her to a stout limb and settled down onto his saddle and pads, rubbing his legs for a few minutes before falling back and making himself comfortable. He would have to wait until daylight to see if he had crossed any sign of the outlaw and Viking. In less than a minute, Skinner was asleep.

In the predawn hour the Little Mare had grazed off what little grass was left near the spring, and Skinner had eaten a portion of the food tucked into his kit. As the light rose, he returned to where the mare had dropped her head the previous night and found a stain made from urine. Skinner lay on his belly and sniffed the wet spot; the odor was faint, but he was sure it was horse urine. Besides that, no other animal he knew of that lived out here was capable of making such a large stain. He followed the tracks, which were only scratches on the hard ground. He hoped at some point he would find a clear print in softer ground. Skinner knew that Viking had a spade shape to his hind left foot that was distinct from other horses. The mare trailed along led by the reins as Skinner walked and kept an eye on the scratches in the hard ground, making sure he never lost the faint trail. It was a mile before he found what he was looking for. In the bottom of a shallow wash in firmly packed sand he found clear prints. One print showed the unmistakable pointed toe with flat sides running back to the quarters, and a sharp turn at the heels. It was Viking. Skinner climbed into the saddle. His bloodshot eyes burned, and the inside of his calves were chafed raw. The small of his back ached relentlessly, and every quick movement brought on the pain in his side, but he didn't care. His legs now held a resolute form of energy as he pushed down against the stirrup. He pulled his hat down low over his eyes and looked at the lay of the land. A long, low ridge ran in a southerly direction to his left; another ran southeast to his right. The valley between stretched towards Mexico. Skinner asked Little Mare for a slow trot.

"Okay, you devil. Enjoy breathing 'cause you're suckin' in some of the last air you're ever gonna."

Little Mare put her ears back, questioning the anger in the man's voice. A spur eased up against her and told her how wrong she was. "I'm plumb smitten with you," said her rider.

Ten hours and twenty-five miles later Little Mare showed the first sign of real fatigue, and Skinner stepped down and moved on afoot. The mare's real challenge was not the miles but the lack of water. The air had turned cold, and darkness was almost upon them. Skinner stopped again at a patch of grass, stripped his saddle, and while the mare ate, he drained the last water from his canteen and spoke to his horse.

"We're out of water Little Mare." he said. "They are too, I reckon."

At dawn the next morning Skinner was again moving south, following the tracks. The ground was so hard now that he only found scrapes on the ground every fifty feet. The outlaw was traveling over this hard ground intending to hide his trail. Skinner reached forward and patted the mare.

"If you hadn't smelled that spot, we woulda ridden' right past 'em."

The pair of them followed the sign into a desolate piece of desert with no suggestion or hope of water to be had anywhere, but the trail continued to lead south towards Mexico.

"Sooner or later we're gonna find the Colorado. We're gonna be in trouble if we don't find it soon."

Skinner considered Little Mare's condition. She'd had all the water she wanted the night before. If he took his time, she could go another twenty miles; after that it was going to become a problem. But it was going to be a problem for all four of them. On their left a round hill rose three hundred feet or more above the desert floor. Skinner quit watching the tracks, dismounted, and led his horse to the summit, confident the outlaw had done the same. The need to find water was incumbent on all of them, and the vantage point of the hilltop was the best place to go.

At the summit the ground was covered in Viking's tracks and the outlaw's boot prints. Skinner stared west, and at the far edge of the horizon he could see the outline of greenery that traced the edges of the Colorado River.

He stripped the saddle and gave the mare a long rubdown with his hands and let her rest. In half an hour she tugged on the reins in Skinner's hand. She wanted to move out; she smelled water.

Skinner mounted and let her pick her way down the far side. When they hit the flats at the bottom of the hill, he pressed a spur into her side and trotted west, not bothering to follow the outlaw's tracks. Instead he concentrated on selecting the smoothest terrain for Little Mare's sake, confident that he would be able to pick up the outlaw's trail somewhere at the river's edge. Skinner knew that the outlaw would be reluctant to leave the river, and he was doubly sure he would be heading south along its shoreline. The outlaw was hungry; he'd be looking for game to shoot and eat—or better yet, someone along the river to rob and kill, to fill his belly, maybe find a fresh horse, and continue on to Mexico. The outlaw would, in Skinner's estimation, be gaining confidence that he had eluded pursuit, having successfully crossed this vast stretch of remote desert, and would be resorting to old habits of killing for a living and moving on. Skinner kept the mare in a slow steady trot; he was gaining confidence as well. He had a good horse. She was tired and in desperate need of water, but they would be at the river soon enough. They could rest and fill up on water. The grass would be thick and nutritious. If he let her graze, rest, and drink all night, she would be able to travel again in the morning. Skinner and Little Mare were gaining ground.

At dusk Skinner stepped down at the edge of the Colorado River. He stripped his saddle and bridle quickly and turned the mare loose. She walked belly deep into the river and buried her muzzle in the water. She drank for a full minute then raised her head and looked around. She took another longer drink before she turned and trudged back through the muddy bottom to the shore. She vaulted up the bank, searched out the best grass, and fed for fifteen minutes before she lay down to rest.

A moment later Skinner heard a gunshot down river. It was a long way off, and he froze waiting to hear another shot, but it didn't happen. He considered how far off it was. He knew that in the evening sound traveled upriver well, and he decided it could be as far away as three miles. Skinner pulled the jerked beef and tortillas out of his kit. He ate slowly and watched the mare. He took long drinks from his canteen and waited patiently until the mare stood and began to feed and drink again. Skinner placed his rifle across his lap, wiped it free of dust and checked its load. A slight breeze began to build, and it brought in a wave of much colder air. The smooth surface of the river now turned into ripples. Skinner reached for his coat, shrugged it on, and spoke to the mare.

"One shot. Must have killed an animal."

Little Mare turned and stared at her rider. Her eyes dropped shut. They opened and closed as she watched him. She brought a hind leg forward and stood hipshot.

"He's hungry. It's cold." Skinner buttoned his coat. "He has an animal down. You think he's dumb enough to start a fire and cook it?" Skinner asked the mare.

Little Mare shifted her hind legs and stood hip shot on the other. She closed her eyes and held them shut, ignoring Skinner.

"I'll give ya an hour," he said.

Skinner saw the glow of a campfire a quarter mile out. He stuck his finger in his mouth, wet it with spit, then held it high above his head. One side cooled quickly, telling him which direction the breeze was blowing from. He pulled the Springfield and checked the load again, then circled downwind from the campfire. He put five extra rounds in his breast pocket and walked the mare straight towards the firelight. He focused on the horse tied to a tree. Even forty yards out he recognized Viking. Skinner kicked the little mare into a trot. When she was moving well on her stiff legs, he sunk spurs into her sides and charged forward.

Viking heard them and pulled back on his lead. Jessup scrambled for his rifle and Skinner fired. The bullet ripped through Jessup's right hand and mangled all four fingers at the top of his palm. He had enough time to load another round before Little Mare jumped a thick clump of cholla just at the edge of the firelight. When she landed, her feet slid on the loose gravel and her tired legs failed. She lost her footing and somersaulted. Skinner swung his left leg forward over the mare's neck and hurled himself to the right. The mare slid along the ground and rolled across the fire pit, sending sparks and coals skittering across the ground. Viking pulled back so hard the branch he was tied to broke, and he ran into the darkness, dragging the limb tied to his lead. Skinner landed on his feet but couldn't check his momentum, so he rolled, then regained his feet and took two quick steps towards Jessup. He brought the butt end of his rifle around and whacked the outlaw across the side of his face. More sparks and embers fell off the mare as she struggled to her feet. She hobbled a few steps, then stopped and held a leg forward in pain.

Skinner moved closer to Jessup, who tried to get to his feet, and hit him with the rifle butt in the chest, knocking him down for good.

Skinner's thumb pulled back the hammer. "You ready to go to hell?"

Jessup rolled his eyes in Skinner's direction.

"I figure I'll give you enough time to mess yourself before I kill ya."

Jessup slid backwards across the gravel. He growled; saliva oozed down his jaw.

"How you like it now? Huh?" Skinner raised his rifle and shot. The bullet slammed into the ground between Jessup's legs, gravel exploded upwards and buried into the flesh on his face.

"You scared? Are ya scared now?" Skinner moved closer and stuck the tip of his rifle against Jessup's chest. "You ready?" His finger curled around the trigger.

Jessup looked at him through one eye; the other was filled with gravel and oozed blood. More blood squirted off his fingerless right hand, and onto his clothes.

Little Mare hobbled on three legs farther away. She whinnied at Viking, desperate for companionship, desperate to get away from the anger and the smell of blood coming from the two men behind her. She held her leg off the ground, pulled in a huge breath, and called out again, louder and stronger. Her whinny was shrill, high-pitched and with a long finish: the call of a mare.

Viking answered. The stallion blew, the sharp exhalation of air whistled out of the darkness.

Skinner's eyelids clamped down over his burning eyes rapidly. The distant sound came from a fine animal, a stallion, a horse that had introduced Skinner to the woman he loved. He remembered sitting on the rails and watching the stallion get acquainted with the mare in the next pen. He remembered the stallion charging across the confines of its pen and locking its eyes on him. He remembered falling in love with Veronica just moments before, on the streets of Prescott, as she walked arm in arm with her mother. He thought about that hot blush that had risen into her cheeks when she had turned to look at him.

"Veronica," he called out. She needed him. Needed him to be there for her. Needed him to be strong. He pressed the tip of the barrel against Jerssup's chest. He leaned into the rifle, pushing the outlaw down against the earth. His finger moved off the trigger.

Jessup saw Skinner's rage dissipate. He pushed the rifle barrel away. His good hand folded over the mangled fingers on his other hand, and he ducked his head in pain.

"That's right." Skinner stepped back. He tilted the rifle upwards and stared down at Jessup. "You won't die today. I'm gonna let someone else have that job."

Jessup's good hand readjusted over his wounded hand to try and stem the flow of blood. He met and held Skinner's gaze despite the dirt in his eyes. "You won't kill me, 'cause you're one of them kind. The ones that let everyone walk all over 'em."

Skinner straightened and exhaled through clenched teeth.

"What's your plan now, huh? You'll never get me back there. People of your ilk make mistakes."

Skinner stared back. "Ilk? Is that the fanciest word you know?"

"I don't let anyone boss me or tell me what to do. I'll kill ya before you get me back there."

"No, you won't kill me. You're gonna be too busy nursing the pain in your hand and beggin' for water." Skinner looked at the blood pouring off Jessup's hand. He shook his head and grimaced.

"Give me something to stop the bleeding."

Skinner planted a foot in Jessup's chest and pushed him backwards, flat on the ground. He ran a hand through Jessup's clothing looking for a hidden weapon and only found a small pocketknife. Skinner ripped at Jessup's shirt and pulled off a long strip.

"Here." He stood and grimaced again as he tossed the cloth scrap to Jessup. "You getting a clearer picture now?

That and what's left of your shirt is all you got to nurse that hand over a four-day ride."

"Let's go to Yuma. It's closer than going back. I won't make it back there."

"Nope."

Jessup groaned and his good hand trembled as he wrapped the shirt scrap over his wound. "I'll die before I make it back there."

"Wrong again. You won't kill me, and I won't let you die. You can make a tall wager on that."

"Damn you," Jessup yelled. His eyes rolled upward, and he started to fall backwards before he caught himself. He cursed Skinner again and gingerly pressed both hands up against chest. "You gotta help me. Damn you," he said again, his voice just above a whisper.

"I'm only gonna help you get back to Prescott."

"You won't get me back there. I won't make it. I'll bleed to death. What kind of person are ya?"

"I'm just the opposite of you, that's what kind I am. The way I see it, people of my ilk are going to be the ones that decide how big a drop you get. We wouldn't want to see your head snap off when we can give you time to dangle and think."

CHAPTER 32

Skinner heard the door slam out in the office. Voices rose louder as they approached the inner door that led to the cells. Strong light poured through the door and Sheriff Boozenbark entered with two of his deputies.

"Okay, Skinner. Your time will be up in a few minutes."

"Gotta admit, I'm ready to go." Skinner stood and grabbed a pile of letters bound with a rubber band. He sucked in his gut and stuffed the bundle behind his belt.

The sheriff chuckled as he opened the cell-door lock. "You got some friends outside; they're waiting down the street. Been there since daybreak. I figured I better let you loose, just to be polite to them." Boozenbark swung the door open. "Your personals are laid out in the main office. Little Mare is in the small corral by the main gate." Boozenbark looked at his watch. "I won't be keeping you in here even one second longer than your ninety days, Skinner. The whole damn town is mad through and through that you did any time at all."

"I know, and I appreciate all the great care, Sheriff."

Boozenbark followed Skinner out into the front room of the jail house and talked the whole way. "When General Miles let me know he was sending you up here because he couldn't be sure they wouldn't try and break you out of jail down there, I was honored." Boozenbark looked at his watch again. "To think that that idiot colonel wanted to slap you with desertion charge for doing your duty was the last straw. I'm telling you, if he had done that, every man at the fort and for a hundred miles around would have tried to bust you outta there. Good thing General Miles had that colonel transferred somewhere else or he was going to be meat."

Skinner smiled. "You told me all this twenty times now."

"I know, but I'm still hot that you even got the ninety days for breaking orders. They should have just let it go after what you and your men did."

Skinner smiled. "It wasn't anything to do the time with you. Feel like I been on vacation with all the good food and company. Best part is that my discharge was administrative not dishonorable." Skinner pointed to Boozenbark's pocket, where he kept his watch. "Can I go yet?"

Boozenbark jerked like someone had just come up behind him unannounced. He yanked out his watch then quickly put out his hand. "You're free to go Tom Skinner."

Skinner reached out and shook the sheriff's hand. He shrugged his shoulders and took two deep breaths as he looked at her belongings. His saddle, saddle pads, and bridle sat on the floor. The leather was polished to a high sheen. His canteen, coat, and hat had been placed on the corner of a table. He put his hat on and tried to pull the brim low over his eyes, but the hat band had shrunk, and it sat high on his head. Skinner looked out the window as he gathered his belongings. The street didn't look all that busy, mainly because it was still early, and he was happy about that. Skinner looped the leather thong of the canteen around his saddle horn and tied his bridle on with the saddle strings. He put on his coat, took the letters from behind his belt and switched them into a coat pocket. He looked back at the sheriff and the two deputies as he slung the load onto his hip.

"You done your time Tom Skinner," said Boozenbark. "Far as I'm concerned, and just about everyone else, it was time didn't need serving. Good luck to ya."

Skinner nodded at them, then he turned, opened the door, and walked out. At the end of the street, two blocks to the east, spread the stock pens. Most were empty. Monte and Courtney sat on the top rail of one pen looking at a small herd of milling horses. Their backs were turned to him, and they didn't see him walk out.

Veronica sat on the tailgate of a new buckboard, her back against the sideboard and her legs stretched out, one leather riding boot crossed over the other. When she saw him step out onto the boardwalk, she slid off the tailgate and swept her hands down the front of a calf-length dark-tan riding skirt to flatten any wrinkles. She shook her hair, pushed one lock behind an ear, and let the rest drape over a crisp tan blouse. She stood by the rear wheel of the buckboard with her hands clasped in front of her waist and watched him approach.

In her final letter to him she'd told him she was going to be there when he got out and that she wanted him to stay with her and the boys until he decided what he wanted to do. She'd shared a lot of thoughts with him in her letters. Quite a few sentences had been devoted to her opinion of the army and one of its leaders in particular. She'd also told him what she and the twins had been doing and how they lived up in the red-rock country. She'd reminisced about her parents and her upbringing and how she now had to be strong for her brothers. Her letters had also included what she and the twins thought of what he'd done to avenge her parents and sister, but not once did she say anything about how she was coping with what had happened to her. Skinner had written her back letter for letter, but his had been cautious, shorter, and more restrained.

Skinner was sure Boozenbark had filled his boots with mud as he began to walk towards her. *I'm damaged goods*, he thought.

She looked older somehow, and she never dropped her gaze from him as he moved up the lane. Her eyes told him what he already knew. She'd suffered loss, been abused, and had been shouldered with a responsibility for two younger brothers. Skinner stopped ten feet from her and dropped his saddle in the dirt.

"I done my time. I'm free now."

Veronica took a step forward. "You've occupied a lot of my thoughts."

"I bet I got you beat on that account." Skinner pointed his thumb over his shoulder at the jailhouse behind. He took a step forward; only ten feet separated them.

"You think so?" Veronica took two more steps forward.

"Yep. I do." Skinner moved forward.

She wrapped her arms around his neck and buried her face against his chest.

Skinner reached around her and held her tight. "You two gonna keep looking at them horses or you gonna come over here and say hello?" he shouted over her shoulder.

Startled the twins twirled around. They jumped off the rails and ran over. The four of them held each other in a tangle of arms.

"You both look good." Skinner pushed the boys back and looked them over but kept an arm around Veronica's shoulders.

"Your sister has invited me to come stay with you for a while."

"That was our idea," said Monte.

Skinner felt Veronica's fingers squeeze into his arm. "Is that right? Well, I guess I'm asking the wrong person then." Skinner swung his eyes onto Veronica. "Mind if I come stay for a while?"

Veronica's face turned red. She pulled away, picked up Skinner's saddle, and heaved it over the side of the buckboard as an answer.

Her riding skirt swirled lightly over her boots, and it reminded Skinner of being in the hunting camp up above the Mogollon, when Veronica had burned her fingers. "You look good too, Veronica. You look beautiful."

"Thank you, Tom. I had a chance to shop yesterday."

"You might need that," Monte said, pointing at Skinner's saddle.

"Whatcha mean?" said Skinner.

"Nothing." Monte vaulted into the back of the wagon to grab Skinner's saddle. He startled the two mares in harness at the front of the wagon and they jolted forward. "Woah." Monte yelled.

"Relax, you meatheads." Courtney scooted in front of the mares and grabbed a bridle. "They're young. Ain't got any sense yet."

"Ain't isn't a word. How many times have I got to tell you?" Veronica admonished Courtney.

Monte picked up Skinner's saddle and swung it out over the sideboard of the wagon. He pointed down the street. "Looks like you'll be riding home."

At the far end of Gurley Street, a heavily loaded wagon had turned towards them.

The wagon was being pulled by two black mules; a stocky chestnut horse walked on one side of the wagon ahead of the dust. The bed of the wagon was piled high with cargo and covered with a gray tarp. On the other side, on a long lead line, a younger horse glided along, obviously bored by the slow pace of the wagon. Its forelock hung well below its eyes. It was thin, a little ribby, and it was tall. Taller than any other horse along the length of the street. It had one white sock.

"I'll be damned, here comes Maria . . . and my friend."

"Tom?" Veronica squeezed his arm.

"Yeah."

"He's not your friend, he's my friend."

"What?"

"Here comes your brother."

Skinner smiled.

Veronica gripped his arm. "We've been working hard on our camp over in the red-rock country."

"You took your father's advice didn't you."

"We have seven mares and a sturdy stud pen for Viking."

"It could be eight. I own Little Mare," said Skinner.

"Eight sounds good to me." Veronica leaned in tighter against him.

"What else have you gotten done up there?"

"We have four-wall tents, all with wooden floors. That's how we started up on the Mogollon. We have a possible irrigation project lined out."

"You've been busy."

Skinner, Veronica, Monte, and Courtney stood four abreast and watched Chaco and Maria roll up the lane.

"Maria wrote me a while back. She told me that when you got out, she and Chaco would be here. I invited them to come live with us too. We need all the help we can get."

"They're good help all right."

"I hope you don't laugh at how little we have done. It's just that . . ."

"I'm in need of some help too."

"What do you need, Tom?"

"Need somebody to love, or I think I'm gonna go crazy."

"You do?" Veronica whispered. "You have anyone in mind?"

"Yup. I sure do."